◄ KAMOME ►
SHIRAHAMA

Witch Hat Atelier

◄ VOLUME ►

2

CONTENTS

WITCH HAT ATELIER

♦

KAMOME
SHIRAHAMA

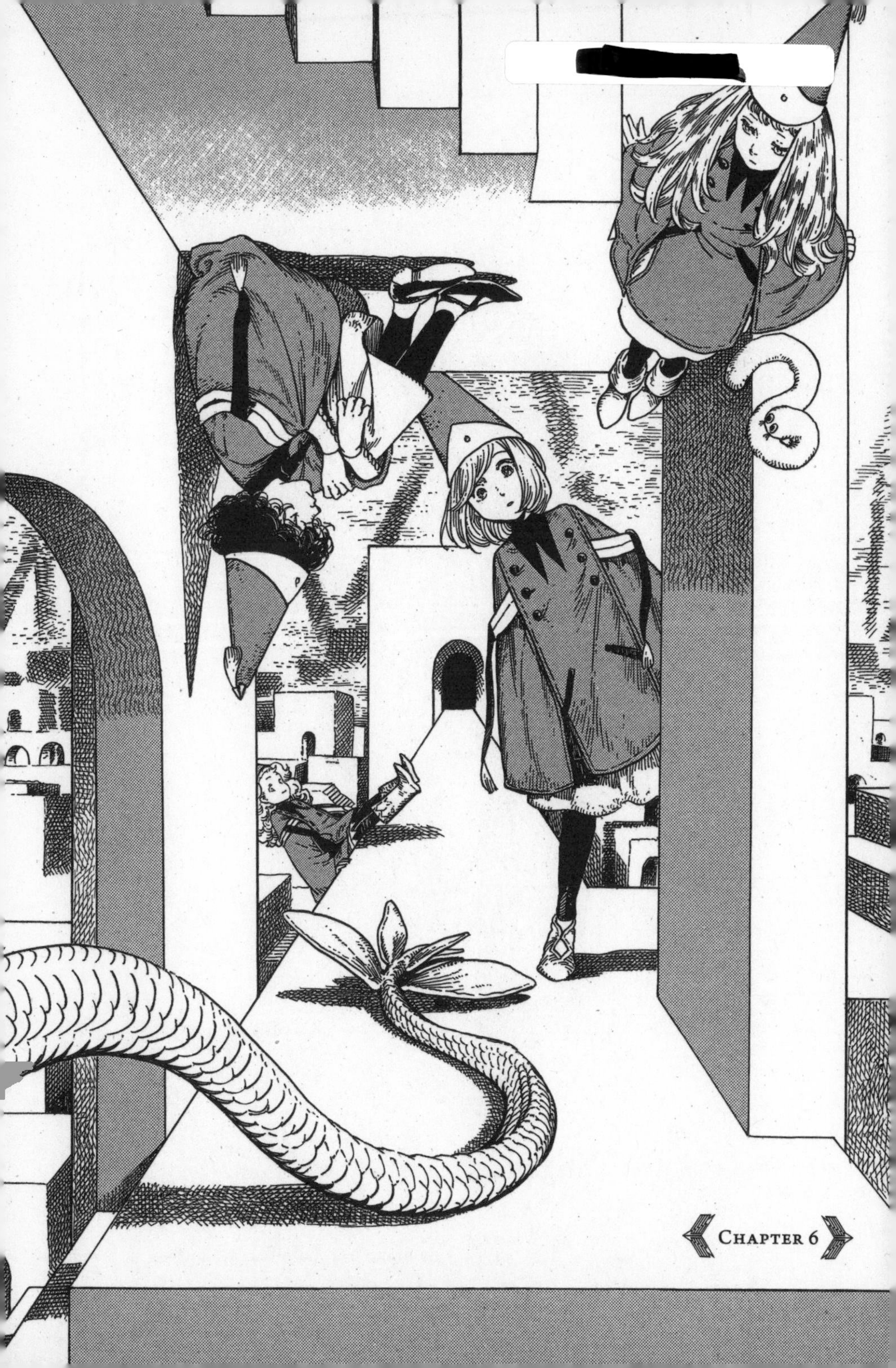
[redacted]
Chapter 6

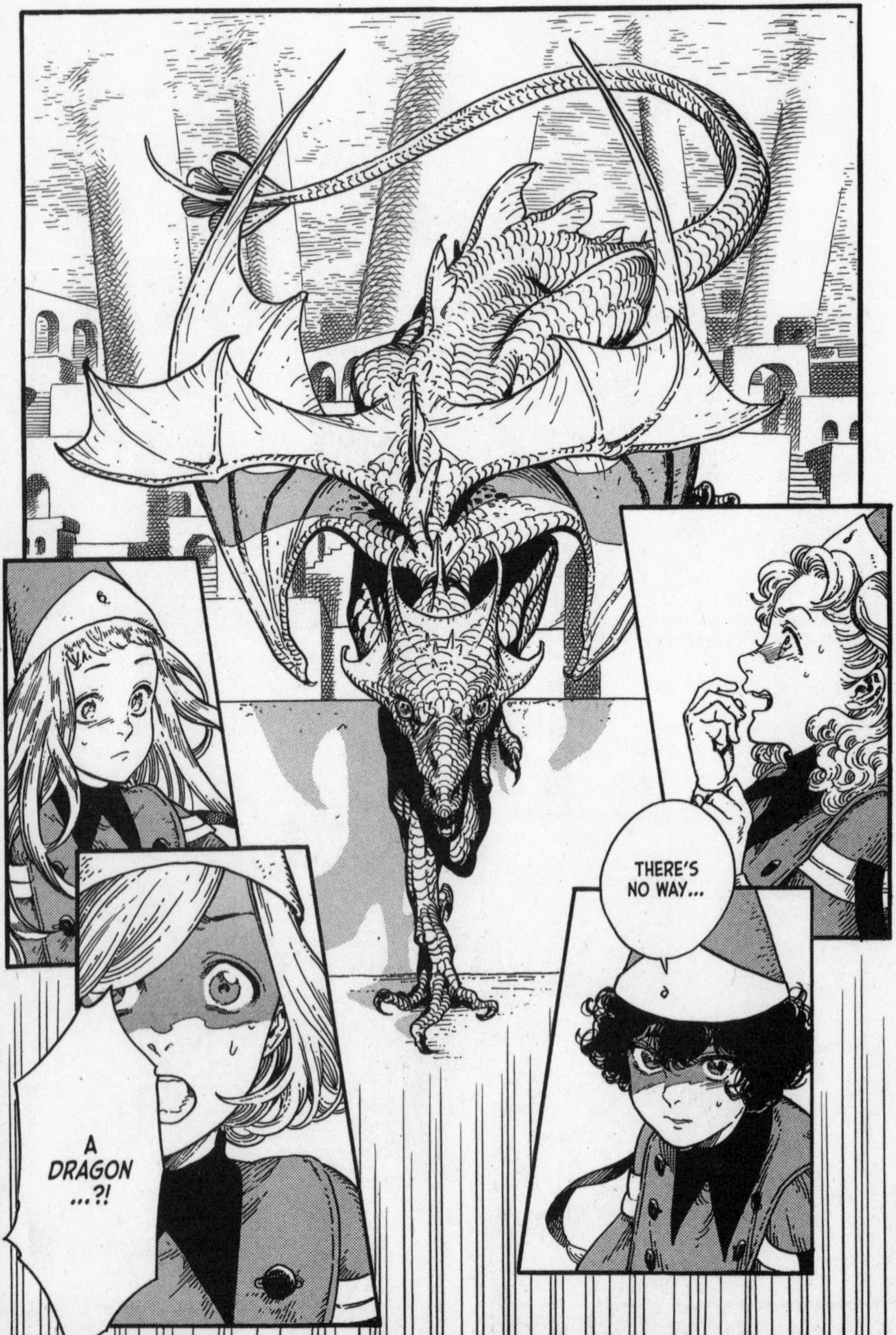
THERE'S NO WAY...
A DRAGON ...?!

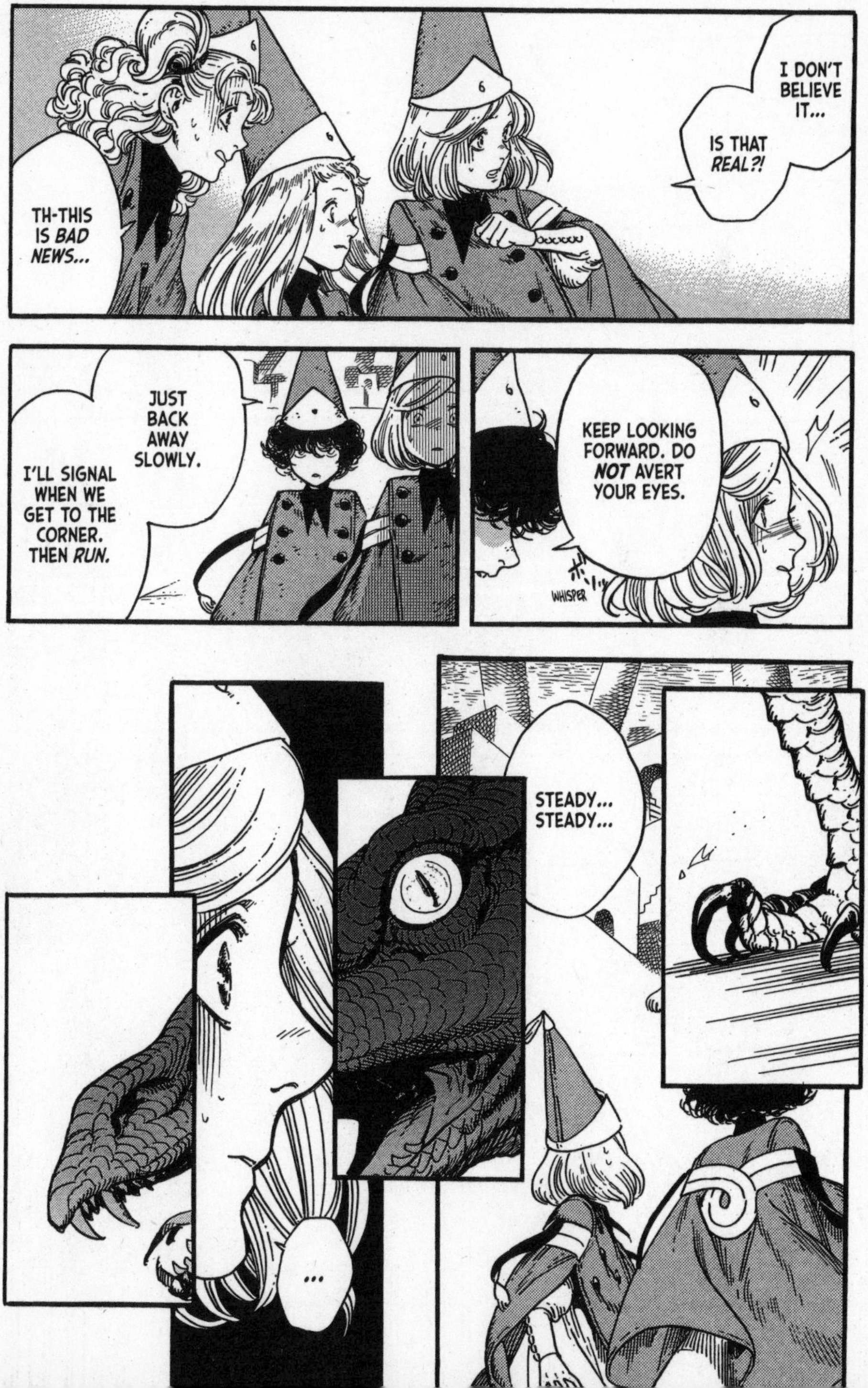
I DON'T BELIEVE IT...
IS THAT REAL?!
TH-THIS IS BAD NEWS...
KEEP LOOKING FORWARD. DO NOT AVERT YOUR EYES.
WHISPER
JUST BACK AWAY SLOWLY.
I'LL SIGNAL WHEN WE GET TO THE CORNER. THEN RUN.
STEADY... STEADY...
...

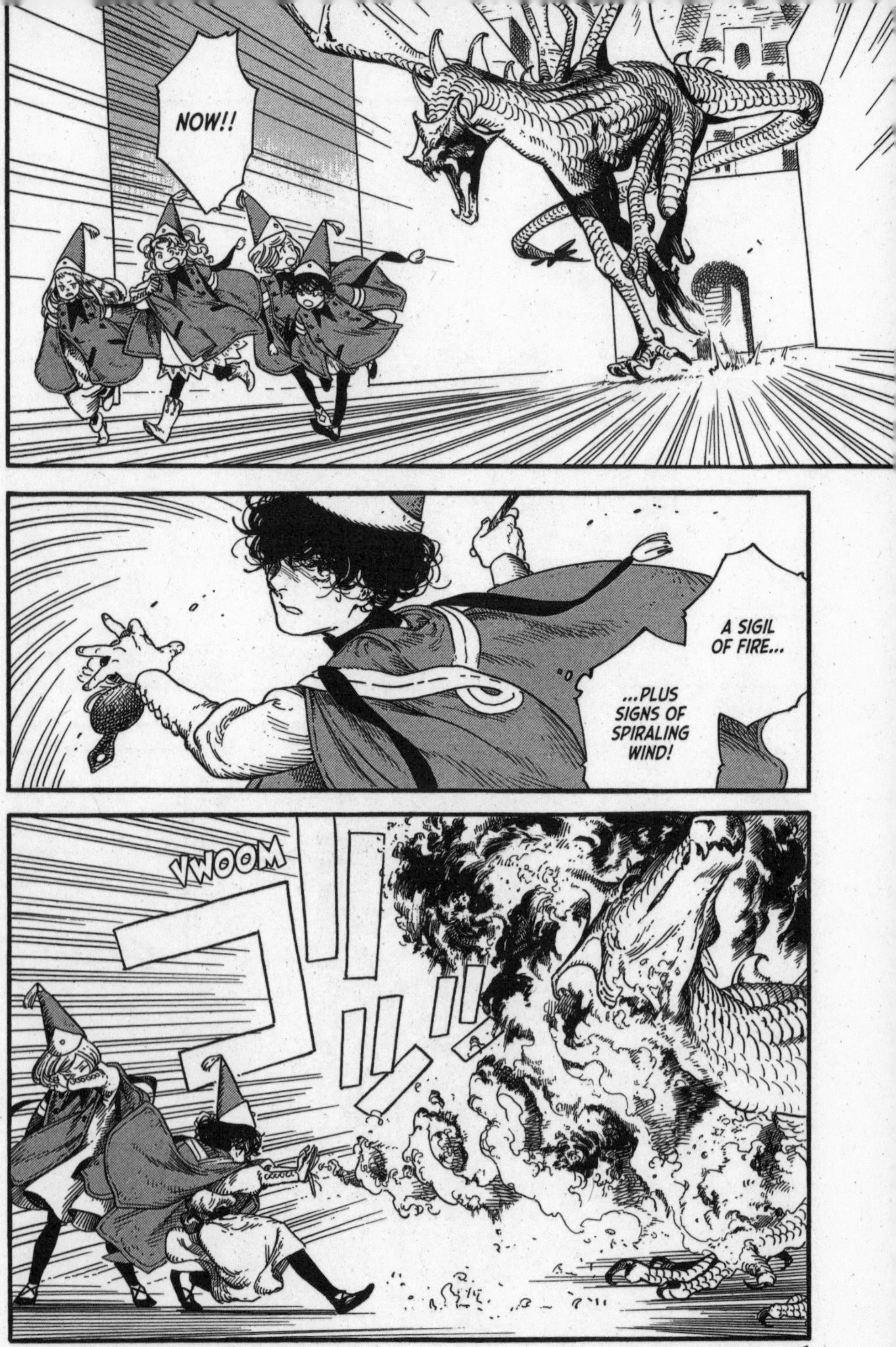
NOW!!
A SIGIL OF FIRE...
...PLUS SIGNS OF SPIRALING WIND!
VWOOM

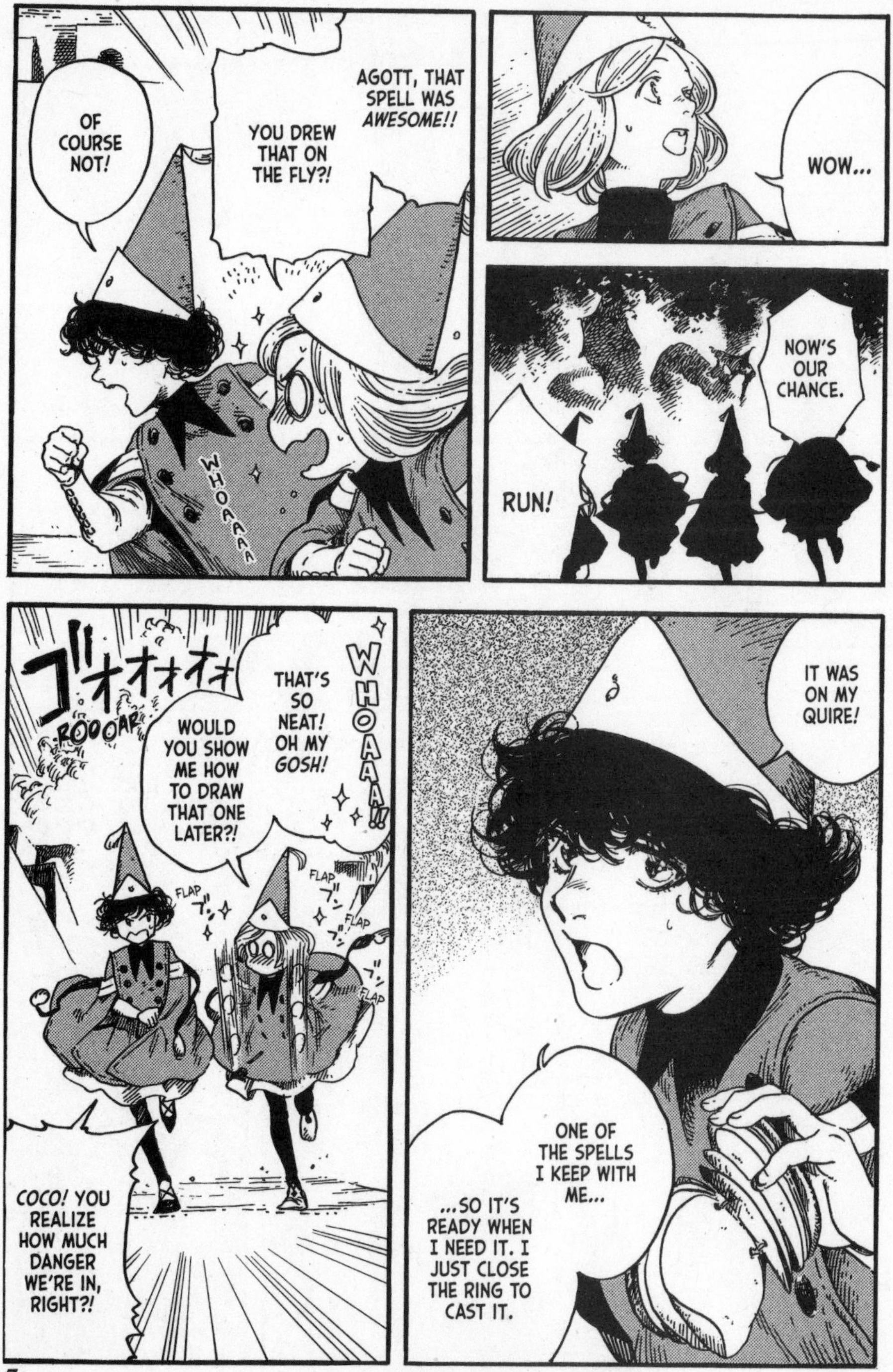
WOW...
NOW'S OUR CHANCE.
RUN!
AGOTT, THAT SPELL WAS *AWESOME!!*
YOU DREW THAT ON THE FLY?!
OF COURSE NOT!
WHOAAAA
IT WAS ON MY QUIRE!
ONE OF THE SPELLS I KEEP WITH ME...
...SO IT'S READY WHEN I NEED IT. I JUST CLOSE THE RING TO CAST IT.
WHOAAAA!!
THAT'S SO NEAT! OH MY *GOSH!*
WOULD YOU SHOW ME HOW TO DRAW THAT ONE LATER?!
ゴオオオオオ
ROOOAR
FLAP
FLAP
FLAP
FLAP
COCO! YOU REALIZE HOW MUCH DANGER WE'RE IN, RIGHT?!

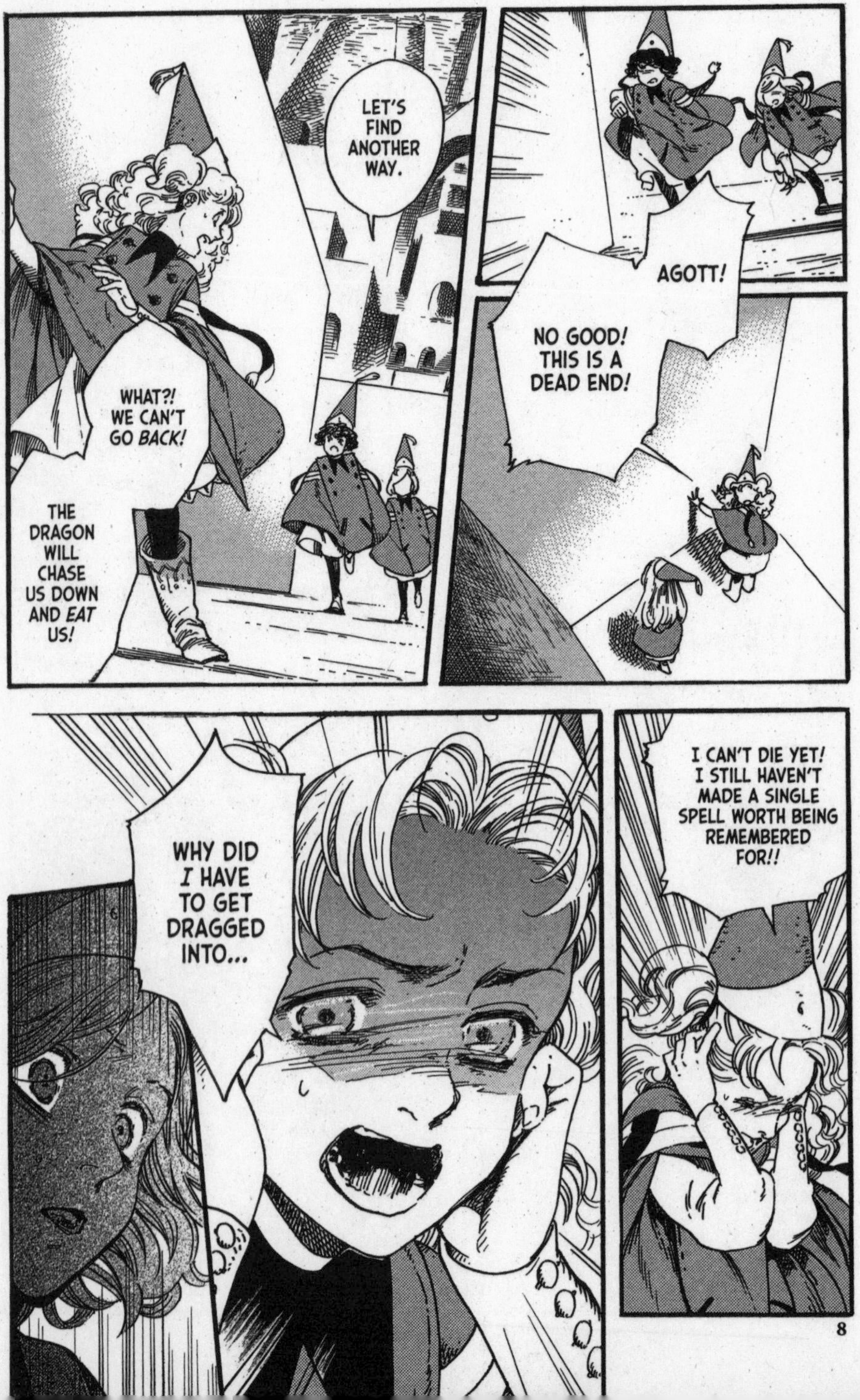
AGOTT!
NO GOOD! THIS IS A DEAD END!
LET'S FIND ANOTHER WAY.
WHAT?! WE CAN'T GO *BACK*!
THE DRAGON WILL CHASE US DOWN AND *EAT* US!
I CAN'T DIE YET! I STILL HAVEN'T MADE A SINGLE SPELL WORTH BEING REMEMBERED FOR!!
WHY DID *I* HAVE TO GET DRAGGED INTO...

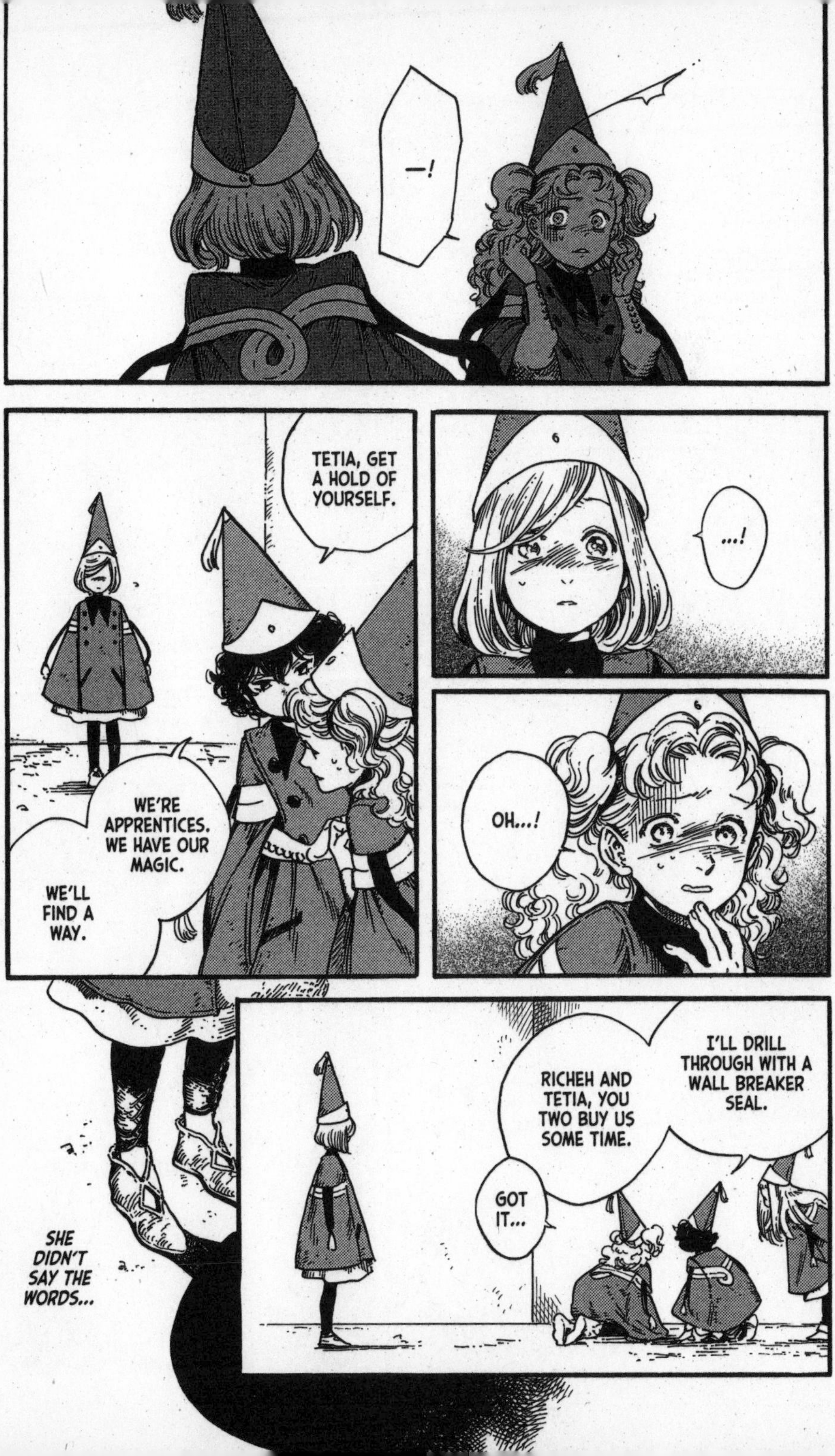
—!
...!
OH...!
TETIA, GET A HOLD OF YOURSELF.
WE'RE APPRENTICES. WE HAVE OUR MAGIC.
WE'LL FIND A WAY.
I'LL DRILL THROUGH WITH A WALL BREAKER SEAL.
RICHEH AND TETIA, YOU TWO BUY US SOME TIME.
GOT IT...
SHE DIDN'T SAY THE WORDS...

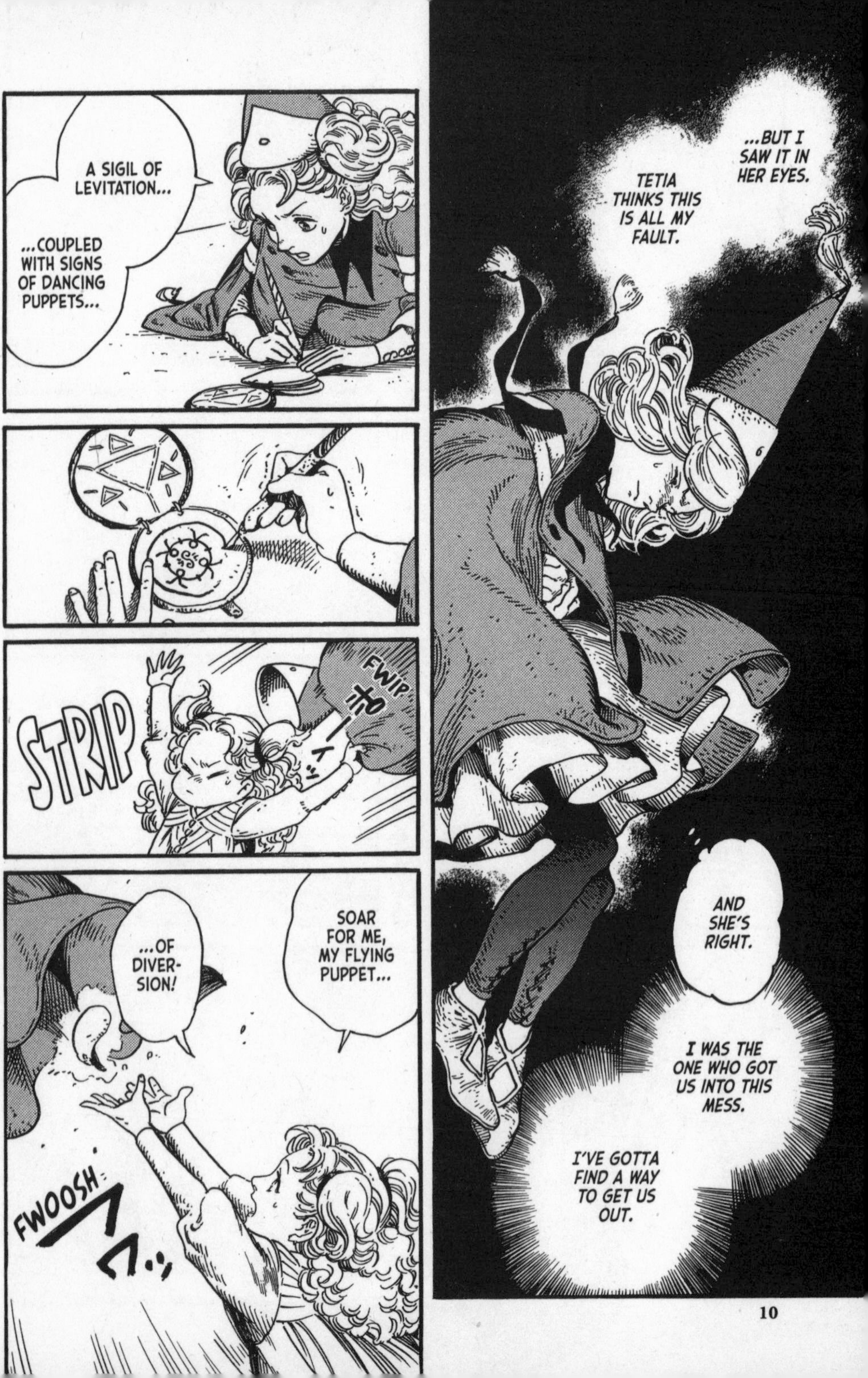
TETIA THINKS THIS IS ALL MY FAULT.
...BUT I SAW IT IN HER EYES.
AND SHE'S RIGHT.
I WAS THE ONE WHO GOT US INTO THIS MESS.
I'VE GOTTA FIND A WAY TO GET US OUT.
A SIGIL OF LEVITATION...
...COUPLED WITH SIGNS OF DANCING PUPPETS...
FWIP
STRIP
SOAR FOR ME, MY FLYING PUPPET...
...OF DIVERSION!
FWOOSH

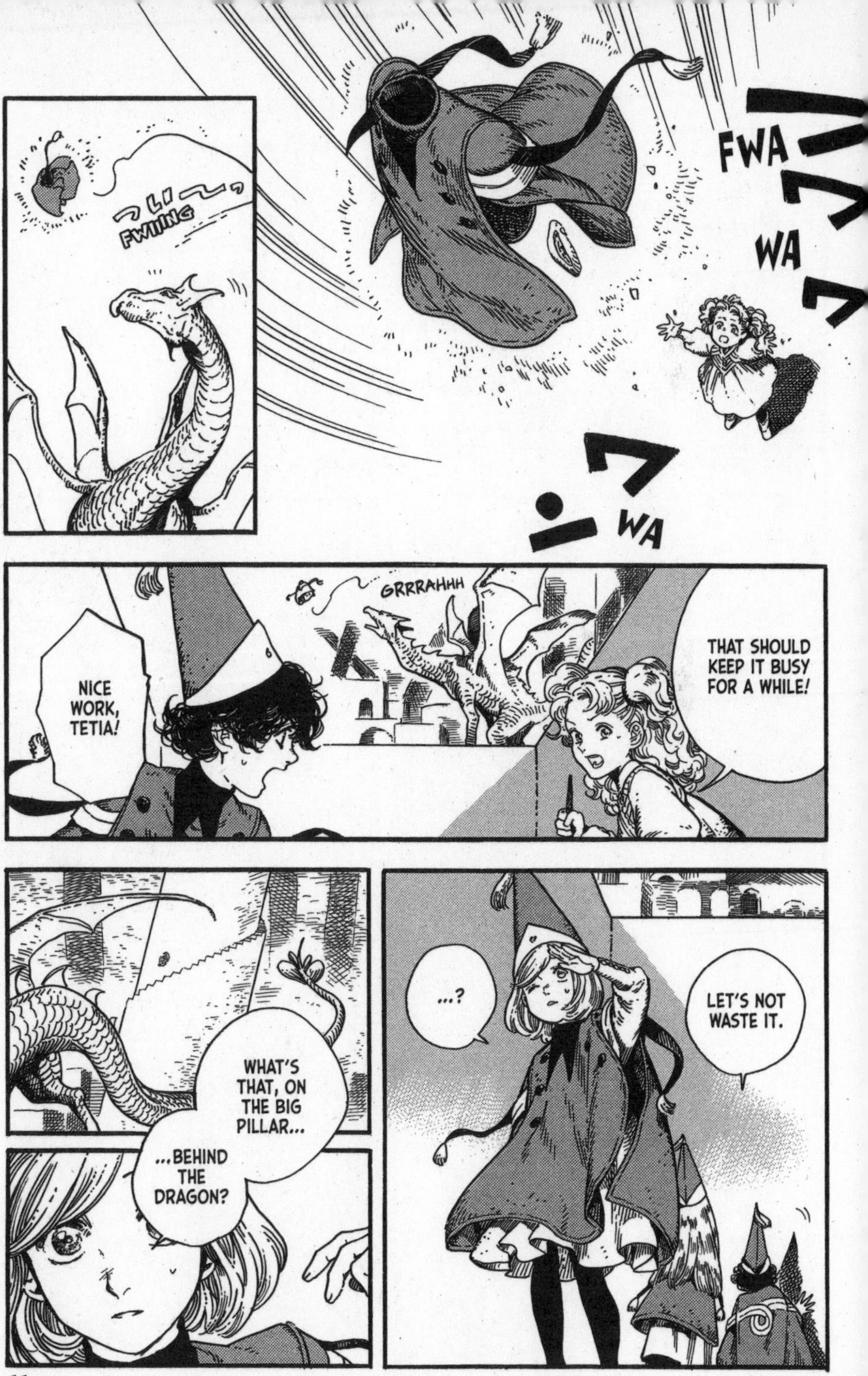
FWA
WA
WA
FWIIING
THAT SHOULD KEEP IT BUSY FOR A WHILE!
GRRRAHHH
NICE WORK, TETIA!
LET'S NOT WASTE IT.
...?
WHAT'S THAT, ON THE BIG PILLAR...
...BEHIND THE DRAGON?

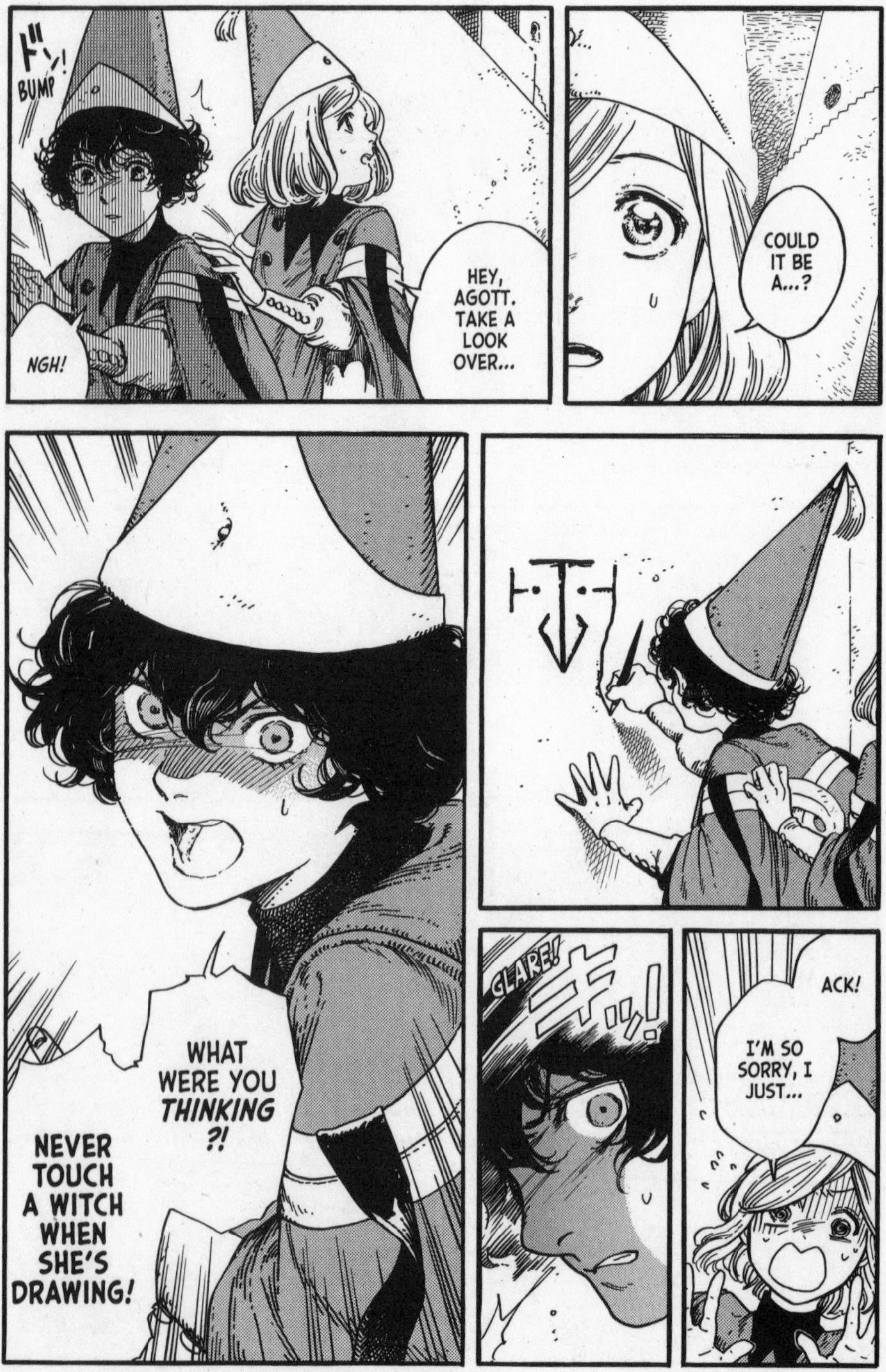
COULD IT BE A...?
ドン!
BUMP
HEY, AGOTT. TAKE A LOOK OVER...
NGH!
ACK!
I'M SO SORRY, I JUST...
GLARE!
WHAT WERE YOU THINKING ?!
NEVER TOUCH A WITCH WHEN SHE'S DRAWING!

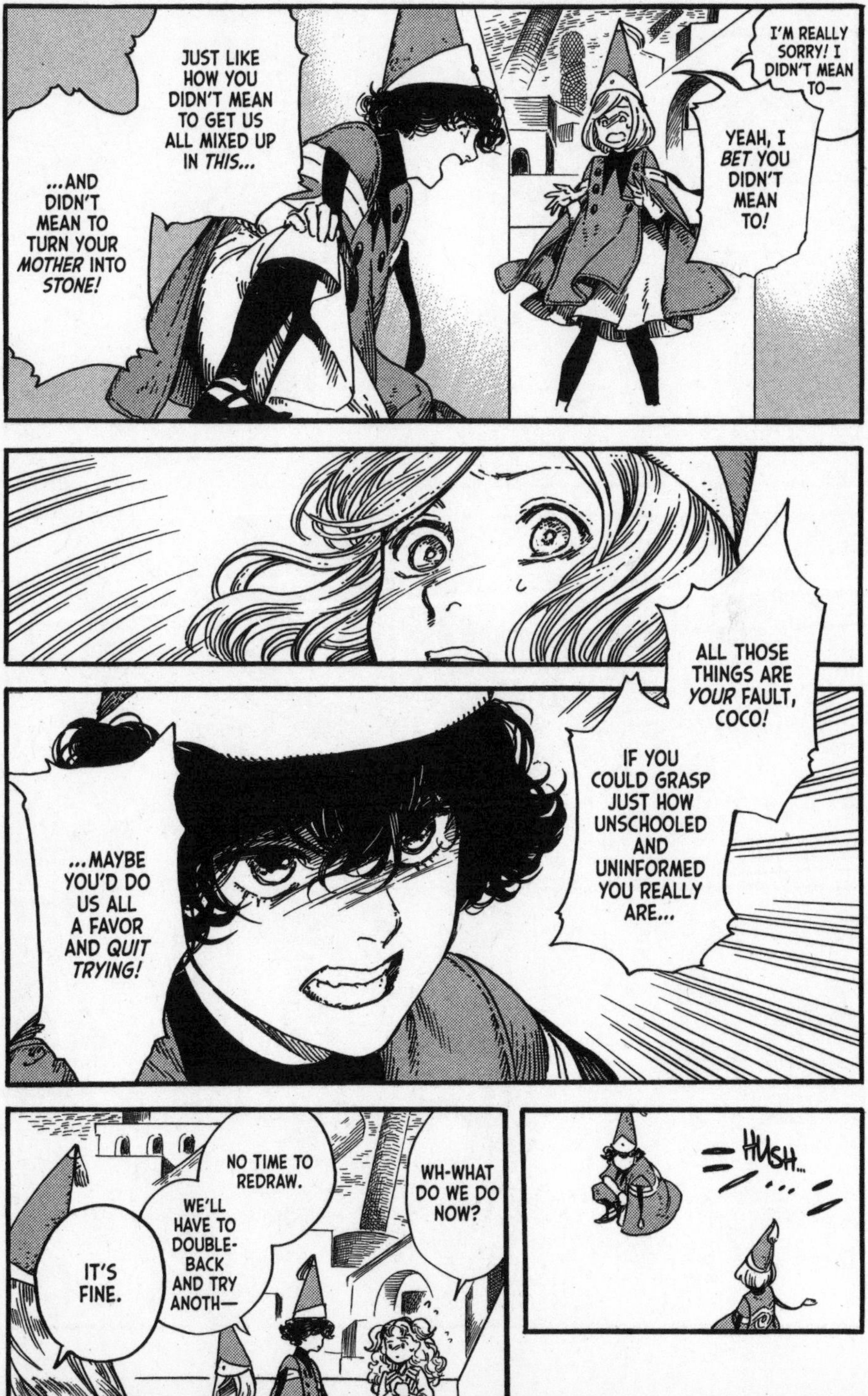
I'M REALLY SORRY! I DIDN'T MEAN TO—
YEAH, I *BET* YOU DIDN'T MEAN TO!
JUST LIKE HOW YOU DIDN'T MEAN TO GET US ALL MIXED UP IN *THIS*...
...AND DIDN'T MEAN TO TURN YOUR *MOTHER* INTO *STONE!*
ALL THOSE THINGS ARE *YOUR* FAULT, COCO!
IF YOU COULD GRASP JUST HOW UNSCHOOLED AND UNINFORMED YOU REALLY ARE...
...MAYBE YOU'D DO US ALL A FAVOR AND *QUIT TRYING!*
HUSH...
...
WH-WHAT DO WE DO NOW?
NO TIME TO REDRAW.
WE'LL HAVE TO DOUBLE-BACK AND TRY ANOTH—
IT'S FINE.

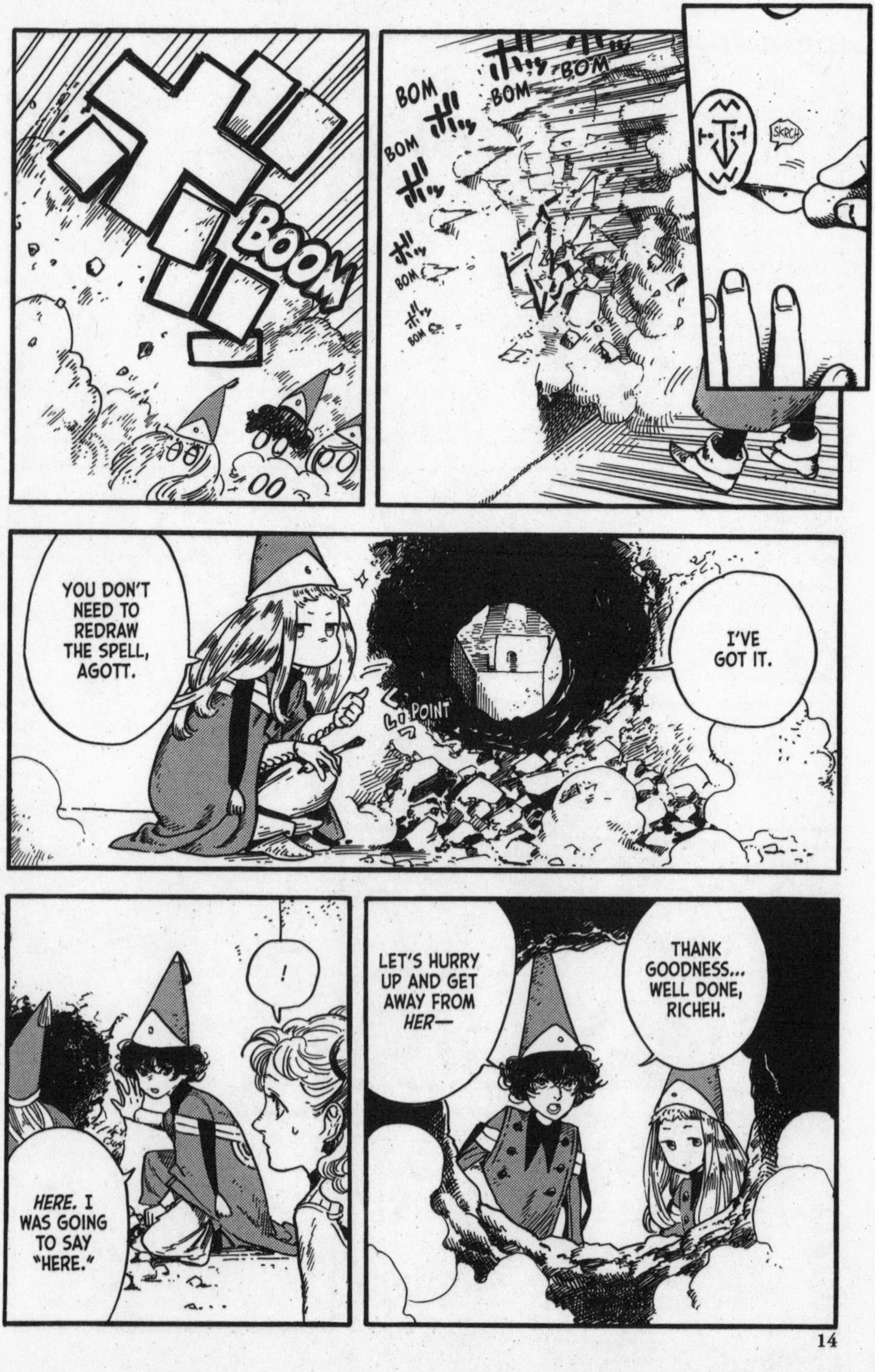
SKRCH
BOM BOM BOM BOM BOM BOM
BOOM
I'VE GOT IT.
YOU DON'T NEED TO REDRAW THE SPELL, AGOTT.
POINT
THANK GOODNESS... WELL DONE, RICHEH.
LET'S HURRY UP AND GET AWAY FROM *HER*—
!
HERE. I WAS GOING TO SAY "HERE."

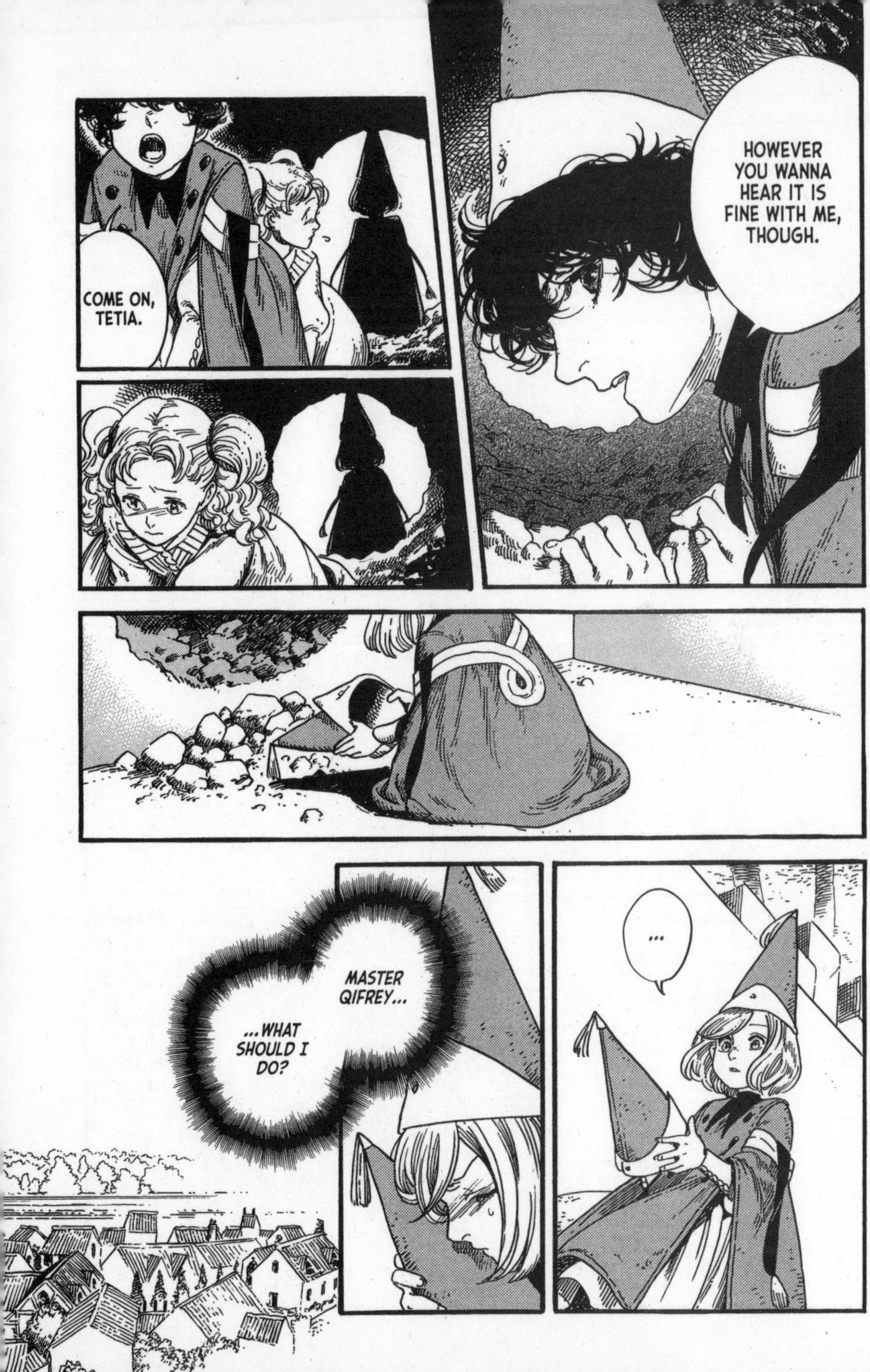
HOWEVER YOU WANNA HEAR IT IS FINE WITH ME, THOUGH.
COME ON, TETIA.
...
MASTER QIFREY...
...WHAT SHOULD I DO?

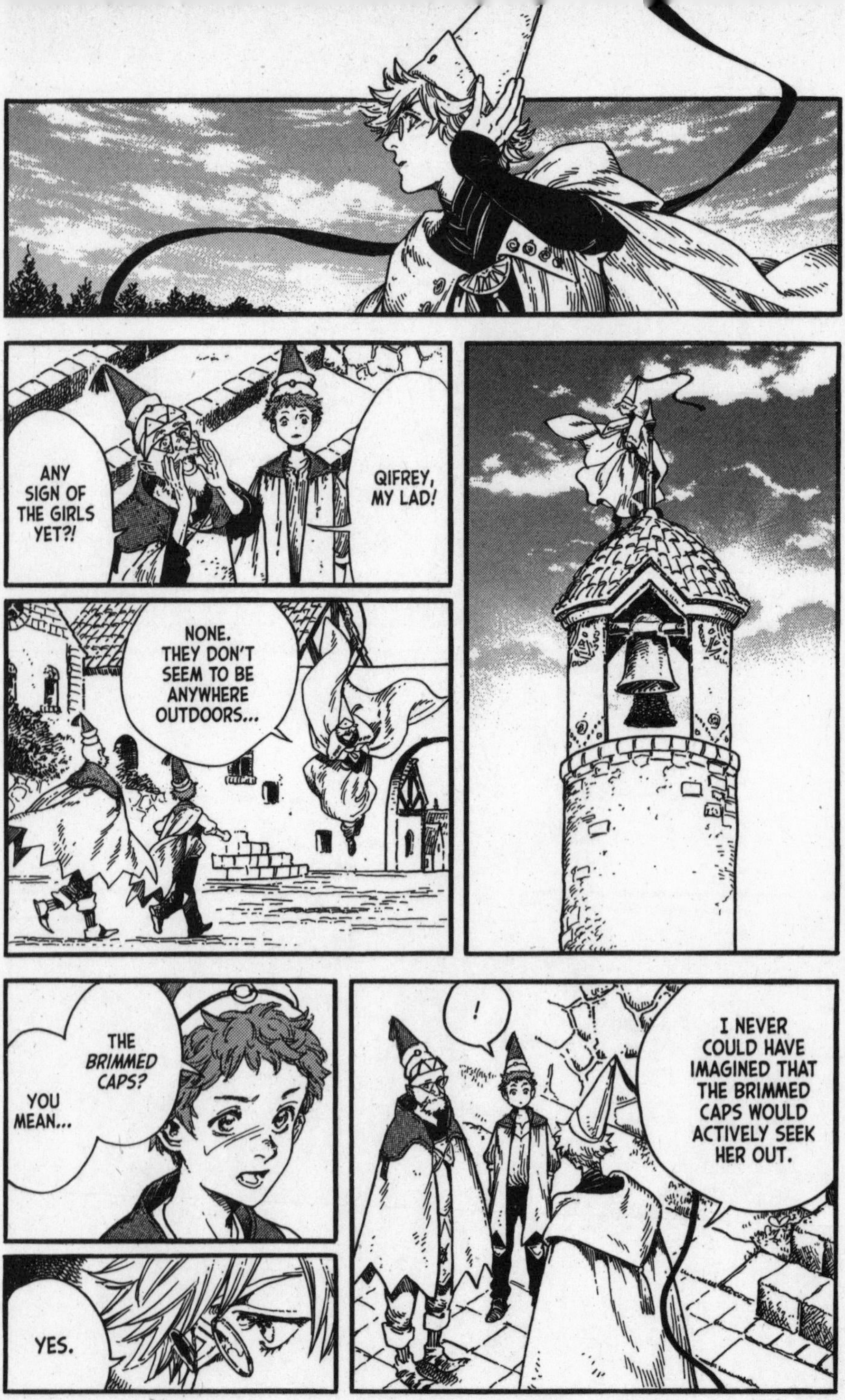
QIFREY, MY LAD!
ANY SIGN OF THE GIRLS YET?!
NONE. THEY DON'T SEEM TO BE ANYWHERE OUTDOORS...
!
I NEVER COULD HAVE IMAGINED THAT THE BRIMMED CAPS WOULD ACTIVELY SEEK HER OUT.
THE *BRIMMED CAPS*?
YOU MEAN...
YES.

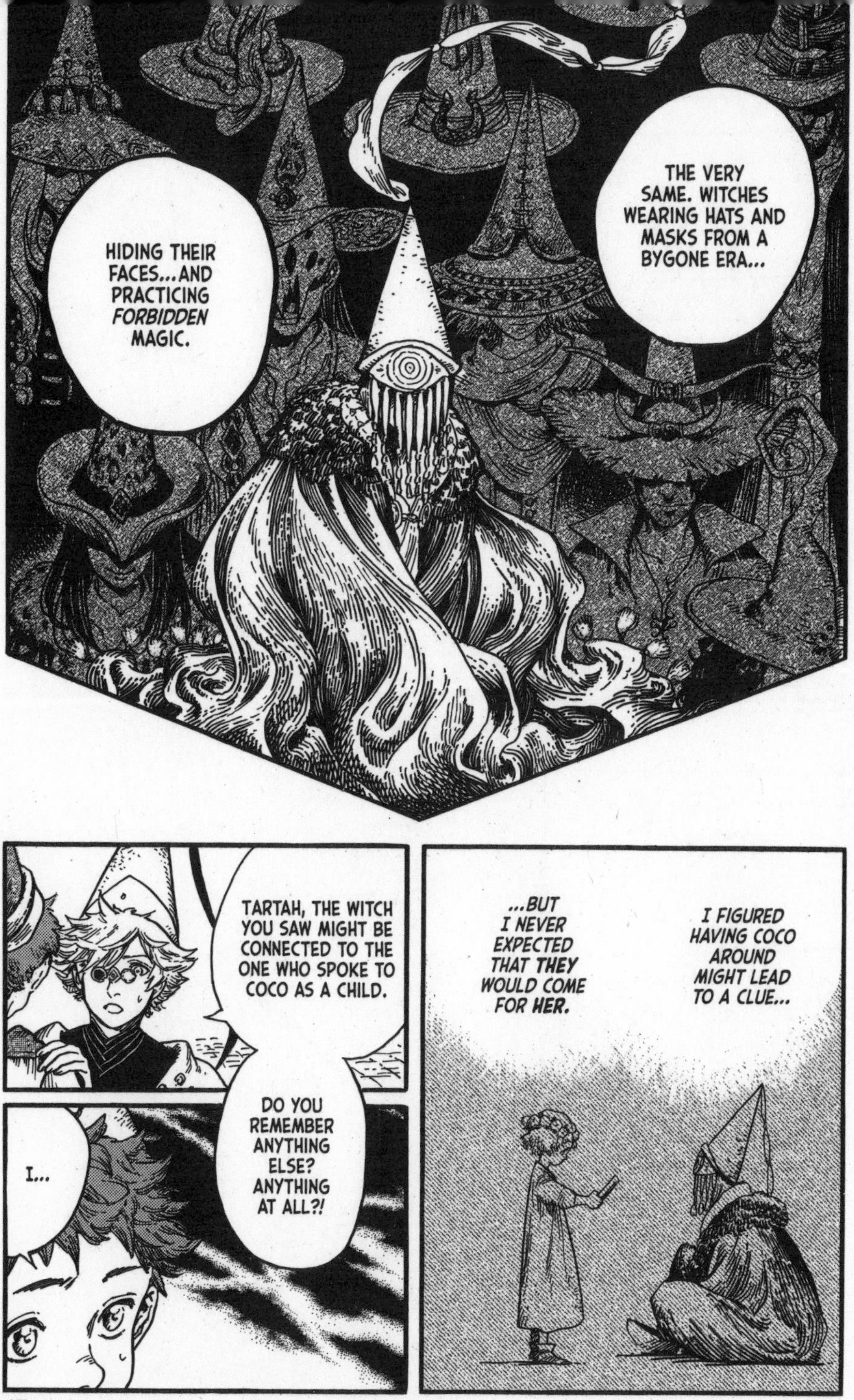
THE VERY SAME. WITCHES WEARING HATS AND MASKS FROM A BYGONE ERA...
HIDING THEIR FACES...AND PRACTICING *FORBIDDEN* MAGIC.
I FIGURED HAVING COCO AROUND MIGHT LEAD TO A CLUE...
...BUT I NEVER EXPECTED THAT ***THEY*** *WOULD COME FOR* ***HER.***
TARTAH, THE WITCH YOU SAW MIGHT BE CONNECTED TO THE ONE WHO SPOKE TO COCO AS A CHILD.
DO YOU REMEMBER ANYTHING ELSE? ANYTHING AT ALL?!
I...

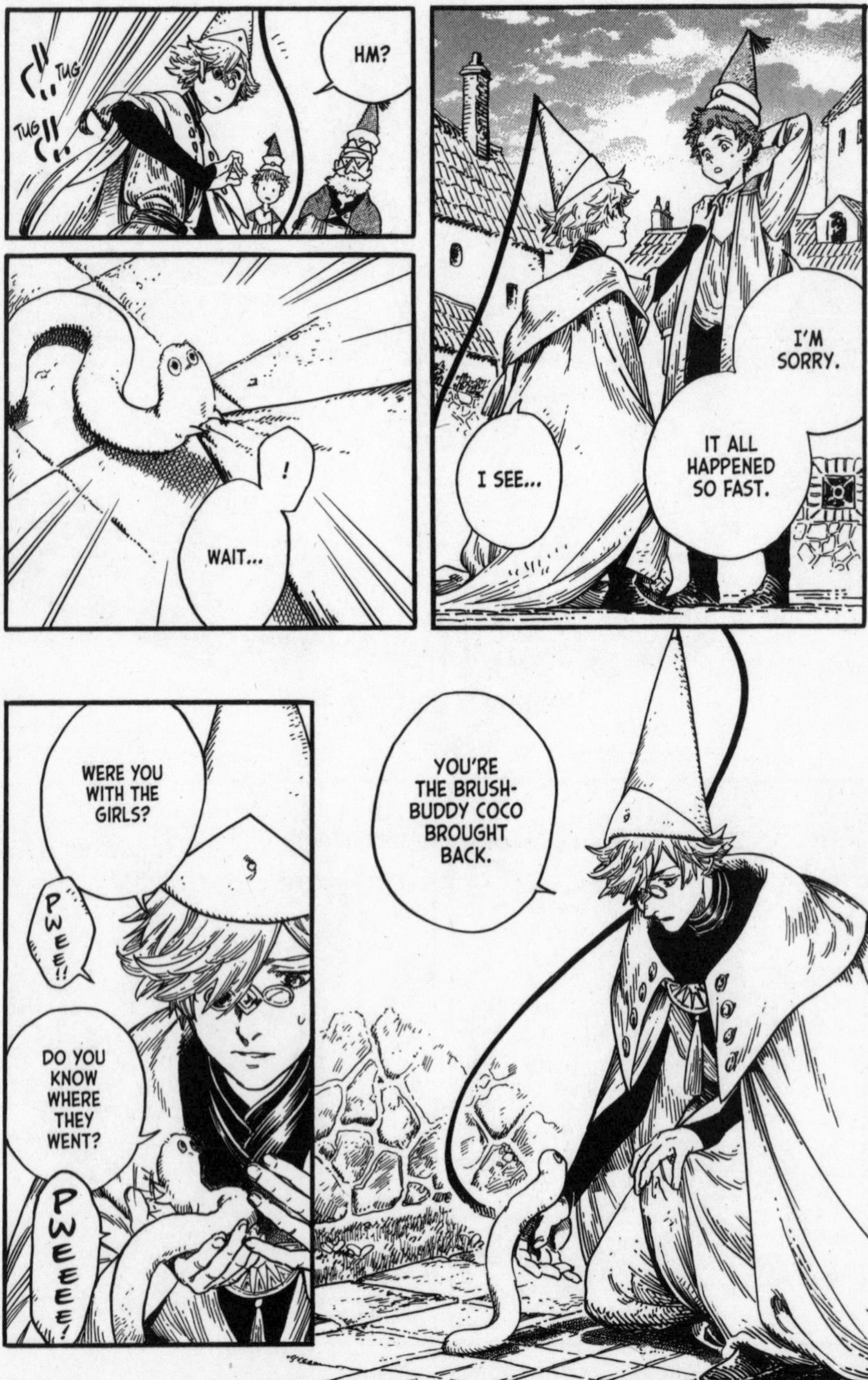
I'M SORRY.
IT ALL HAPPENED SO FAST.
I SEE...
HM?
TUG
TUG
!
WAIT...
YOU'RE THE BRUSH-BUDDY COCO BROUGHT BACK.
WERE YOU WITH THE GIRLS?
PWEE!!
DO YOU KNOW WHERE THEY WENT?
PWEEEE!

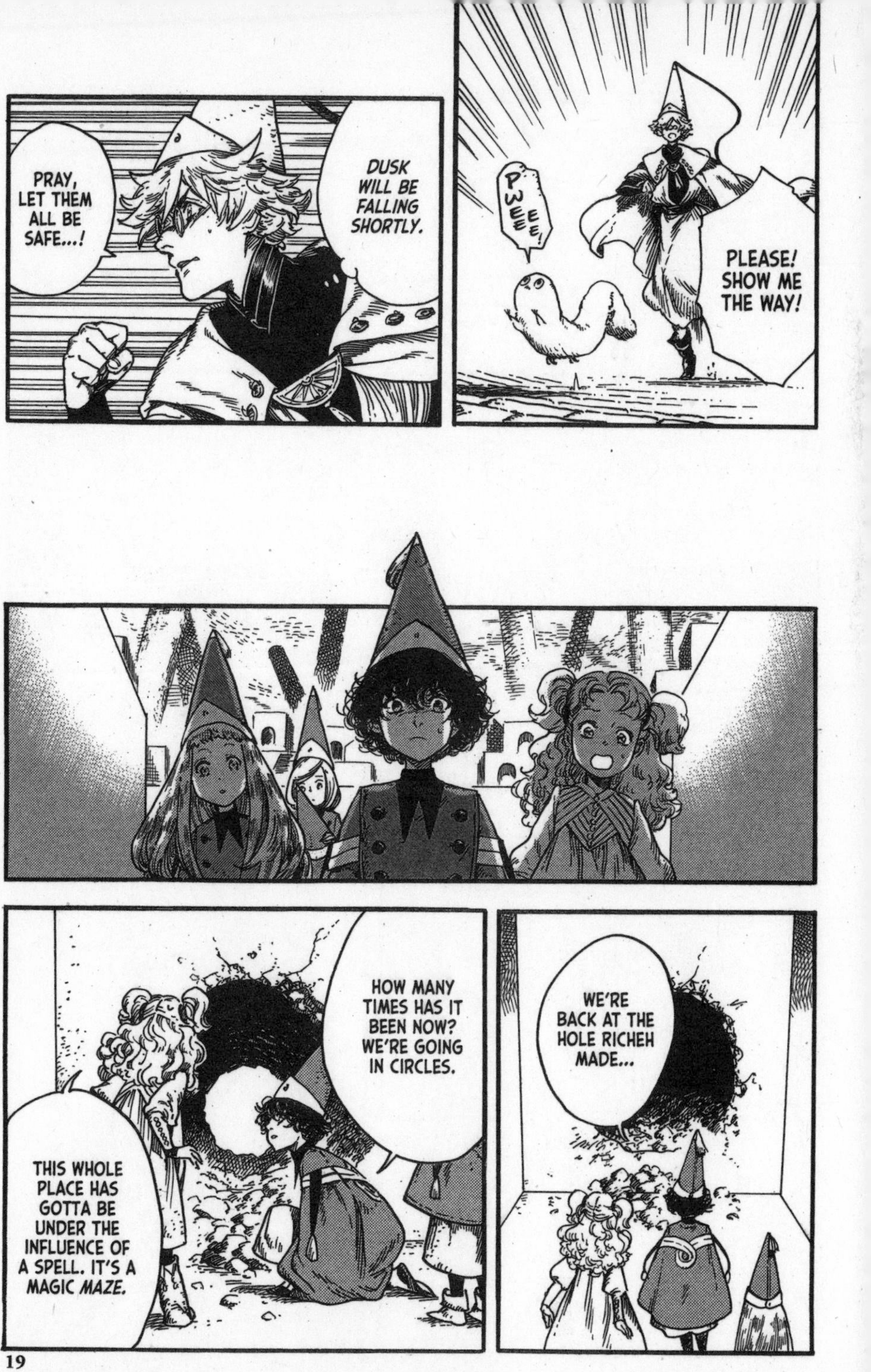
PWEEE
PLEASE! SHOW ME THE WAY!
DUSK WILL BE FALLING SHORTLY.
PRAY, LET THEM ALL BE SAFE...!
WE'RE BACK AT THE HOLE RICHEH MADE...
HOW MANY TIMES HAS IT BEEN NOW? WE'RE GOING IN CIRCLES.
THIS WHOLE PLACE HAS GOTTA BE UNDER THE INFLUENCE OF A SPELL. IT'S A MAGIC *MAZE*.

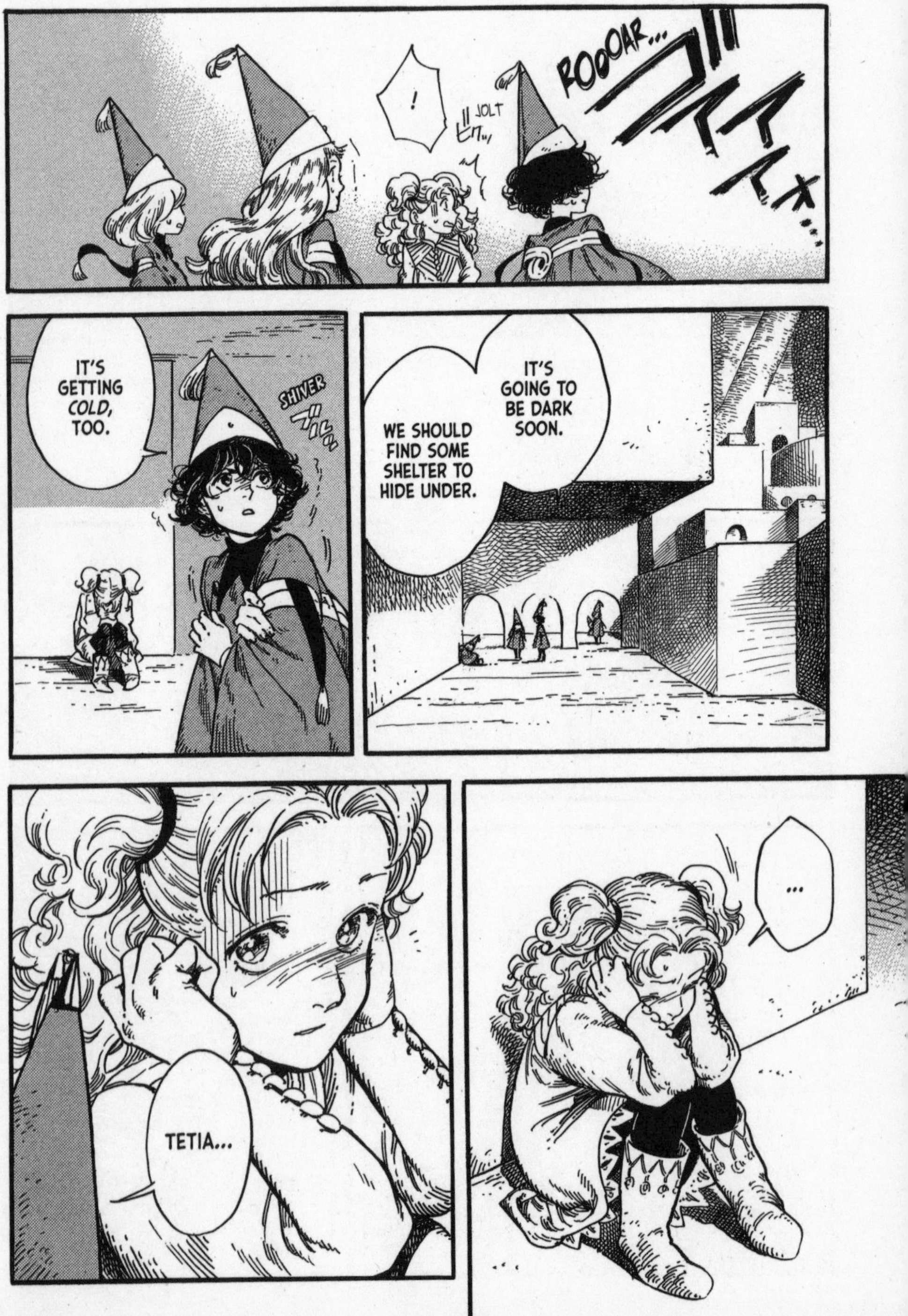
ROOOAR...
JOLT
!
IT'S GOING TO BE DARK SOON.
WE SHOULD FIND SOME SHELTER TO HIDE UNDER.
SHIVER
IT'S GETTING *COLD*, TOO.
...
TETIA...

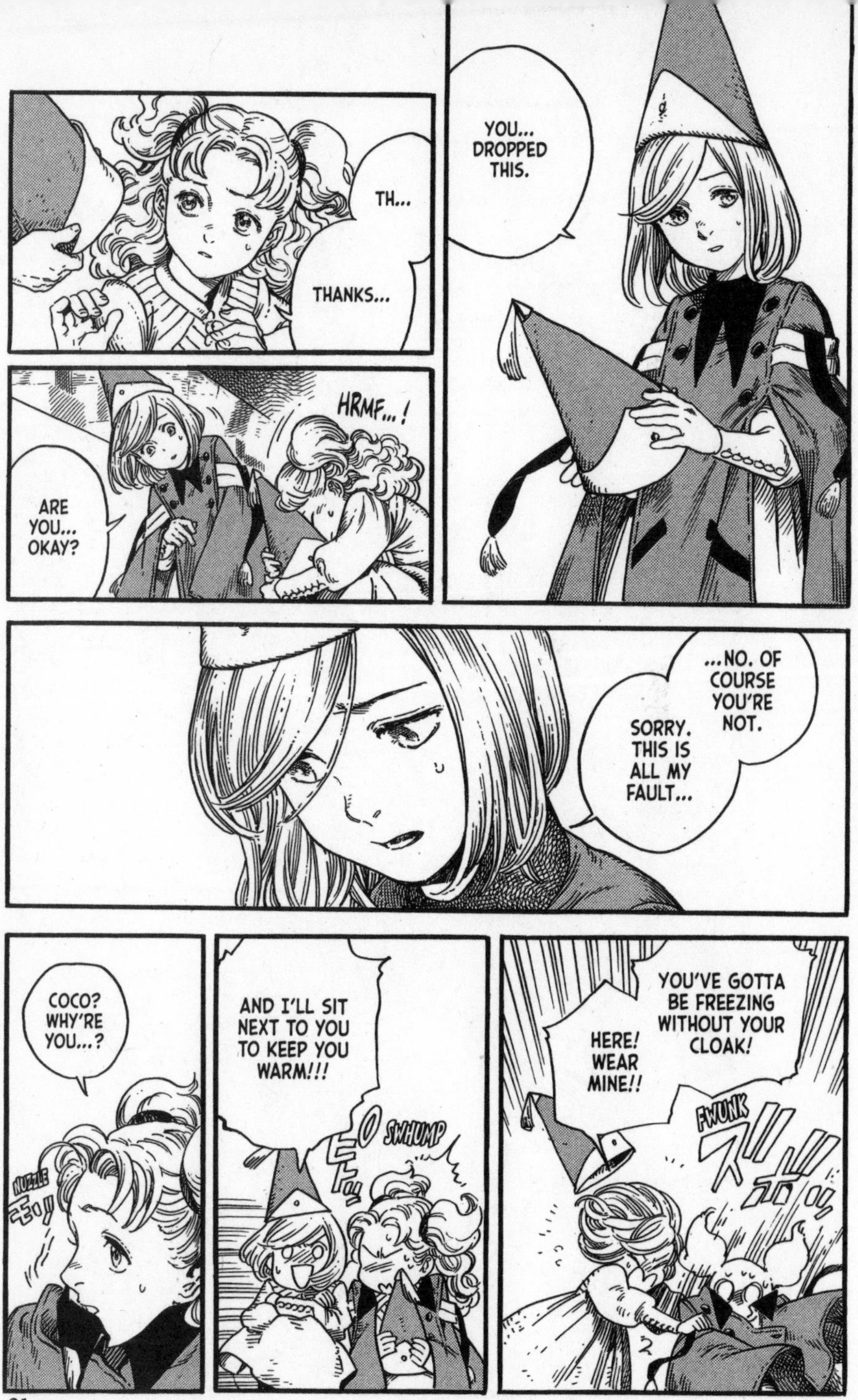
YOU... DROPPED THIS.
TH...
THANKS...
HRMF...!
ARE YOU... OKAY?
...NO. OF COURSE YOU'RE NOT.
SORRY. THIS IS ALL MY FAULT...
YOU'VE GOTTA BE FREEZING WITHOUT YOUR CLOAK!
HERE! WEAR MINE!!
FWUNK
AND I'LL SIT NEXT TO YOU TO KEEP YOU WARM!!!
SWHUMP
COCO? WHY'RE YOU...?
NUZZLE

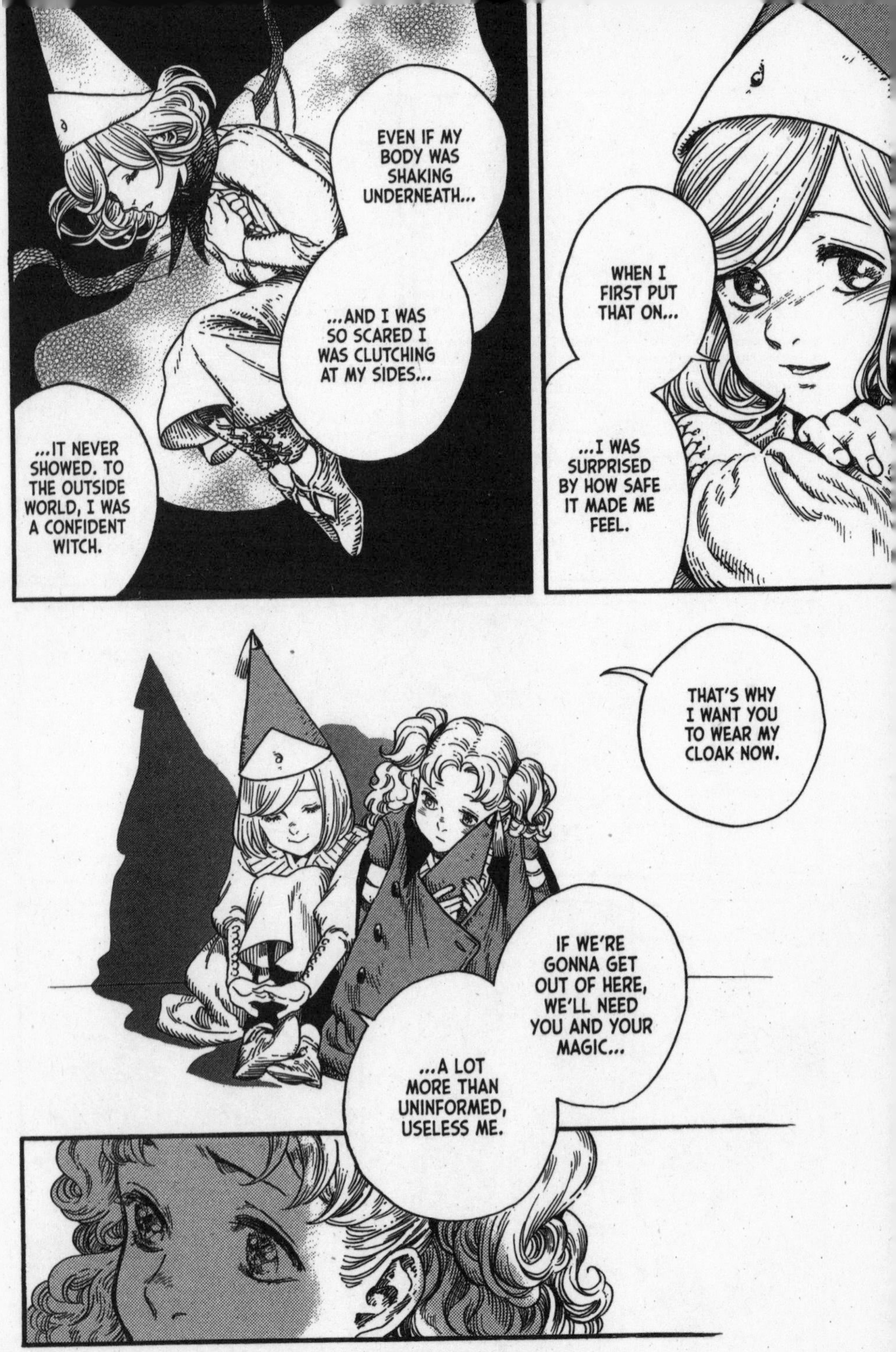
WHEN I FIRST PUT THAT ON...
...I WAS SURPRISED BY HOW SAFE IT MADE ME FEEL.
EVEN IF MY BODY WAS SHAKING UNDERNEATH...
...AND I WAS SO SCARED I WAS CLUTCHING AT MY SIDES...
...IT NEVER SHOWED. TO THE OUTSIDE WORLD, I WAS A CONFIDENT WITCH.
THAT'S WHY I WANT YOU TO WEAR MY CLOAK NOW.
IF WE'RE GONNA GET OUT OF HERE, WE'LL NEED YOU AND YOUR MAGIC...
...A LOT MORE THAN UNINFORMED, USELESS ME.

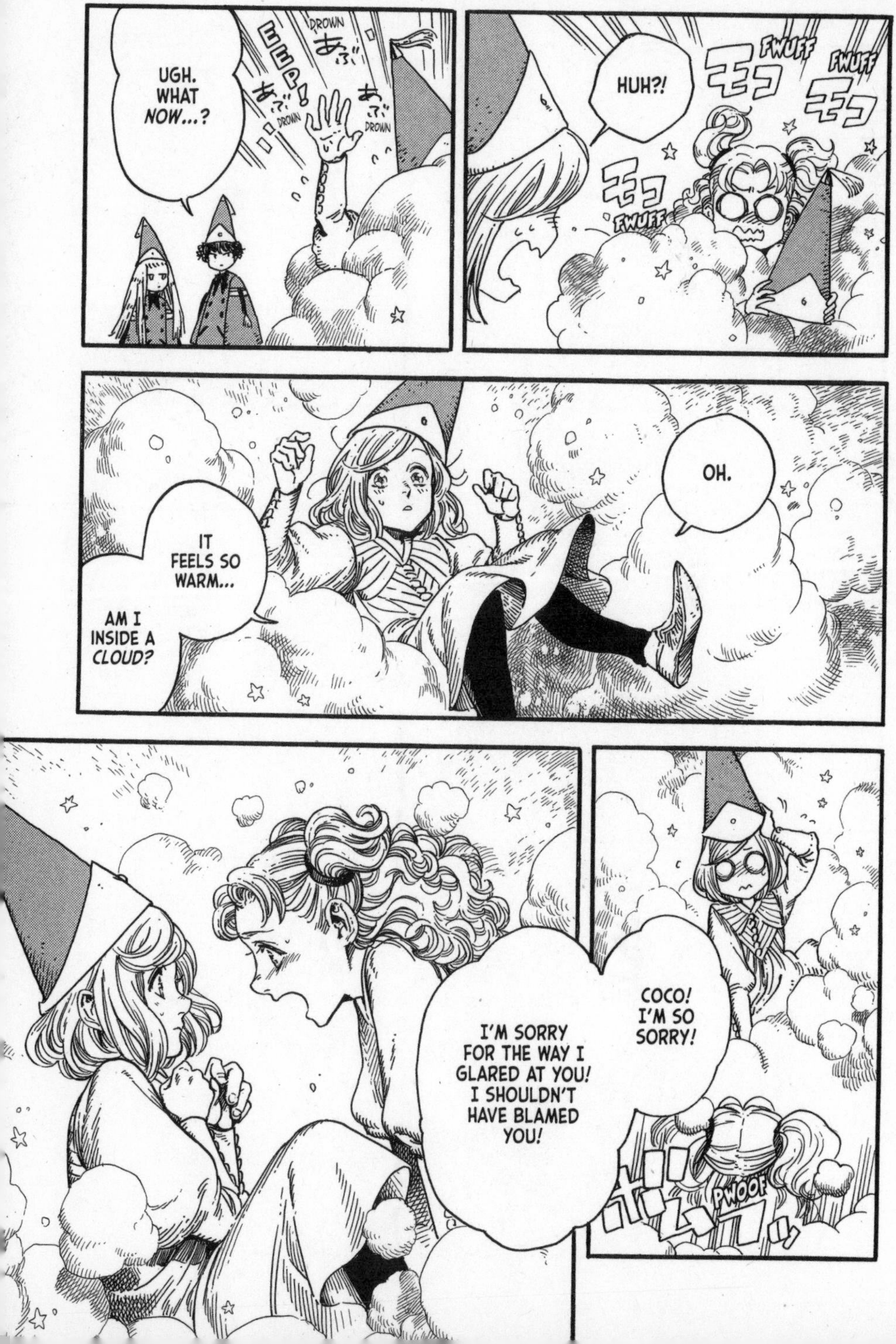
HUH?!
FWUFF
モコ
FWUFF
モコ
モコ
FWUFF
UGH. WHAT NOW...?
EEEP!
DROWN
あぶ
あぶ
DROWN
あぶ
DROWN
OH.
IT FEELS SO WARM...
AM I INSIDE A CLOUD?
COCO! I'M SO SORRY!
I'M SORRY FOR THE WAY I GLARED AT YOU! I SHOULDN'T HAVE BLAMED YOU!
PWOOF

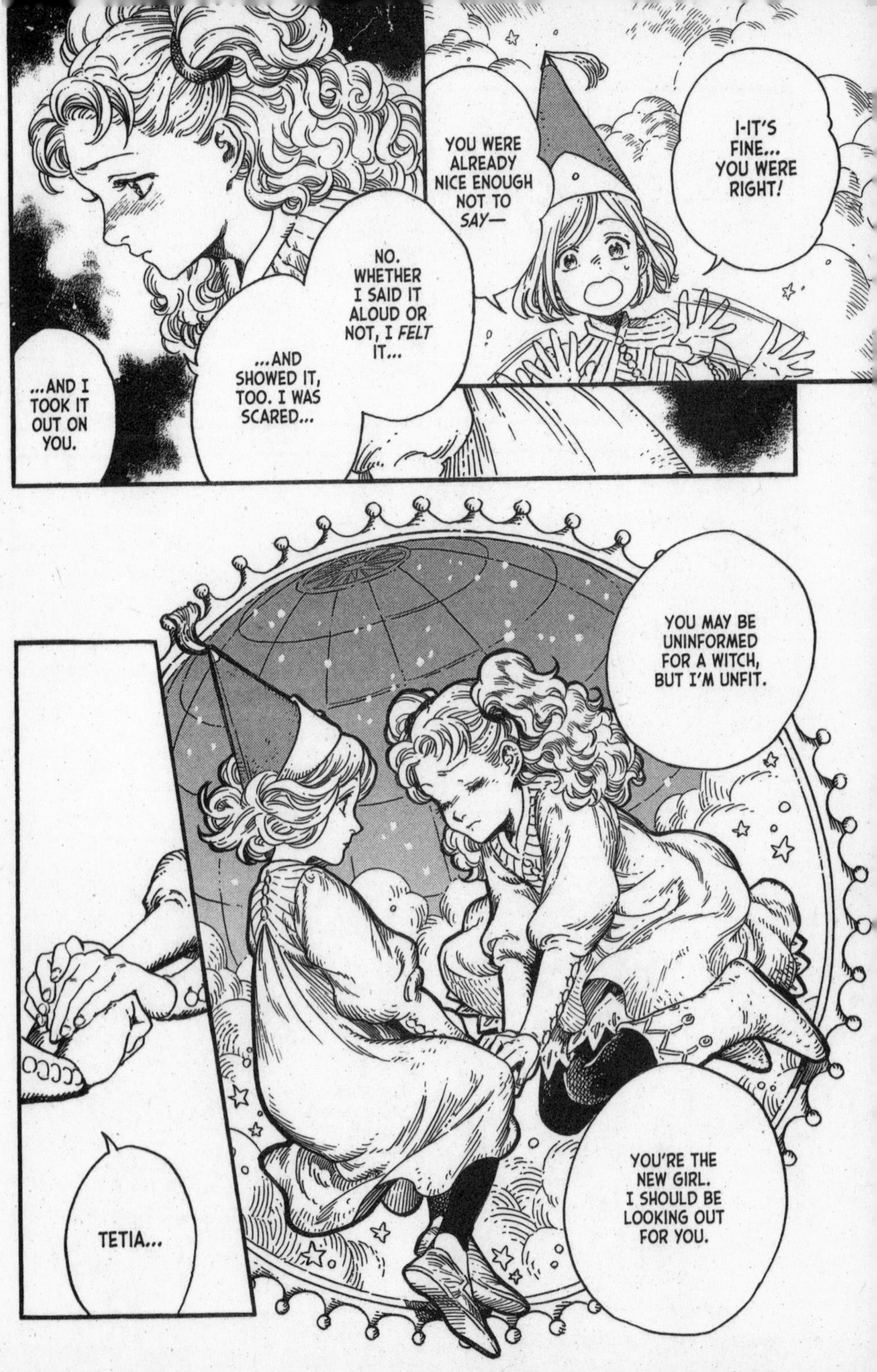
I-IT'S FINE... YOU WERE RIGHT!
YOU WERE ALREADY NICE ENOUGH NOT TO *SAY*—
NO. WHETHER I SAID IT ALOUD OR NOT, I *FELT* IT...
...AND SHOWED IT, TOO. I WAS SCARED...
...AND I TOOK IT OUT ON YOU.
YOU MAY BE UNINFORMED FOR A WITCH, BUT I'M UNFIT.
YOU'RE THE NEW GIRL. I SHOULD BE LOOKING OUT FOR YOU.
TETIA...

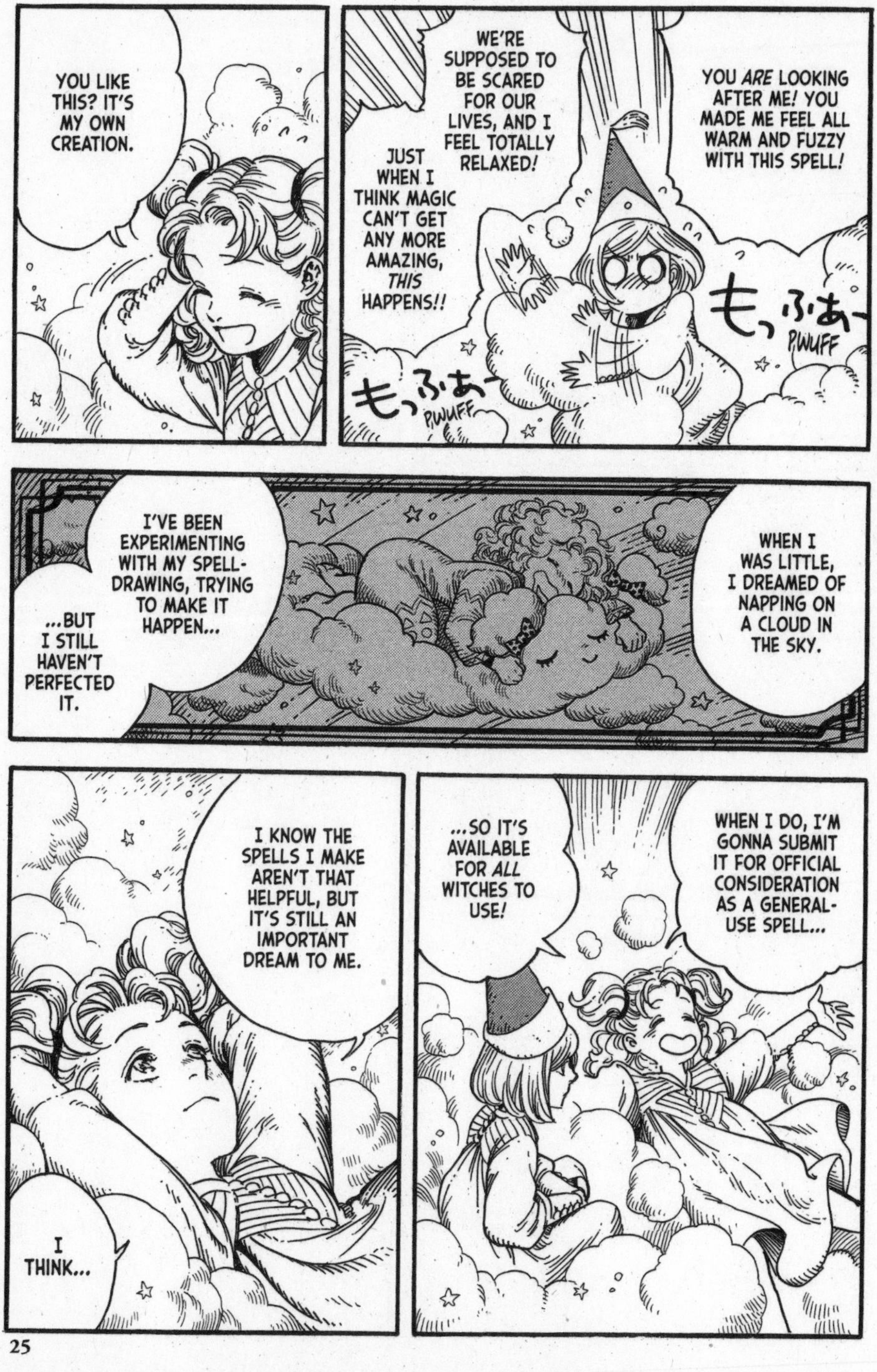
YOU *ARE* LOOKING AFTER ME! YOU MADE ME FEEL ALL WARM AND FUZZY WITH THIS SPELL!
WE'RE SUPPOSED TO BE SCARED FOR OUR LIVES, AND I FEEL TOTALLY RELAXED!
JUST WHEN I THINK MAGIC CAN'T GET ANY MORE AMAZING, *THIS* HAPPENS!!
もっふぁー P.WUFF
もっふぁー P.WUFF
YOU LIKE THIS? IT'S MY OWN CREATION.
WHEN I WAS LITTLE, I DREAMED OF NAPPING ON A CLOUD IN THE SKY.
I'VE BEEN EXPERIMENTING WITH MY SPELL-DRAWING, TRYING TO MAKE IT HAPPEN...
...BUT I STILL HAVEN'T PERFECTED IT.
WHEN I DO, I'M GONNA SUBMIT IT FOR OFFICIAL CONSIDERATION AS A GENERAL-USE SPELL...
...SO IT'S AVAILABLE FOR *ALL* WITCHES TO USE!
I KNOW THE SPELLS I MAKE AREN'T THAT HELPFUL, BUT IT'S STILL AN IMPORTANT DREAM TO ME.
I THINK...

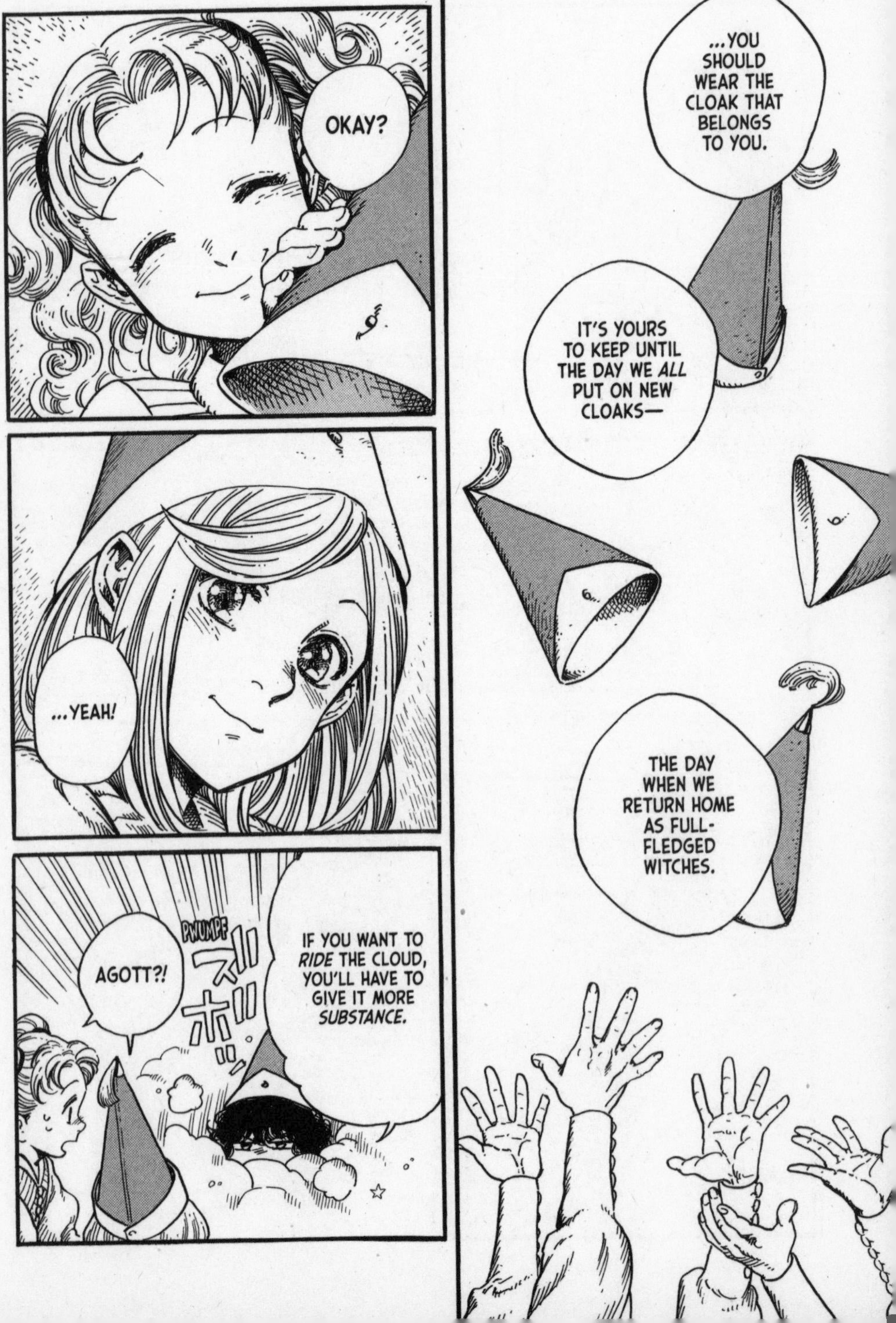
...YOU SHOULD WEAR THE CLOAK THAT BELONGS TO YOU.
IT'S YOURS TO KEEP UNTIL THE DAY WE *ALL* PUT ON NEW CLOAKS—
THE DAY WHEN WE RETURN HOME AS FULL-FLEDGED WITCHES.
OKAY?
...YEAH!
IF YOU WANT TO *RIDE* THE CLOUD, YOU'LL HAVE TO GIVE IT MORE *SUBSTANCE*.
PWUMPF
AGOTT?!

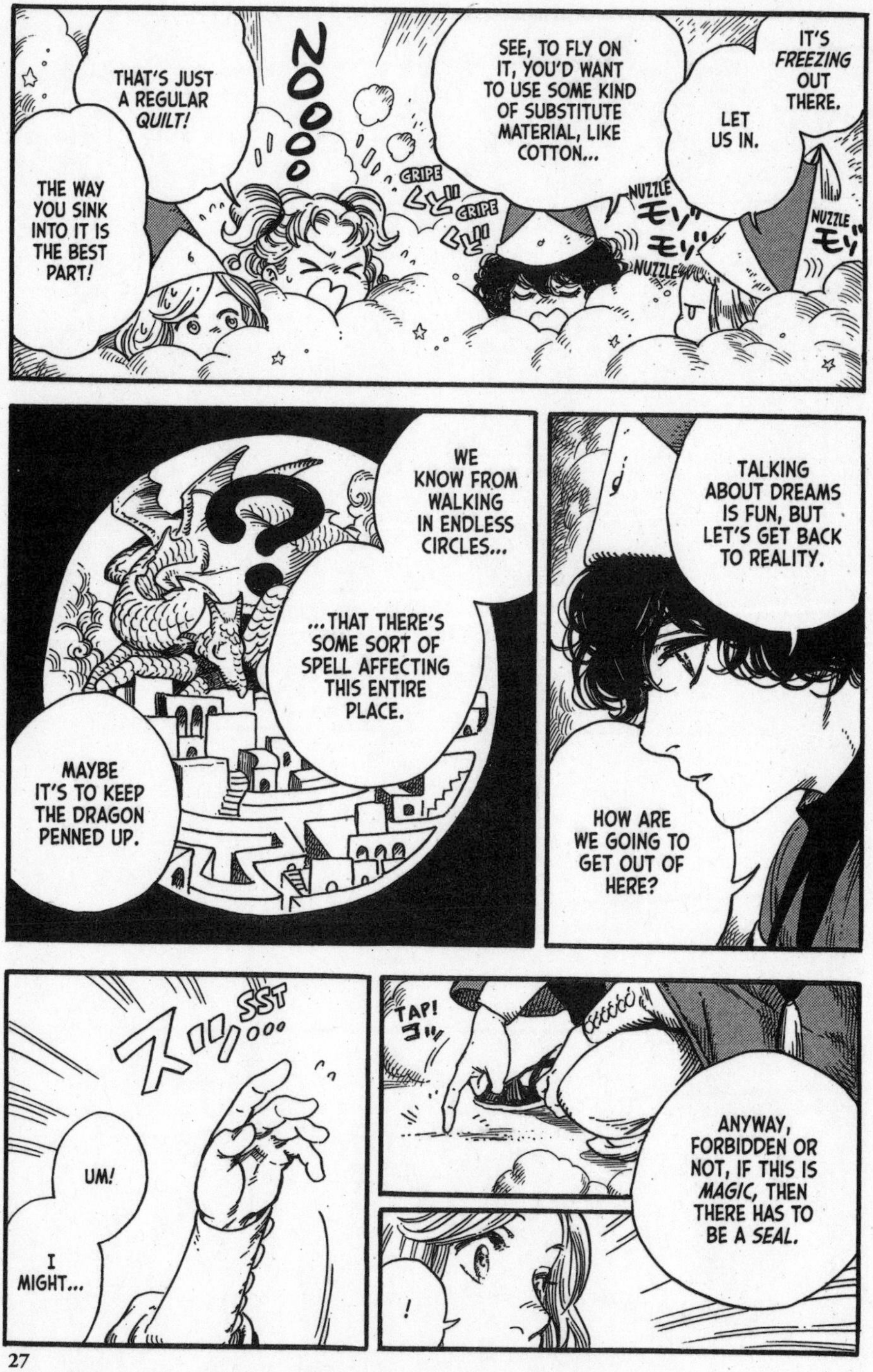
IT'S FREEZING OUT THERE.
LET US IN.
NUZZLE
NUZZLE
NUZZLE
SEE, TO FLY ON IT, YOU'D WANT TO USE SOME KIND OF SUBSTITUTE MATERIAL, LIKE COTTON...
GRIPE
GRIPE
NOOOOO
THAT'S JUST A REGULAR QUILT!
THE WAY YOU SINK INTO IT IS THE BEST PART!
TALKING ABOUT DREAMS IS FUN, BUT LET'S GET BACK TO REALITY.
HOW ARE WE GOING TO GET OUT OF HERE?
WE KNOW FROM WALKING IN ENDLESS CIRCLES...
...THAT THERE'S SOME SORT OF SPELL AFFECTING THIS ENTIRE PLACE.
MAYBE IT'S TO KEEP THE DRAGON PENNED UP.
TAP!
ANYWAY, FORBIDDEN OR NOT, IF THIS IS MAGIC, THEN THERE HAS TO BE A SEAL.
!
SST
UM!
I MIGHT...

...IS.

MAYBE.

...WHERE THE SEAL...

...KNOW...

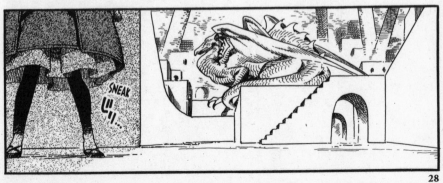

SNEAK

28

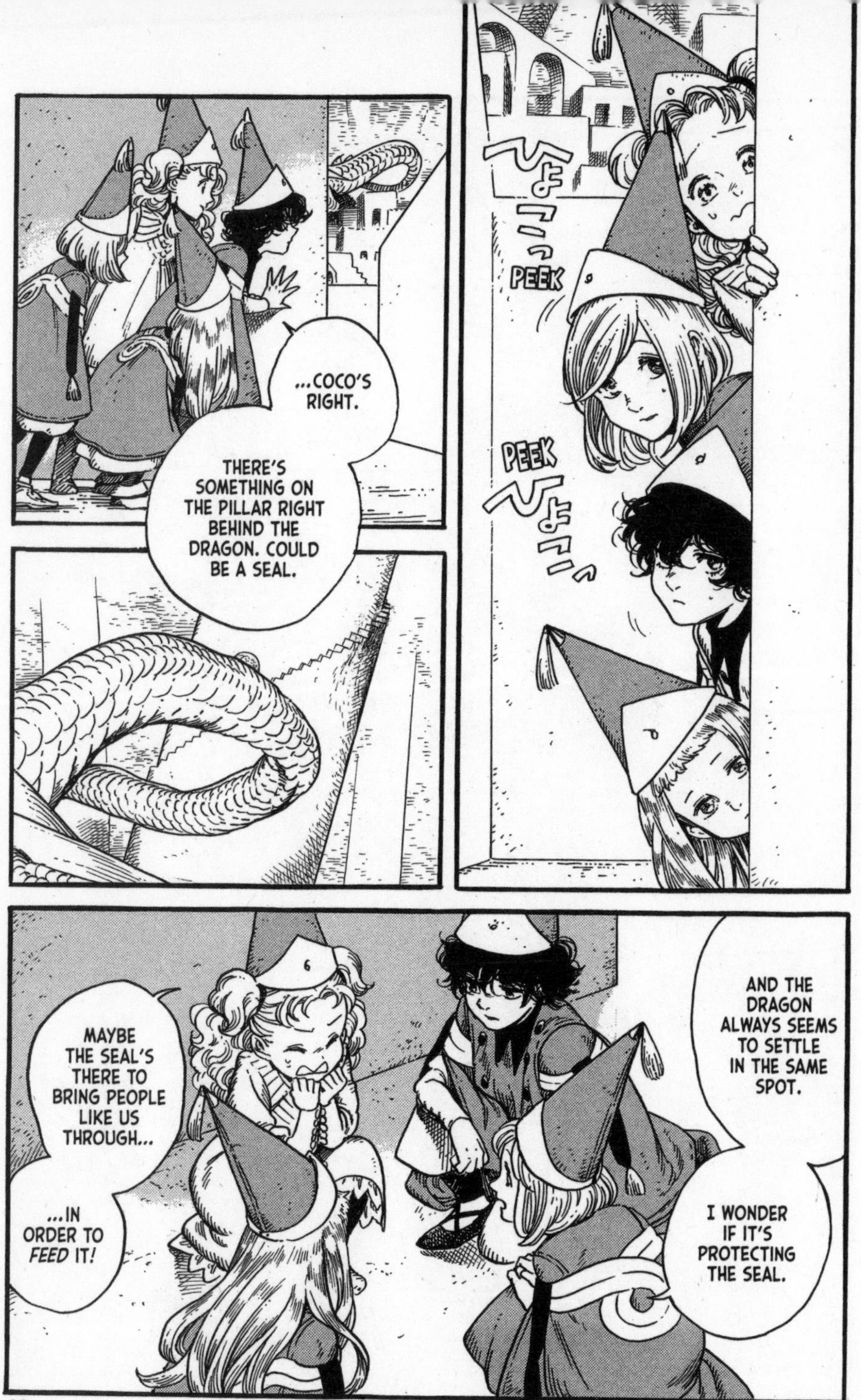
ひょこっ
PEEK
PEEK
ひょこっ
...COCO'S RIGHT.
THERE'S SOMETHING ON THE PILLAR RIGHT BEHIND THE DRAGON. COULD BE A SEAL.
AND THE DRAGON ALWAYS SEEMS TO SETTLE IN THE SAME SPOT.
I WONDER IF IT'S PROTECTING THE SEAL.
MAYBE THE SEAL'S THERE TO BRING PEOPLE LIKE US THROUGH...
...IN ORDER TO *FEED* IT!

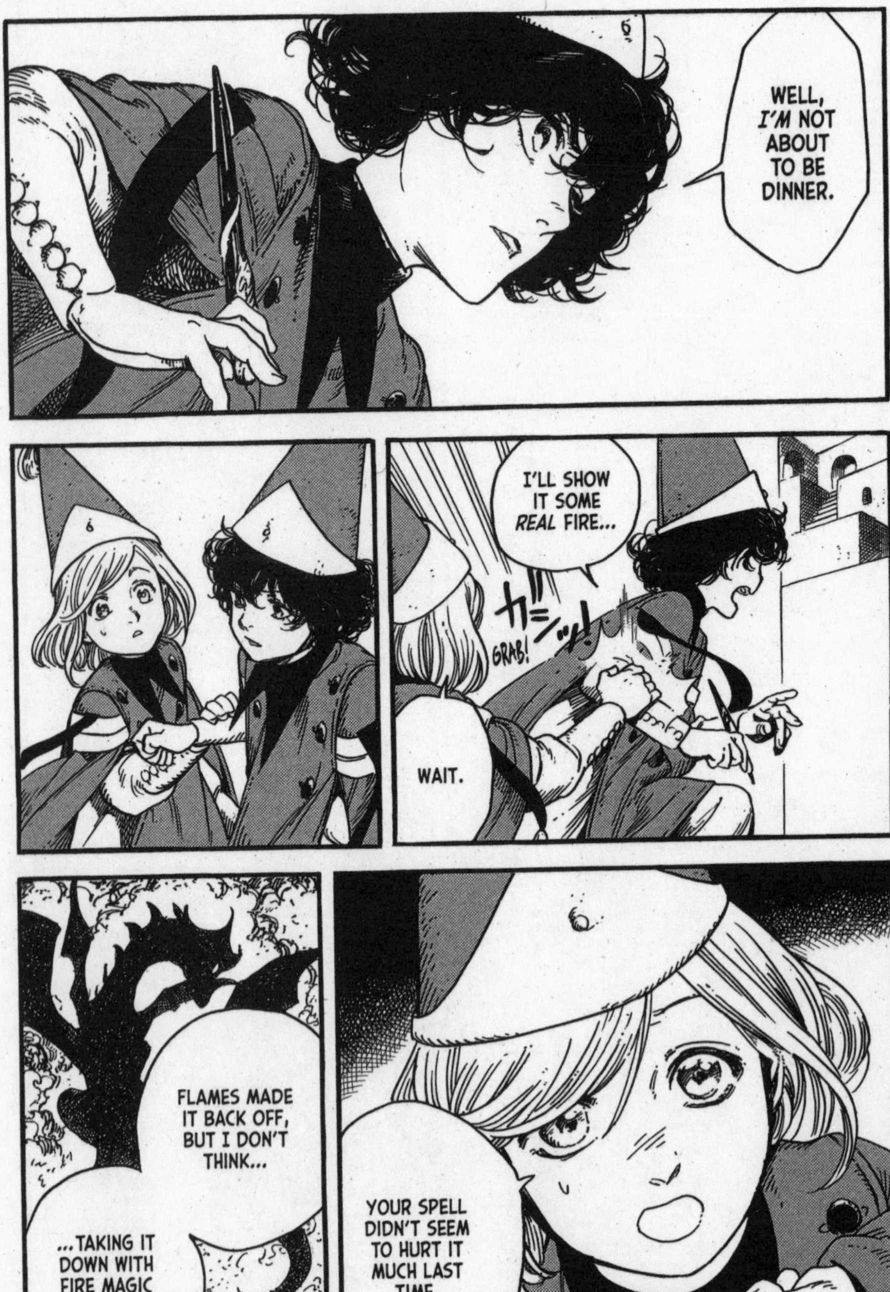
WELL, *I'M* NOT ABOUT TO BE DINNER.
I'LL SHOW IT SOME *REAL* FIRE...
ガシッ!
GRAB!
WAIT.
YOUR SPELL DIDN'T SEEM TO HURT IT MUCH LAST TIME.
FLAMES MADE IT BACK OFF, BUT I DON'T THINK...
...TAKING IT DOWN WITH FIRE MAGIC WOULD BE EASY.

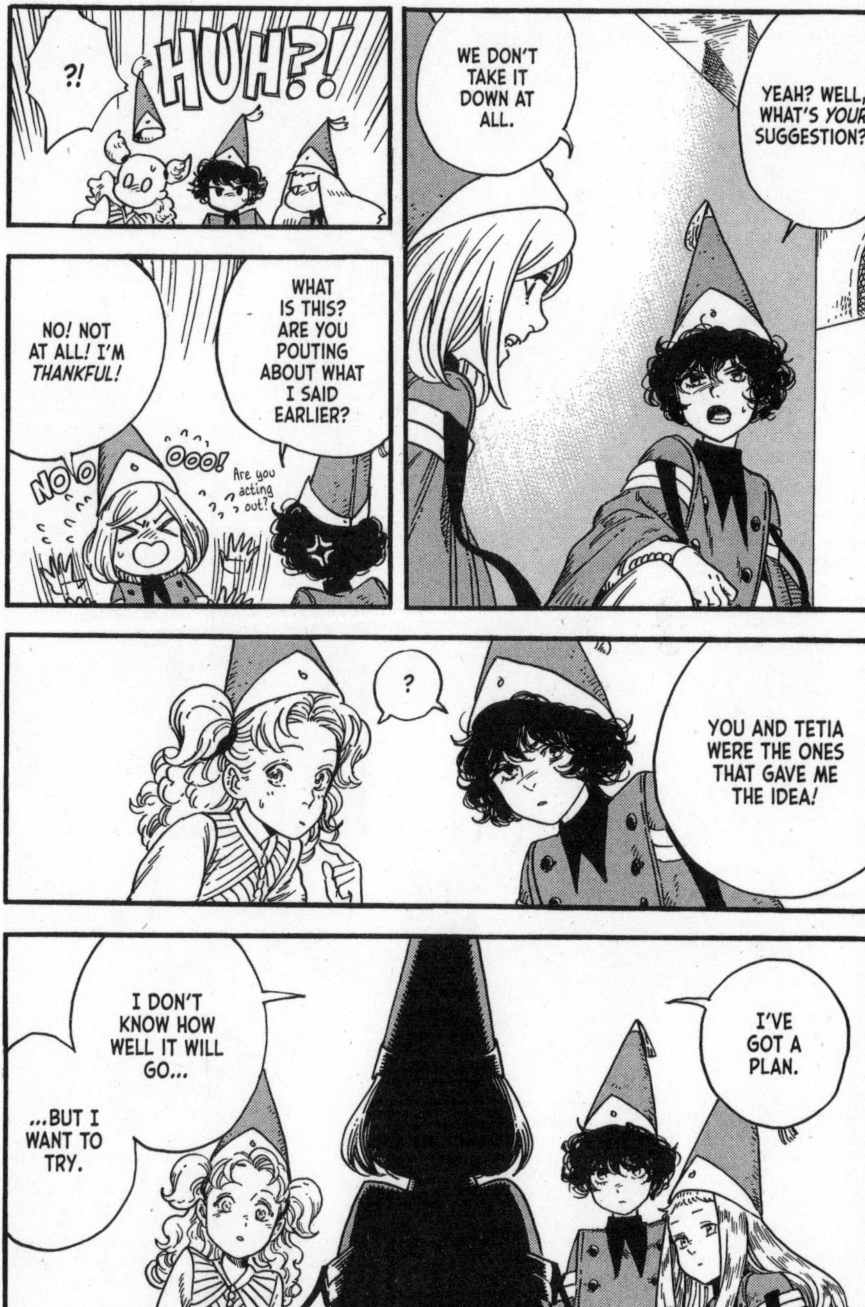
YEAH? WELL, WHAT'S *YOUR* SUGGESTION?!
WE DON'T TAKE IT DOWN AT ALL.
HUH?!
?!
WHAT IS THIS? ARE YOU POUTING ABOUT WHAT I SAID EARLIER?
Are you acting out?
NO! NOT AT ALL! I'M *THANKFUL!*
NOOOO!
YOU AND TETIA WERE THE ONES THAT GAVE ME THE IDEA!
?
I'VE GOT A PLAN.
I DON'T KNOW HOW WELL IT WILL GO...
...BUT I WANT TO TRY.

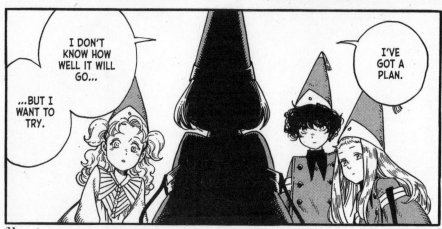

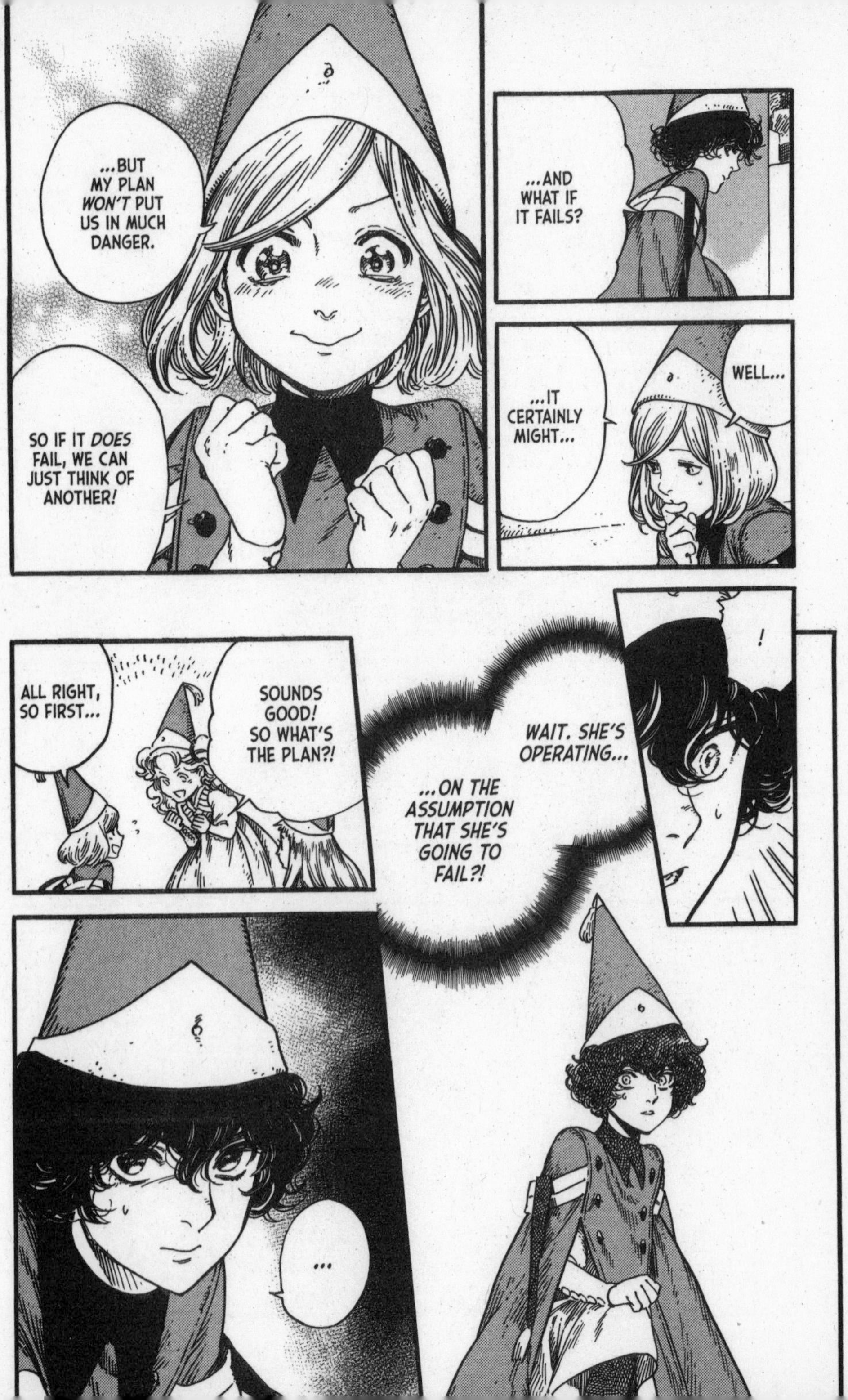
...AND WHAT IF IT FAILS?
WELL...
...IT CERTAINLY MIGHT...
...BUT MY PLAN *WON'T* PUT US IN MUCH DANGER.
SO IF IT *DOES* FAIL, WE CAN JUST THINK OF ANOTHER!
!
WAIT. SHE'S OPERATING...
...ON THE ASSUMPTION THAT SHE'S GOING TO FAIL?!
SOUNDS GOOD! SO WHAT'S THE PLAN?!
ALL RIGHT, SO FIRST...
...

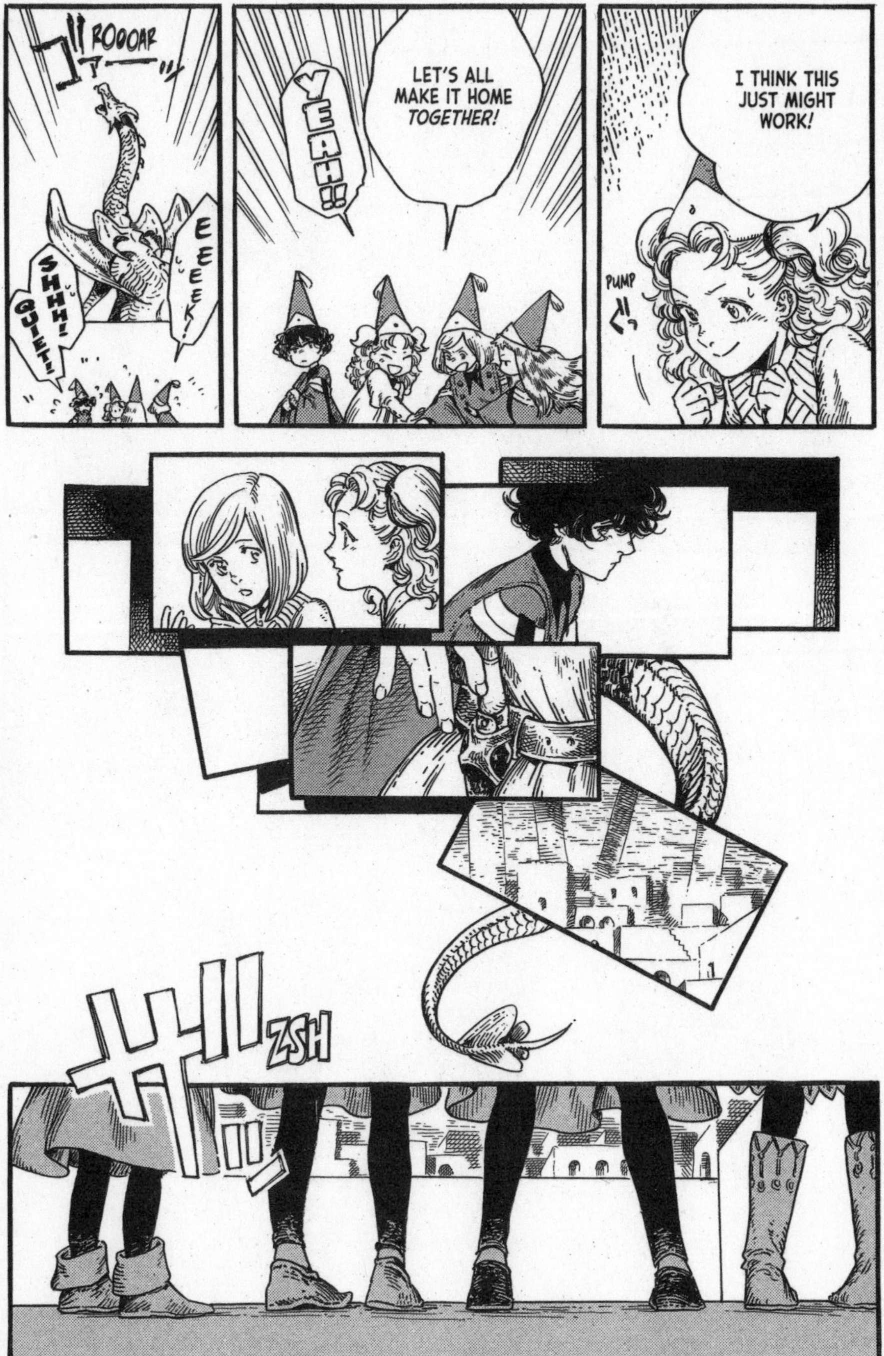
I THINK THIS JUST MIGHT WORK!
PUMP
LET'S ALL MAKE IT HOME TOGETHER!
YEAH!!
ROOOAR
EEEEK!
SHHH! QUIET!
ZSH

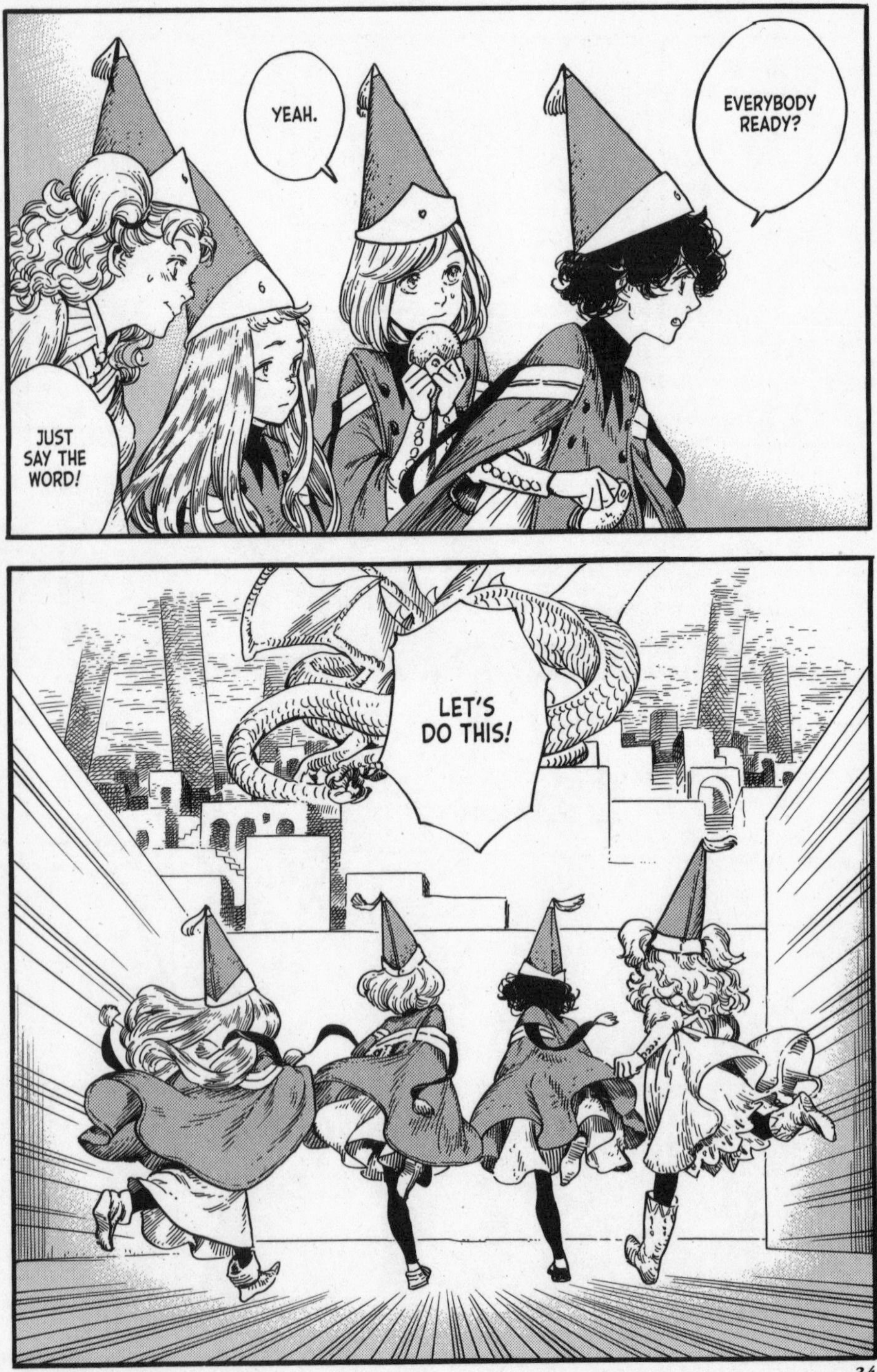
EVERYBODY READY?
YEAH.
JUST SAY THE WORD!
LET'S DO THIS!

Witch Hat Atelier

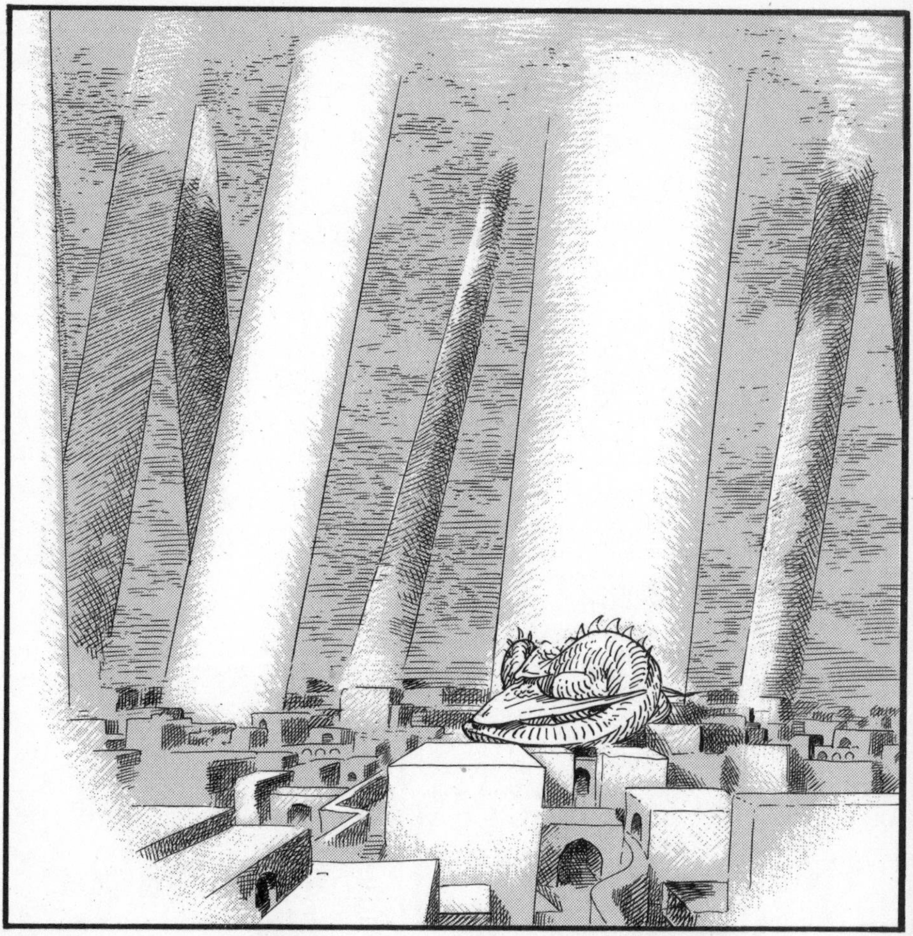

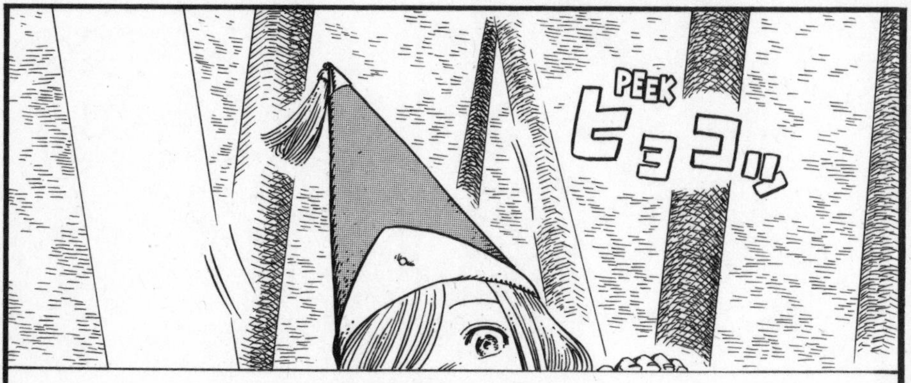
PEEK
ヒョコッ

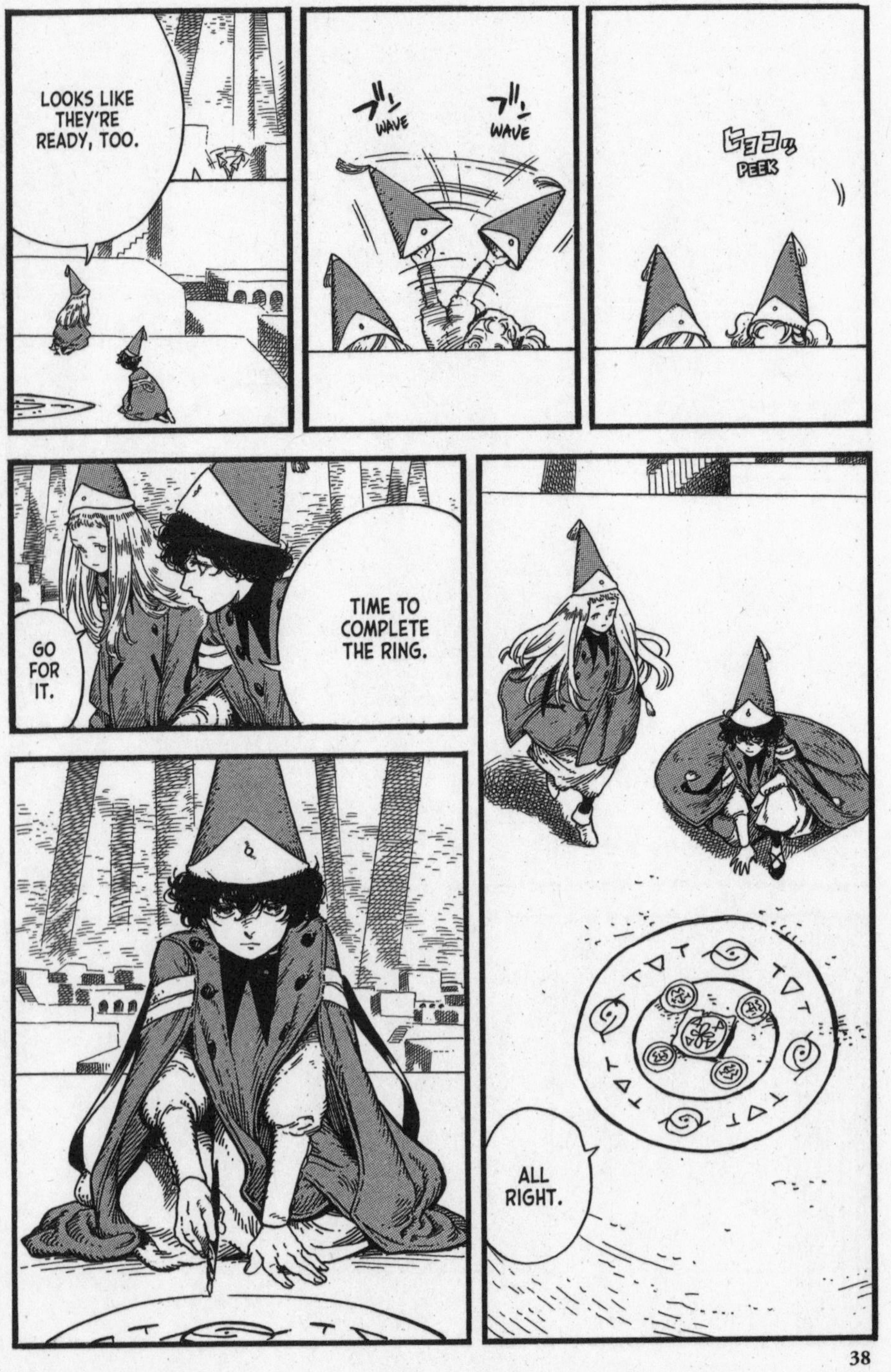
ヒョコッ
PEEK
ブン
WAVE
ブン
WAVE
LOOKS LIKE THEY'RE READY, TOO.
ALL RIGHT.
TIME TO COMPLETE THE RING.
GO FOR IT.

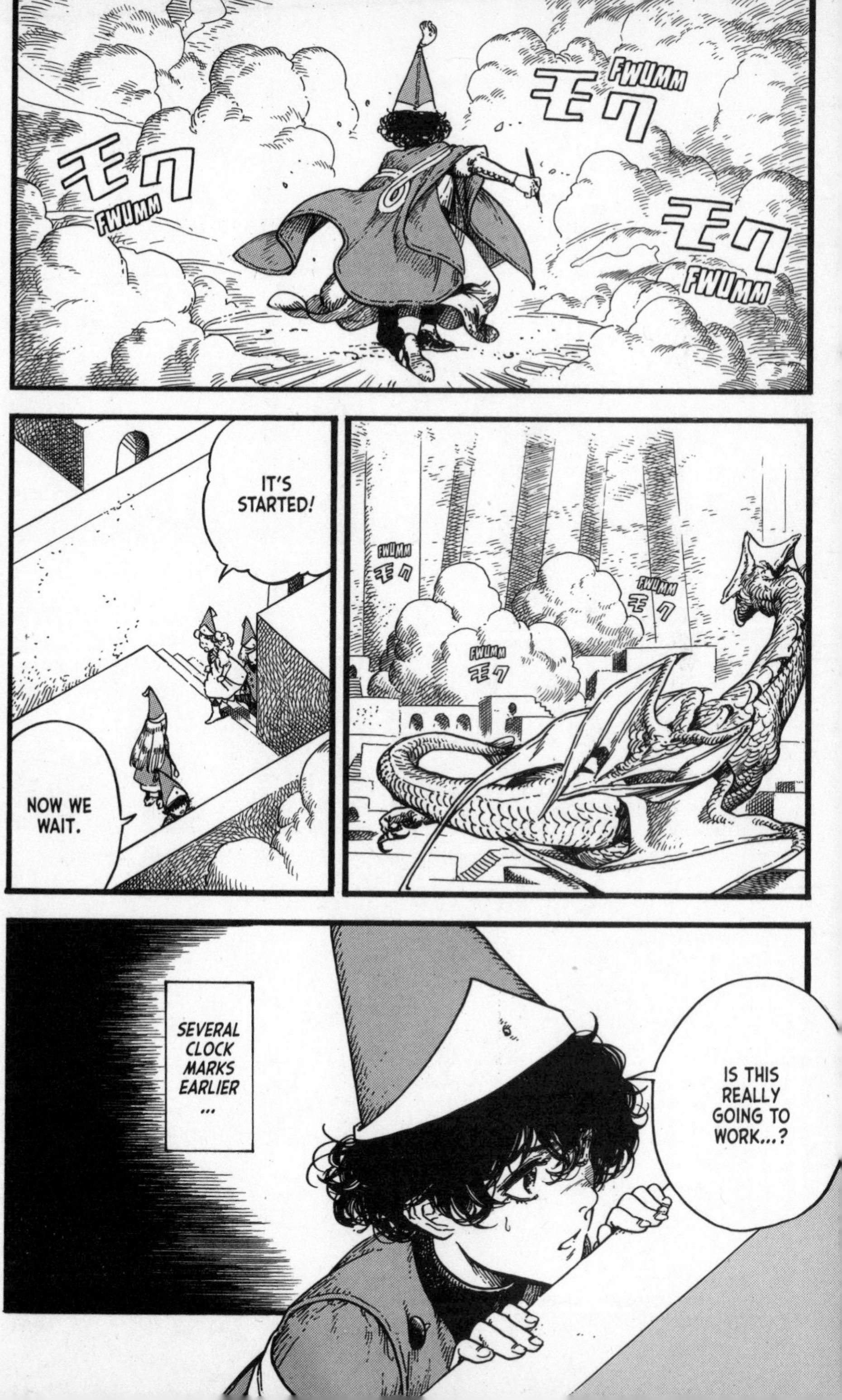
モク
FWUMM
モク
FWUMM
モク
FWUMM
FWUMM
モク
FWUMM
モク
FWUMM
モク
IT'S STARTED!
NOW WE WAIT.
IS THIS REALLY GOING TO WORK...?
SEVERAL CLOCK MARKS EARLIER ...

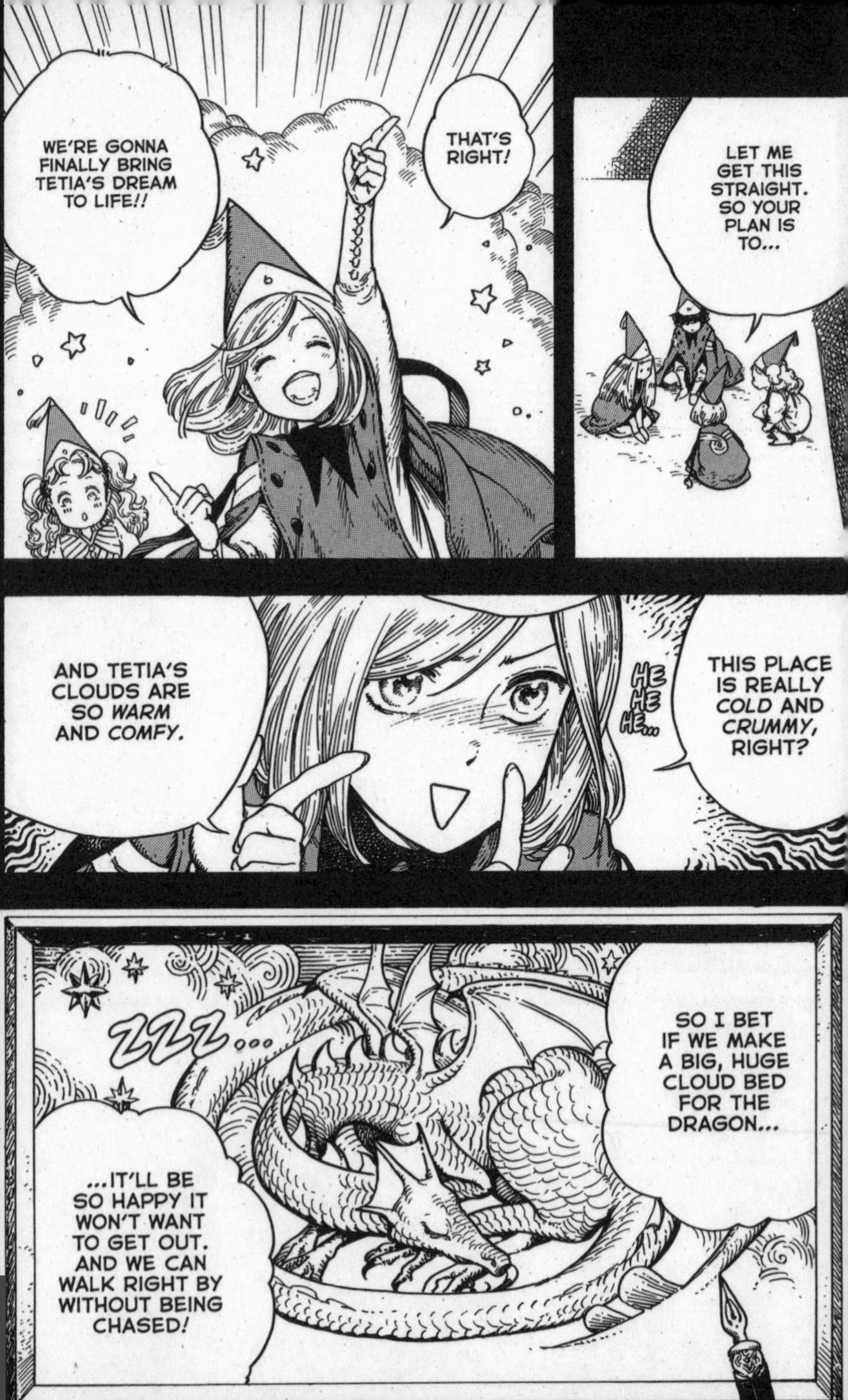
LET ME GET THIS STRAIGHT. SO YOUR PLAN IS TO...
THAT'S RIGHT!
WE'RE GONNA FINALLY BRING TETIA'S DREAM TO LIFE!!
THIS PLACE IS REALLY *COLD* AND *CRUMMY,* RIGHT?
HE HE HE...
AND TETIA'S CLOUDS ARE SO *WARM* AND *COMFY.*
SO I BET IF WE MAKE A BIG, HUGE CLOUD BED FOR THE DRAGON...
ZZZ...
...IT'LL BE SO HAPPY IT WON'T WANT TO GET OUT. AND WE CAN WALK RIGHT BY WITHOUT BEING CHASED!

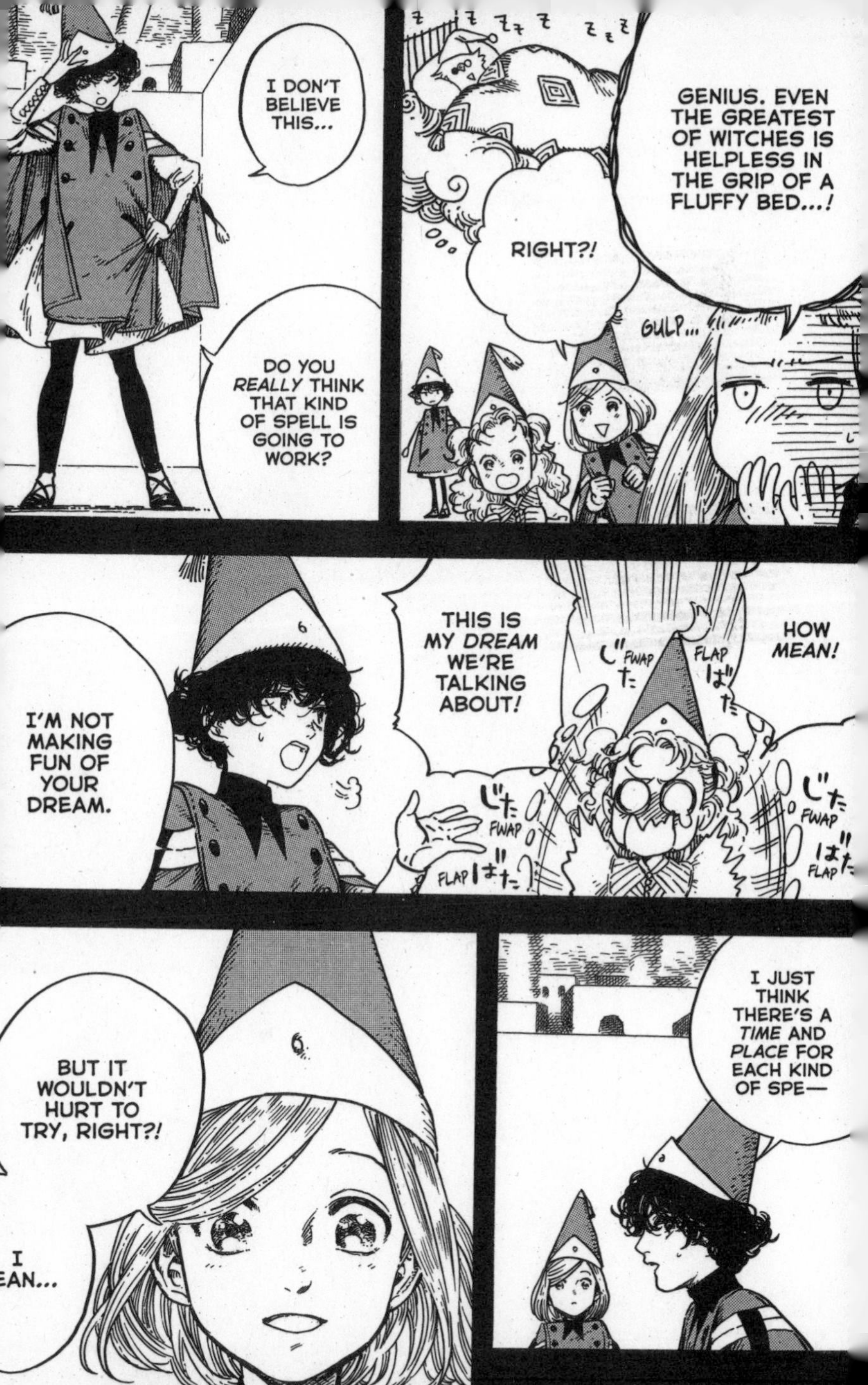
GENIUS. EVEN THE GREATEST OF WITCHES IS HELPLESS IN THE GRIP OF A FLUFFY BED...!
RIGHT?!
GULP...
I DON'T BELIEVE THIS...
DO YOU REALLY THINK THAT KIND OF SPELL IS GOING TO WORK?
HOW MEAN!
FLAP
FWAP
FWAP
FLAP
THIS IS MY DREAM WE'RE TALKING ABOUT!
FWAP
FLAP
I'M NOT MAKING FUN OF YOUR DREAM.
I JUST THINK THERE'S A TIME AND PLACE FOR EACH KIND OF SPE—
BUT IT WOULDN'T HURT TO TRY, RIGHT?!
I
EAN...

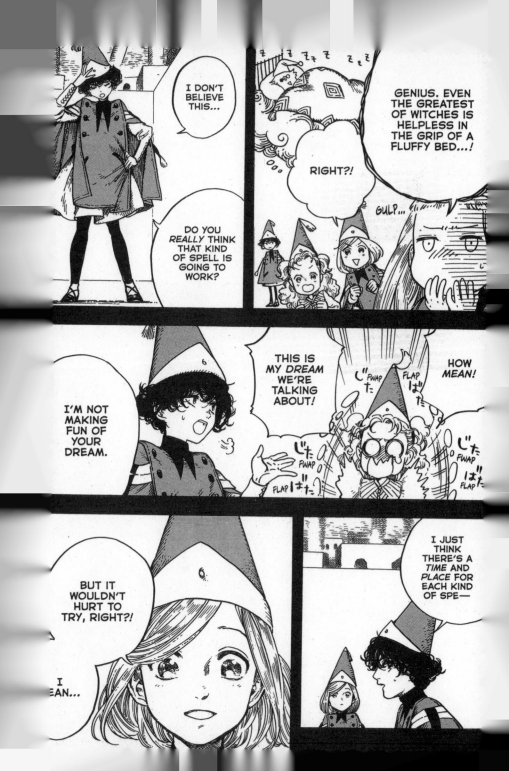

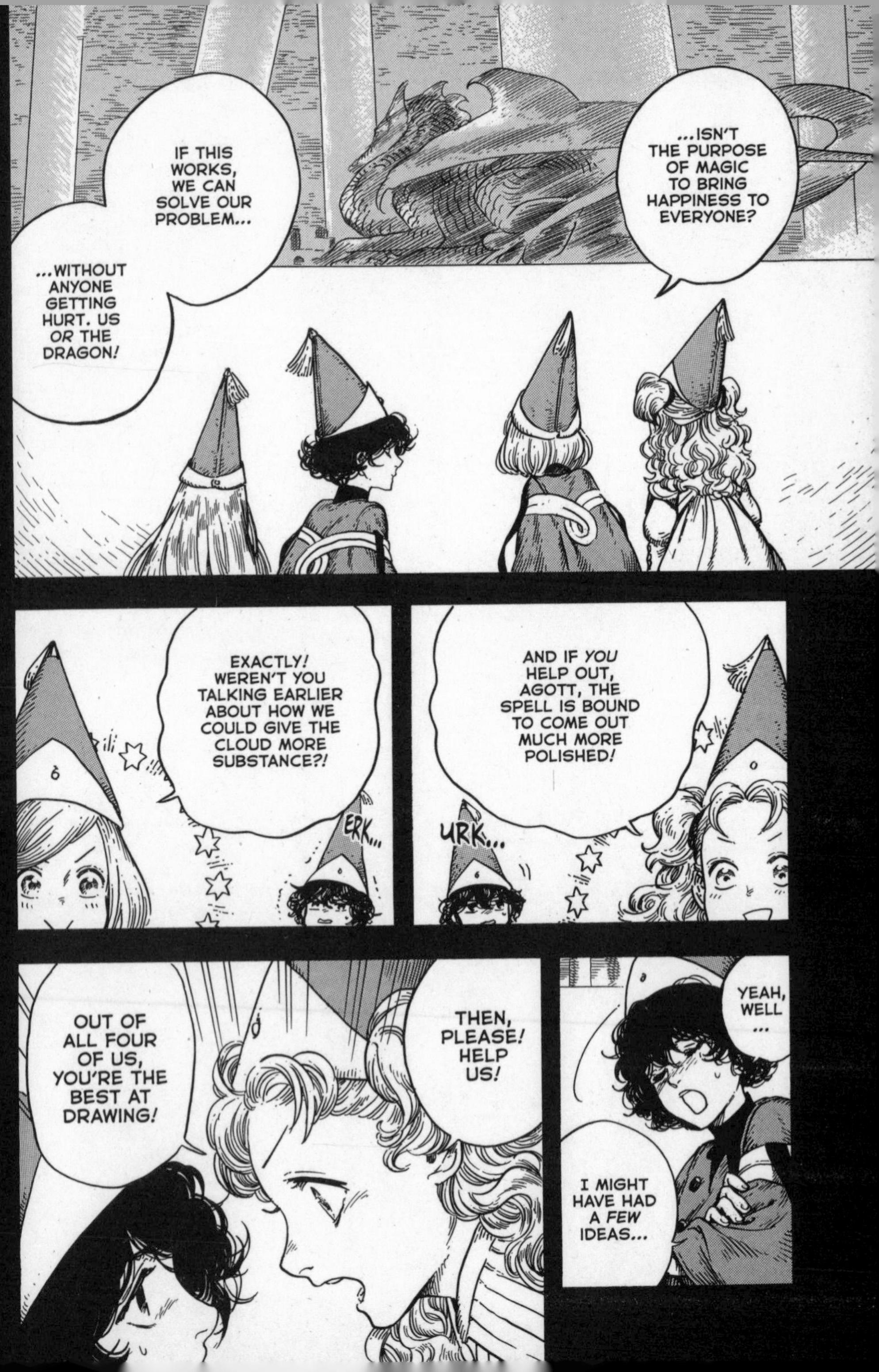
...ISN'T THE PURPOSE OF MAGIC TO BRING HAPPINESS TO EVERYONE?
IF THIS WORKS, WE CAN SOLVE OUR PROBLEM...
...WITHOUT ANYONE GETTING HURT. US *OR* THE DRAGON!
AND IF *YOU* HELP OUT, AGOTT, THE SPELL IS BOUND TO COME OUT MUCH MORE POLISHED!
URK...
EXACTLY! WEREN'T YOU TALKING EARLIER ABOUT HOW WE COULD GIVE THE CLOUD MORE SUBSTANCE?!
ERK...
YEAH, WELL ...
I MIGHT HAVE HAD A *FEW* IDEAS...
THEN, PLEASE! HELP US!
OUT OF ALL FOUR OF US, YOU'RE THE BEST AT DRAWING!

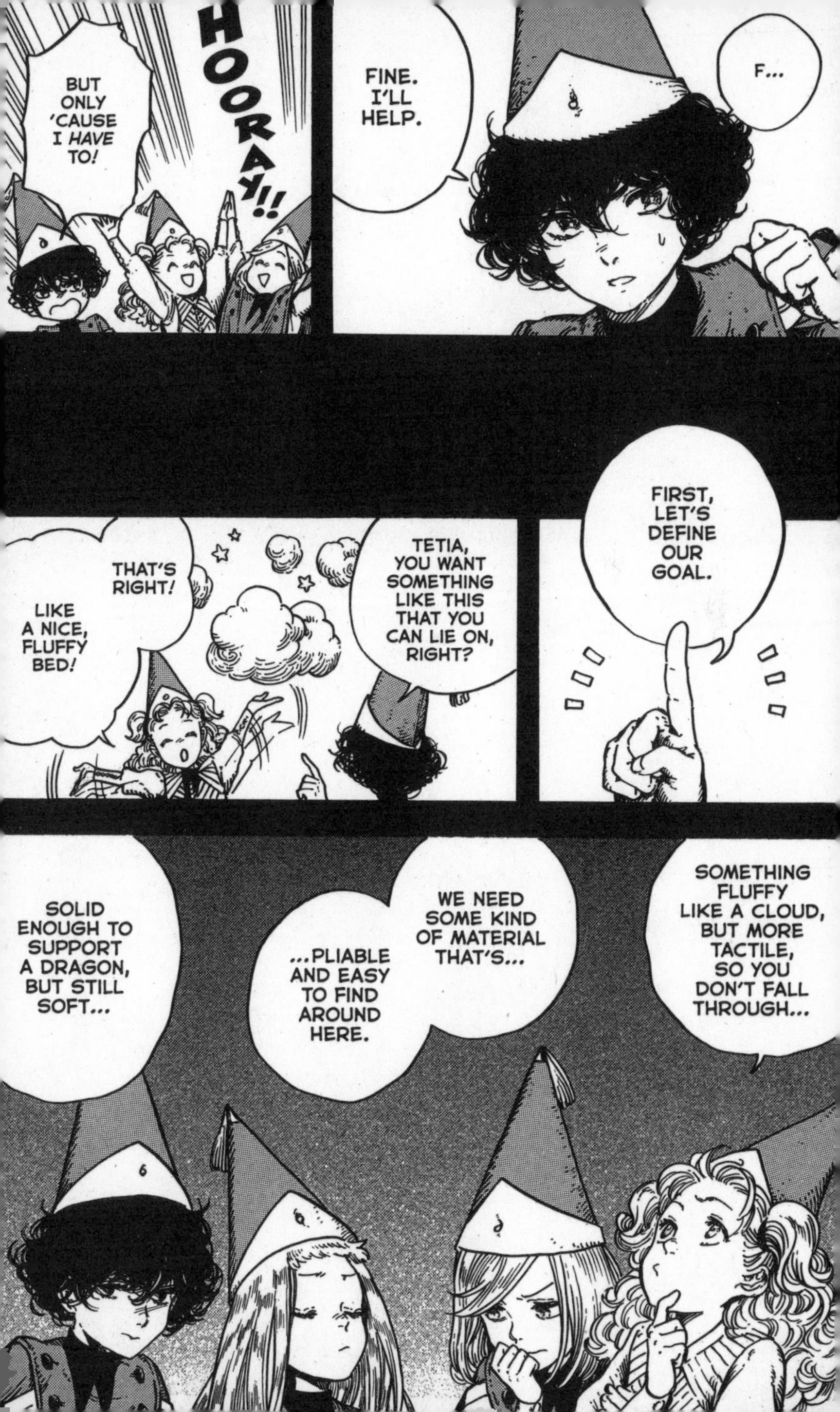
F...
FINE. I'LL HELP.
BUT ONLY 'CAUSE I *HAVE* TO!
HOORAY!!
FIRST, LET'S DEFINE OUR GOAL.
TETIA, YOU WANT SOMETHING LIKE THIS THAT YOU CAN LIE ON, RIGHT?
THAT'S RIGHT!
LIKE A NICE, FLUFFY BED!
SOMETHING FLUFFY LIKE A CLOUD, BUT MORE TACTILE, SO YOU DON'T FALL THROUGH...
WE NEED SOME KIND OF MATERIAL THAT'S...
...PLIABLE AND EASY TO FIND AROUND HERE.
SOLID ENOUGH TO SUPPORT A DRAGON, BUT STILL SOFT...

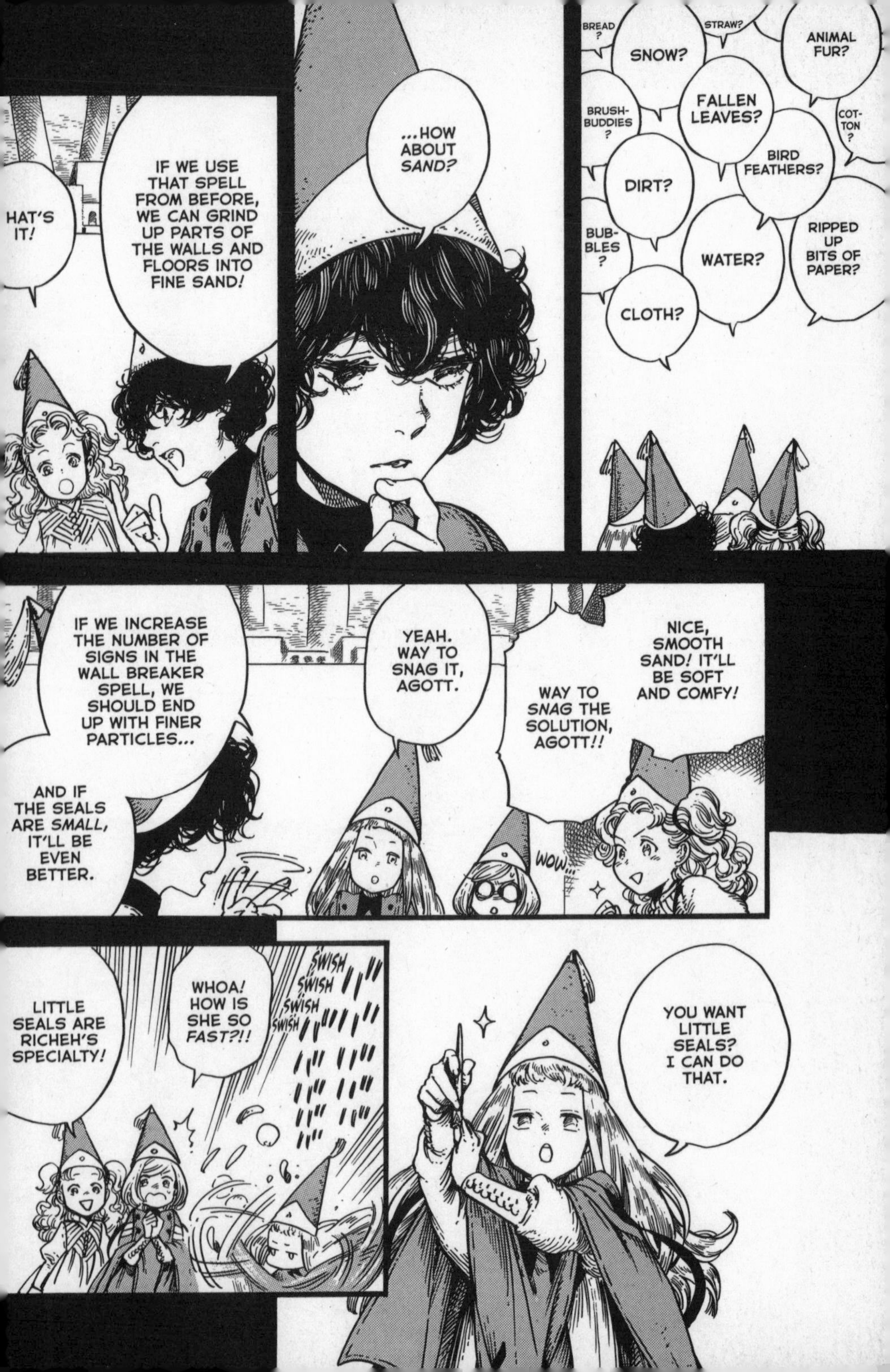
ANIMAL FUR?
STRAW?
SNOW?
BREAD?
COT-TON?
FALLEN LEAVES?
BRUSH-BUDDIES?
BIRD FEATHERS?
DIRT?
RIPPED UP BITS OF PAPER?
WATER?
BUB-BLES?
CLOTH?
...HOW ABOUT *SAND?*
IF WE USE THAT SPELL FROM BEFORE, WE CAN GRIND UP PARTS OF THE WALLS AND FLOORS INTO FINE SAND!
HAT'S IT!
NICE, SMOOTH SAND! IT'LL BE SOFT AND COMFY!
WAY TO *SNAG* THE SOLUTION, AGOTT!!
WOW...
YEAH. WAY TO SNAG IT, AGOTT.
IF WE INCREASE THE NUMBER OF SIGNS IN THE WALL BREAKER SPELL, WE SHOULD END UP WITH FINER PARTICLES...
AND IF THE SEALS ARE *SMALL*, IT'LL BE EVEN BETTER.
YOU WANT LITTLE SEALS? I CAN DO THAT.
SWISH
SWISH
SWISH
SWISH
WHOA! HOW IS SHE SO *FAST?!!*
LITTLE SEALS ARE RICHEH'S SPECIALTY!

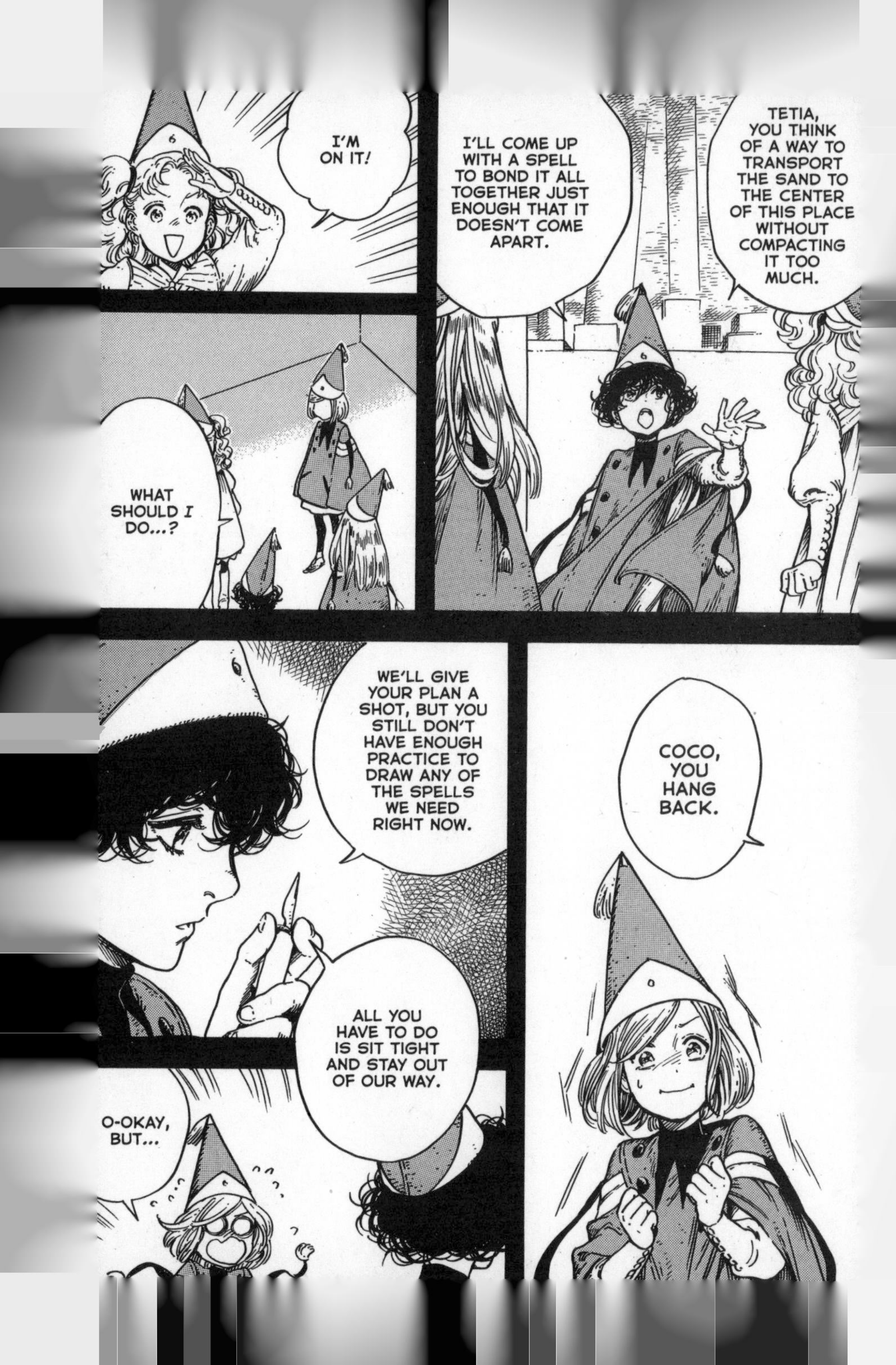

TETIA, YOU THINK OF A WAY TO TRANSPORT THE SAND TO THE CENTER OF THIS PLACE WITHOUT COMPACTING IT TOO MUCH.
I'LL COME UP WITH A SPELL TO BOND IT ALL TOGETHER JUST ENOUGH THAT IT DOESN'T COME APART.
I'M ON IT!
WHAT SHOULD I DO...?
COCO, YOU HANG BACK.
WE'LL GIVE YOUR PLAN A SHOT, BUT YOU STILL DON'T HAVE ENOUGH PRACTICE TO DRAW ANY OF THE SPELLS WE NEED RIGHT NOW.
ALL YOU HAVE TO DO IS SIT TIGHT AND STAY OUT OF OUR WAY.
O-OKAY, BUT...

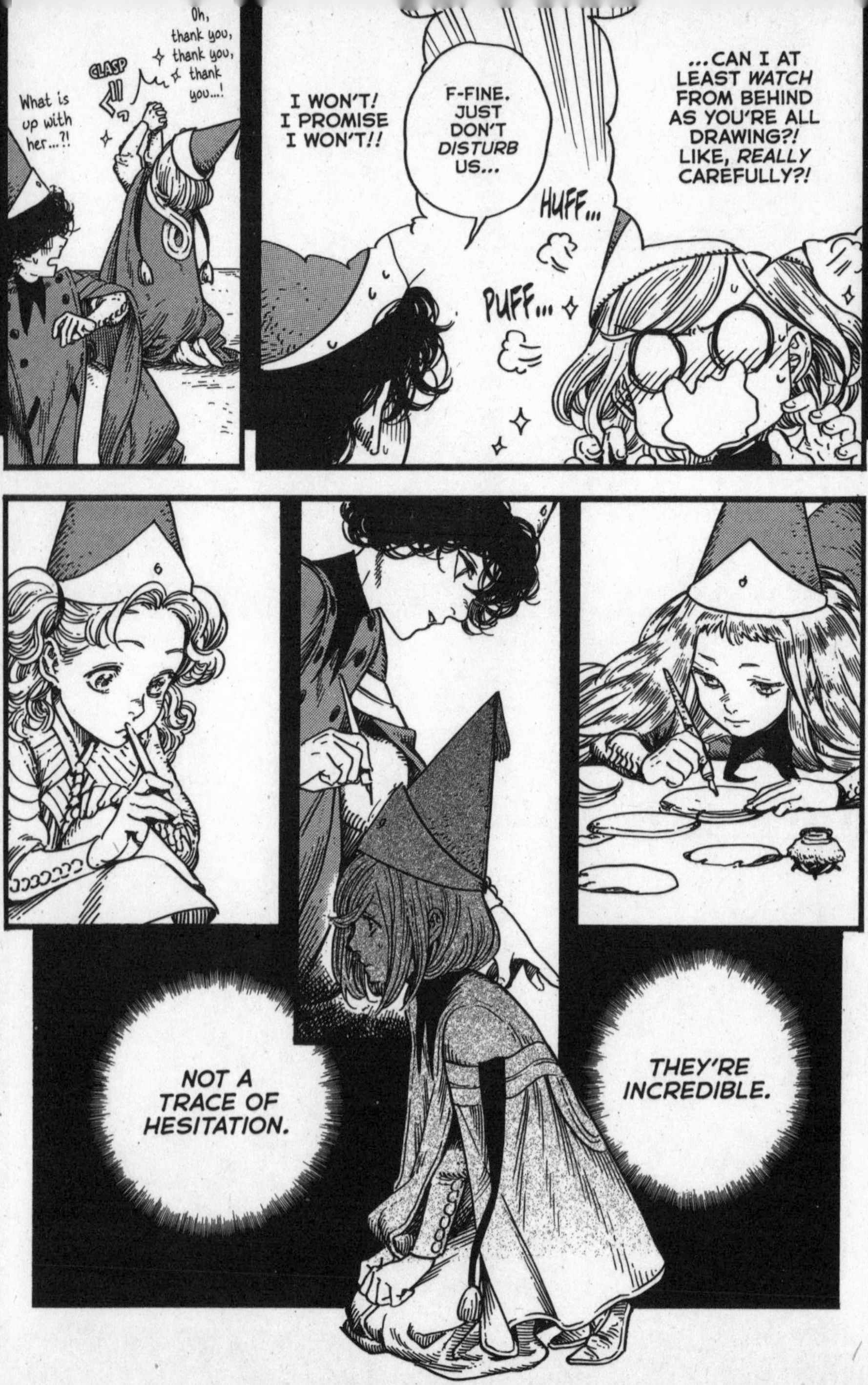
...CAN I AT LEAST WATCH FROM BEHIND AS YOU'RE ALL DRAWING?! LIKE, REALLY CAREFULLY?!
HUFF...
PUFF...
F-FINE. JUST DON'T DISTURB US...
I WON'T! I PROMISE I WON'T!!
Oh, thank you, thank you, thank you...!
CLASP
What is up with her...?!
THEY'RE INCREDIBLE.
NOT A TRACE OF HESITATION.

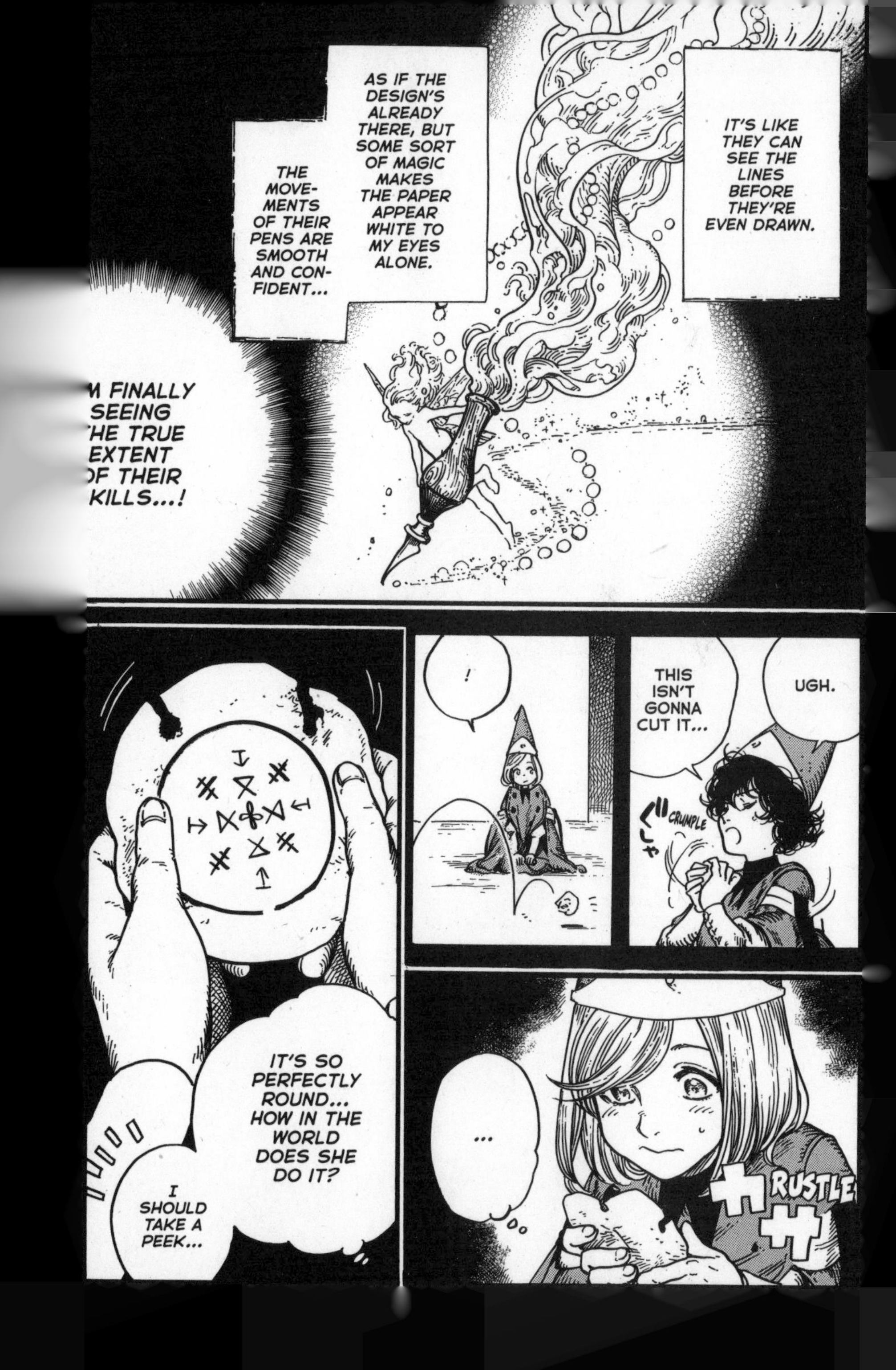
IT'S LIKE THEY CAN SEE THE LINES BEFORE THEY'RE EVEN DRAWN.
AS IF THE DESIGN'S ALREADY THERE, BUT SOME SORT OF MAGIC MAKES THE PAPER APPEAR WHITE TO MY EYES ALONE.
THE MOVEMENTS OF THEIR PENS ARE SMOOTH AND CONFIDENT...
M FINALLY SEEING HE TRUE EXTENT OF THEIR KILLS...!
UGH.
THIS ISN'T GONNA CUT IT...
CRUMPLE
!
...
RUSTLE
IT'S SO PERFECTLY ROUND... HOW IN THE WORLD DOES SHE DO IT?
I SHOULD TAKE A PEEK...

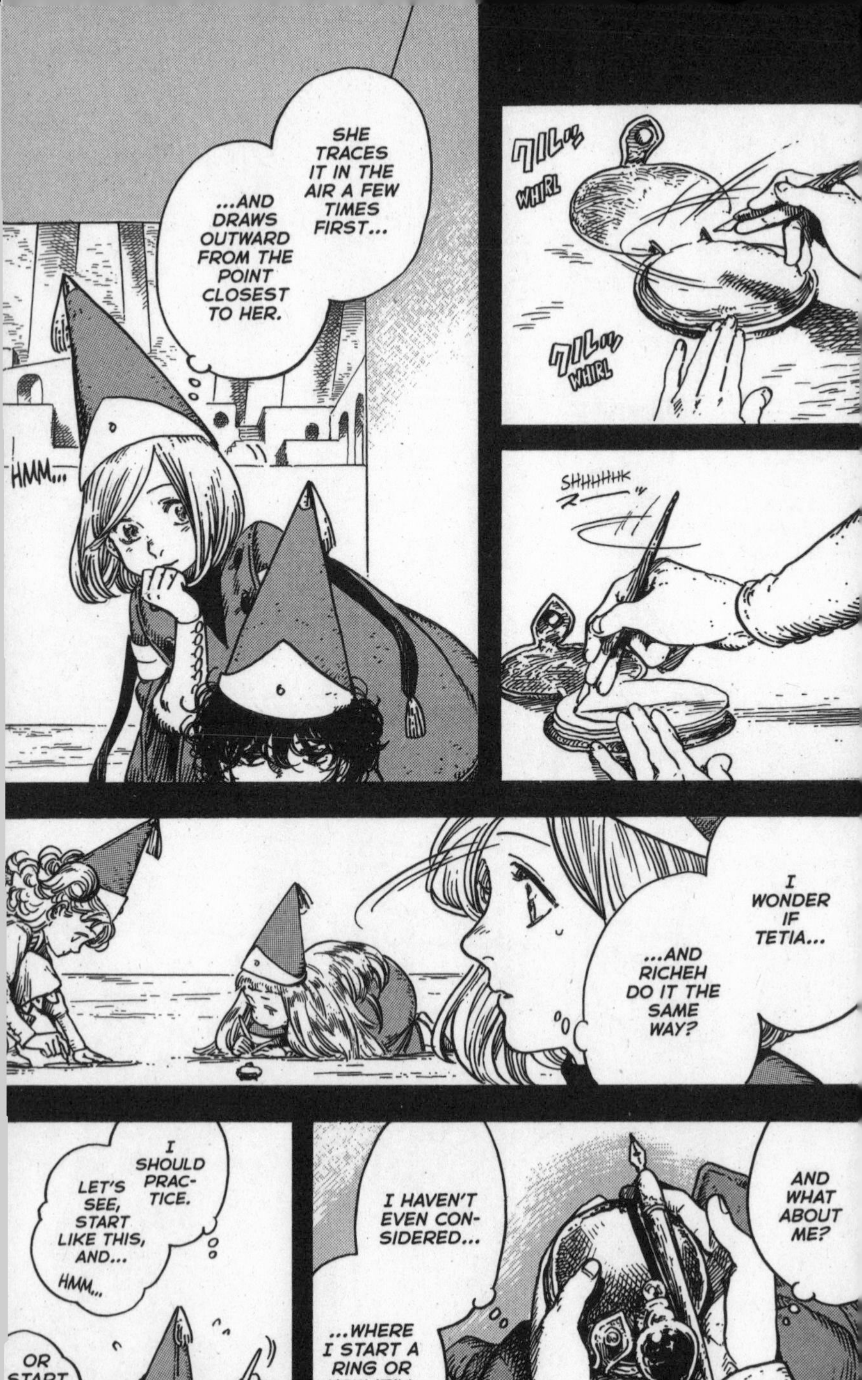
クルッ
WHIRL
クルッ
WHIRL
SHHHHHK
SHE TRACES IT IN THE AIR A FEW TIMES FIRST...
...AND DRAWS OUTWARD FROM THE POINT CLOSEST TO HER.
HMM...
I WONDER IF TETIA...
...AND RICHEH DO IT THE SAME WAY?
AND WHAT ABOUT ME?
I HAVEN'T EVEN CONSIDERED...
...WHERE I START A RING OR HOW IT'LL END UP.
I SHOULD PRACTICE.
LET'S SEE, START LIKE THIS, AND...
HMM...
OR START LIKE THIS, AND...

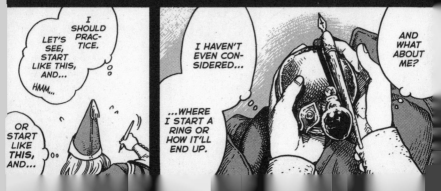

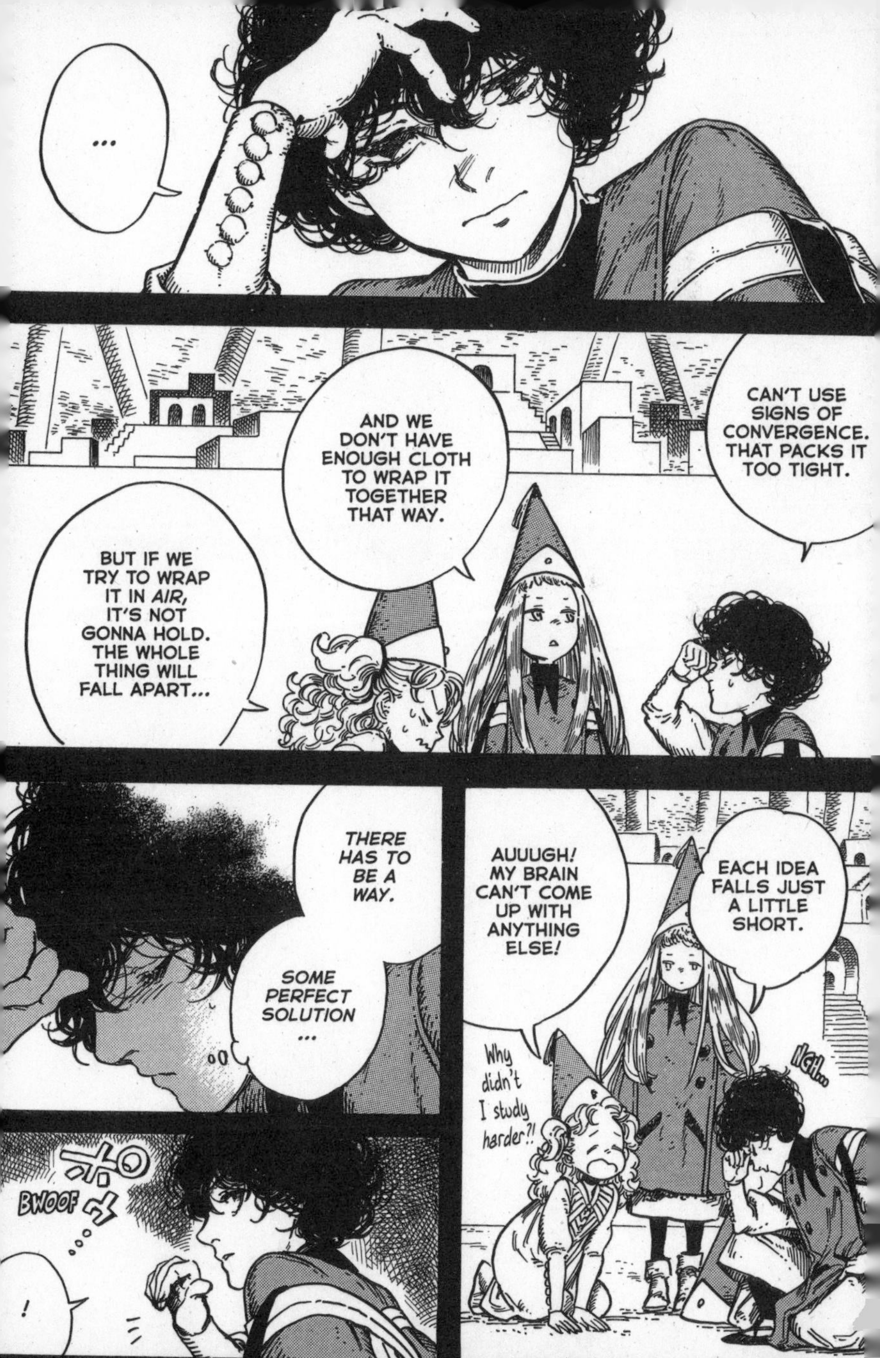
...
CAN'T USE SIGNS OF CONVERGENCE. THAT PACKS IT TOO TIGHT.
AND WE DON'T HAVE ENOUGH CLOTH TO WRAP IT TOGETHER THAT WAY.
BUT IF WE TRY TO WRAP IT IN *AIR*, IT'S NOT GONNA HOLD. THE WHOLE THING WILL FALL APART...
EACH IDEA FALLS JUST A LITTLE SHORT.
AUUUGH! MY BRAIN CAN'T COME UP WITH ANYTHING ELSE!
NGH...
Why didn't I study harder?!
THERE HAS TO BE A WAY.
SOME PERFECT SOLUTION ...
BWOOF
...
!

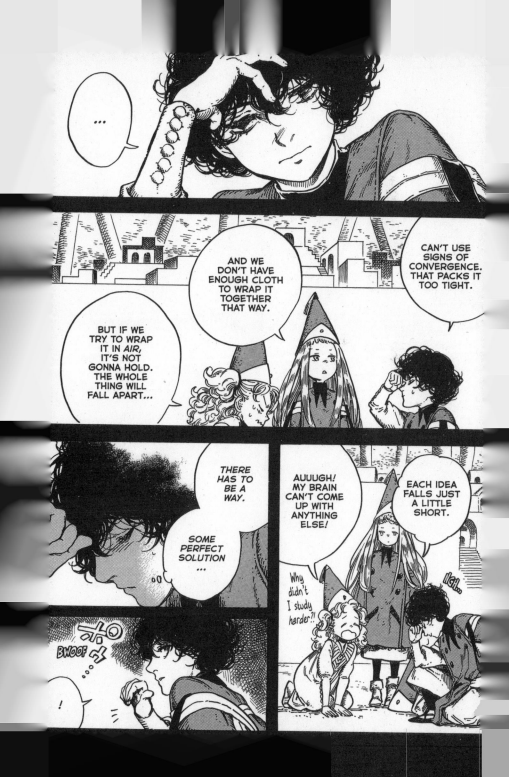

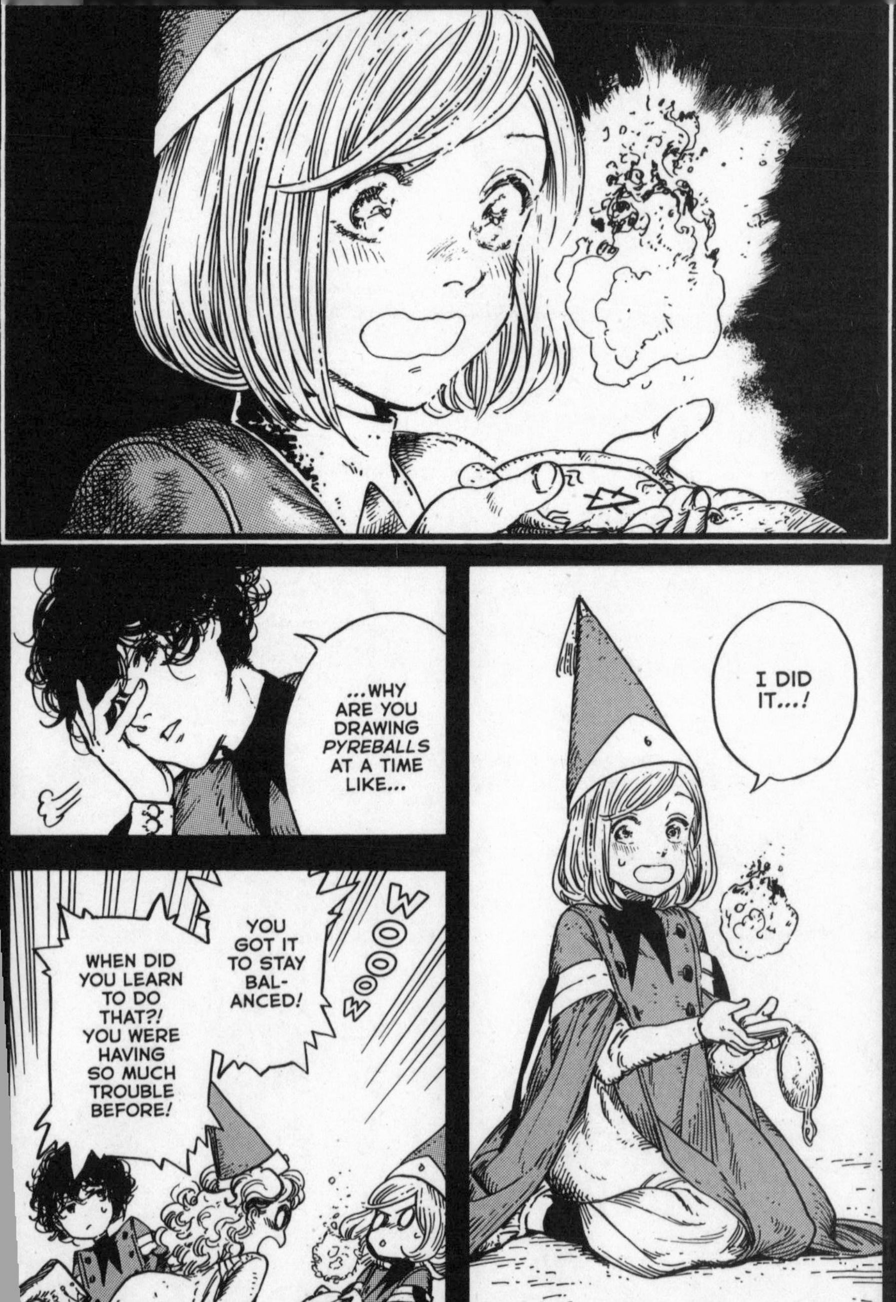
I DID IT...!
...WHY ARE YOU DRAWING *PYREBALLS* AT A TIME LIKE...
WOOOOW
YOU GOT IT TO STAY BAL-ANCED!
WHEN DID YOU LEARN TO DO THAT?! YOU WERE HAVING SO MUCH TROUBLE BEFORE!

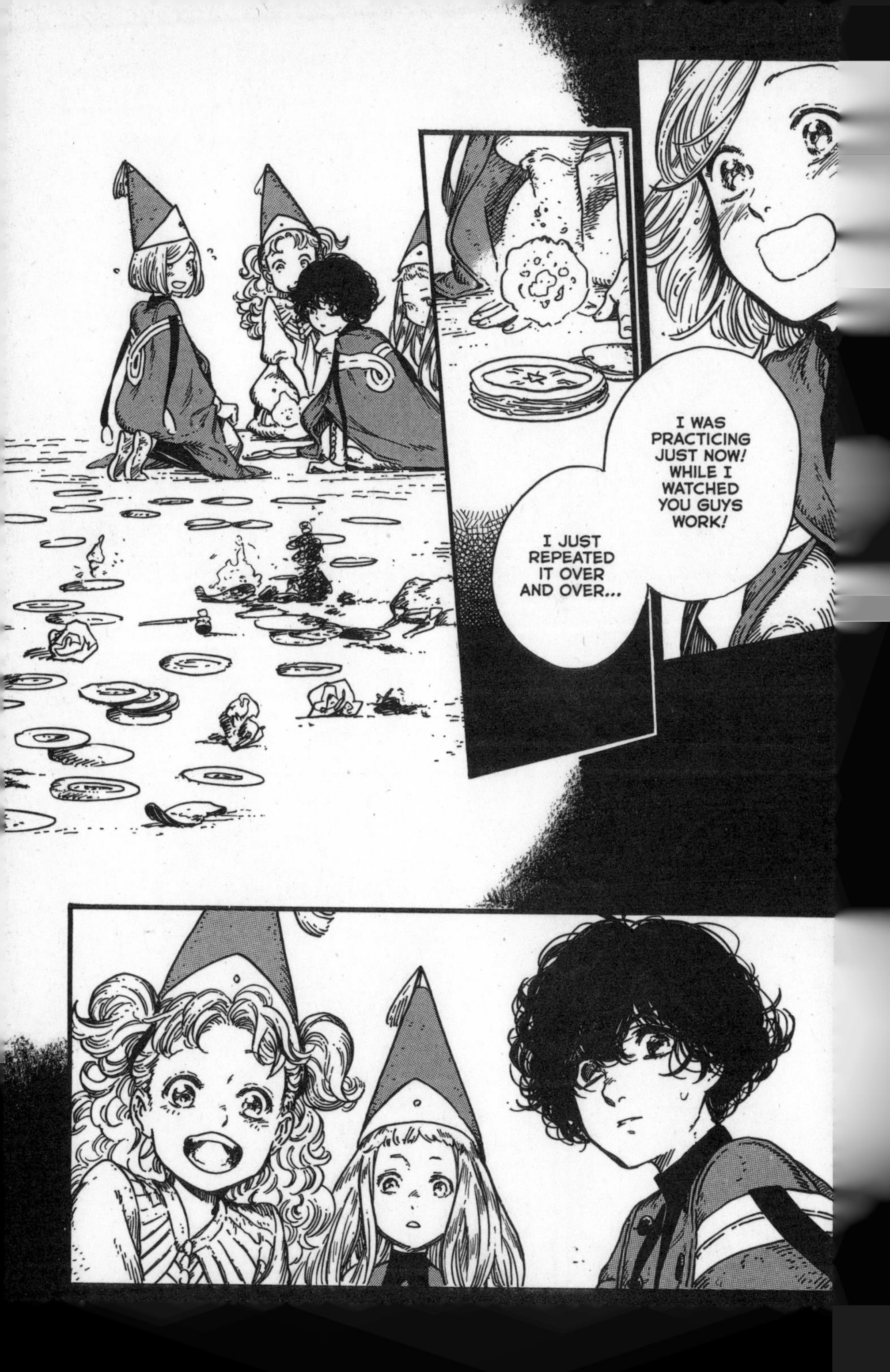
I WAS PRACTICING JUST NOW! WHILE I WATCHED YOU GUYS WORK!
I JUST REPEATED IT OVER AND OVER...

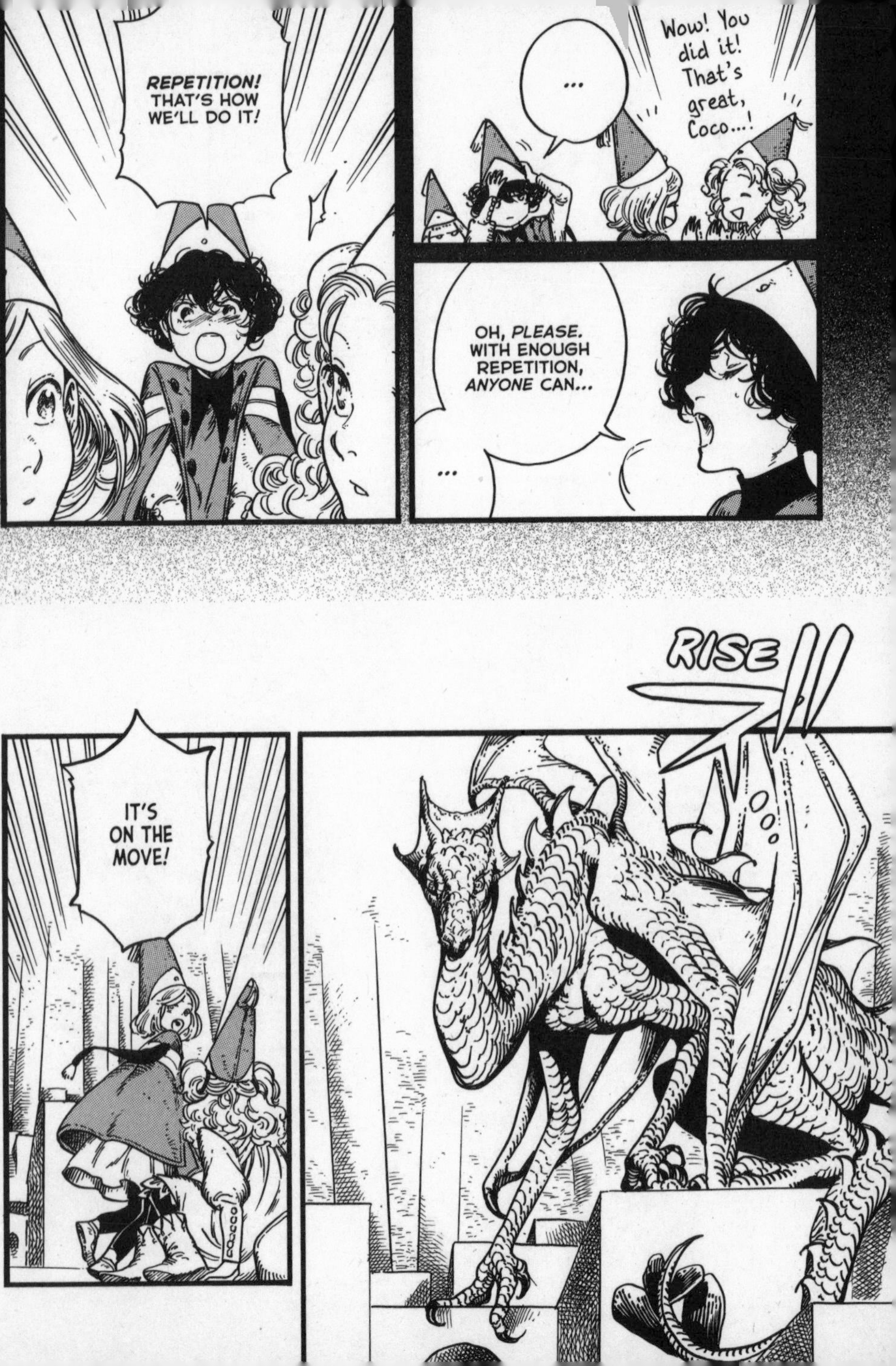
Wow! You did it! That's great, Coco...!
...
OH, *PLEASE.* WITH ENOUGH REPETITION, *ANYONE* CAN...
...
REPETITION! THAT'S HOW WE'LL DO IT!
RISE
IT'S ON THE MOVE!

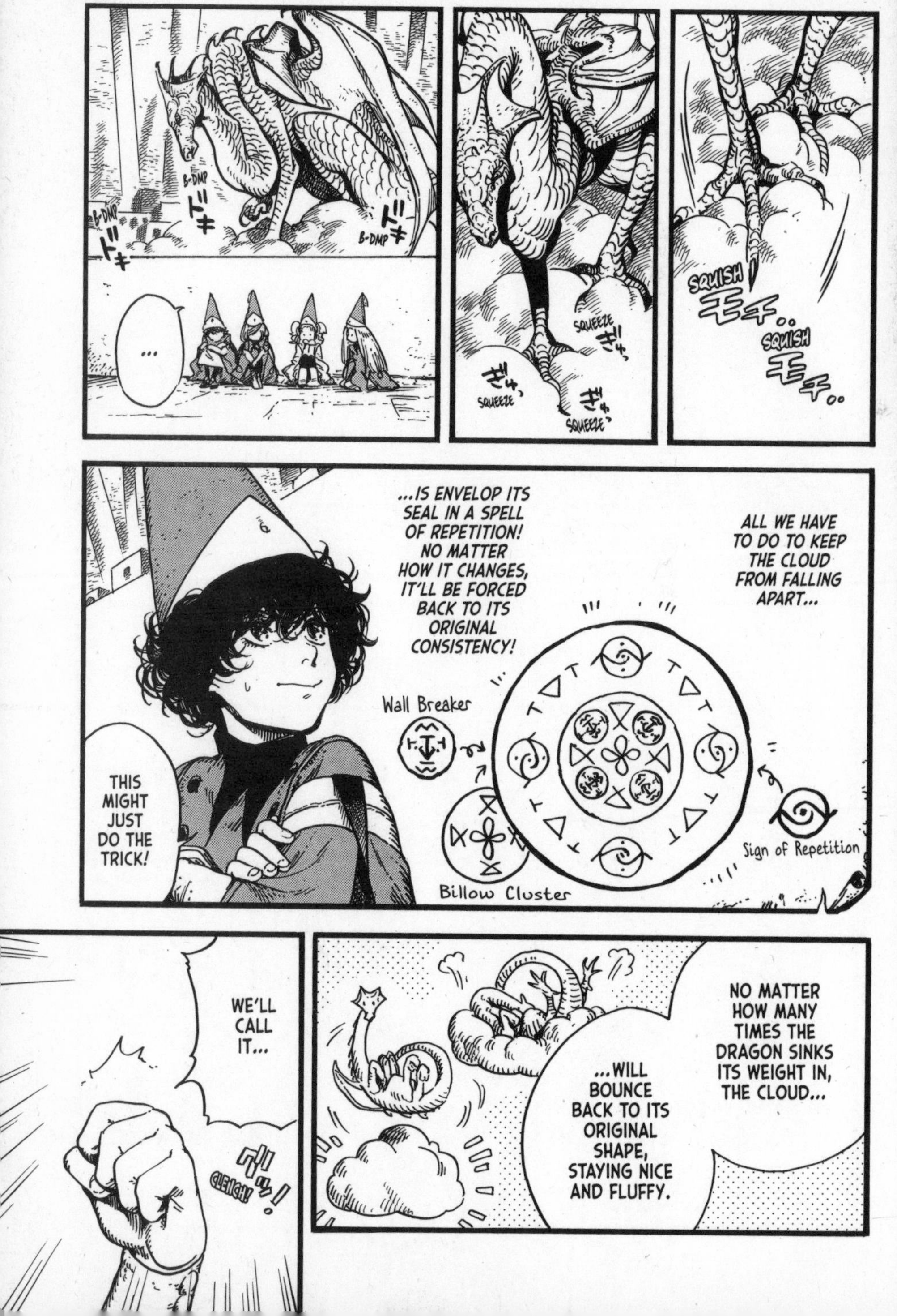
SQUISH
モチ。。
SQUISH
モチ。。
SQUEEZE
ぎゅっ
SQUEEZE
ぎゅっ
SQUEEZE
ぎゅっ
B-DMP
ドキ
B-DMP
ドキ
B-DMP
ドキ
...
ALL WE HAVE TO DO TO KEEP THE CLOUD FROM FALLING APART...
...IS ENVELOP ITS SEAL IN A SPELL OF REPETITION! NO MATTER HOW IT CHANGES, IT'LL BE FORCED BACK TO ITS ORIGINAL CONSISTENCY!
Sign of Repetition
Wall Breaker
Billow Cluster
THIS MIGHT JUST DO THE TRICK!
NO MATTER HOW MANY TIMES THE DRAGON SINKS ITS WEIGHT IN, THE CLOUD...
...WILL BOUNCE BACK TO ITS ORIGINAL SHAPE, STAYING NICE AND FLUFFY.
WE'LL CALL IT...
CLENCH!
ぐっ!

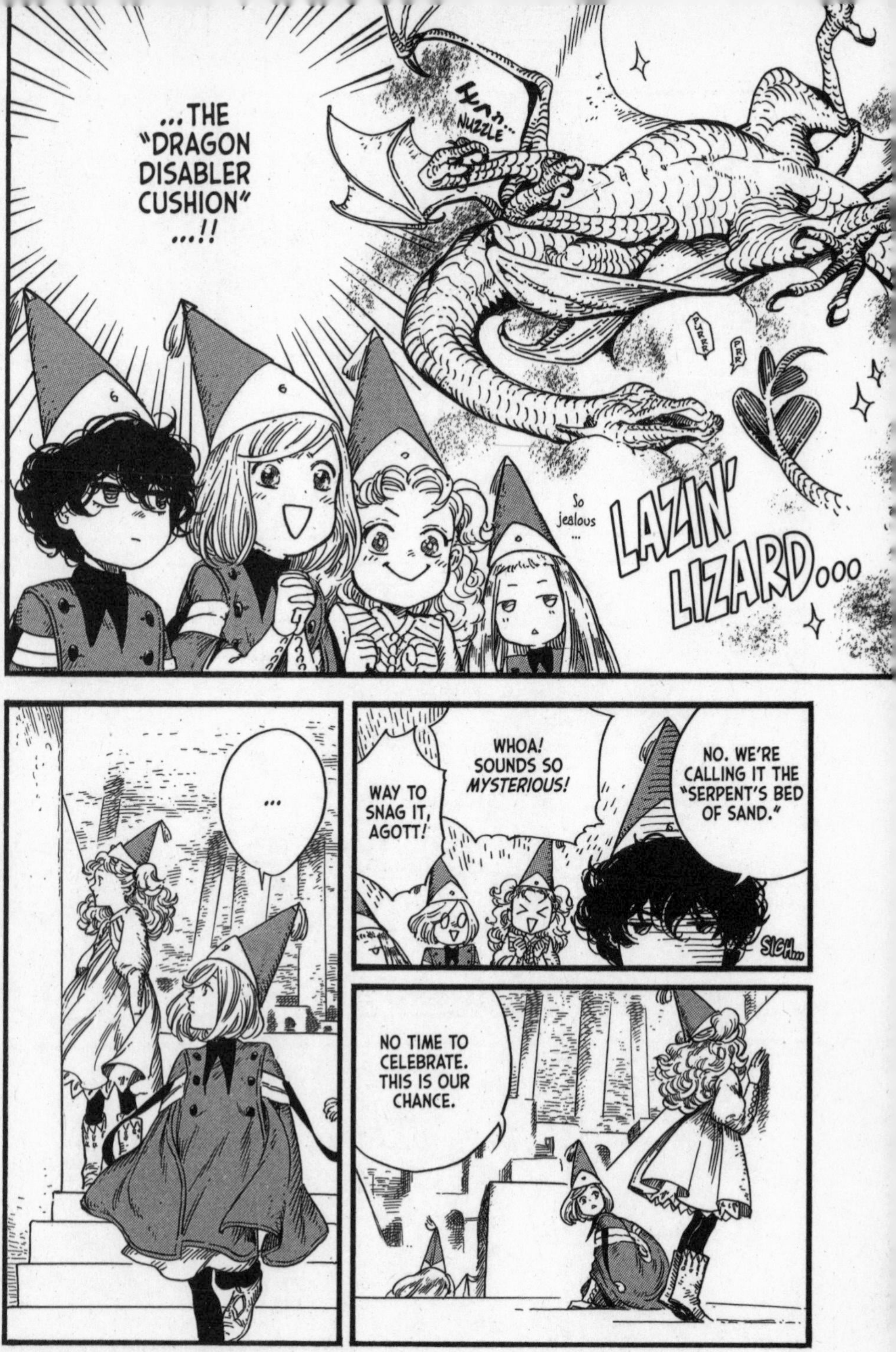
NUZZLE
...THE "DRAGON DISABLER CUSHION" ...!!
PURRR
PRR
LAZIN' LIZARD...
So jealous ...
NO. WE'RE CALLING IT THE "SERPENT'S BED OF SAND."
WHOA! SOUNDS SO *MYSTERIOUS!*
WAY TO SNAG IT, AGOTT!
SIGH...
NO TIME TO CELEBRATE. THIS IS OUR CHANCE.
...

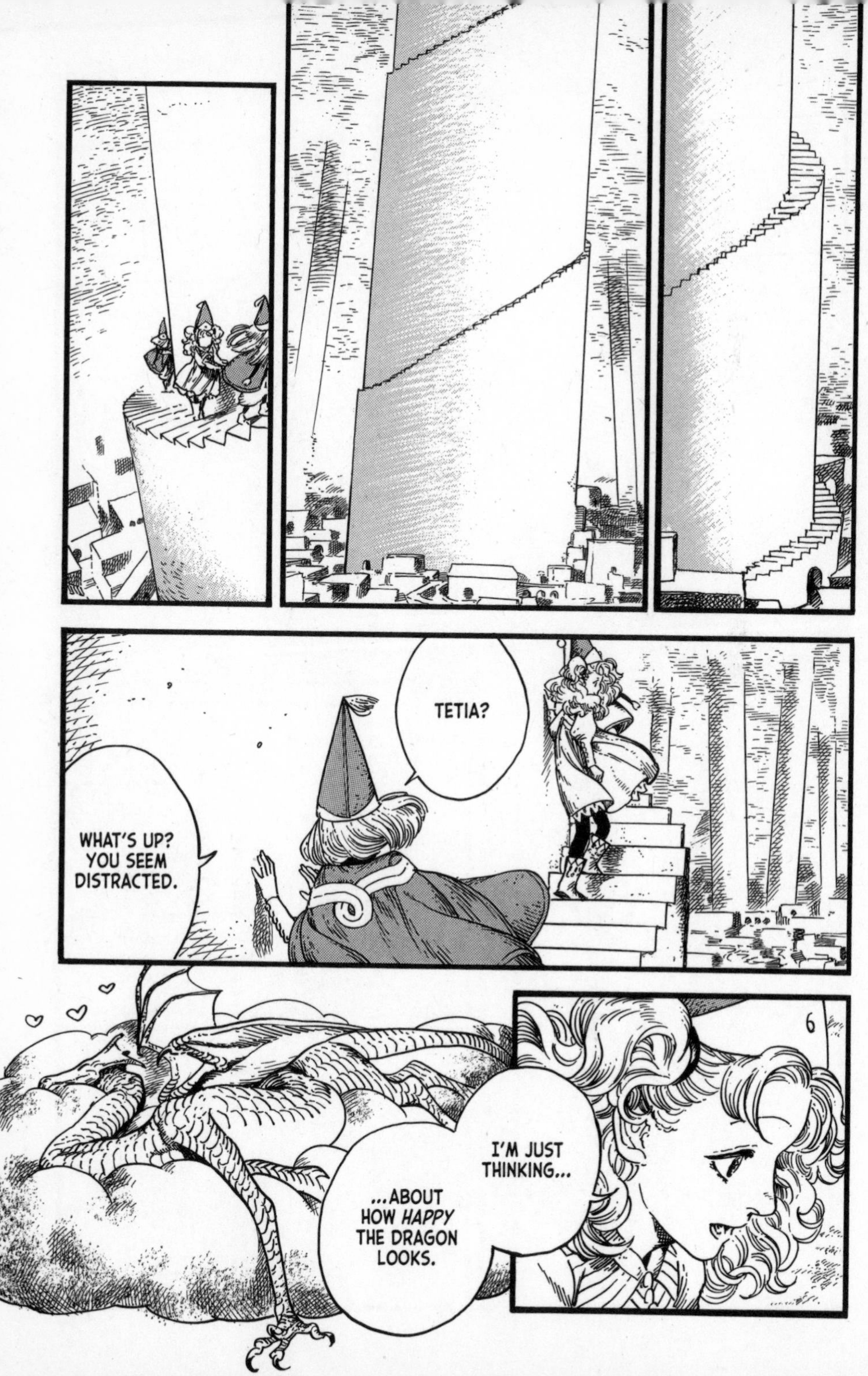
TETIA?
WHAT'S UP? YOU SEEM DISTRACTED.
I'M JUST THINKING...
...ABOUT HOW *HAPPY* THE DRAGON LOOKS.

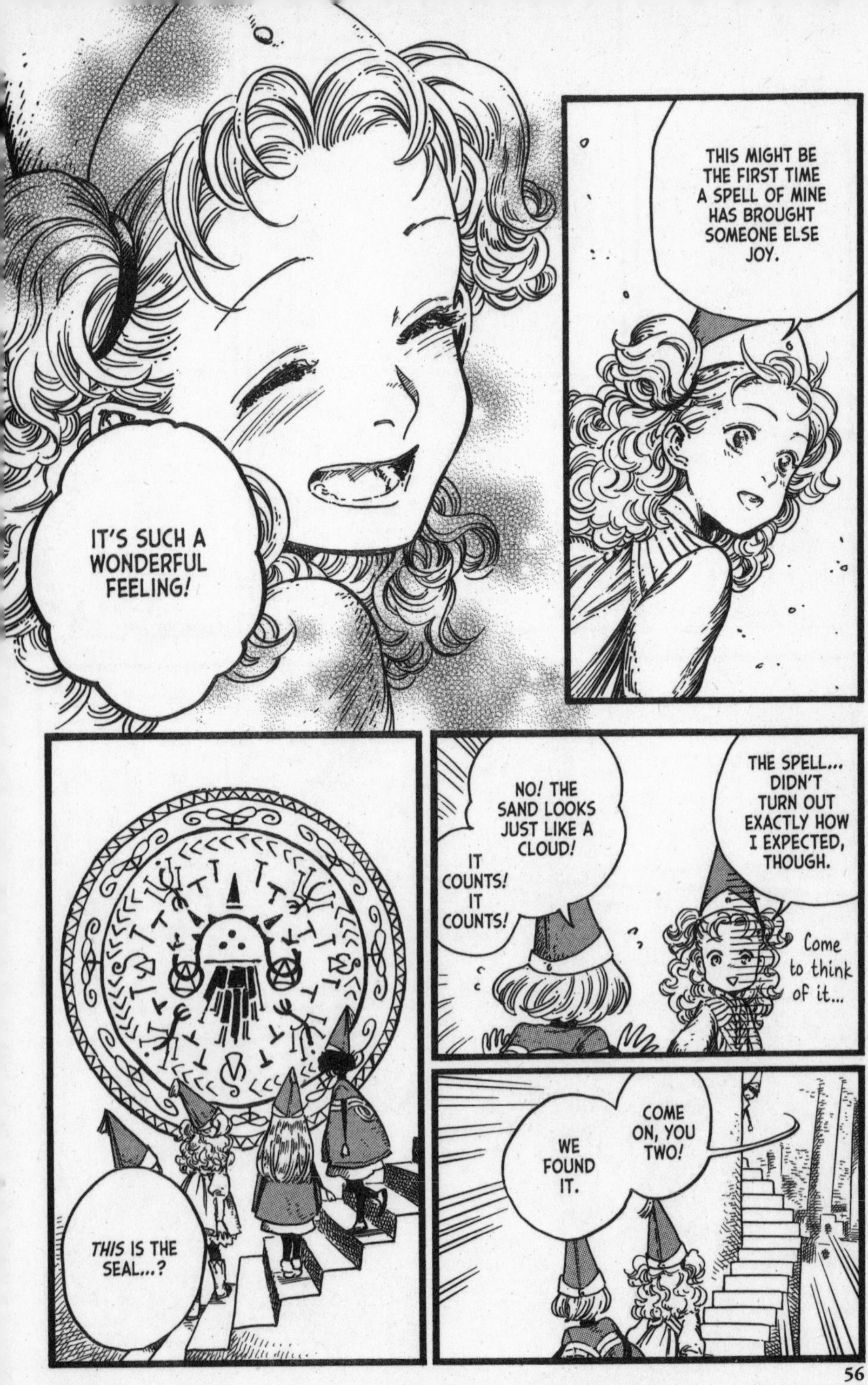
THIS MIGHT BE THE FIRST TIME A SPELL OF MINE HAS BROUGHT SOMEONE ELSE JOY.
IT'S SUCH A WONDERFUL FEELING!
THE SPELL... DIDN'T TURN OUT EXACTLY HOW I EXPECTED, THOUGH.
Come to think of it...
NO! THE SAND LOOKS JUST LIKE A CLOUD!
IT COUNTS! IT COUNTS!
COME ON, YOU TWO!
WE FOUND IT.
THIS IS THE SEAL...?

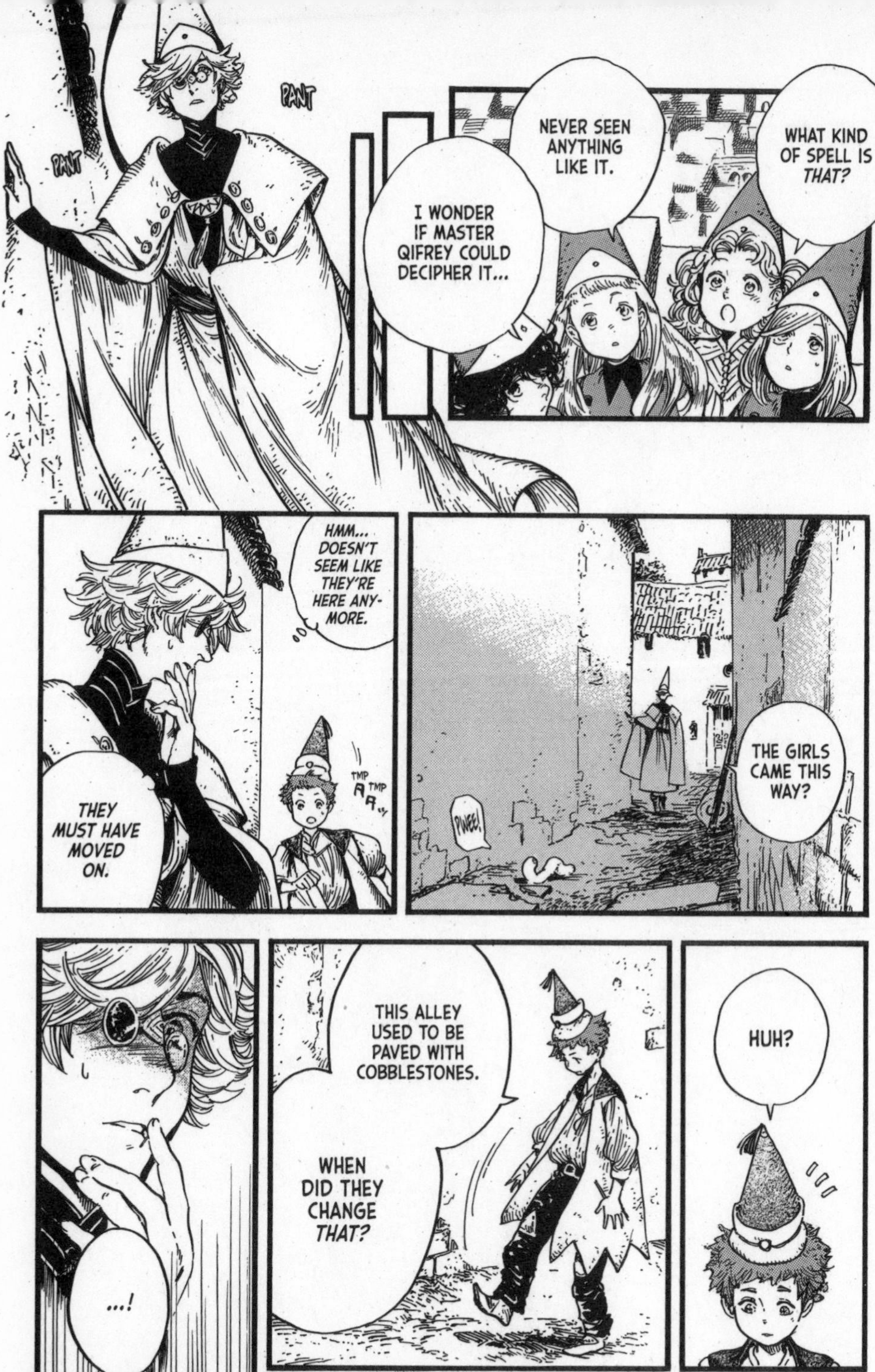

WHAT KIND OF SPELL IS *THAT?*
NEVER SEEN ANYTHING LIKE IT.
I WONDER IF MASTER QIFREY COULD DECIPHER IT...
PANT
PANT
THE GIRLS CAME THIS WAY?
PWEE!
HMM... DOESN'T SEEM LIKE THEY'RE HERE ANY-MORE.
TMP TMP
THEY MUST HAVE MOVED ON.
HUH?
THIS ALLEY USED TO BE PAVED WITH COBBLESTONES.
WHEN DID THEY CHANGE *THAT?*
...!

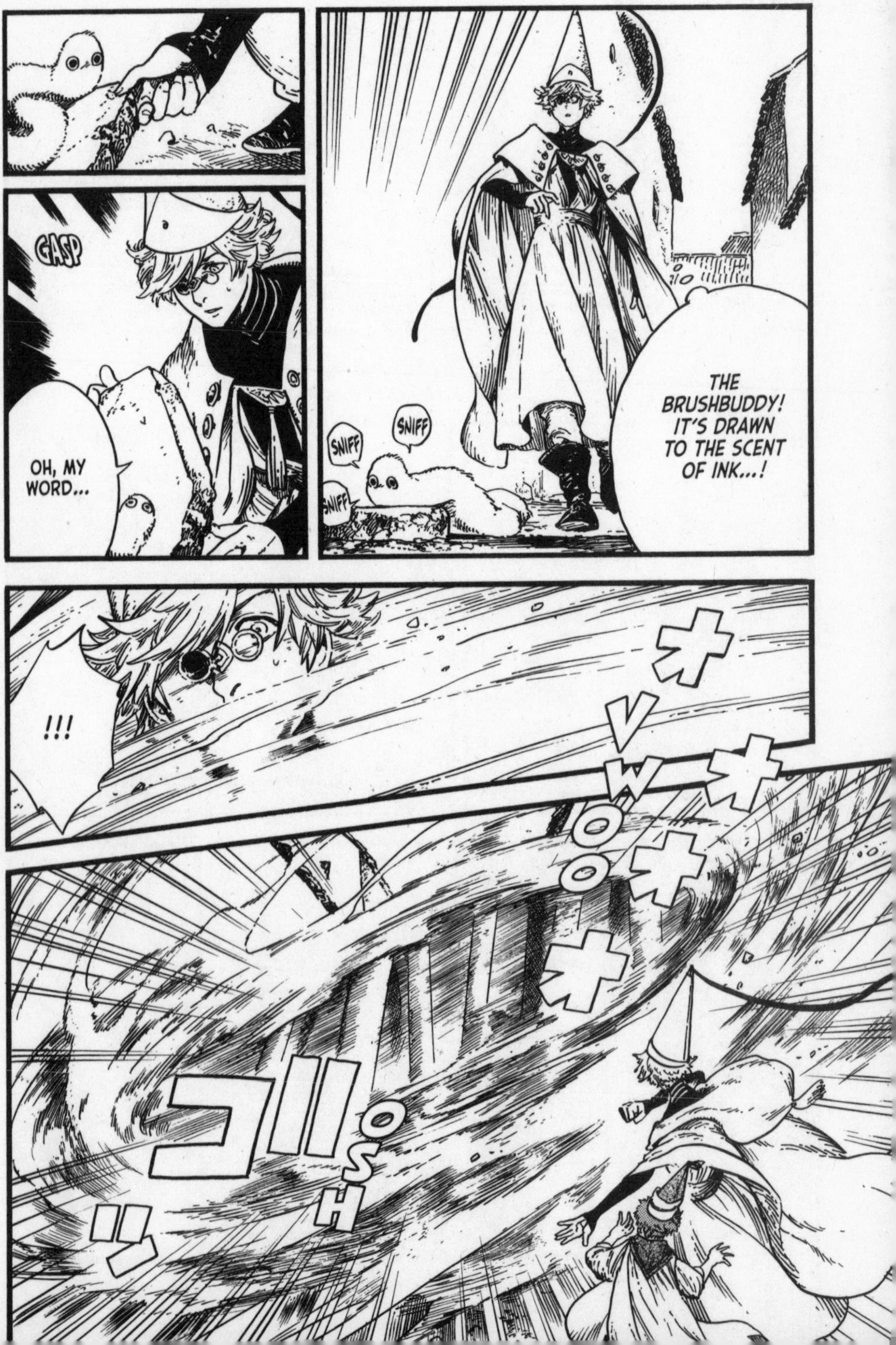
THE BRUSHBUDDY! IT'S DRAWN TO THE SCENT OF INK...!
SNIFF
SNIFF
SNIFF
GASP
OH, MY WORD...
!!!
VWOOO
WHOOSH

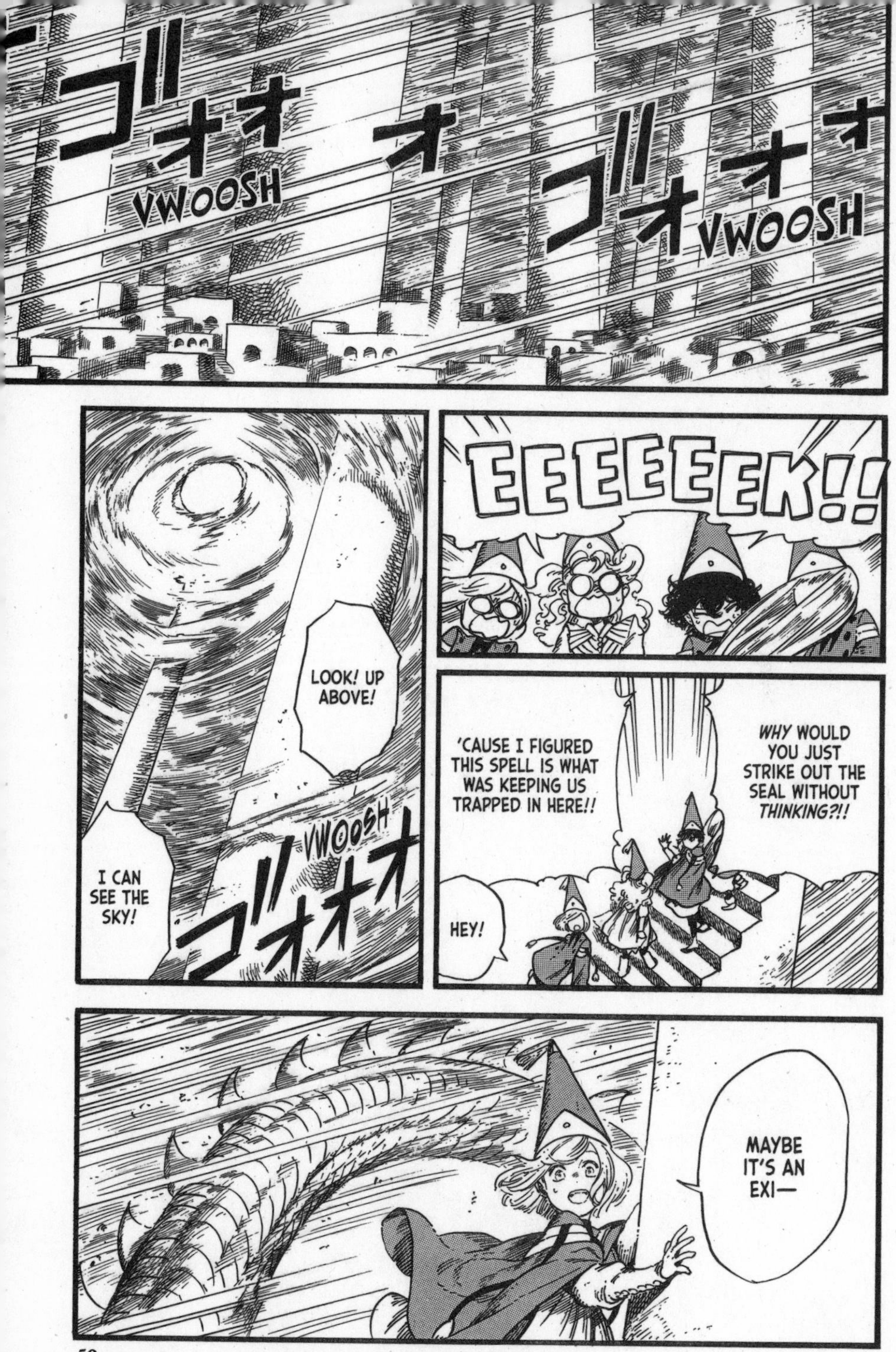
ゴオオ
VWOOSH
ゴオオ
VWOOSH
EEEEEEK!!
WHY WOULD YOU JUST STRIKE OUT THE SEAL WITHOUT *THINKING?!!*
'CAUSE I FIGURED THIS SPELL IS WHAT WAS KEEPING US TRAPPED IN HERE!!
HEY!
LOOK! UP ABOVE!
I CAN SEE THE SKY!
VWOOSH
ゴオオ
MAYBE IT'S AN EXI—

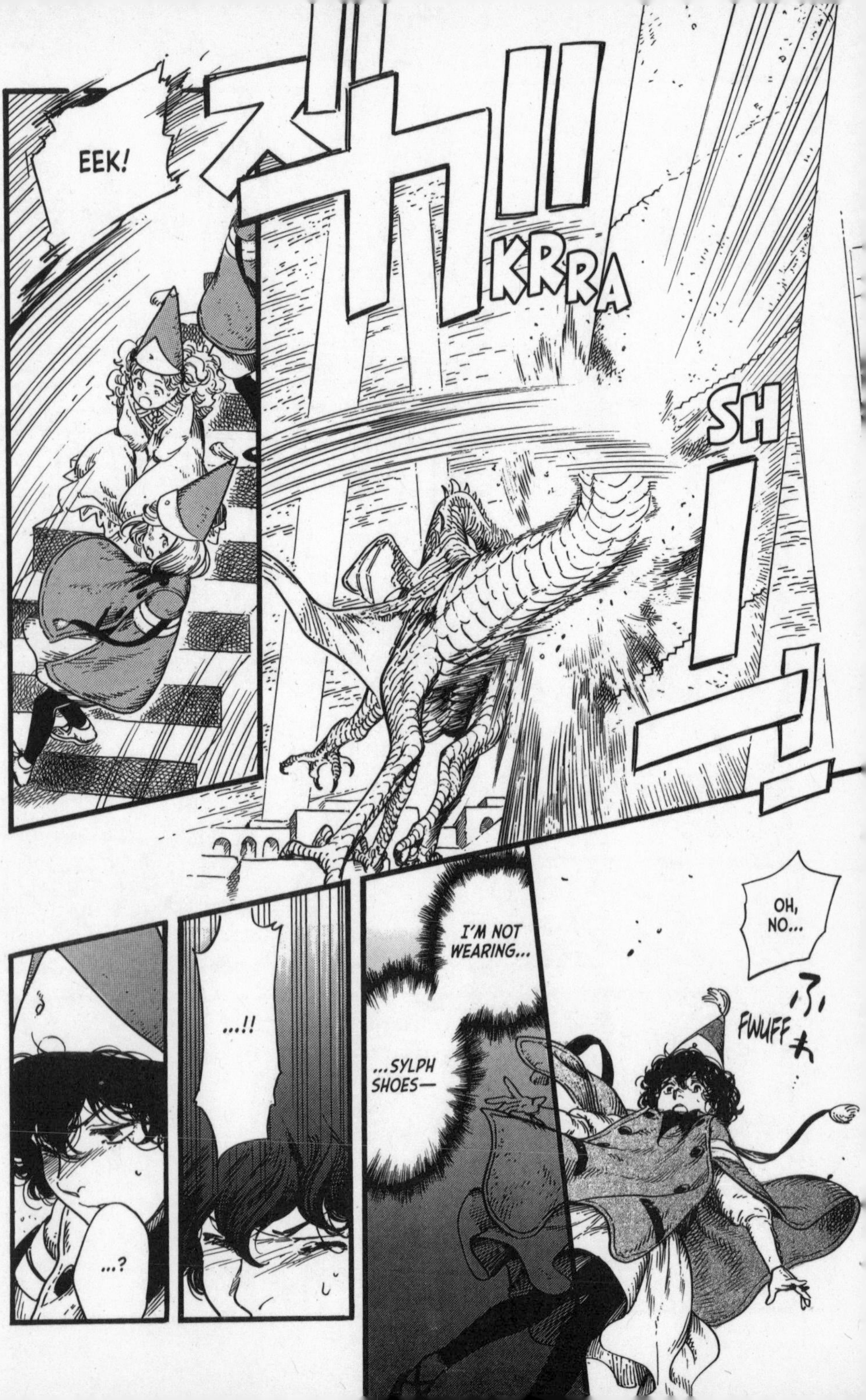
KRRA
SH
EEK!
OH, NO...
FWUFF
I'M NOT WEARING...
...SYLPH SHOES—
...!!
...?

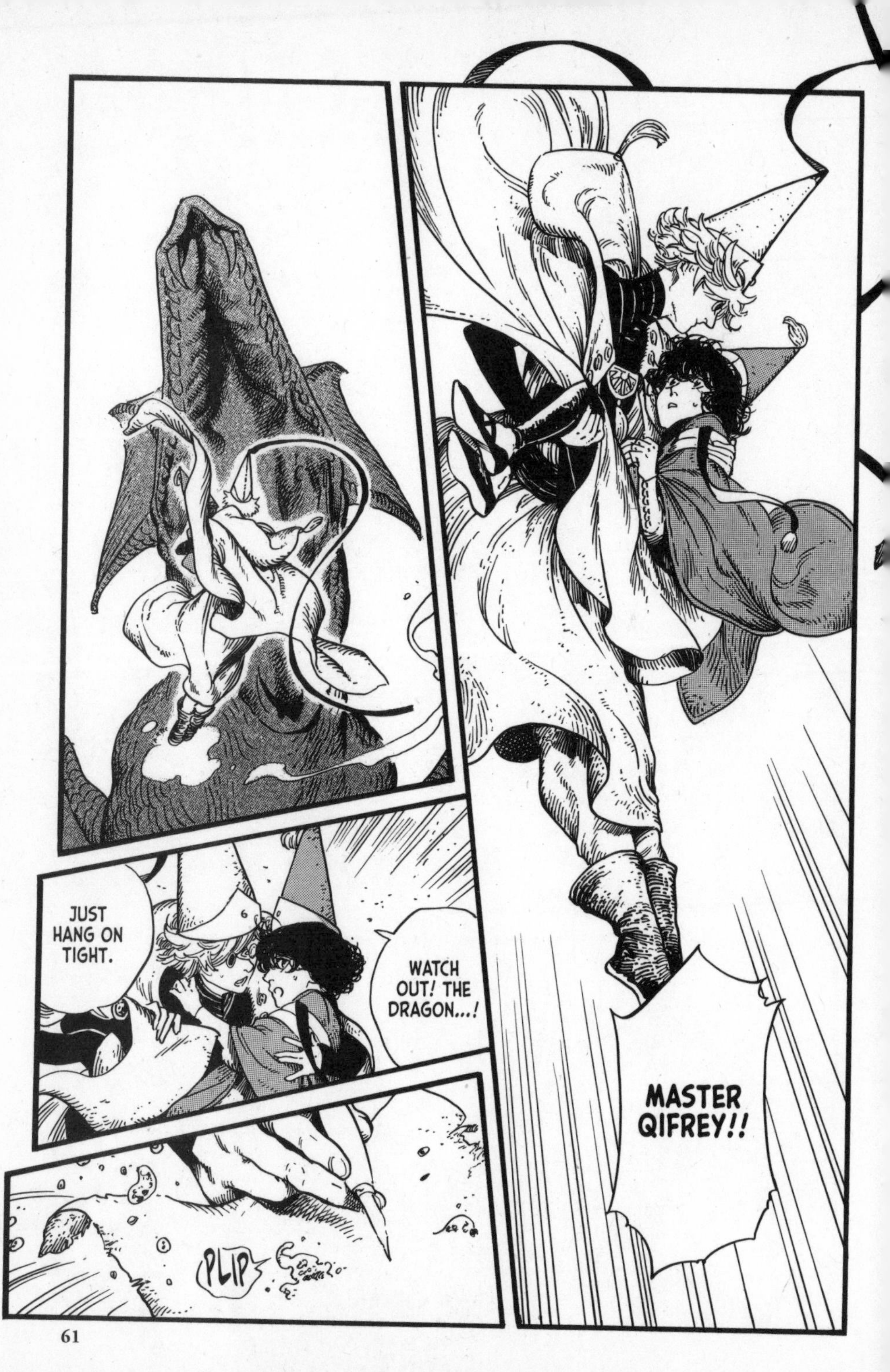
MASTER QIFREY!!
WATCH OUT! THE DRAGON...!
JUST HANG ON TIGHT.
PLIP

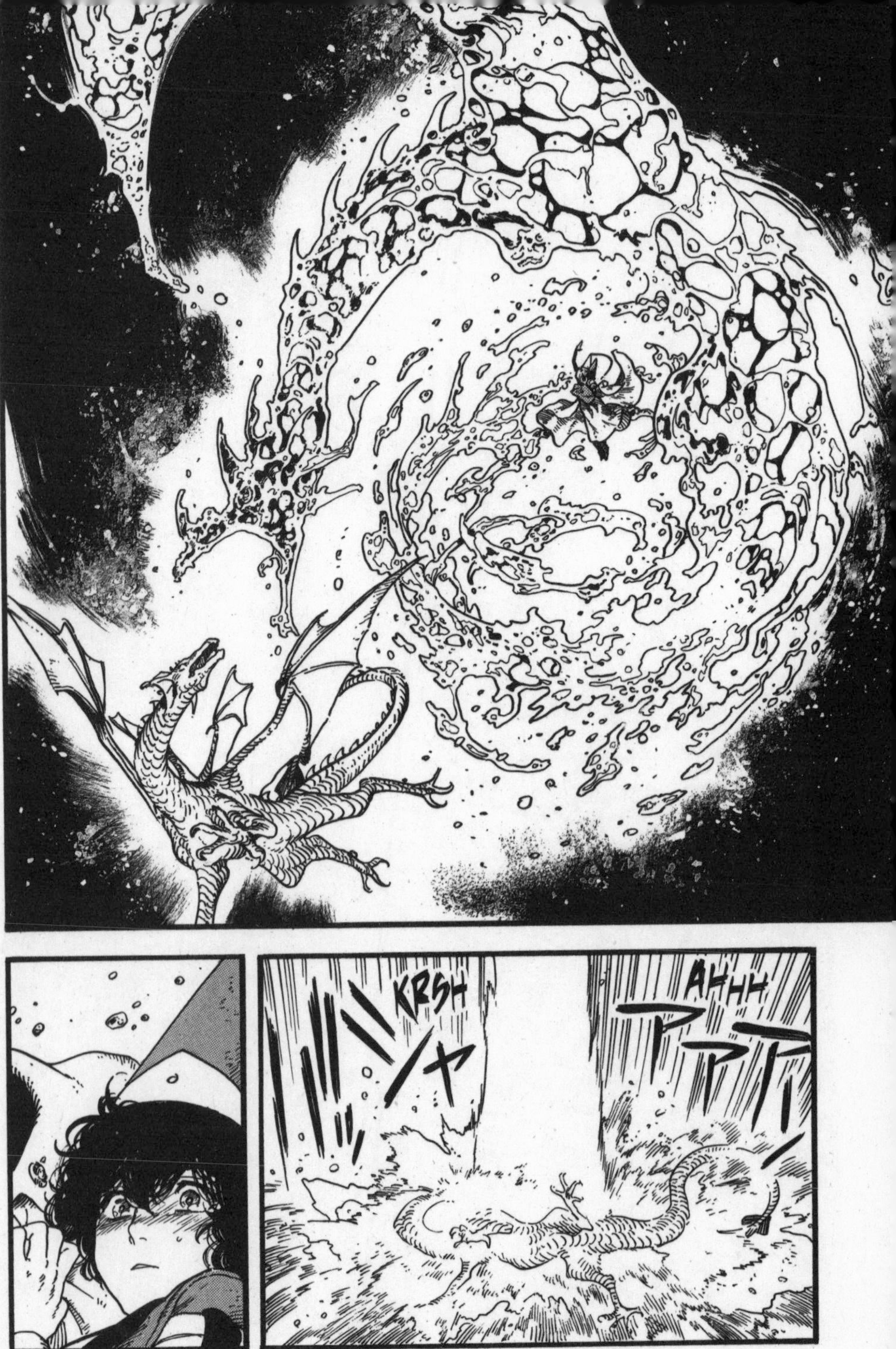
AHHH
KRSH

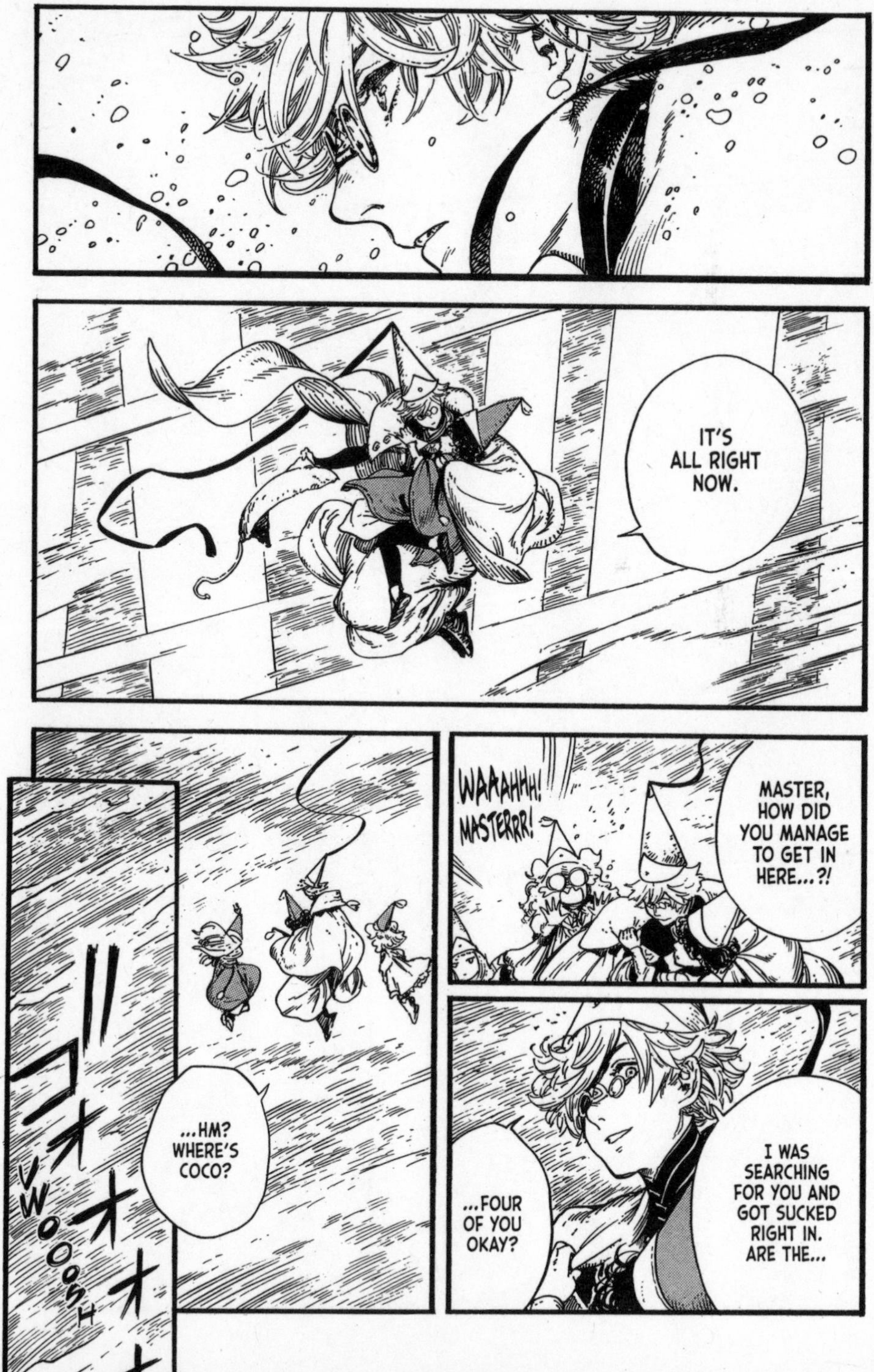
IT'S ALL RIGHT NOW.
MASTER, HOW DID YOU MANAGE TO GET IN HERE...?!
WAAAHHH! MASTERRR!
I WAS SEARCHING FOR YOU AND GOT SUCKED RIGHT IN. ARE THE...
...FOUR OF YOU OKAY?
...HM? WHERE'S COCO?
ゴオオオ
VWOOOSH

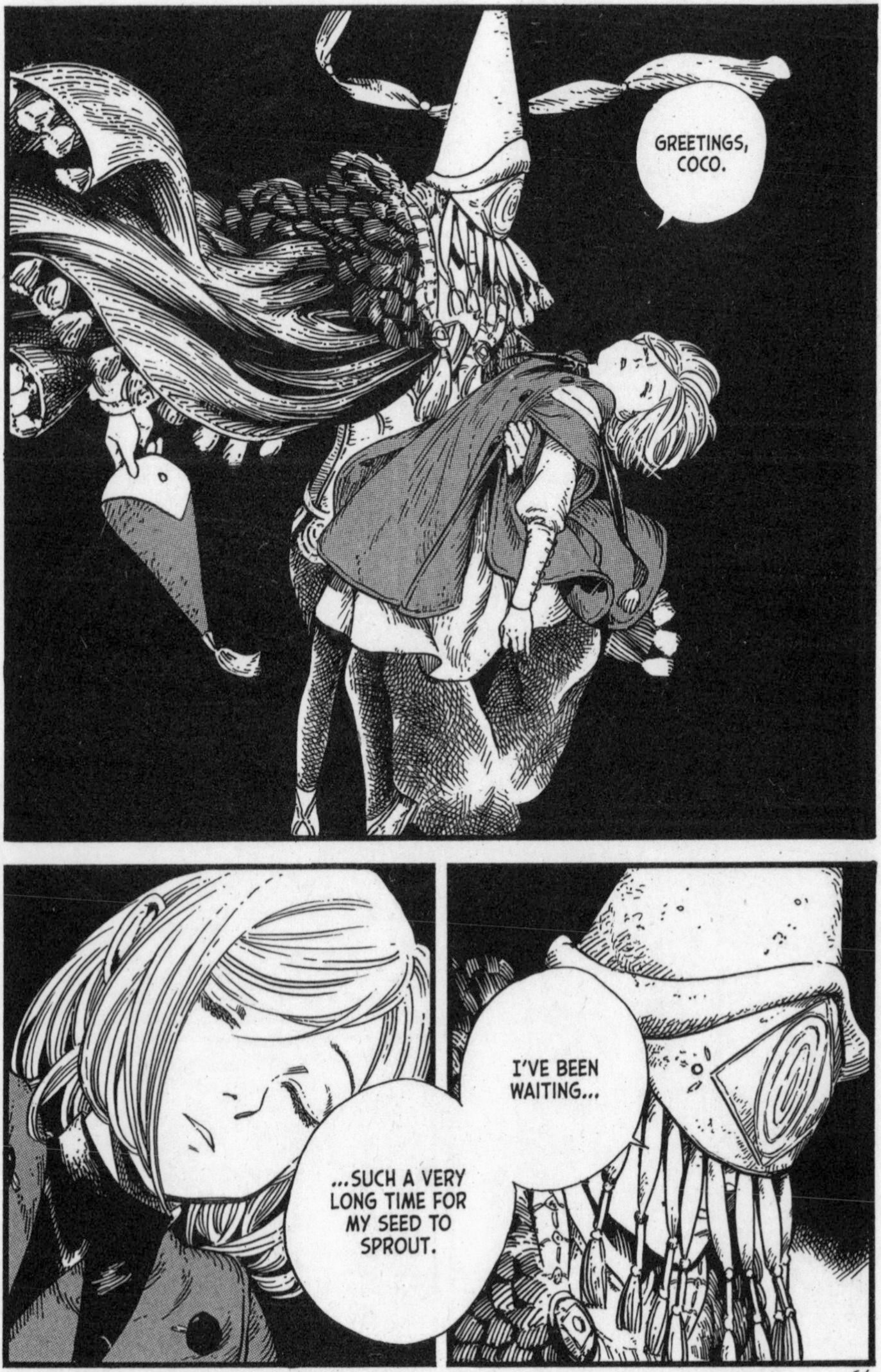
GREETINGS, COCO.
I'VE BEEN WAITING...
...SUCH A VERY LONG TIME FOR MY SEED TO SPROUT.

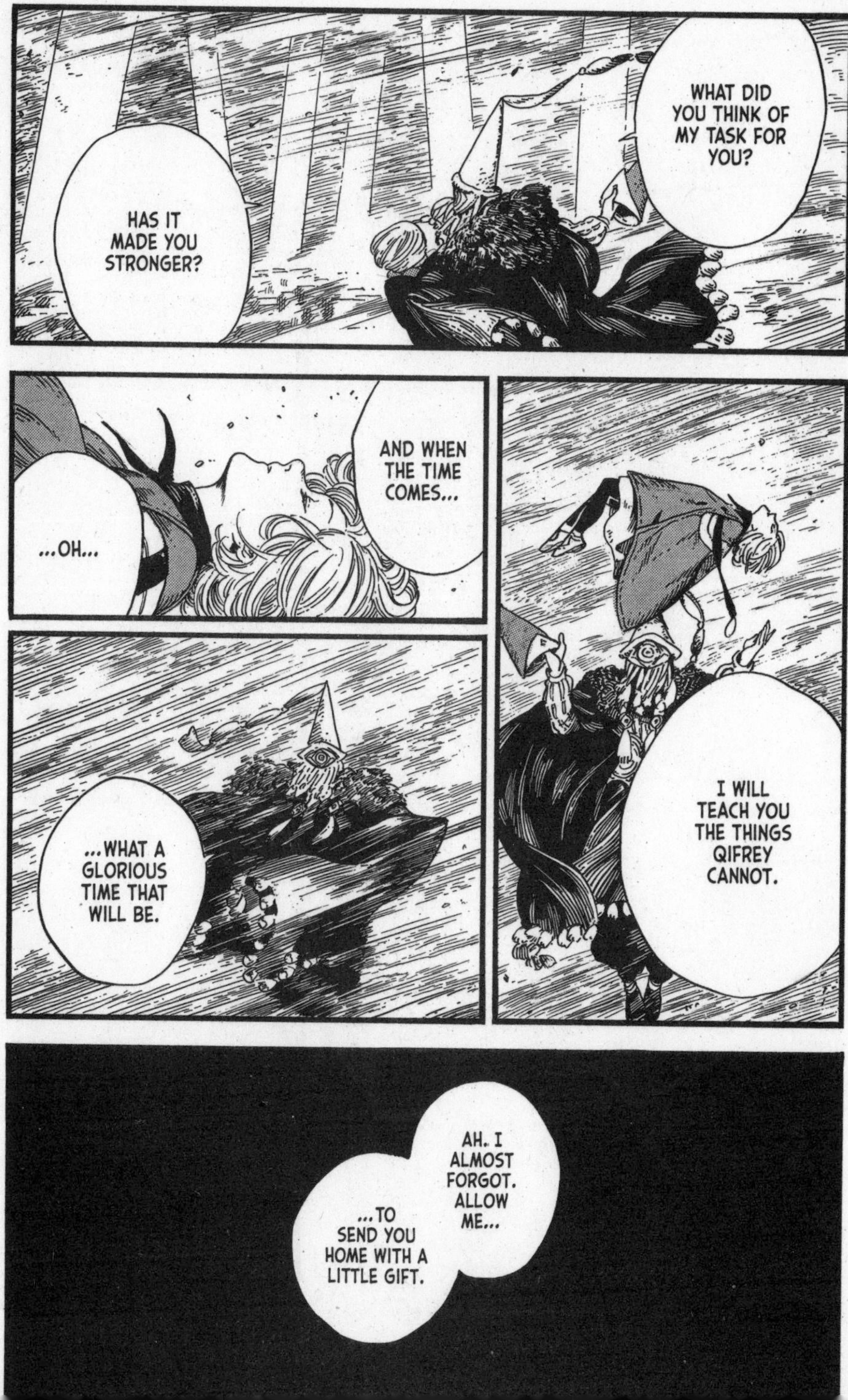
WHAT DID YOU THINK OF MY TASK FOR YOU?
HAS IT MADE YOU STRONGER?
I WILL TEACH YOU THE THINGS QIFREY CANNOT.
AND WHEN THE TIME COMES...
...OH...
...WHAT A GLORIOUS TIME THAT WILL BE.
AH. I ALMOST FORGOT. ALLOW ME...
...TO SEND YOU HOME WITH A LITTLE GIFT.

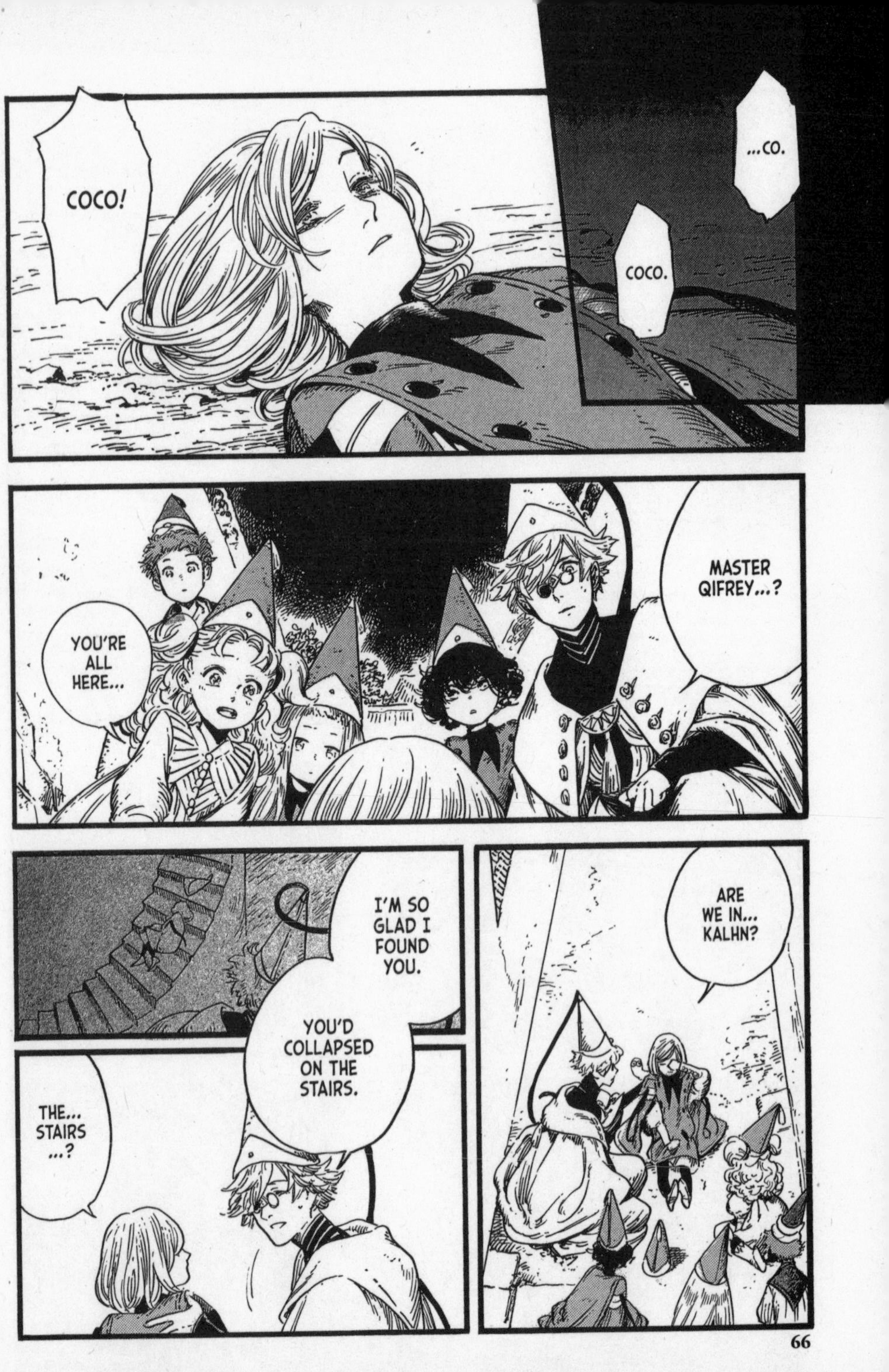
...CO.
COCO.
COCO!
MASTER QIFREY...?
YOU'RE ALL HERE...
ARE WE IN... KALHN?
I'M SO GLAD I FOUND YOU.
YOU'D COLLAPSED ON THE STAIRS.
THE... STAIRS ...?

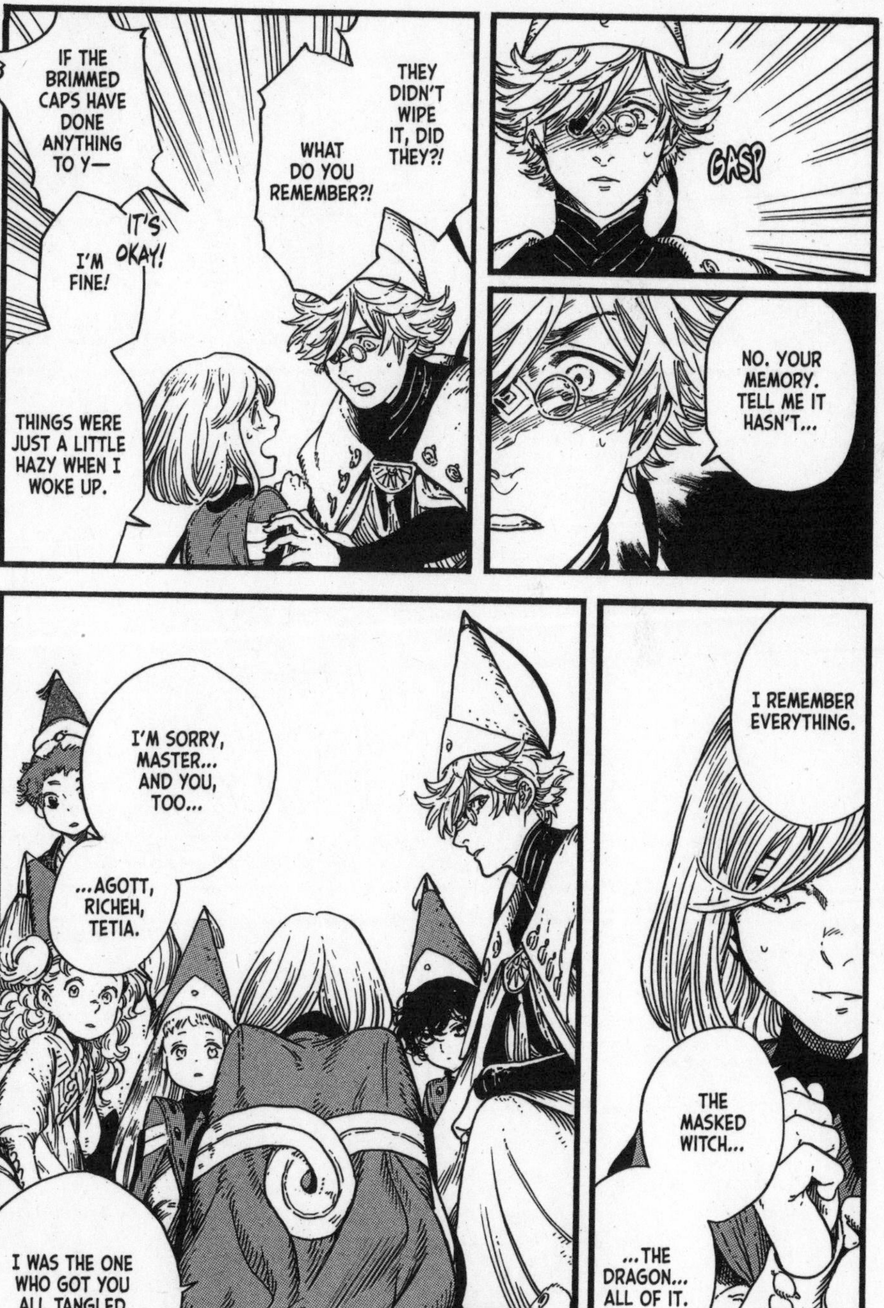
GASP
NO. YOUR MEMORY. TELL ME IT HASN'T...
THEY DIDN'T WIPE IT, DID THEY?!
WHAT DO YOU REMEMBER?!
IF THE BRIMMED CAPS HAVE DONE ANYTHING TO Y—
IT'S OKAY!
I'M FINE!
THINGS WERE JUST A LITTLE HAZY WHEN I WOKE UP.
I REMEMBER EVERYTHING.
THE MASKED WITCH...
...THE DRAGON... ALL OF IT.
I'M SORRY, MASTER... AND YOU, TOO...
...AGOTT, RICHEH, TETIA.
I WAS THE ONE WHO GOT YOU ALL TANGLED UP IN THIS!

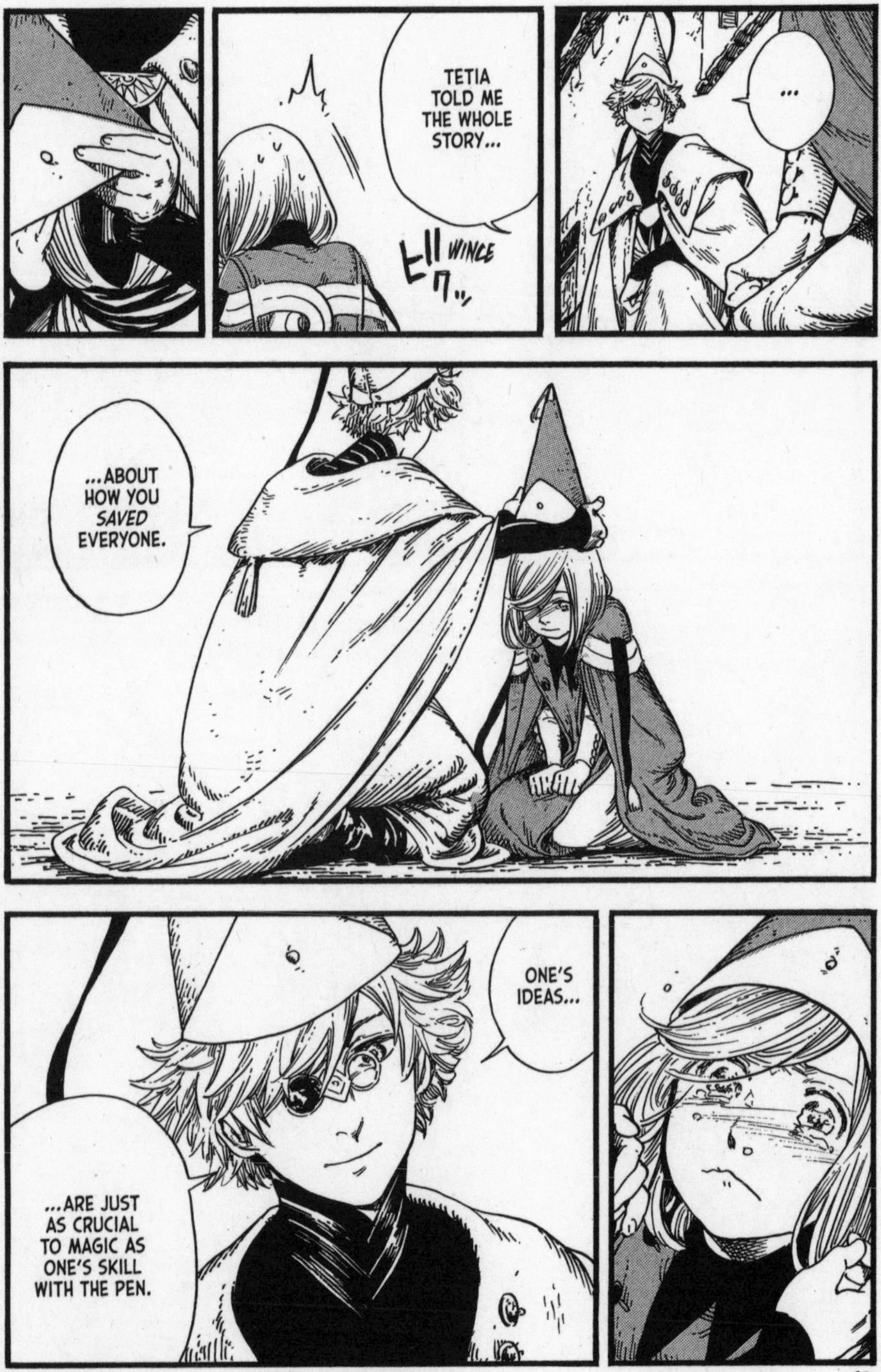
...
TETIA TOLD ME THE WHOLE STORY...
ビクッ WINCE
...ABOUT HOW YOU *SAVED* EVERYONE.
ONE'S IDEAS...
...ARE JUST AS CRUCIAL TO MAGIC AS ONE'S SKILL WITH THE PEN.

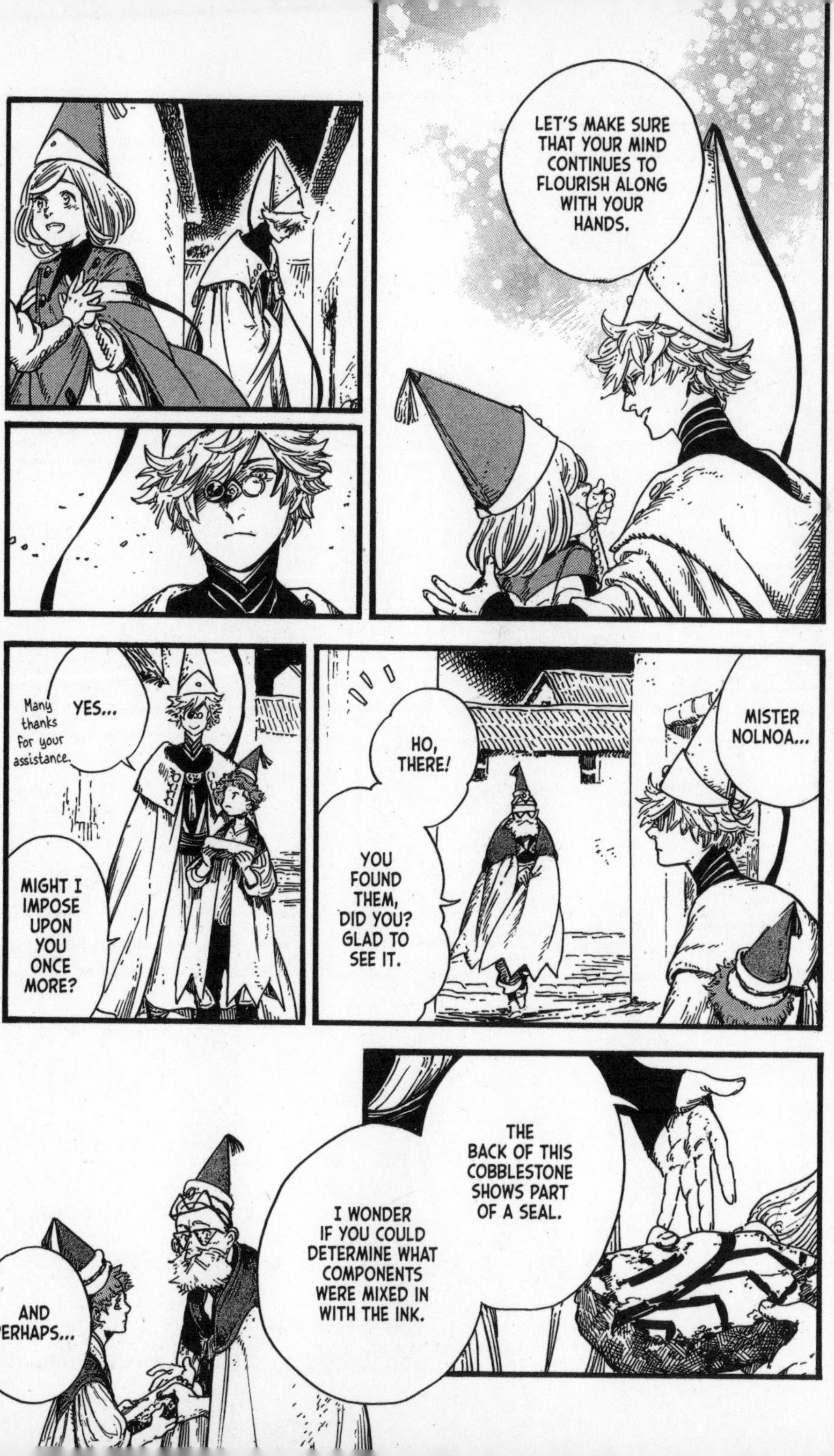
LET'S MAKE SURE THAT YOUR MIND CONTINUES TO FLOURISH ALONG WITH YOUR HANDS.
MISTER NOLNOA...
HO, THERE!
YOU FOUND THEM, DID YOU? GLAD TO SEE IT.
YES...
Many thanks for your assistance.
MIGHT I IMPOSE UPON YOU ONCE MORE?
THE BACK OF THIS COBBLESTONE SHOWS PART OF A SEAL.
I WONDER IF YOU COULD DETERMINE WHAT COMPONENTS WERE MIXED IN WITH THE INK.
AND PERHAPS...

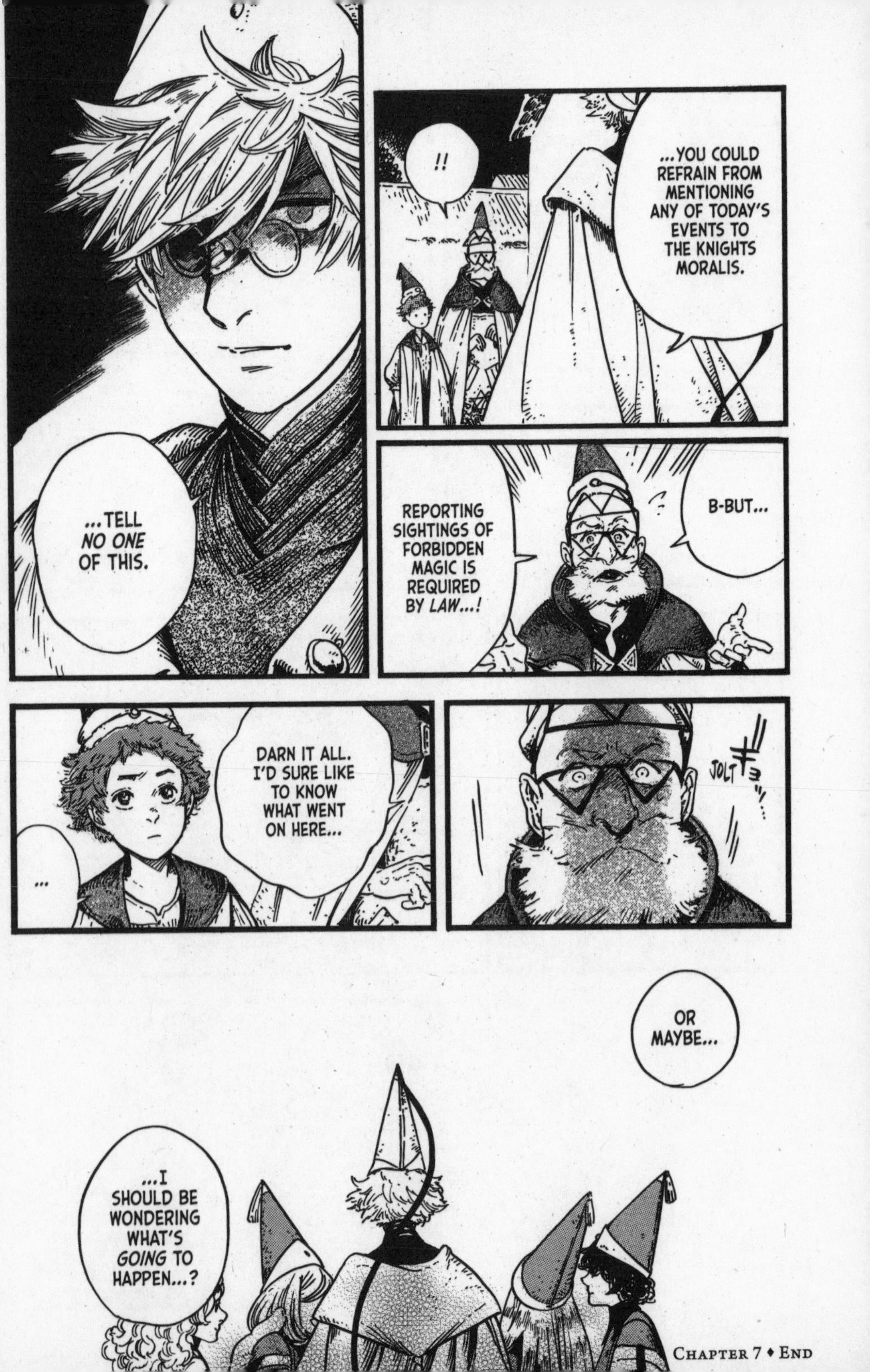
...YOU COULD REFRAIN FROM MENTIONING ANY OF TODAY'S EVENTS TO THE KNIGHTS MORALIS.
!!
B-BUT...
REPORTING SIGHTINGS OF FORBIDDEN MAGIC IS REQUIRED BY *LAW*...!
...TELL *NO ONE* OF THIS.
JOLT
DARN IT ALL. I'D SURE LIKE TO KNOW WHAT WENT ON HERE...
...
OR MAYBE...
...I SHOULD BE WONDERING WHAT'S *GOING* TO HAPPEN...?
Chapter 7 ♦ End

Witch Hat Atelier

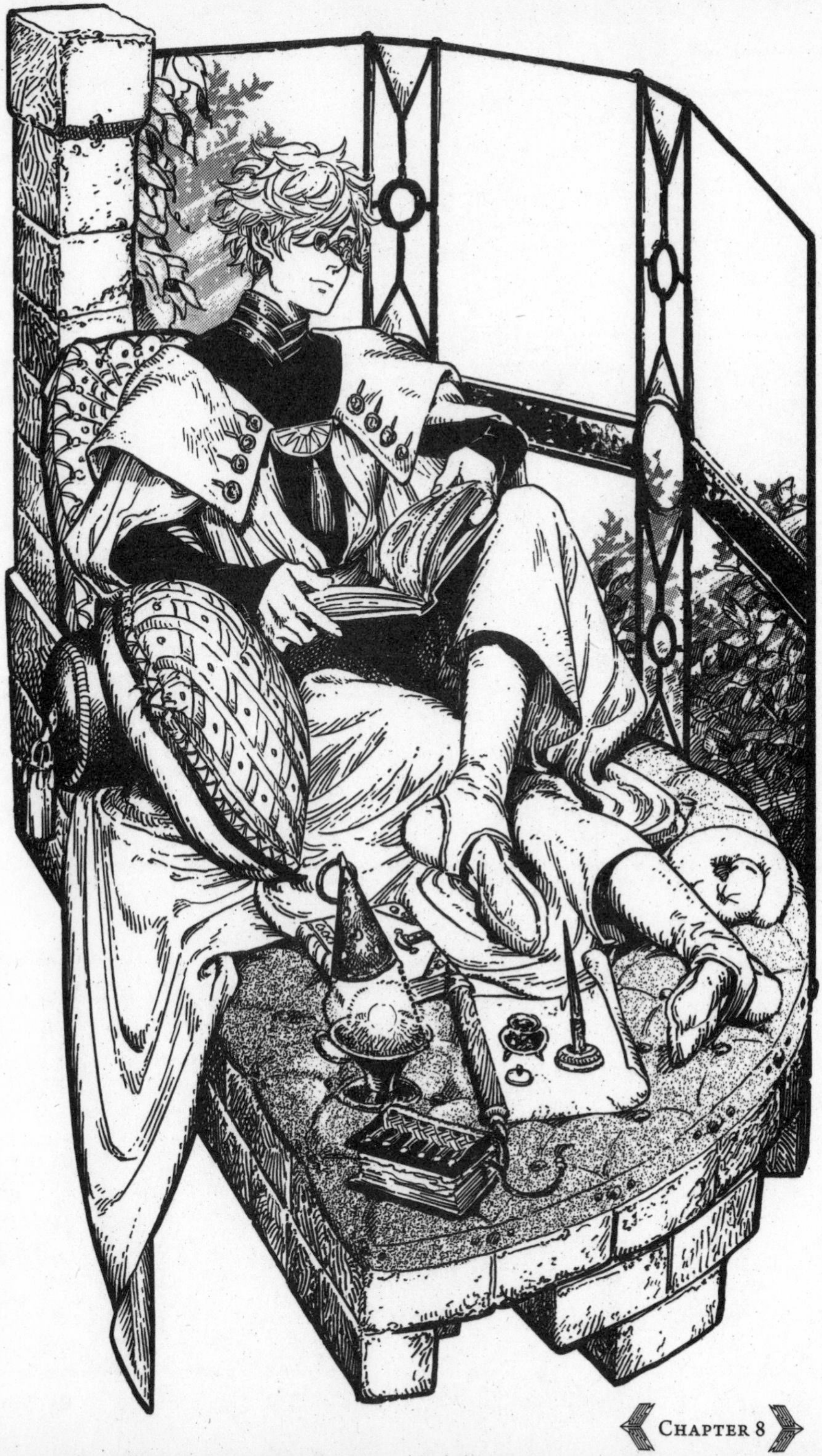

Chapter 8

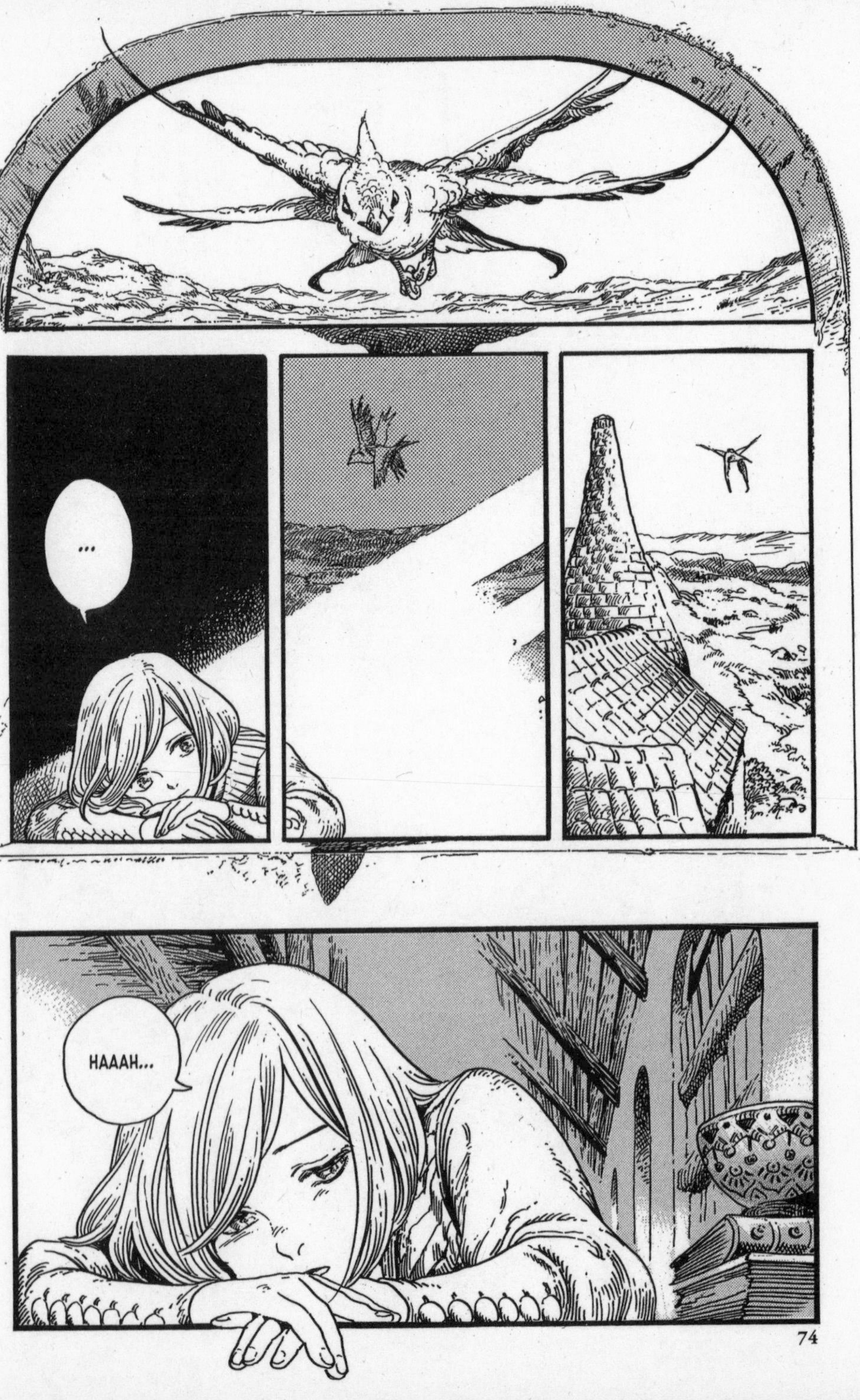
...
HAAAH...

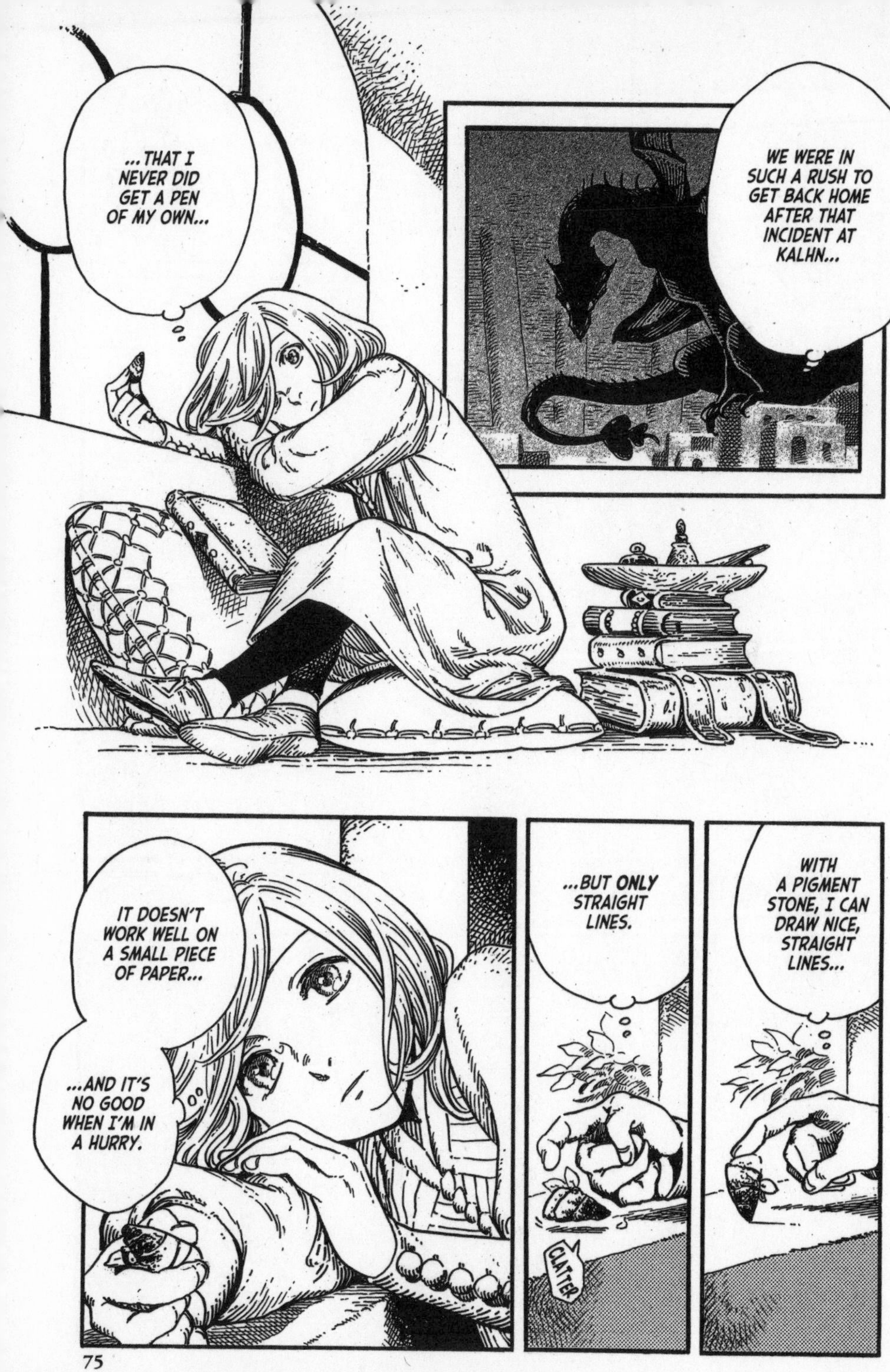
WE WERE IN SUCH A RUSH TO GET BACK HOME AFTER THAT INCIDENT AT KALHN...
...THAT I NEVER DID GET A PEN OF MY OWN...
WITH A PIGMENT STONE, I CAN DRAW NICE, STRAIGHT LINES...
...BUT ONLY STRAIGHT LINES.
CLATTER
IT DOESN'T WORK WELL ON A SMALL PIECE OF PAPER...
...AND IT'S NO GOOD WHEN I'M IN A HURRY.

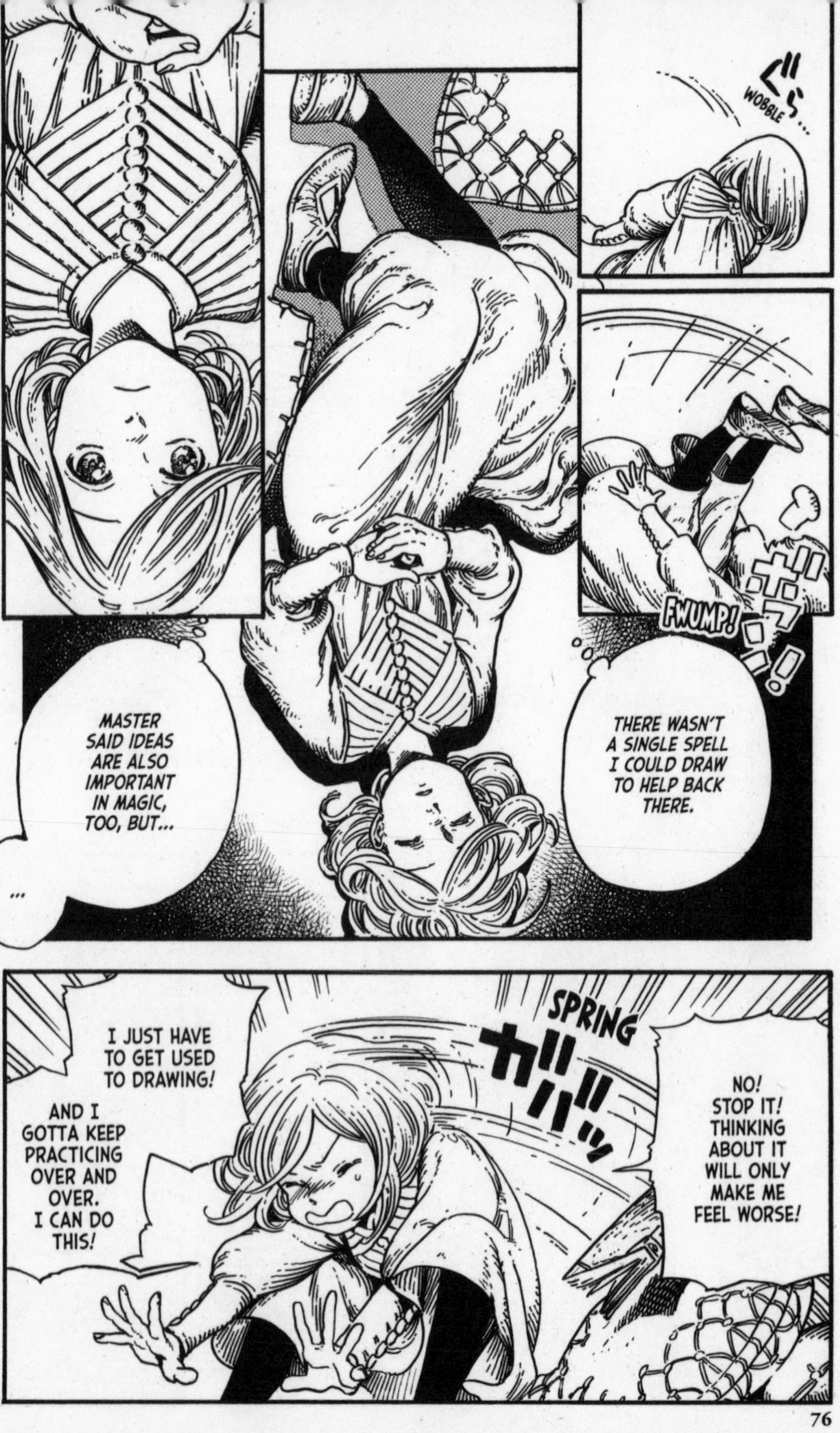
WOBBLE...
FWUMP!
THERE WASN'T A SINGLE SPELL I COULD DRAW TO HELP BACK THERE.
MASTER SAID IDEAS ARE ALSO IMPORTANT IN MAGIC, TOO, BUT...
...
NO! STOP IT! THINKING ABOUT IT WILL ONLY MAKE ME FEEL WORSE!
SPRING
I JUST HAVE TO GET USED TO DRAWING!
AND I GOTTA KEEP PRACTICING OVER AND OVER. I CAN DO THIS!

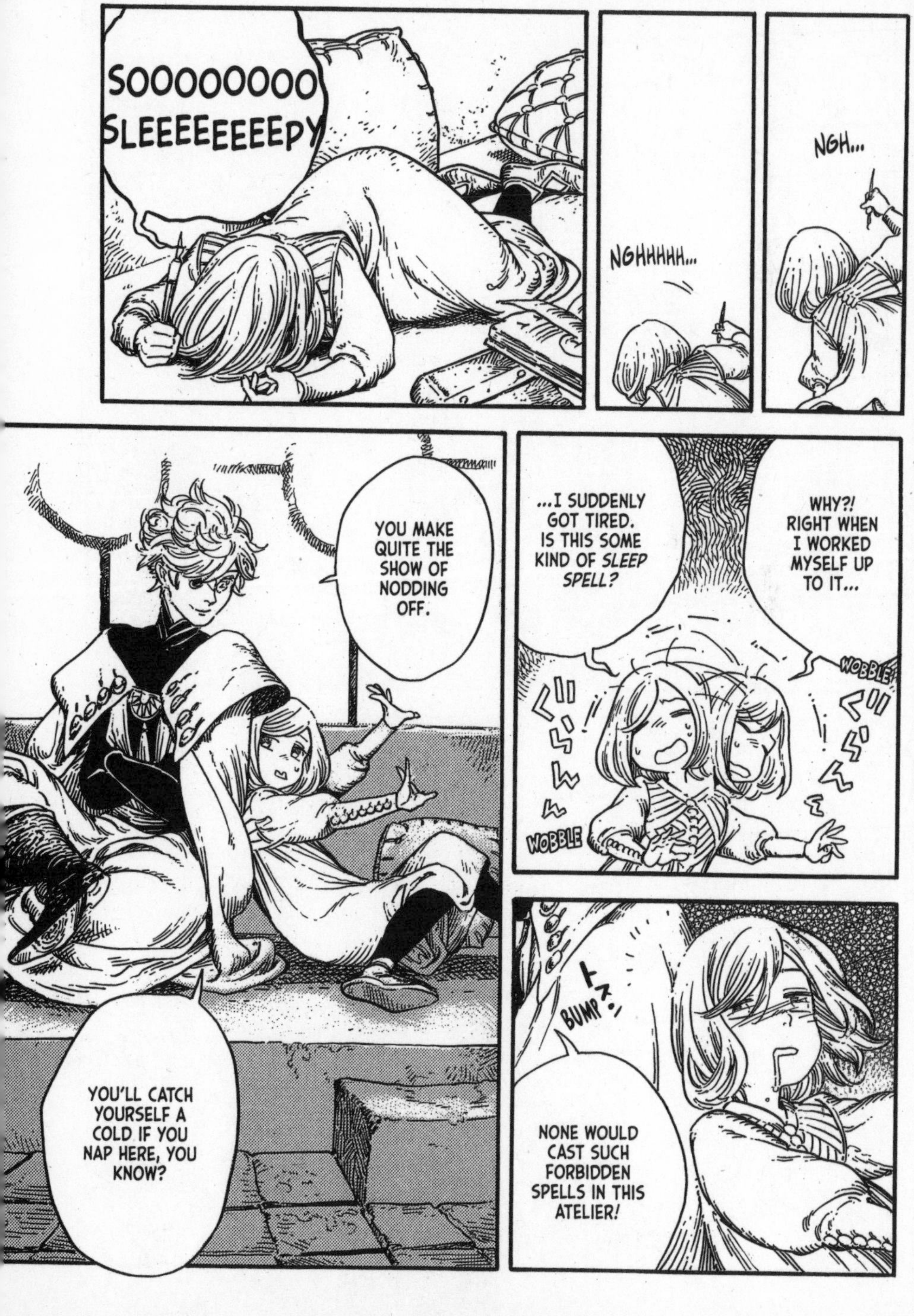
NGH...
NGHHHHH...
SOOOOOOOO SLEEEEEEEEPY
WHY?! RIGHT WHEN I WORKED MYSELF UP TO IT...
...I SUDDENLY GOT TIRED. IS THIS SOME KIND OF *SLEEP SPELL?*
WOBBLE
WOBBLE
BUMP
NONE WOULD CAST SUCH FORBIDDEN SPELLS IN THIS ATELIER!
YOU MAKE QUITE THE SHOW OF NODDING OFF.
YOU'LL CATCH YOURSELF A COLD IF YOU NAP HERE, YOU KNOW?

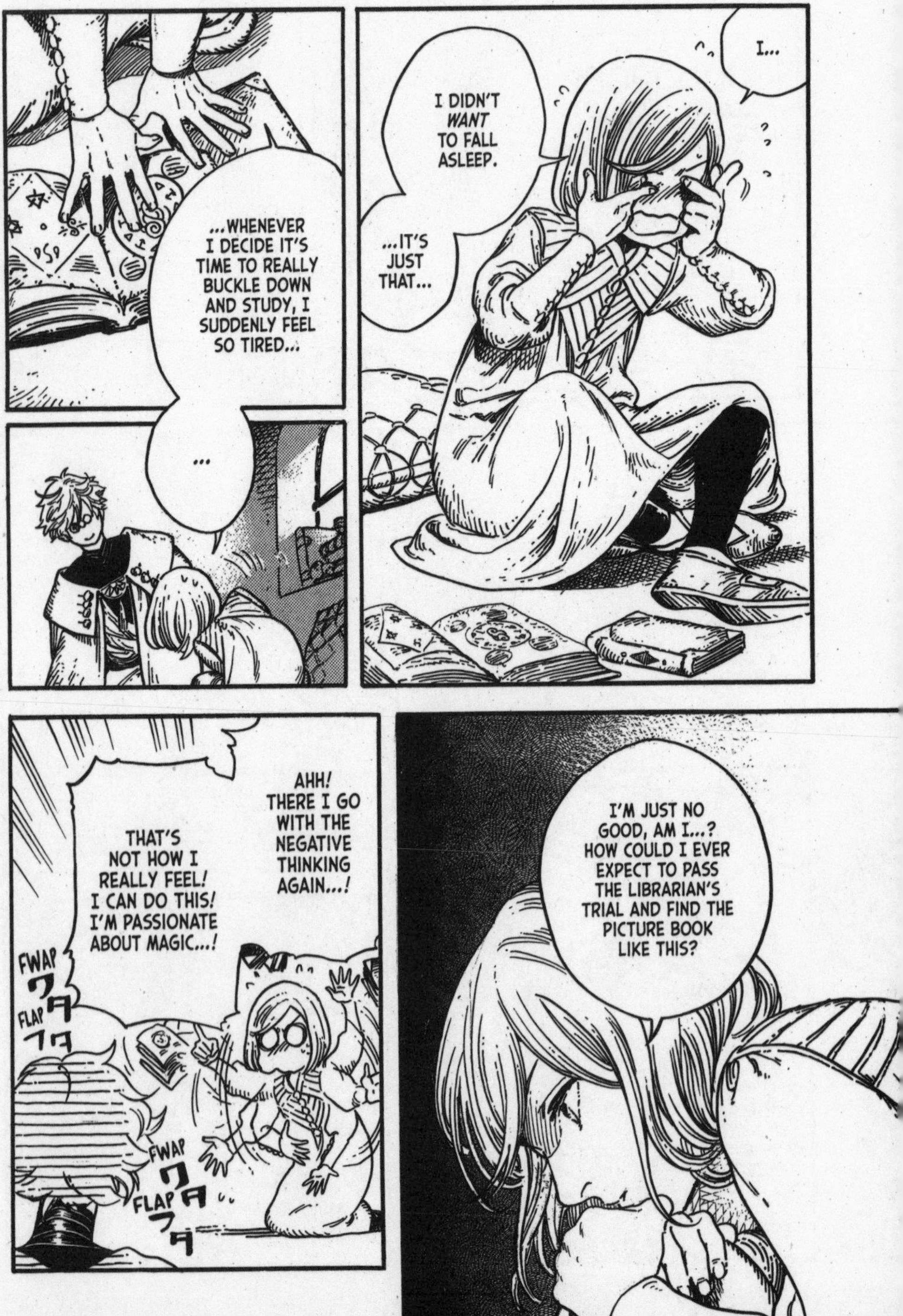
I...
I DIDN'T *WANT* TO FALL ASLEEP.
...IT'S JUST THAT...
...WHENEVER I DECIDE IT'S TIME TO REALLY BUCKLE DOWN AND STUDY, I SUDDENLY FEEL SO TIRED...
...
I'M JUST NO GOOD, AM I...? HOW COULD I EVER EXPECT TO PASS THE LIBRARIAN'S TRIAL AND FIND THE PICTURE BOOK LIKE THIS?
AHH! THERE I GO WITH THE NEGATIVE THINKING AGAIN...!
THAT'S NOT HOW I REALLY FEEL! I CAN DO THIS! I'M PASSIONATE ABOUT MAGIC...!
FWAP ワタ FLAP フタ
FWAP ワタ FLAP フタ

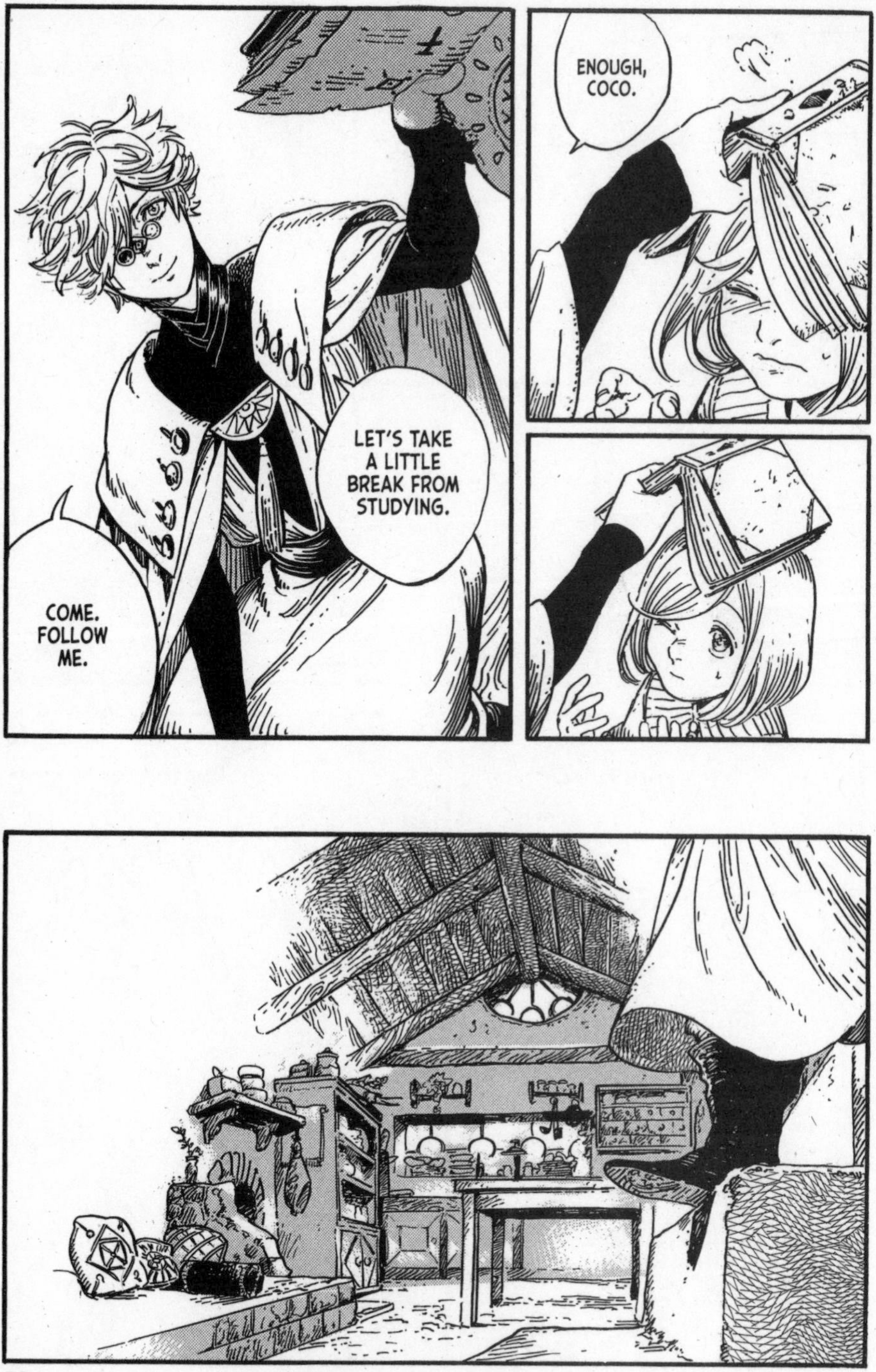
ENOUGH, COCO.
LET'S TAKE A LITTLE BREAK FROM STUDYING.
COME. FOLLOW ME.

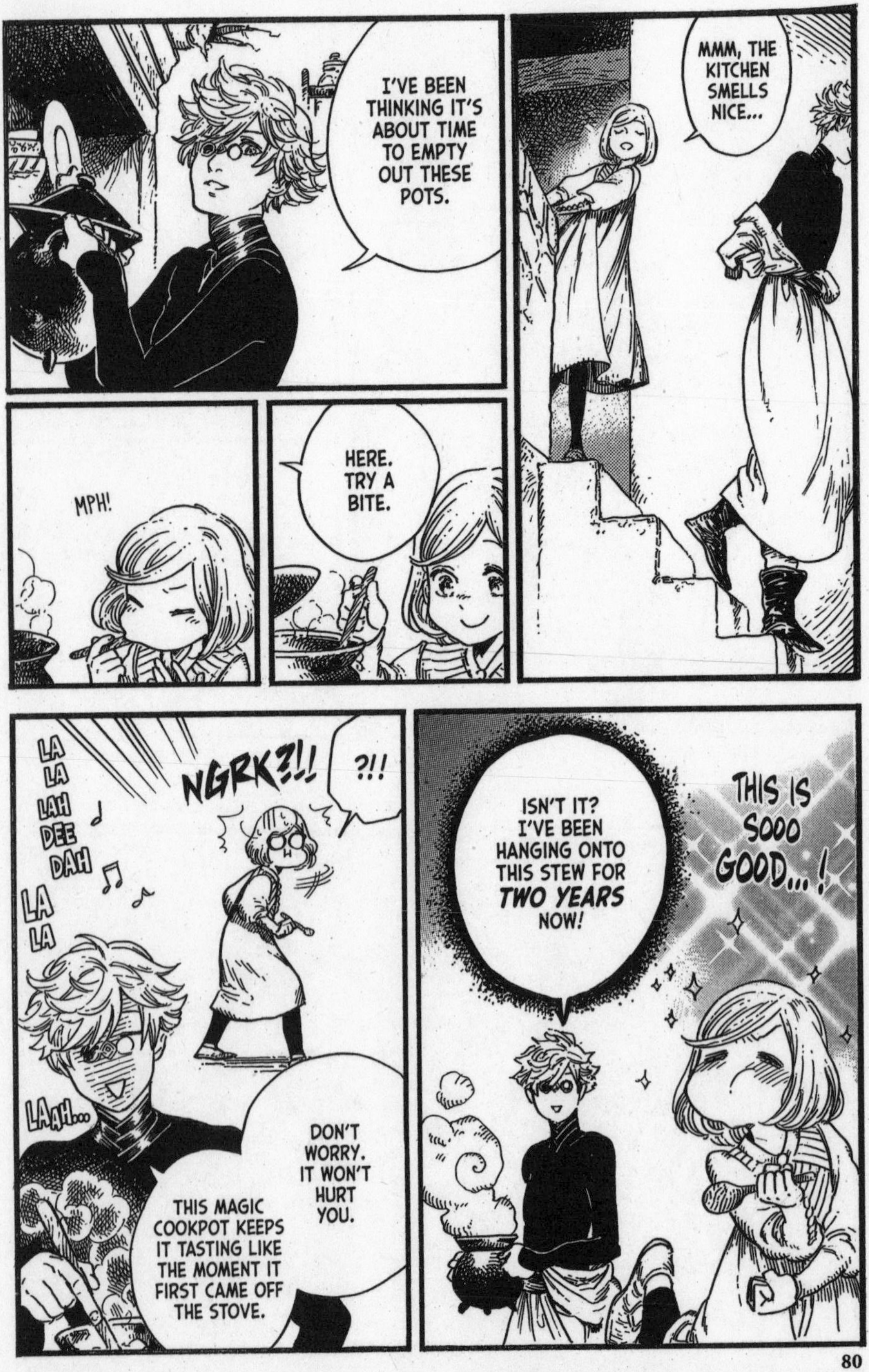
MMM, THE KITCHEN SMELLS NICE...
I'VE BEEN THINKING IT'S ABOUT TIME TO EMPTY OUT THESE POTS.
HERE. TRY A BITE.
MPH!
THIS IS SOOO GOOD...!
ISN'T IT? I'VE BEEN HANGING ONTO THIS STEW FOR *TWO YEARS* NOW!
?!!
NGRK?!!
LA LA LAH DEE DAH
LA LA
LAAH...
DON'T WORRY. IT WON'T HURT YOU.
THIS MAGIC COOKPOT KEEPS IT TASTING LIKE THE MOMENT IT FIRST CAME OFF THE STOVE.

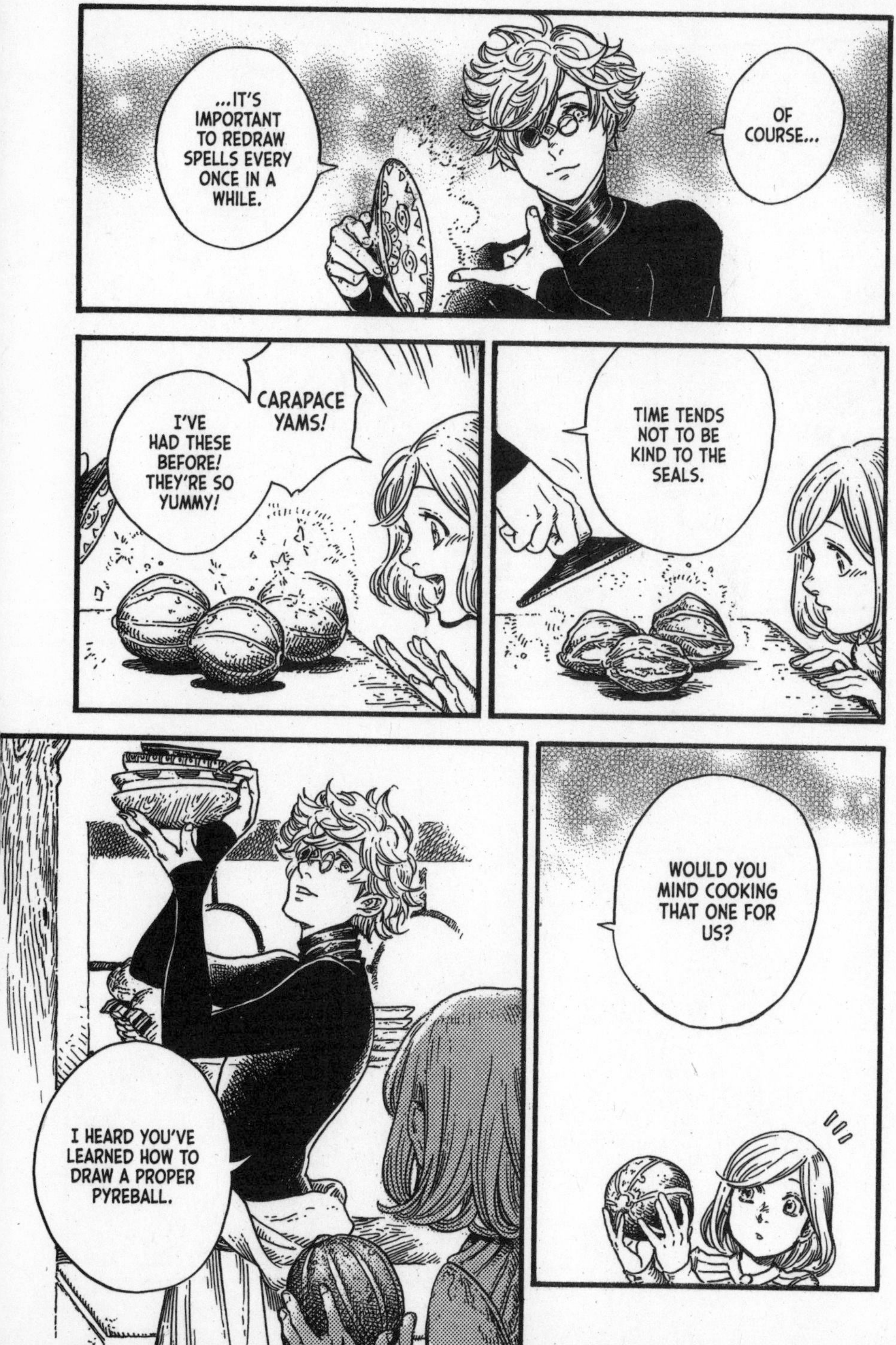
OF COURSE...
...IT'S IMPORTANT TO REDRAW SPELLS EVERY ONCE IN A WHILE.
TIME TENDS NOT TO BE KIND TO THE SEALS.
CARAPACE YAMS!
I'VE HAD THESE BEFORE! THEY'RE SO YUMMY!
WOULD YOU MIND COOKING THAT ONE FOR US?
I HEARD YOU'VE LEARNED HOW TO DRAW A PROPER PYREBALL.

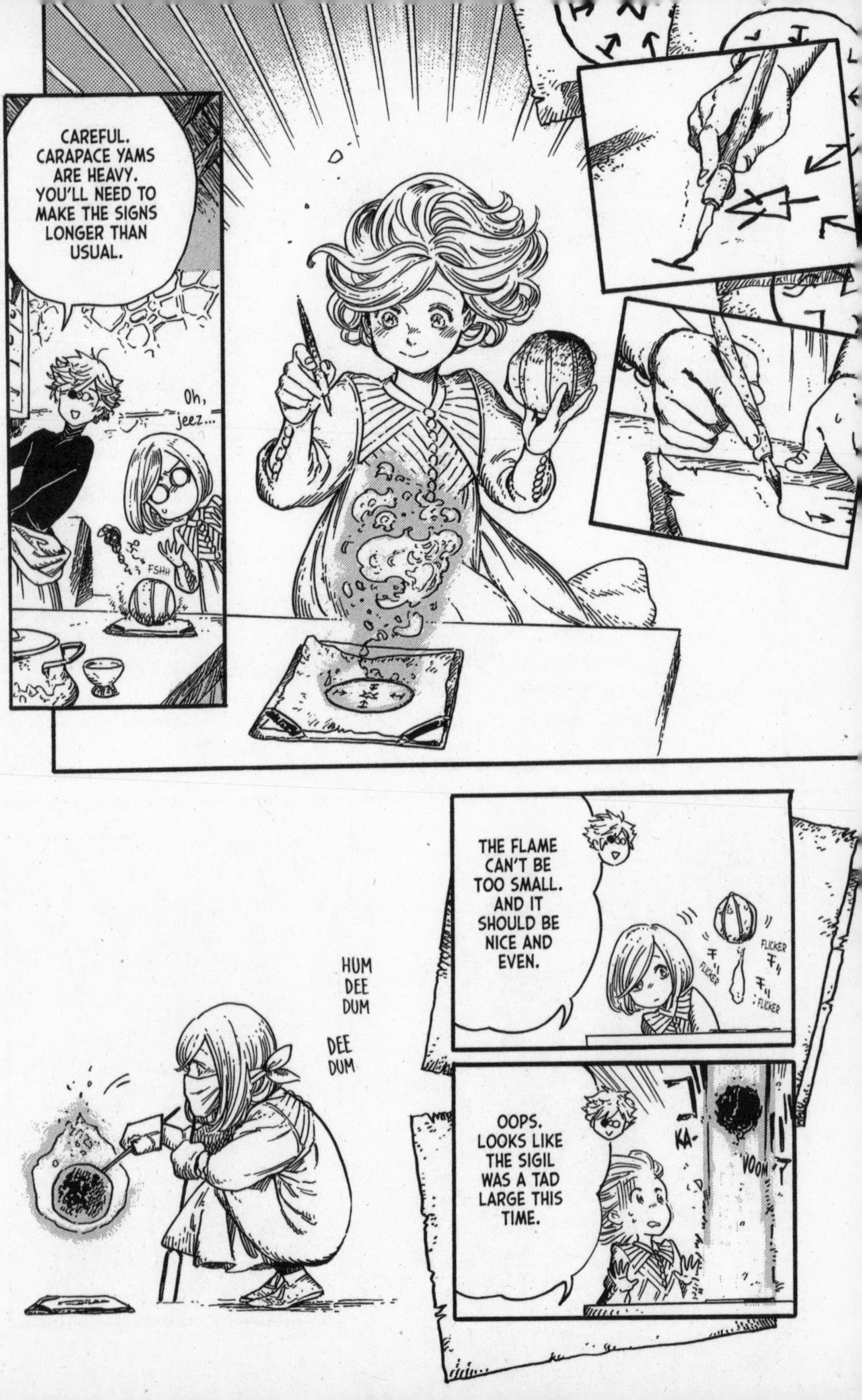
CAREFUL. CARAPACE YAMS ARE HEAVY. YOU'LL NEED TO MAKE THE SIGNS LONGER THAN USUAL.
Oh, jeez...
FSHH
THE FLAME CAN'T BE TOO SMALL. AND IT SHOULD BE NICE AND EVEN.
FLICKER
FLICKER
FLICKER
OOPS. LOOKS LIKE THE SIGIL WAS A TAD LARGE THIS TIME.
KA-VOOM
HUM DEE DUM
DEE DUM

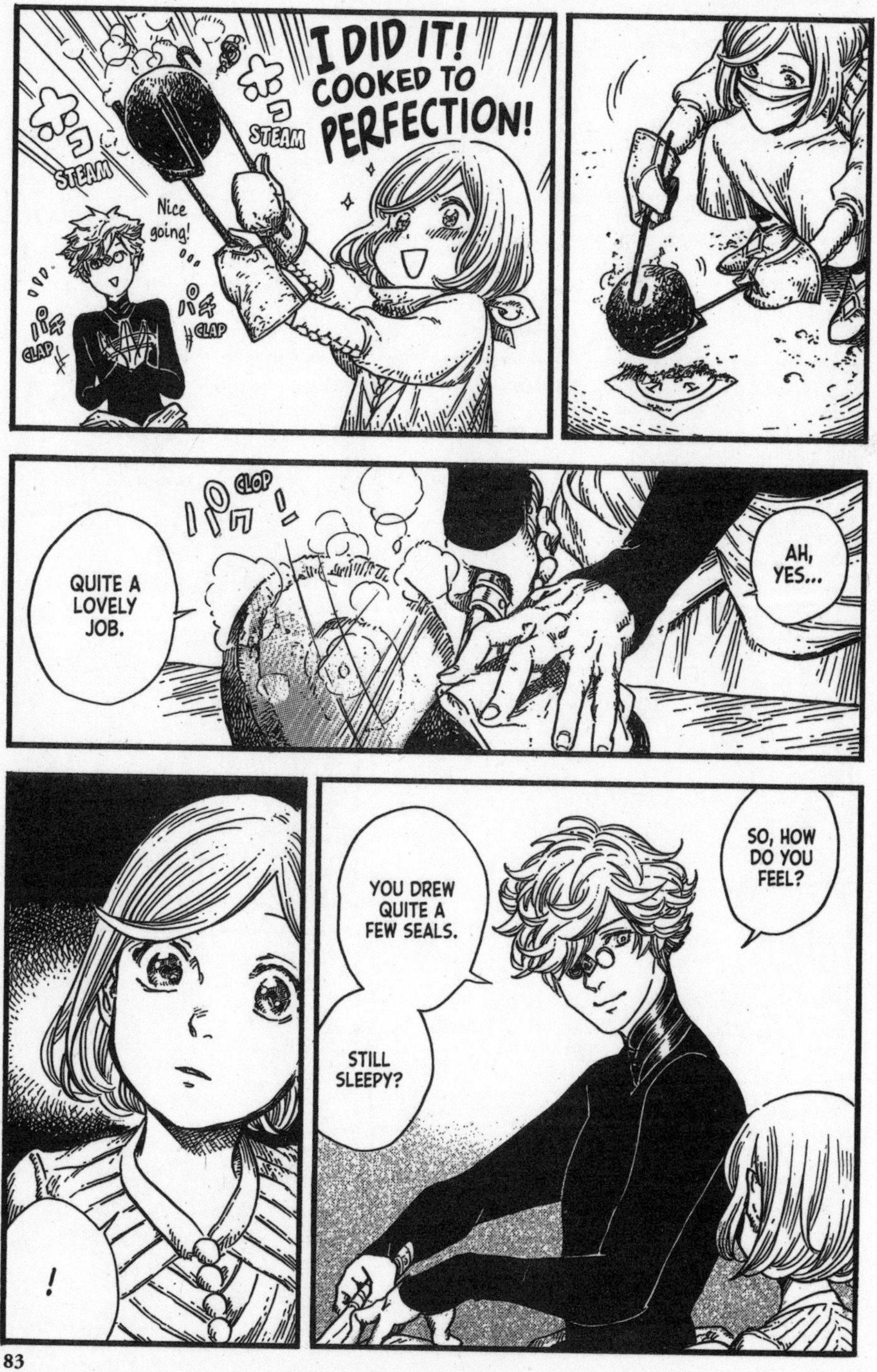
I DID IT! COOKED TO PERFECTION!
STEAM
STEAM
Nice going!
CLAP
CLAP
AH, YES...
CLOP
QUITE A LOVELY JOB.
SO, HOW DO YOU FEEL?
YOU DREW QUITE A FEW SEALS.
STILL SLEEPY?
!

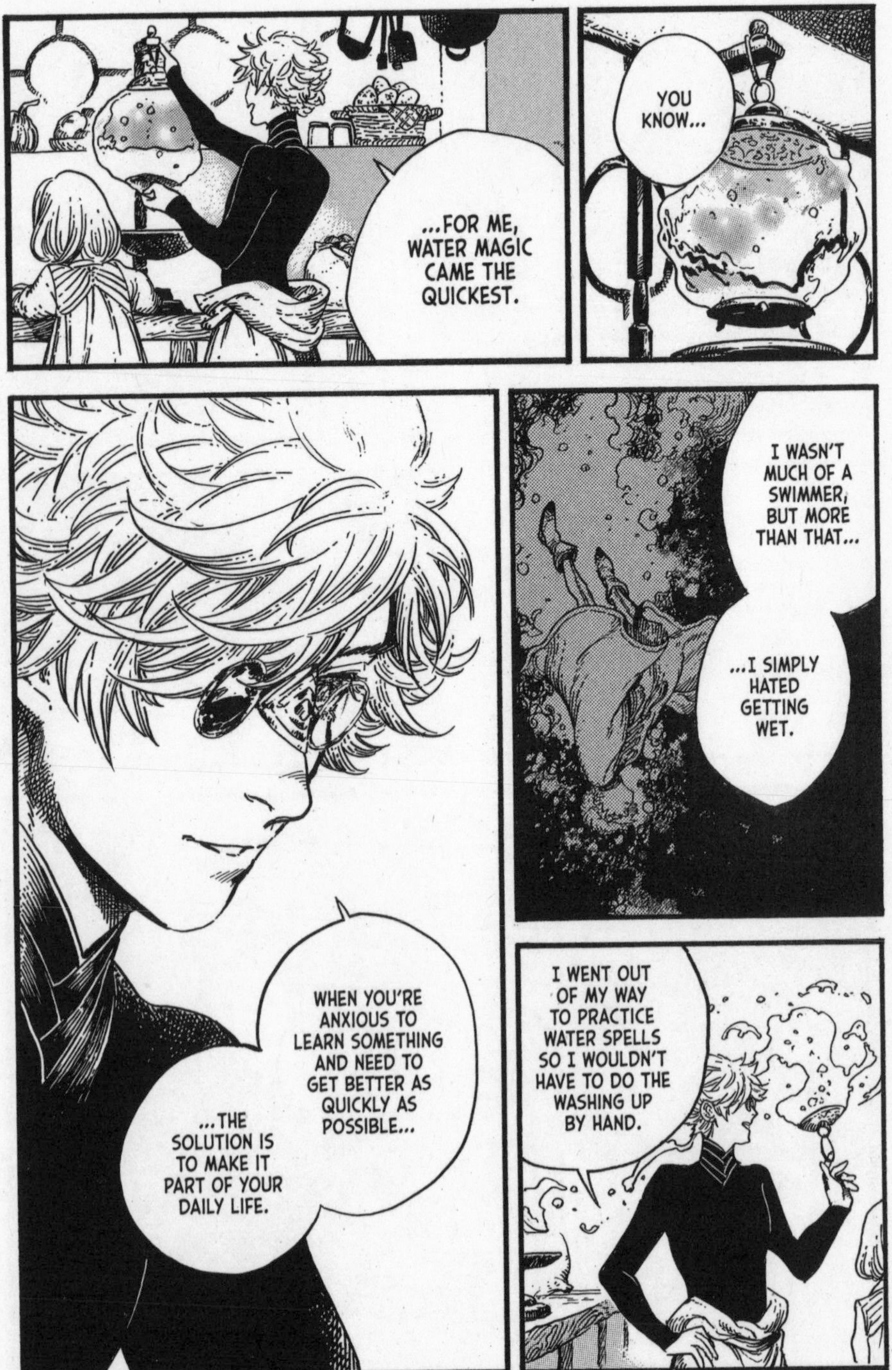
YOU KNOW...
...FOR ME, WATER MAGIC CAME THE QUICKEST.
I WASN'T MUCH OF A SWIMMER, BUT MORE THAN THAT...
...I SIMPLY HATED GETTING WET.
I WENT OUT OF MY WAY TO PRACTICE WATER SPELLS SO I WOULDN'T HAVE TO DO THE WASHING UP BY HAND.
WHEN YOU'RE ANXIOUS TO LEARN SOMETHING AND NEED TO GET BETTER AS QUICKLY AS POSSIBLE...
...THE SOLUTION IS TO MAKE IT PART OF YOUR DAILY LIFE.

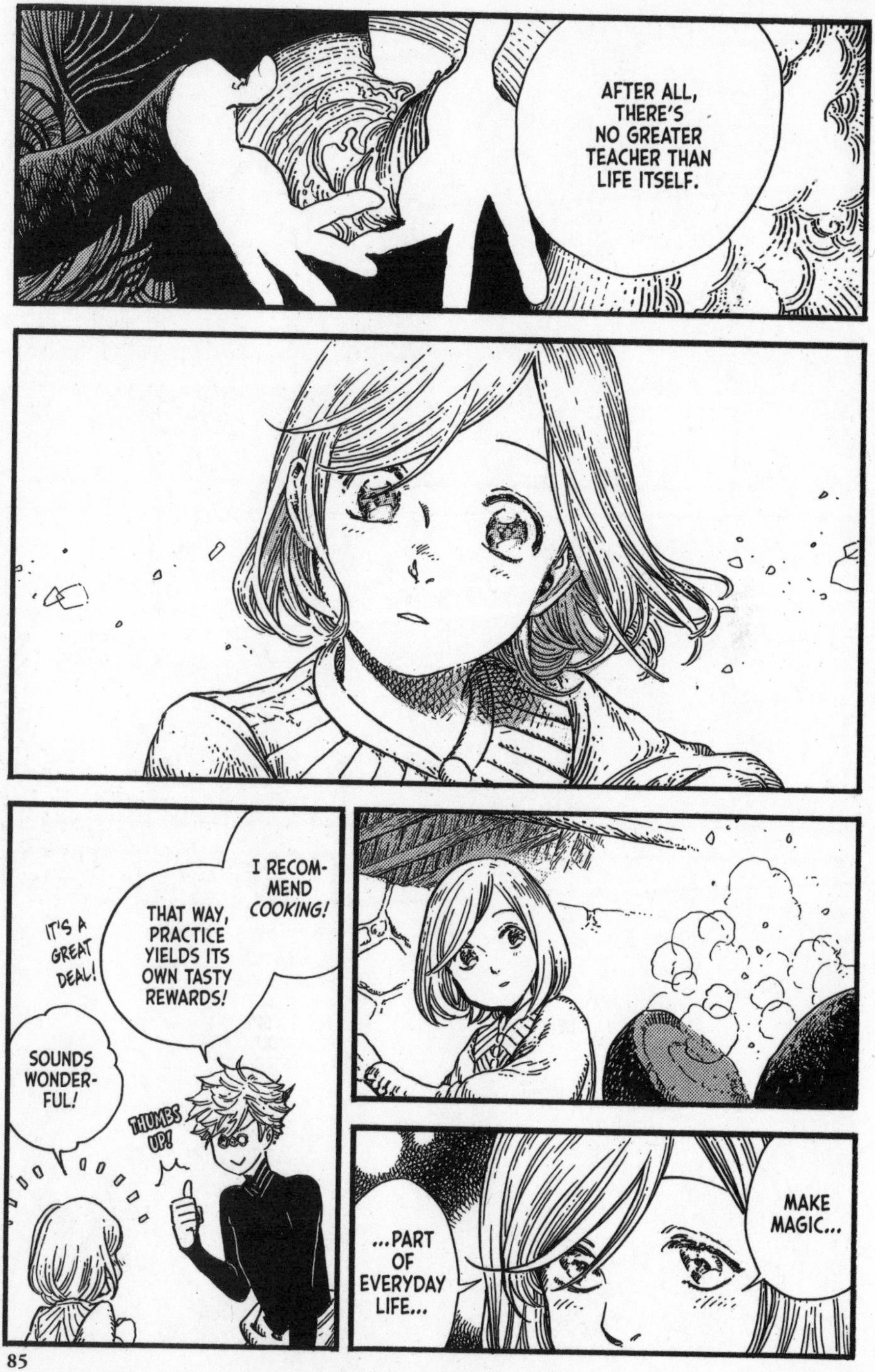
AFTER ALL, THERE'S NO GREATER TEACHER THAN LIFE ITSELF.
MAKE MAGIC...
...PART OF EVERYDAY LIFE...
I RECOMMEND COOKING!
THAT WAY, PRACTICE YIELDS ITS OWN TASTY REWARDS!
IT'S A GREAT DEAL!
SOUNDS WONDERFUL!
THUMBS UP!

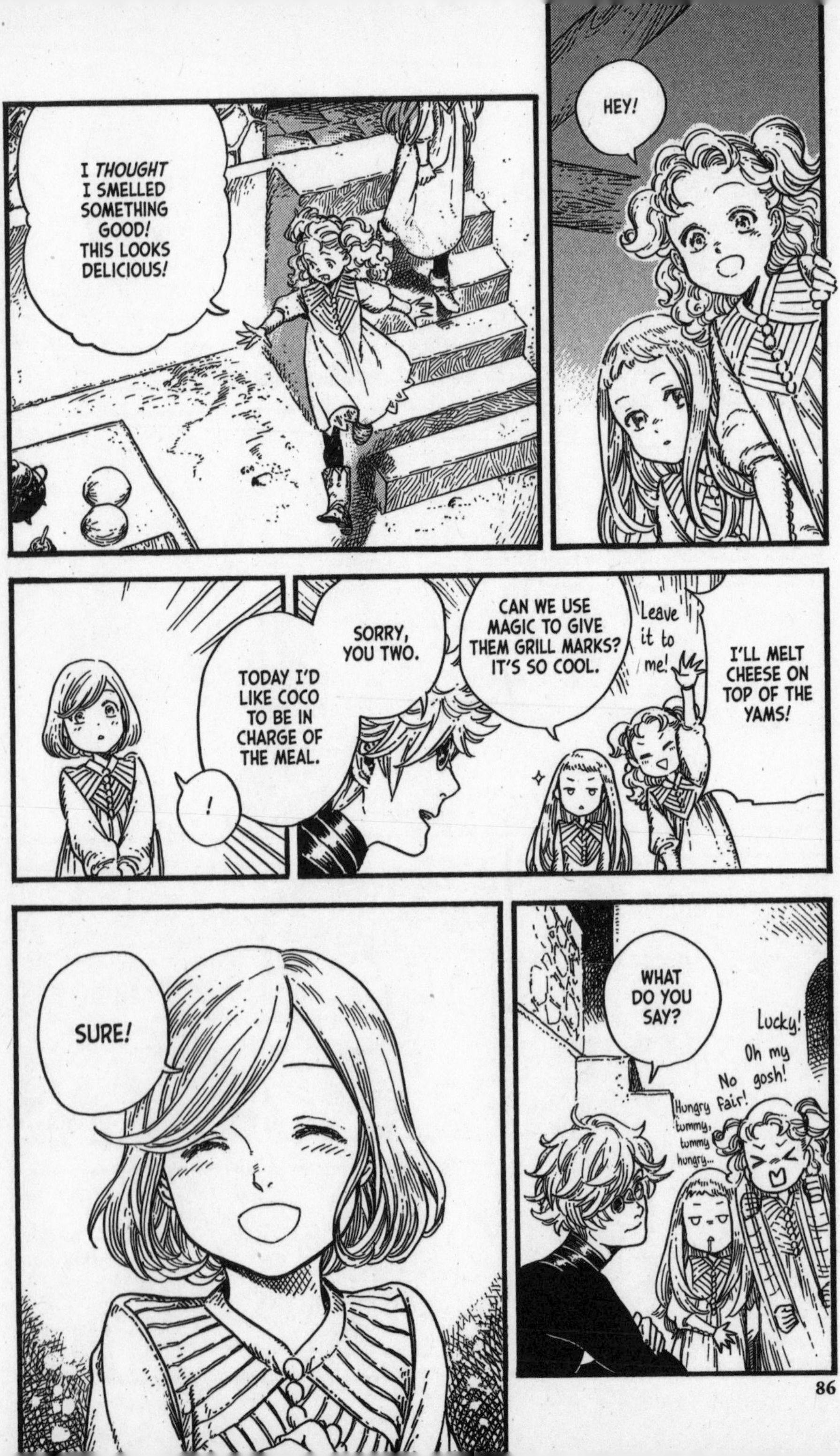

HEY!
I *THOUGHT* I SMELLED SOMETHING GOOD! THIS LOOKS DELICIOUS!
I'LL MELT CHEESE ON TOP OF THE YAMS!
Leave it to me!
CAN WE USE MAGIC TO GIVE THEM GRILL MARKS? IT'S SO COOL.
SORRY, YOU TWO.
TODAY I'D LIKE COCO TO BE IN CHARGE OF THE MEAL.
!
Lucky!
Oh my gosh!
WHAT DO YOU SAY?
No fair!
Hungry tummy, tummy hungry...
SURE!

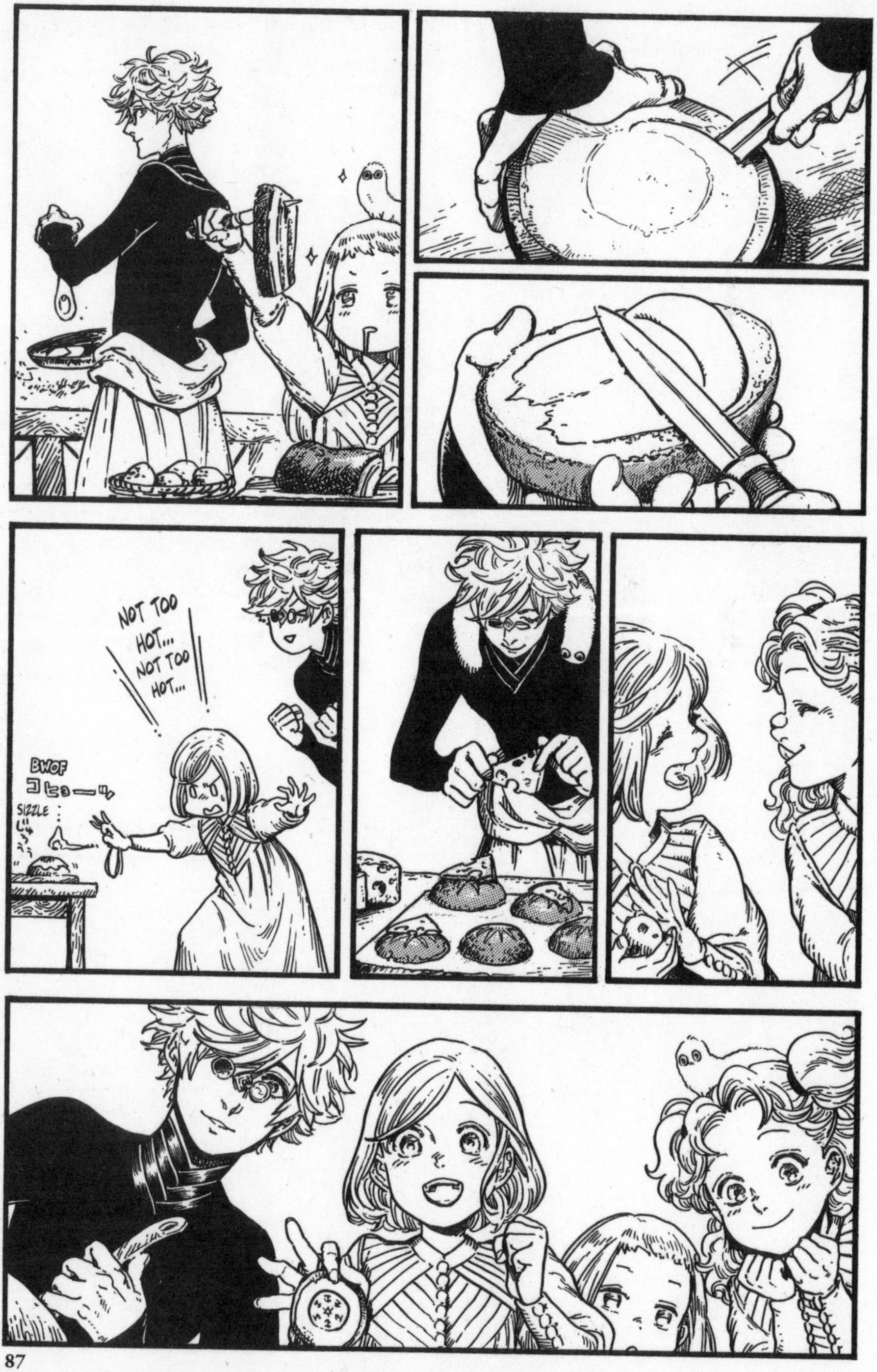
NOT TOO HOT... NOT TOO HOT...
BWOF
コヒョーッ
SIZZLE
じゅぅぅ

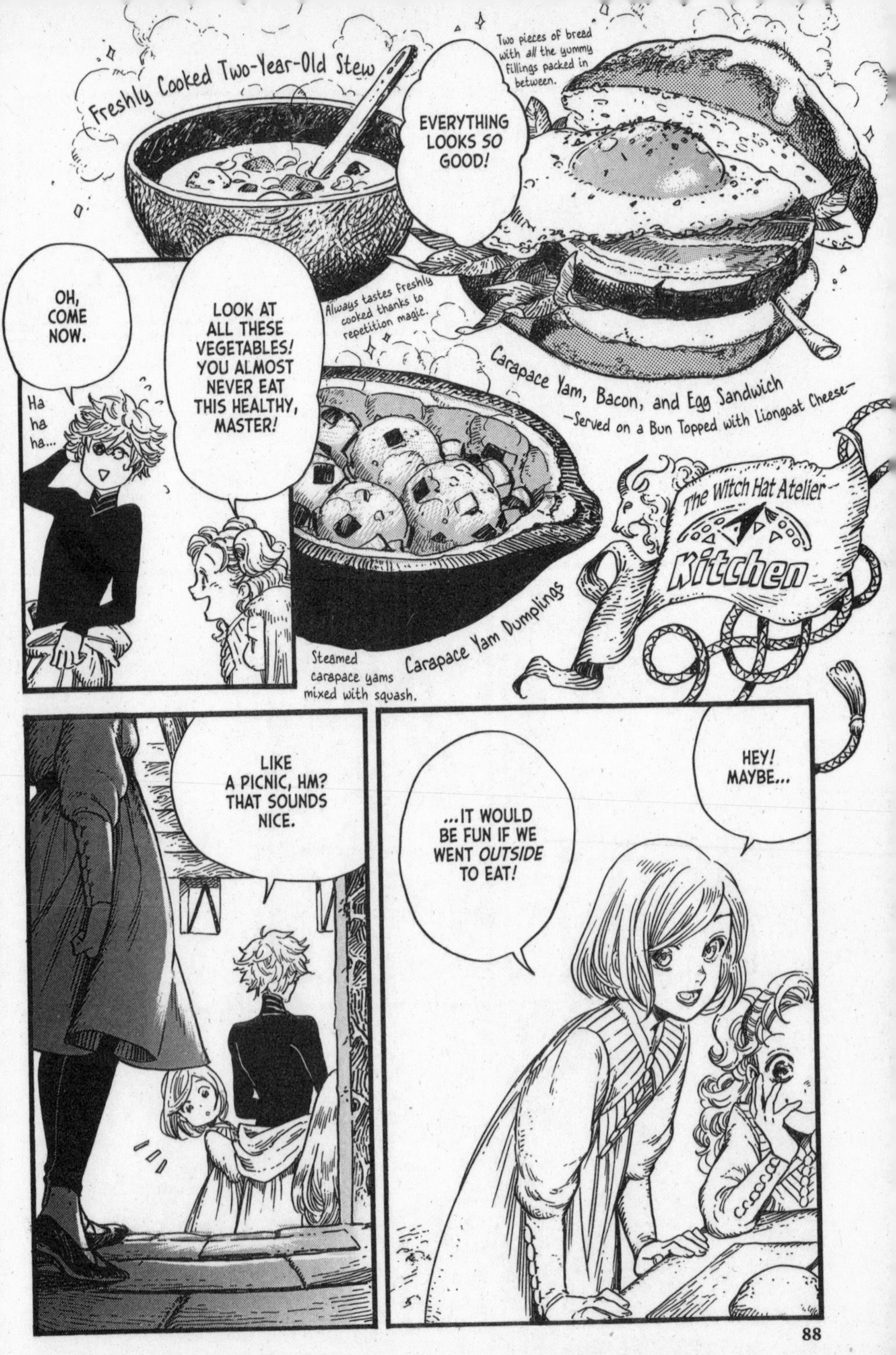
Two pieces of bread with *all* the yummy fillings packed in between.
EVERYTHING LOOKS SO GOOD!
Freshly Cooked Two-Year-Old Stew
Always tastes freshly cooked thanks to repetition magic.
Carapace Yam, Bacon, and Egg Sandwich
—Served on a Bun Topped with Liongoat Cheese—
The Witch Hat Atelier Kitchen
Carapace Yam Dumplings
Steamed carapace yams mixed with squash.
LOOK AT ALL THESE VEGETABLES! YOU ALMOST NEVER EAT THIS HEALTHY, MASTER!
OH, COME NOW.
Ha ha ha...
HEY! MAYBE...
...IT WOULD BE FUN IF WE WENT *OUTSIDE* TO EAT!
LIKE A PICNIC, HM? THAT SOUNDS NICE.

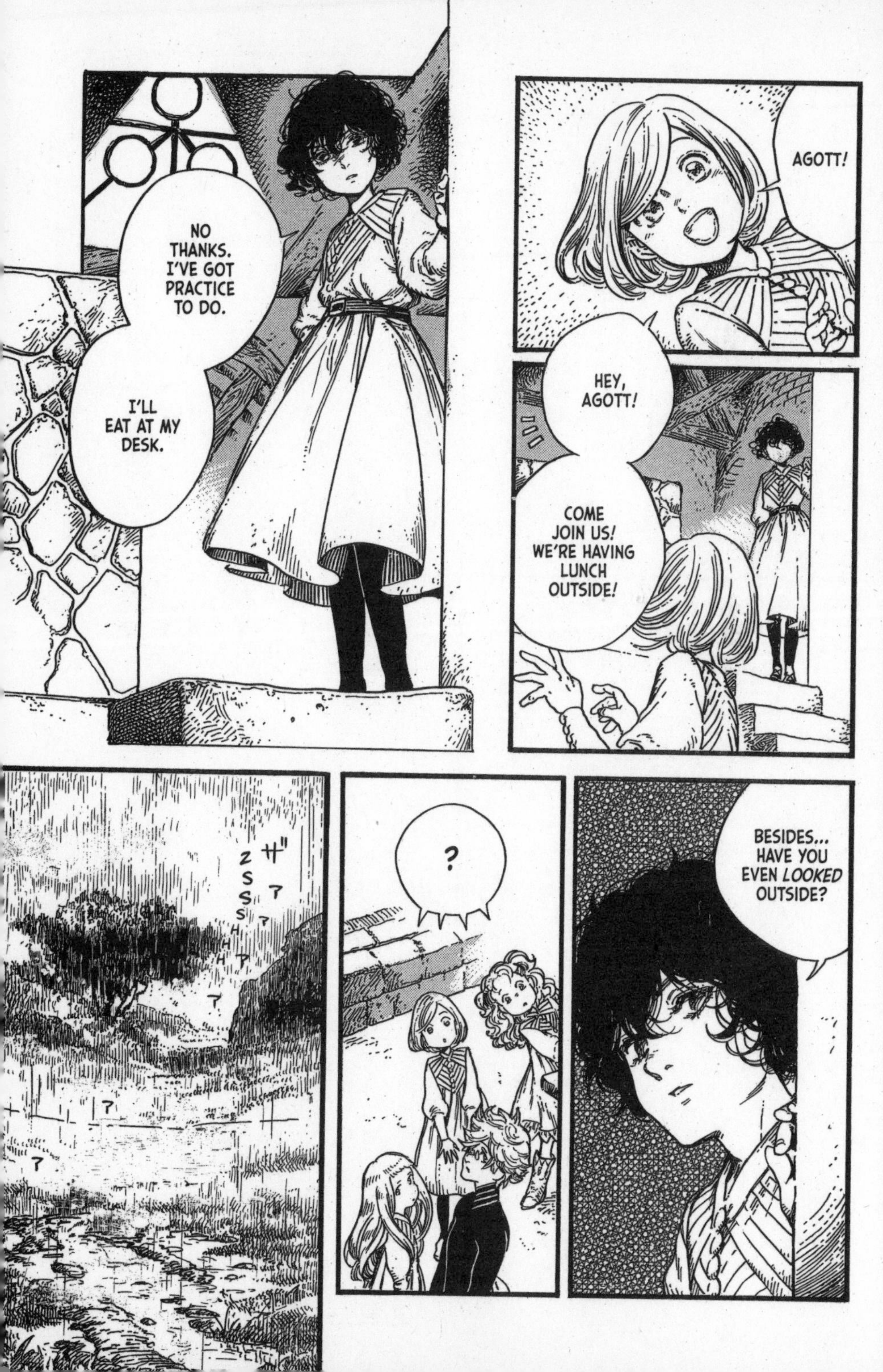
AGOTT!
HEY, AGOTT!
COME JOIN US! WE'RE HAVING LUNCH OUTSIDE!
NO THANKS. I'VE GOT PRACTICE TO DO.
I'LL EAT AT MY DESK.
BESIDES... HAVE YOU EVEN *LOOKED* OUTSIDE?
?
ZSSSHH

THE WEATHER WAS PERFECT EARLIER.

AWWooo

OH, WELL.

LET'S GO BACK INSIDE.

MASTER QIFREY WAS JUST TALKING ABOUT HOW HE DOESN'T LIKE TO GET WET.

WHY WOULD WE LET A LITTLE RAIN STOP US?

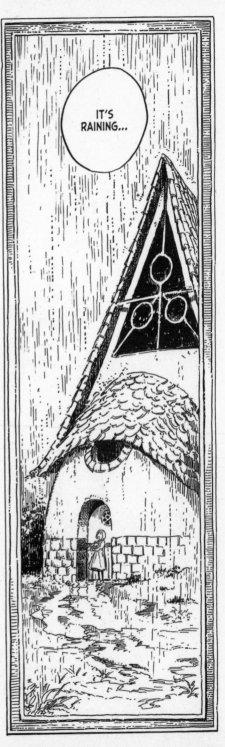

IT'S RAINING...

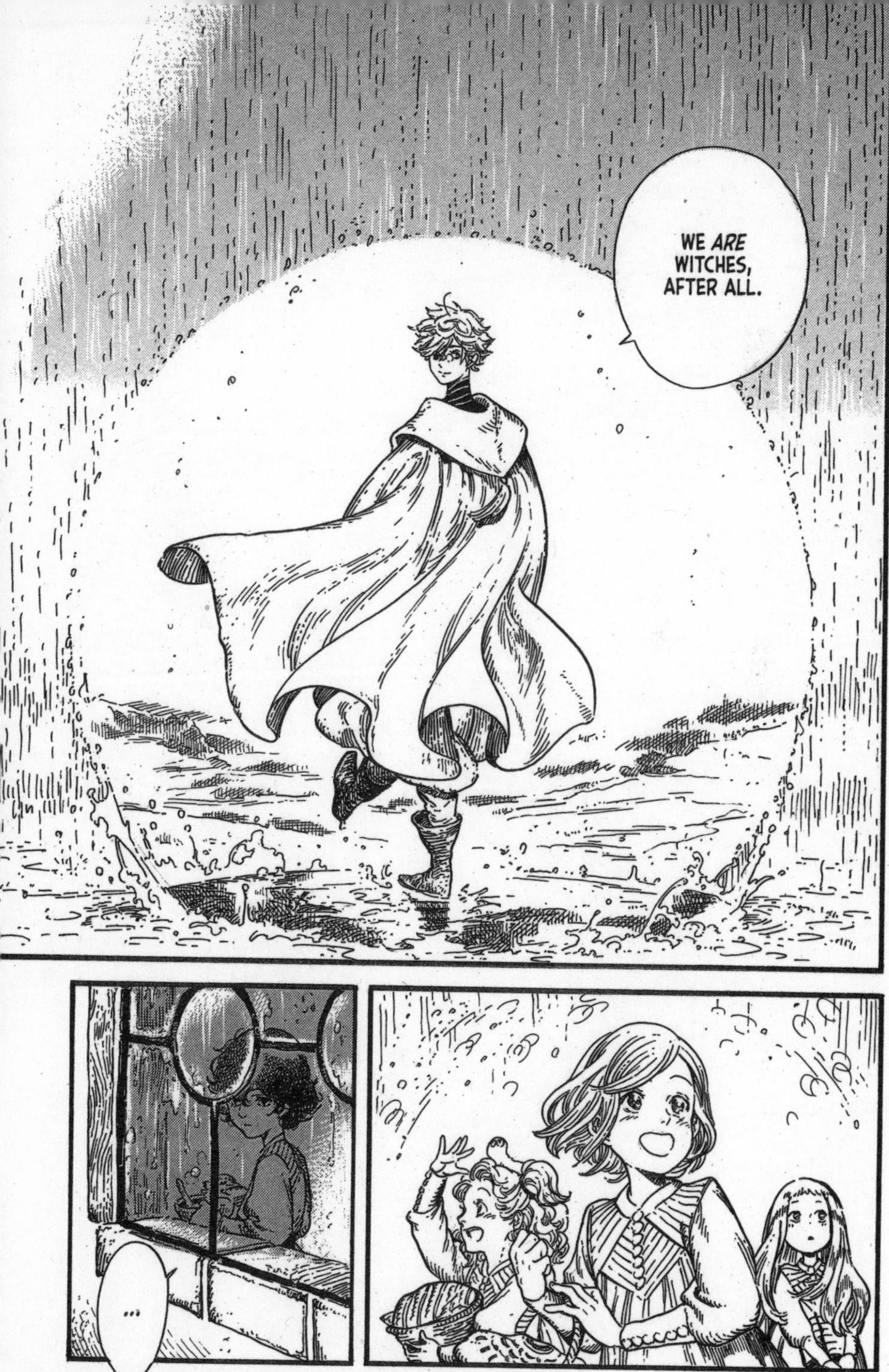
WE *ARE* WITCHES, AFTER ALL.
...

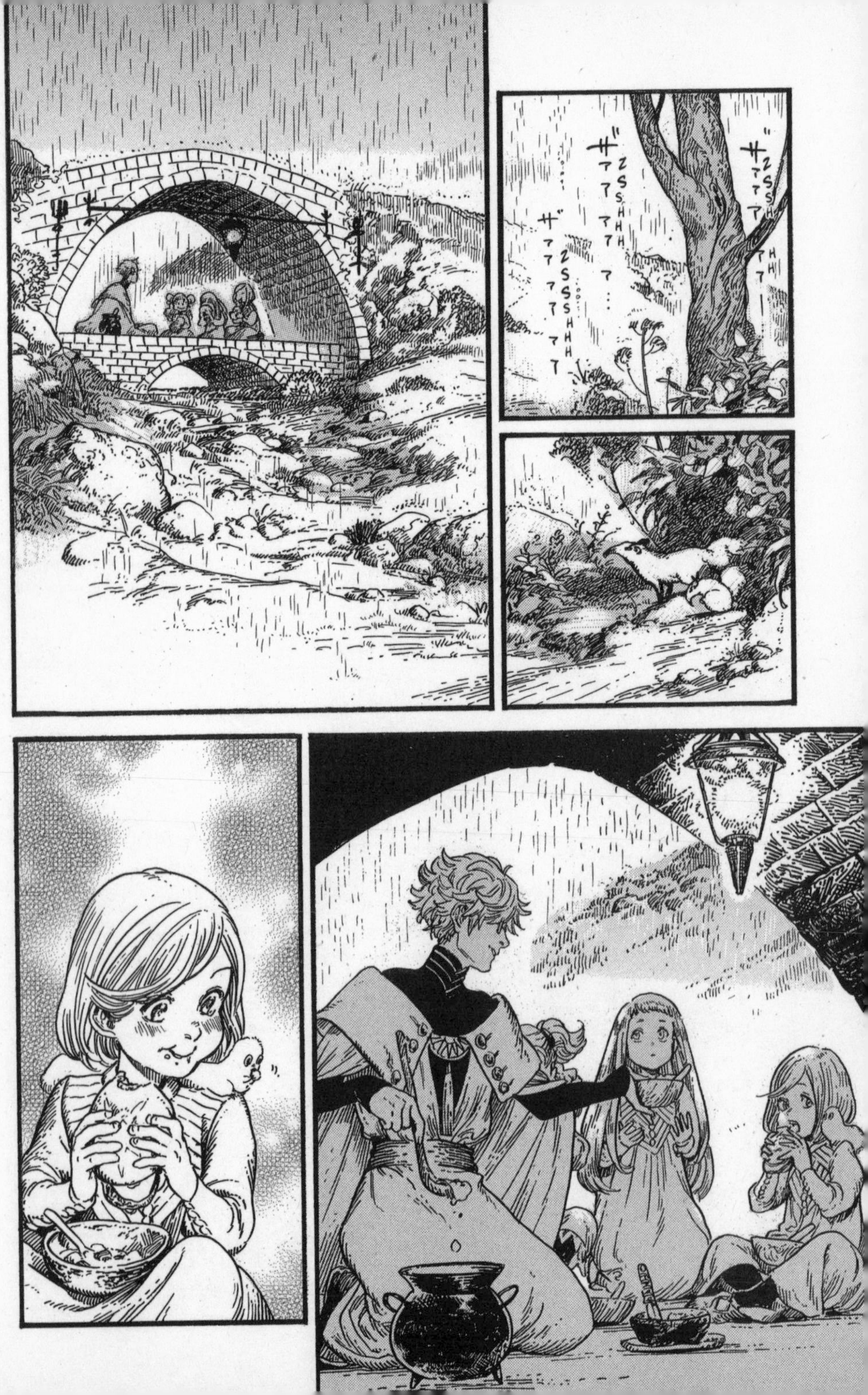
ザァァァァー
ZSSHHHH
ザァァァァァ…
ZSSHHH
ザァァァァァァ
ZSSHHH
…

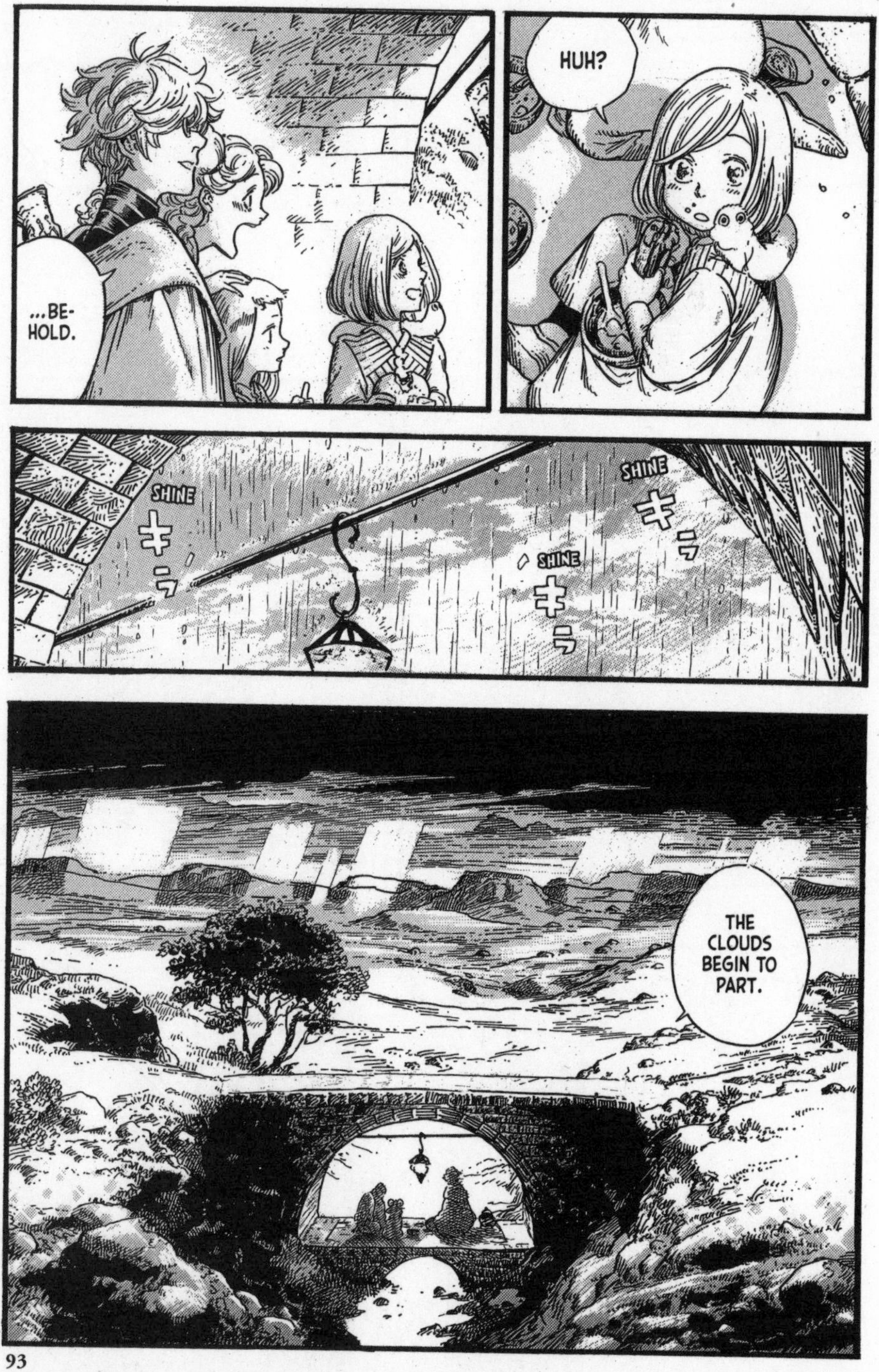
HUH?
...BE-
HOLD.
SHINE
キラ
SHINE
キラ
SHINE
キラ
THE CLOUDS BEGIN TO PART.

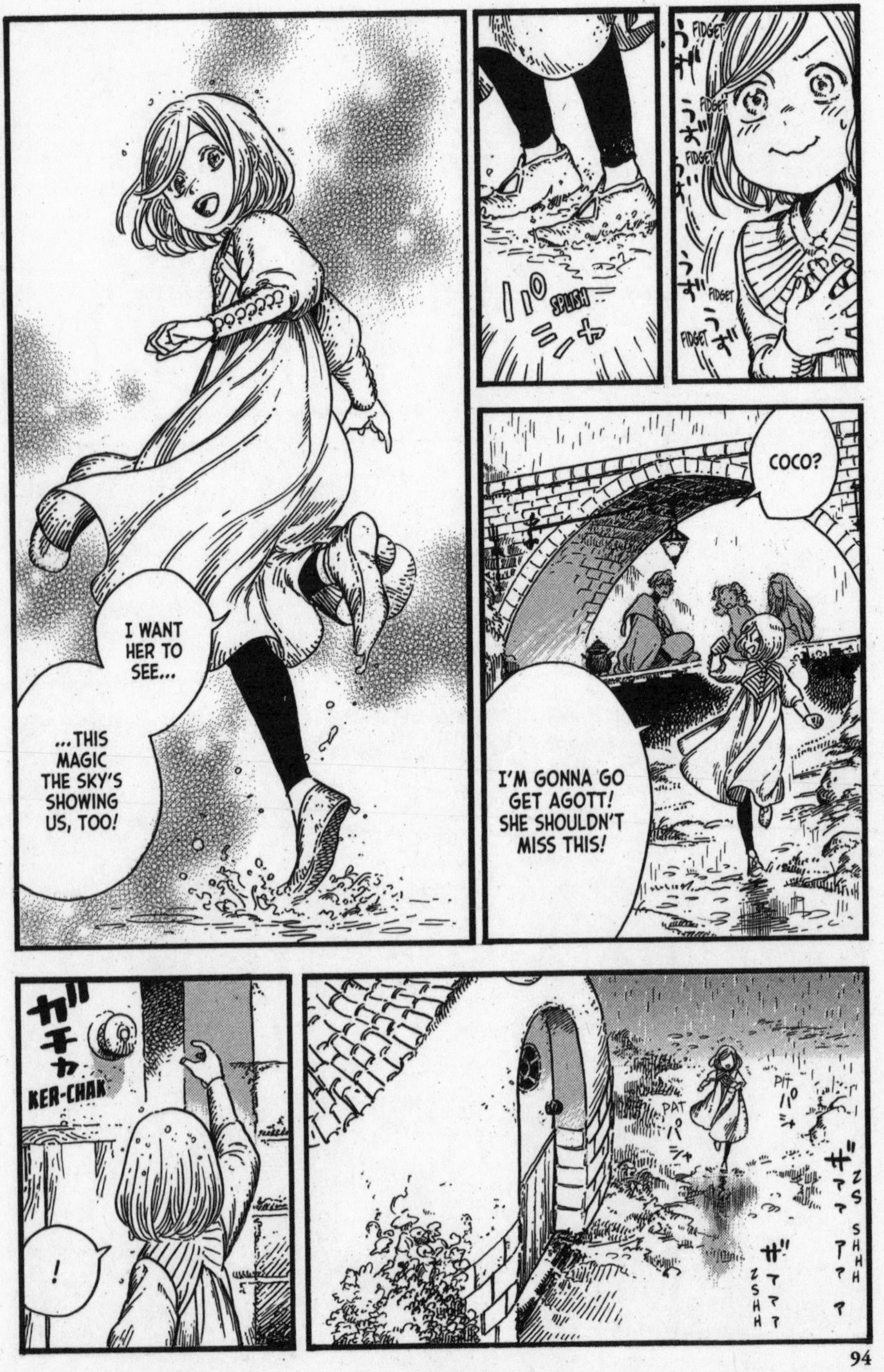
うず FIDGET
うず FIDGET
うず FIDGET
うず FIDGET
うず FIDGET
パシャ
SPLISH
COCO?
I'M GONNA GO GET AGOTT! SHE SHOULDN'T MISS THIS!
I WANT HER TO SEE...
...THIS MAGIC THE SKY'S SHOWING US, TOO!
PIT
パシャ
PAT
パシャ
ザァァ
ZSHH
ザァァ
ZSHH
ガチャ
KER-CHAK
!

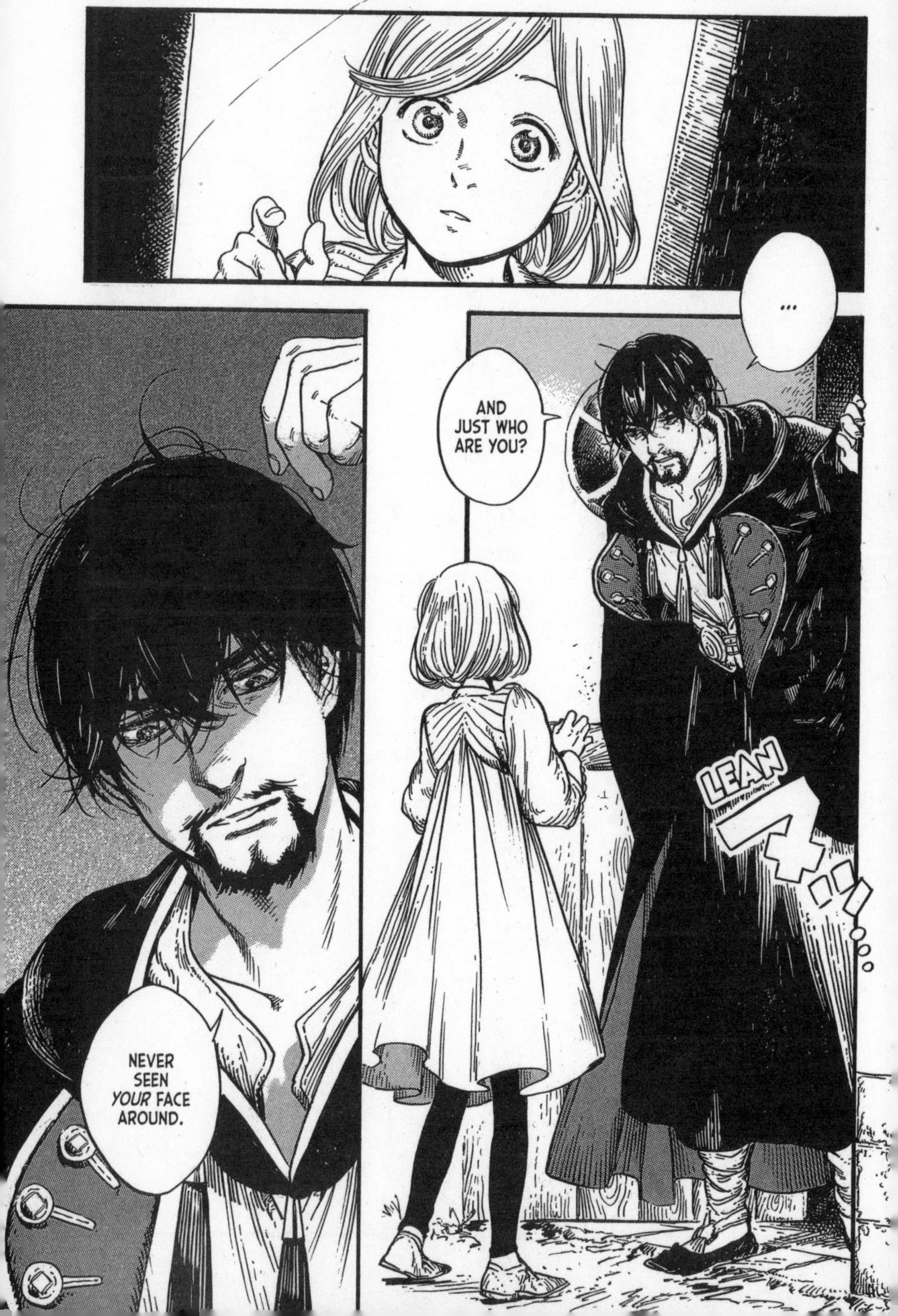
...
AND JUST WHO ARE YOU?
LEAN
NEVER SEEN *YOUR* FACE AROUND.

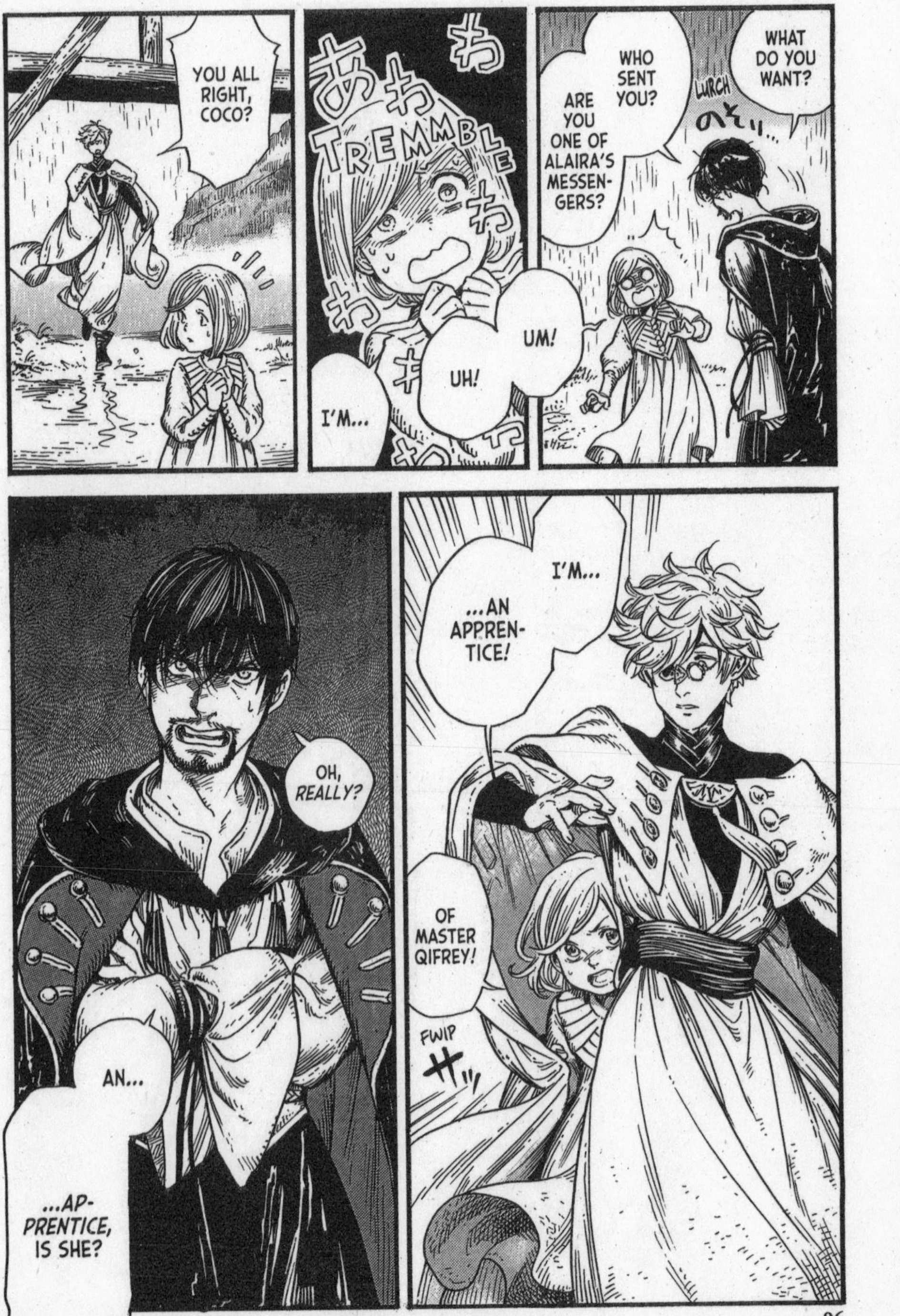
WHAT DO YOU WANT?
LURCH
WHO SENT YOU?
ARE YOU ONE OF ALAIRA'S MESSENGERS?
TREMMBLE
UM!
UH!
I'M...
YOU ALL RIGHT, COCO?
I'M...
...AN APPRENTICE!
OF MASTER QIFREY!
FWIP
OH, REALLY?
AN...
...AP-PRENTICE, IS SHE?

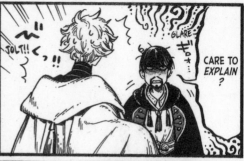

CARE TO EXPLAIN?
GLARE
JOLT!!
GOOD TO SEE YOU, OLRUGIO.
FINISHED YOUR WORK ALREADY?
FIGURED IT WOULD HAVE TAKEN A BIT LONGER—
WHEN EXACTLY DID YOUR LITTLE STABLE OF APPRENTICES MULTIPLY?
THIS IS A SPECIAL CASE.
COCO...
...IS A VICTIM OF FORBIDDEN MAGIC.
THE FORBIDDEN SPELLS?
GRAB

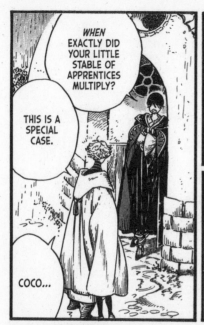

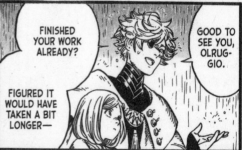

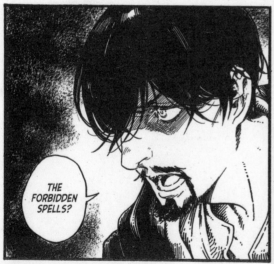

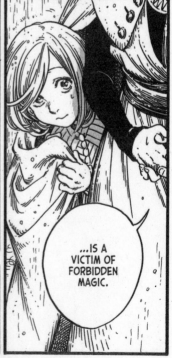

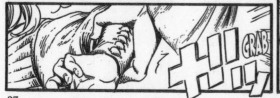

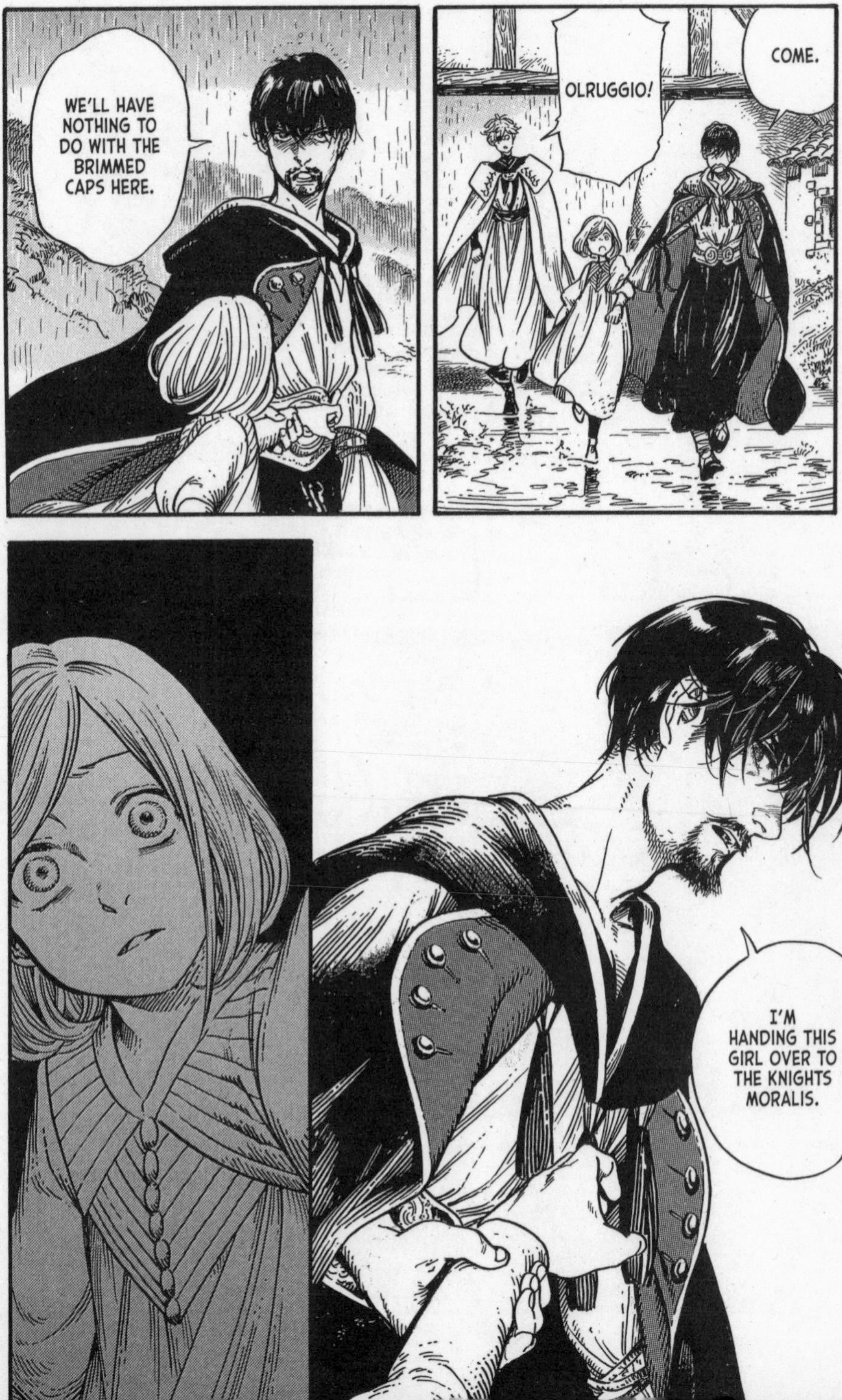
COME.
OLRUGGIO!
WE'LL HAVE NOTHING TO DO WITH THE BRIMMED CAPS HERE.
I'M HANDING THIS GIRL OVER TO THE KNIGHTS MORALIS.

CHAPTER 8 ◆ END

Witch Hat
Atelier

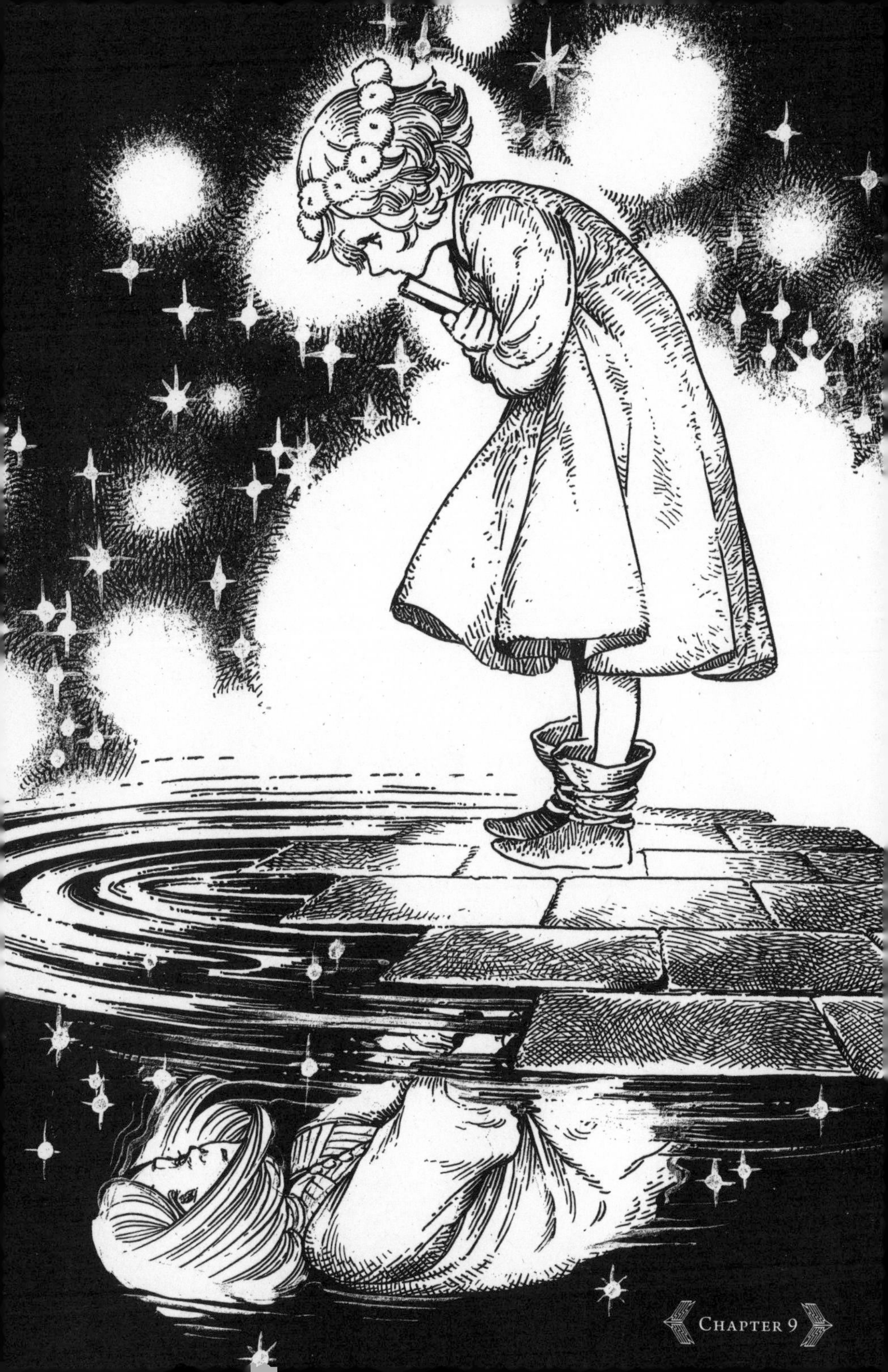

CHAPTER 9

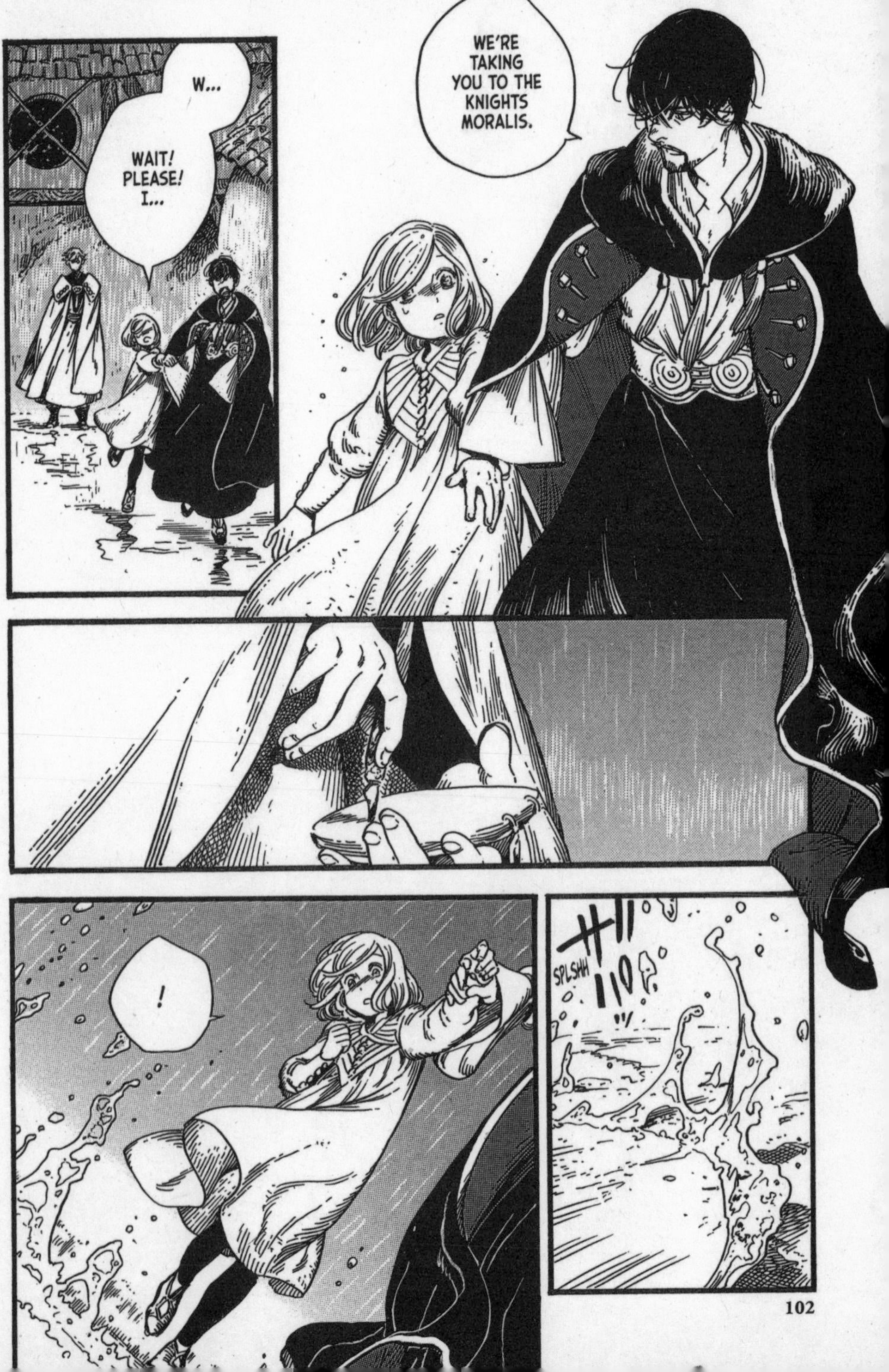

WE'RE TAKING YOU TO THE KNIGHTS MORALIS.
W...
WAIT! PLEASE! I...
SPLSHH
!

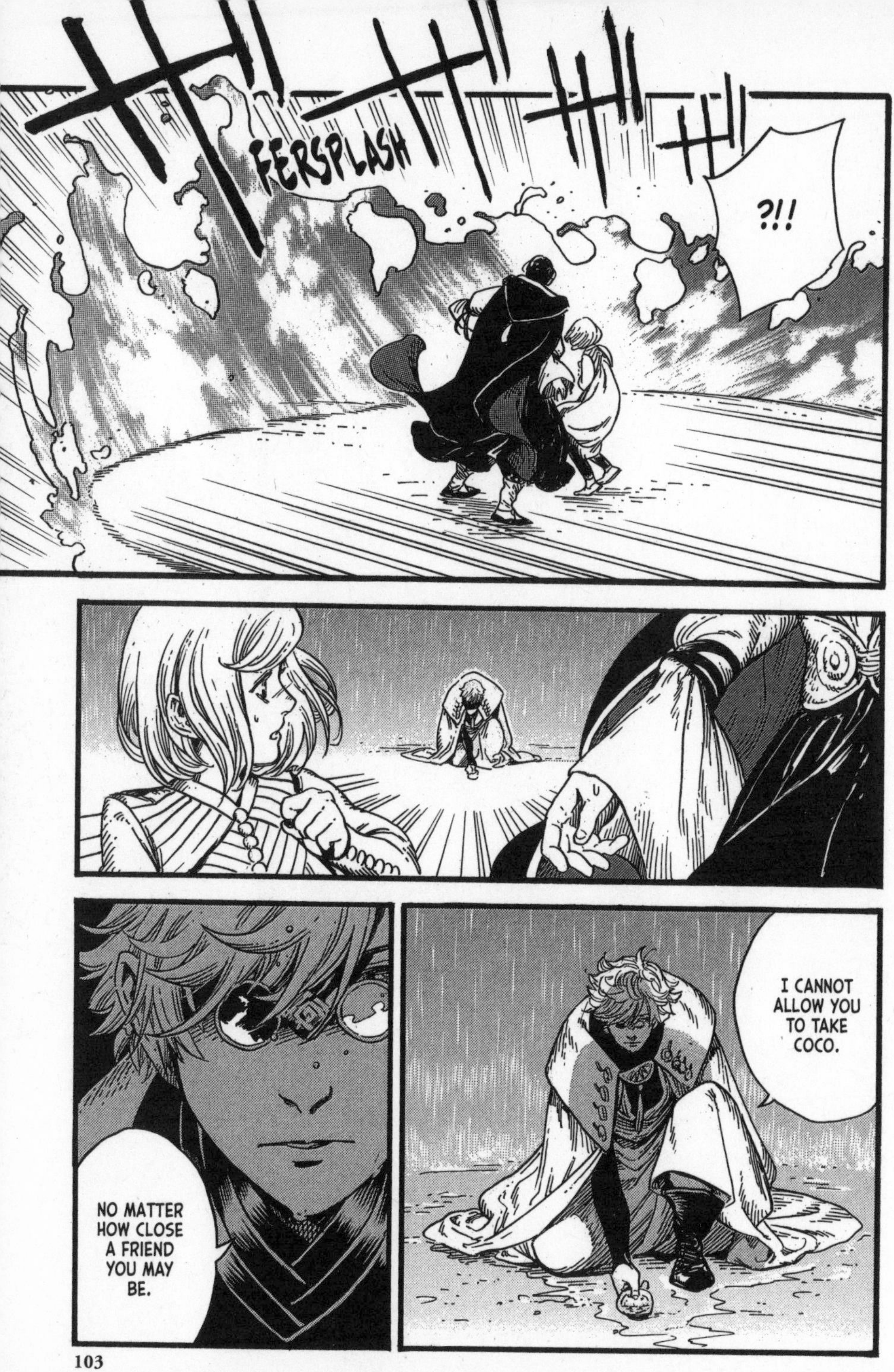
FERSPLASH
?!!
I CANNOT ALLOW YOU TO TAKE COCO.
NO MATTER HOW CLOSE A FRIEND YOU MAY BE.

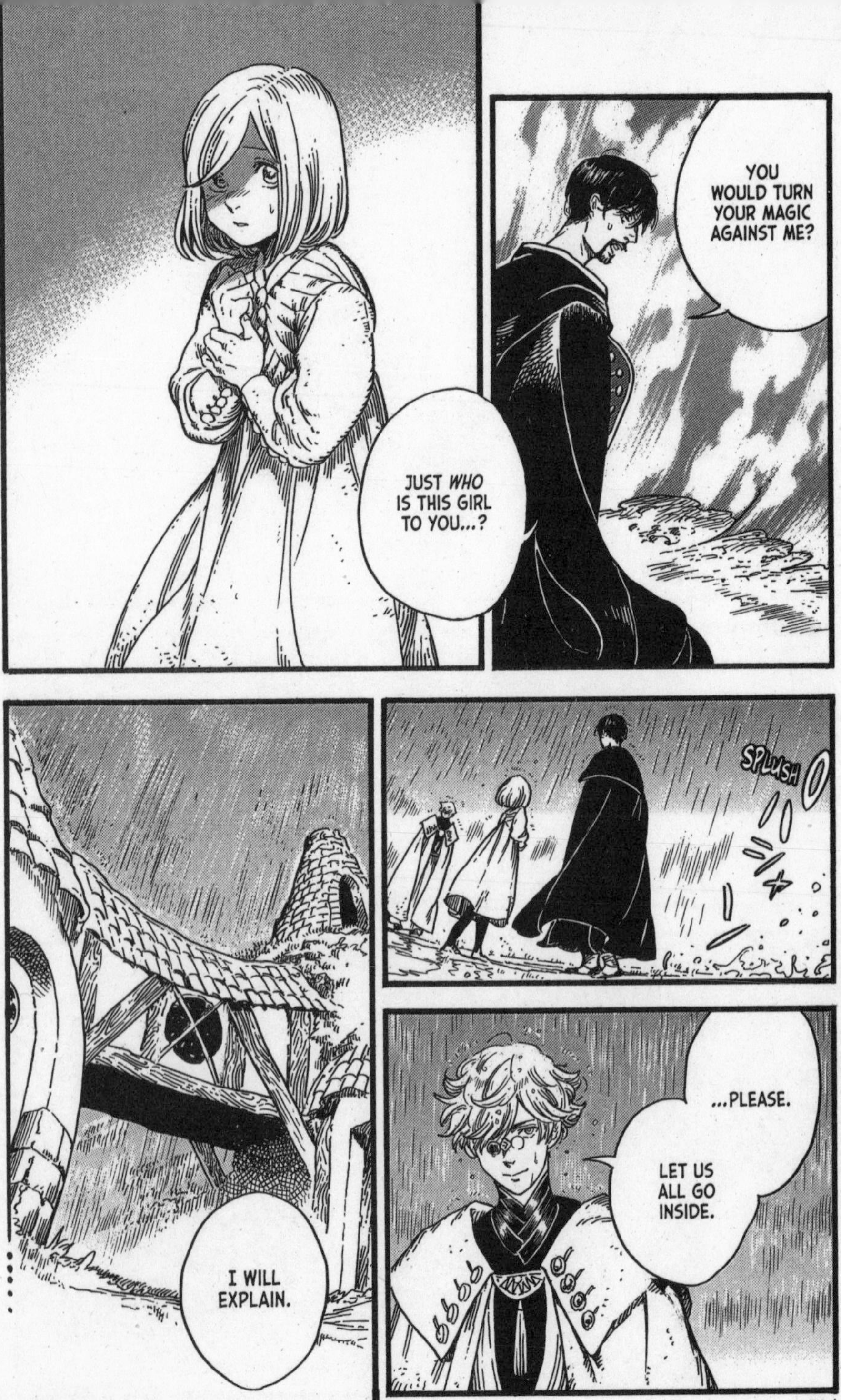

YOU WOULD TURN YOUR MAGIC AGAINST ME?
JUST *WHO* IS THIS GIRL TO YOU...?
SPLUSH
...PLEASE.
LET US ALL GO INSIDE.
I WILL EXPLAIN.

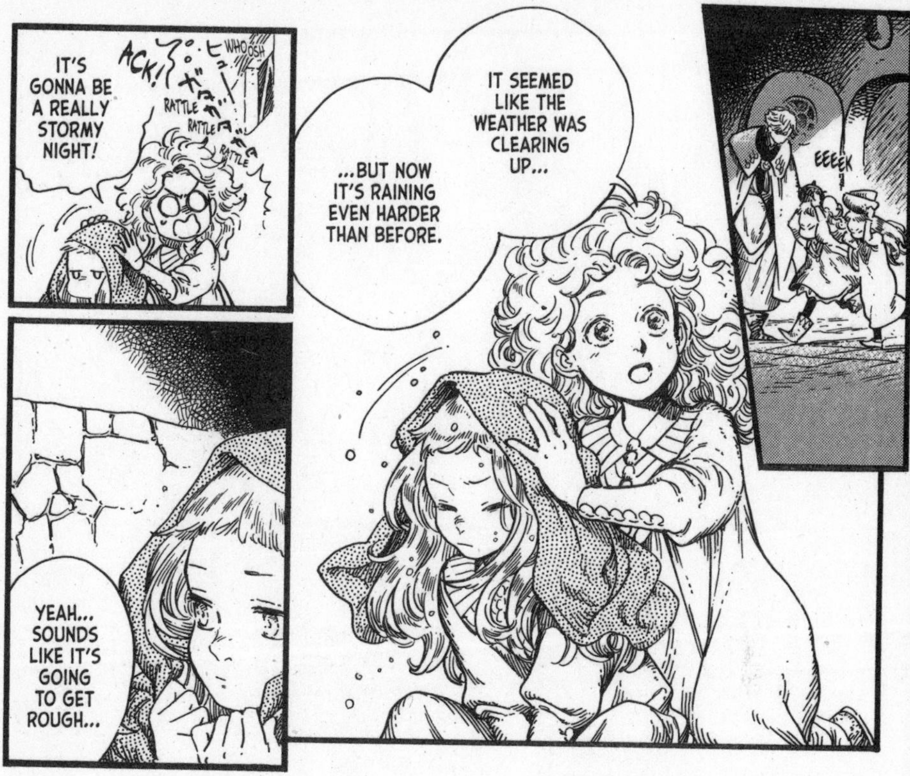
EEEEK
IT SEEMED LIKE THE WEATHER WAS CLEARING UP...
...BUT NOW IT'S RAINING EVEN HARDER THAN BEFORE.
WHOOSH
RATTLE
RATTLE
RATTLE
ACK!
IT'S GONNA BE A REALLY STORMY NIGHT!
YEAH... SOUNDS LIKE IT'S GOING TO GET ROUGH...

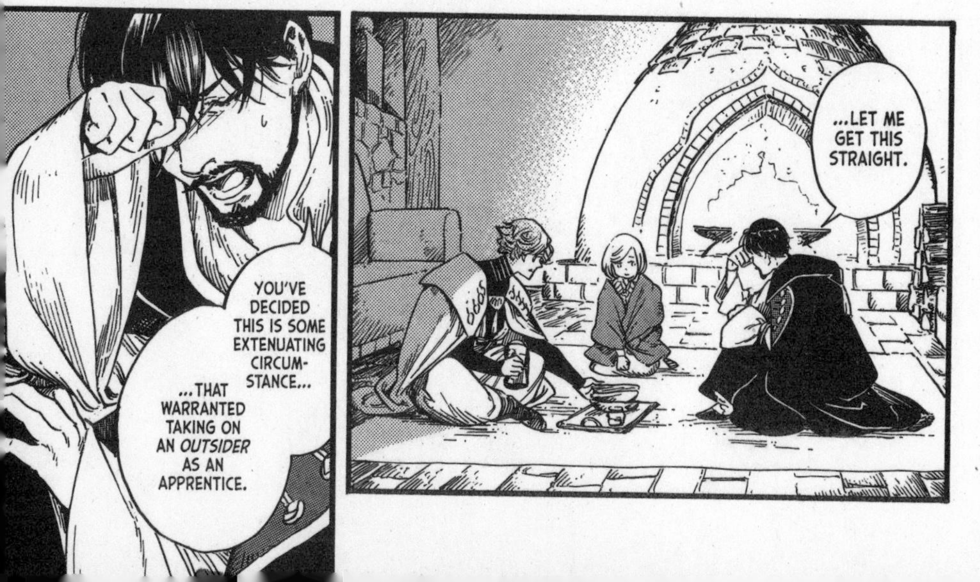
...LET ME GET THIS STRAIGHT.
YOU'VE DECIDED THIS IS SOME EXTENUATING CIRCUM-STANCE...
...THAT WARRANTED TAKING ON AN *OUTSIDER* AS AN APPRENTICE.

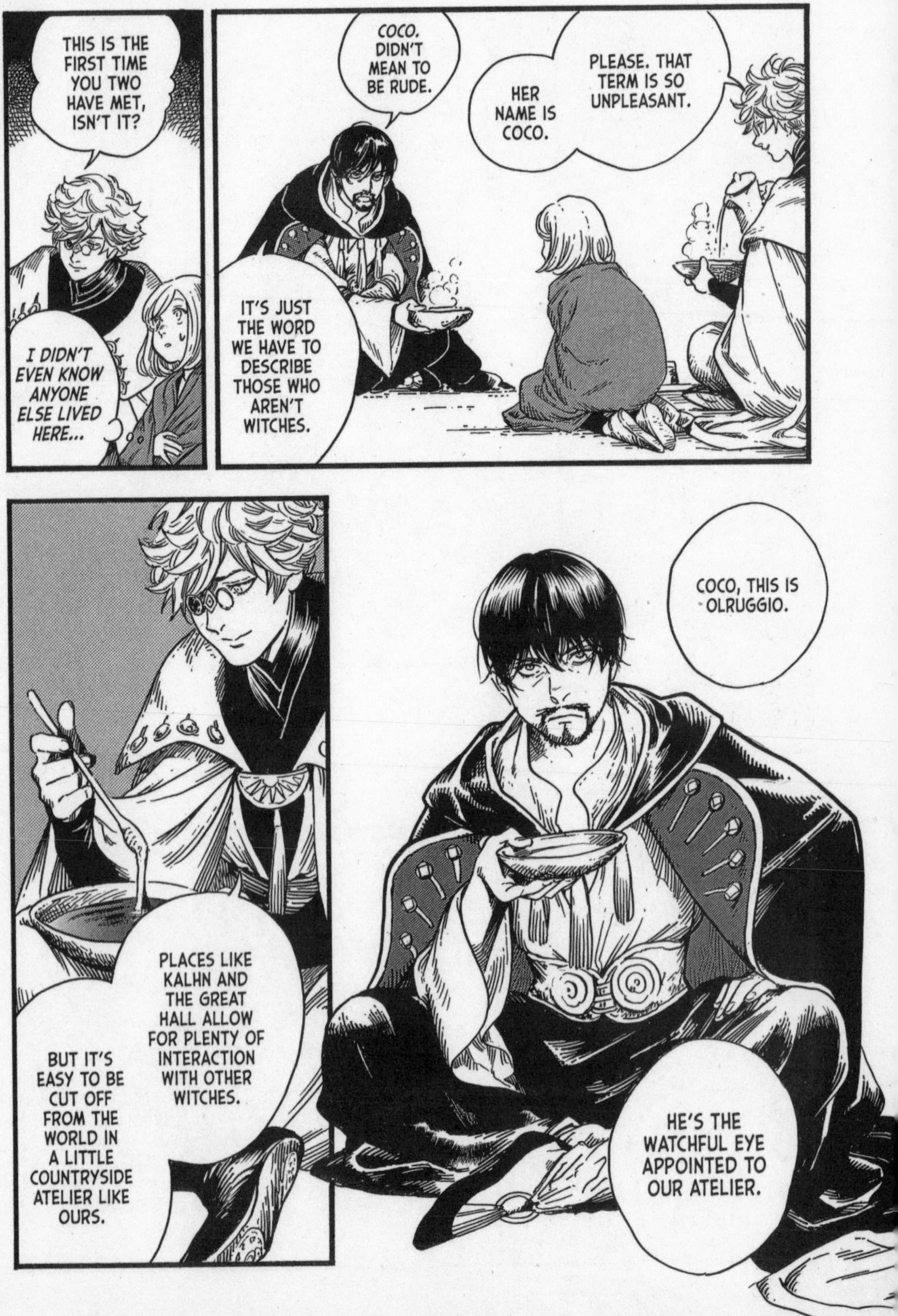
PLEASE. THAT TERM IS SO UNPLEASANT.
HER NAME IS COCO.
COCO. DIDN'T MEAN TO BE RUDE.
IT'S JUST THE WORD WE HAVE TO DESCRIBE THOSE WHO AREN'T WITCHES.
THIS IS THE FIRST TIME YOU TWO HAVE MET, ISN'T IT?
I DIDN'T EVEN KNOW ANYONE ELSE LIVED HERE...
COCO, THIS IS OLRUGGIO.
HE'S THE WATCHFUL EYE APPOINTED TO OUR ATELIER.
PLACES LIKE KALHN AND THE GREAT HALL ALLOW FOR PLENTY OF INTERACTION WITH OTHER WITCHES.
BUT IT'S EASY TO BE CUT OFF FROM THE WORLD IN A LITTLE COUNTRYSIDE ATELIER LIKE OURS.

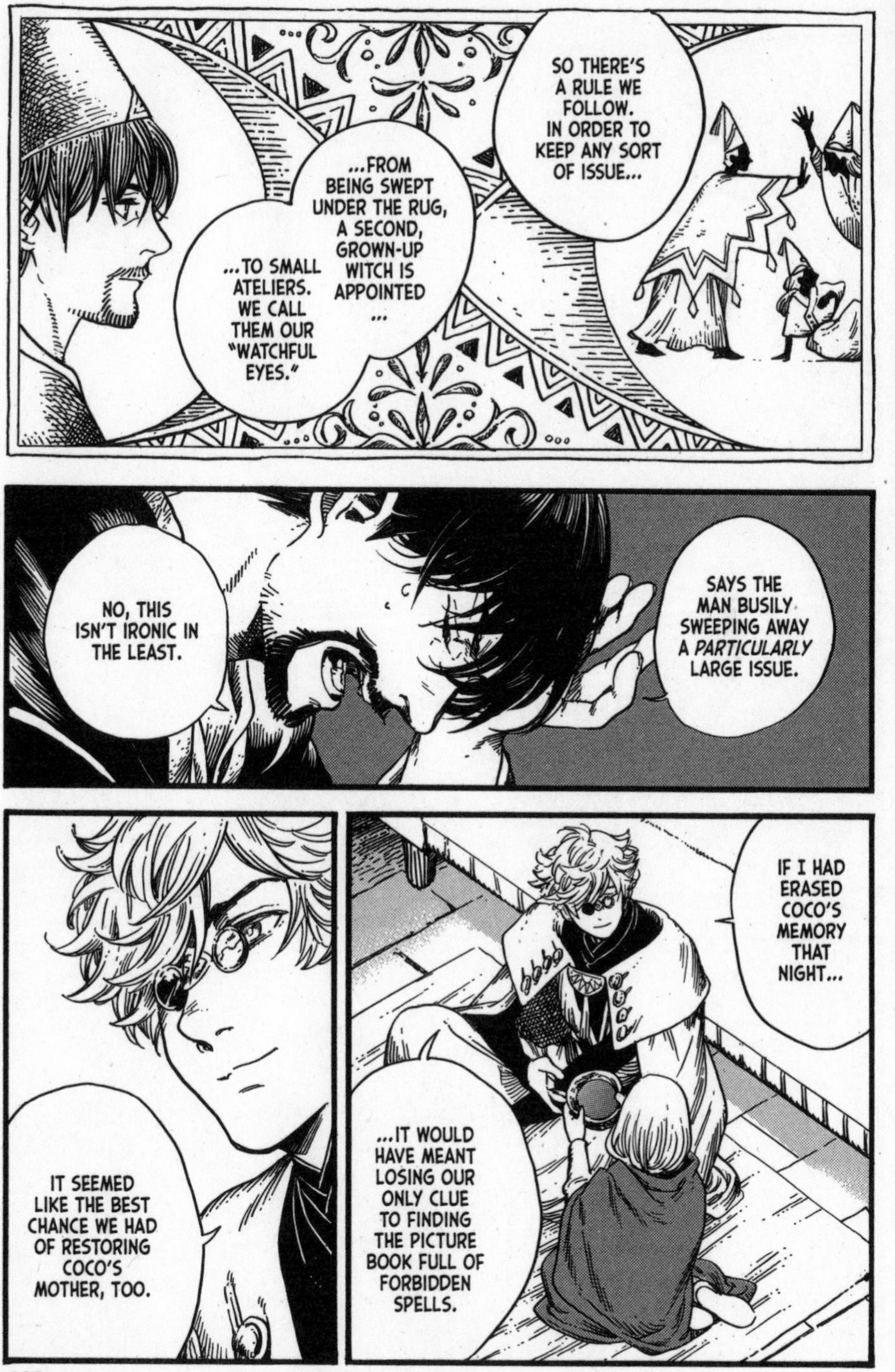
SO THERE'S A RULE WE FOLLOW. IN ORDER TO KEEP ANY SORT OF ISSUE...
...FROM BEING SWEPT UNDER THE RUG, A SECOND, GROWN-UP WITCH IS APPOINTED ...
...TO SMALL ATELIERS. WE CALL THEM OUR "WATCHFUL EYES."
SAYS THE MAN BUSILY SWEEPING AWAY A *PARTICULARLY* LARGE ISSUE.
NO, THIS ISN'T IRONIC IN THE LEAST.
IF I HAD ERASED COCO'S MEMORY THAT NIGHT...
...IT WOULD HAVE MEANT LOSING OUR ONLY CLUE TO FINDING THE PICTURE BOOK FULL OF FORBIDDEN SPELLS.
IT SEEMED LIKE THE BEST CHANCE WE HAD OF RESTORING COCO'S MOTHER, TOO.

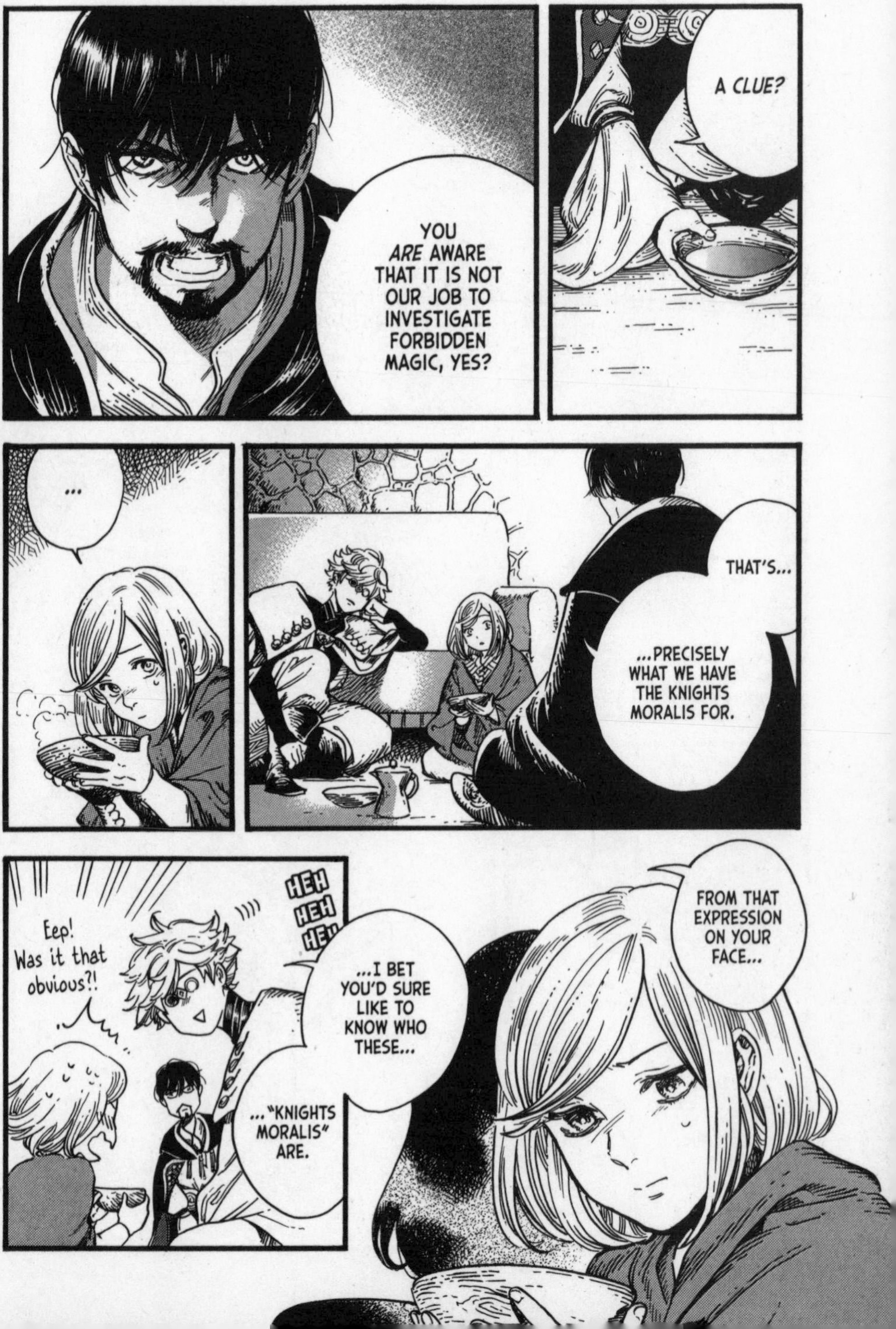
A CLUE?
YOU *ARE* AWARE THAT IT IS NOT OUR JOB TO INVESTIGATE FORBIDDEN MAGIC, YES?
THAT'S...
...PRECISELY WHAT WE HAVE THE KNIGHTS MORALIS FOR.
...
FROM THAT EXPRESSION ON YOUR FACE...
...I BET YOU'D SURE LIKE TO KNOW WHO THESE...
..."KNIGHTS MORALIS" ARE.
HEH HEH HEH
Eep! Was it that obvious?!

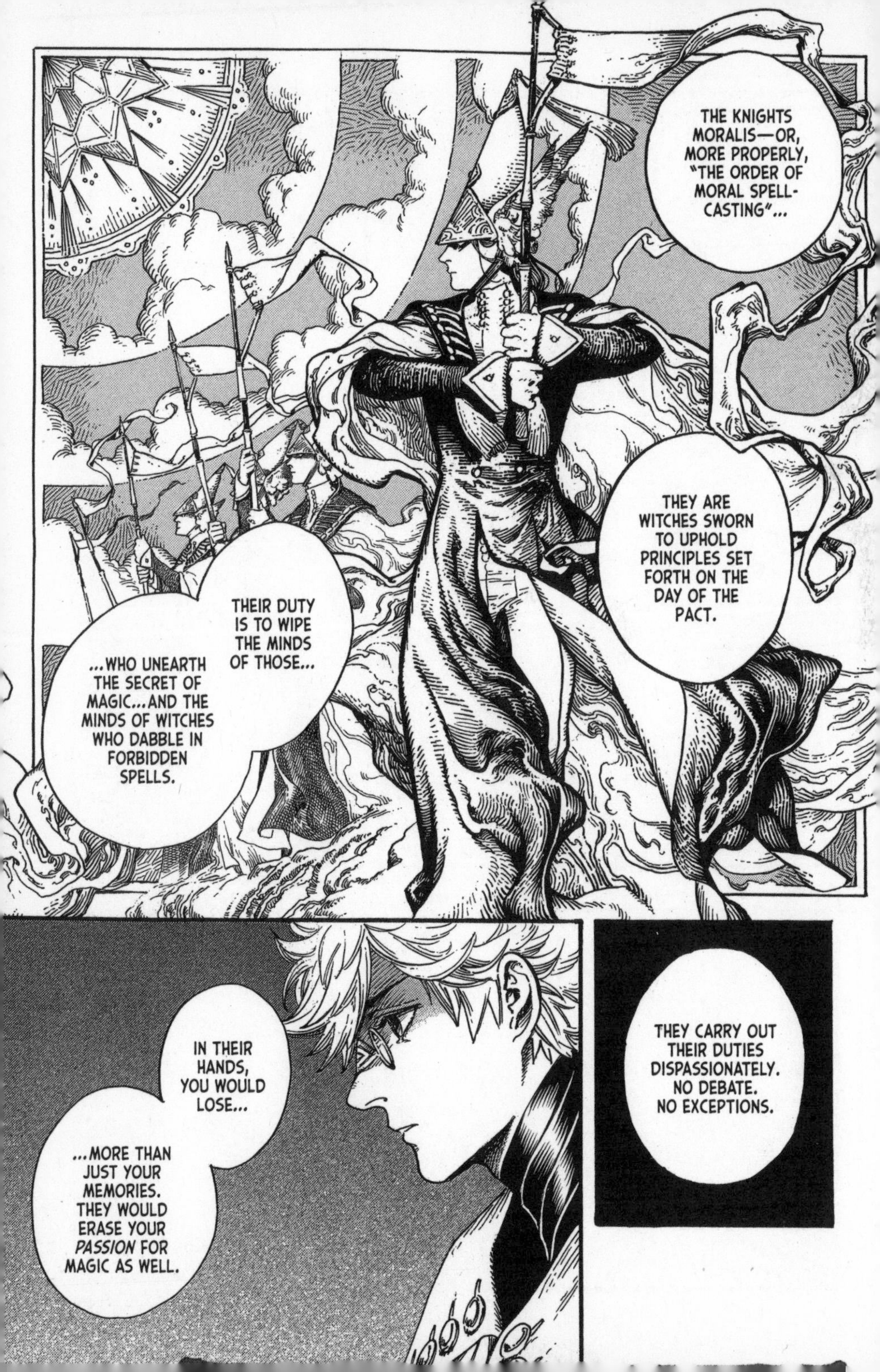
THE KNIGHTS MORALIS—OR, MORE PROPERLY, "THE ORDER OF MORAL SPELL-CASTING"...
THEY ARE WITCHES SWORN TO UPHOLD PRINCIPLES SET FORTH ON THE DAY OF THE PACT.
THEIR DUTY IS TO WIPE THE MINDS OF THOSE...
...WHO UNEARTH THE SECRET OF MAGIC...AND THE MINDS OF WITCHES WHO DABBLE IN FORBIDDEN SPELLS.
THEY CARRY OUT THEIR DUTIES DISPASSIONATELY. NO DEBATE. NO EXCEPTIONS.
IN THEIR HANDS, YOU WOULD LOSE...
...MORE THAN JUST YOUR MEMORIES. THEY WOULD ERASE YOUR *PASSION* FOR MAGIC AS WELL.

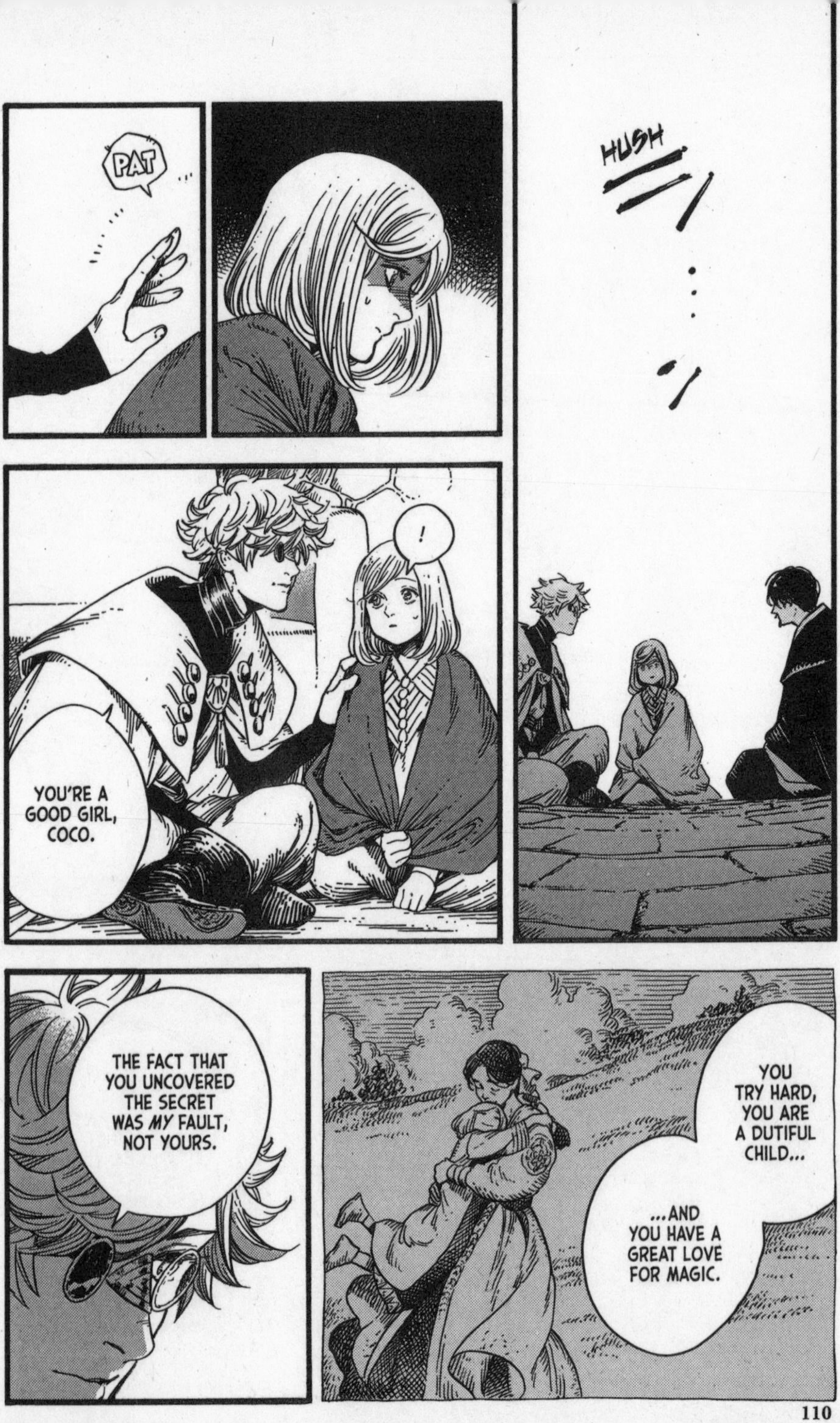
HUSH
...
PAT
!
YOU'RE A GOOD GIRL, COCO.
YOU TRY HARD, YOU ARE A DUTIFUL CHILD...
...AND YOU HAVE A GREAT LOVE FOR MAGIC.
THE FACT THAT YOU UNCOVERED THE SECRET WAS *MY* FAULT, NOT YOURS.

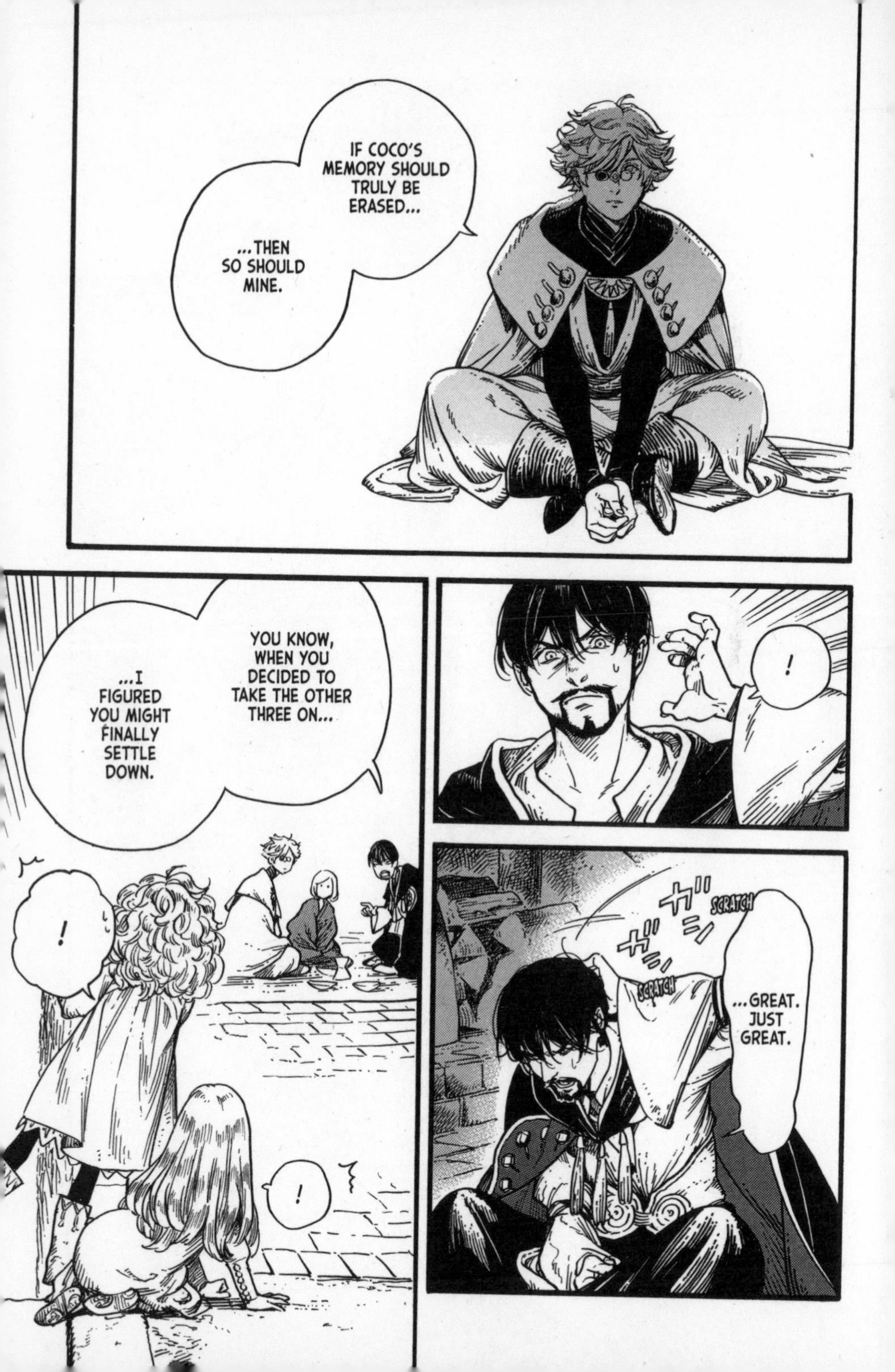
IF COCO'S MEMORY SHOULD TRULY BE ERASED...
...THEN SO SHOULD MINE.
!
SCRATCH
SCRATCH
...GREAT. JUST GREAT.
YOU KNOW, WHEN YOU DECIDED TO TAKE THE OTHER THREE ON...
...I FIGURED YOU MIGHT FINALLY SETTLE DOWN.
!
!

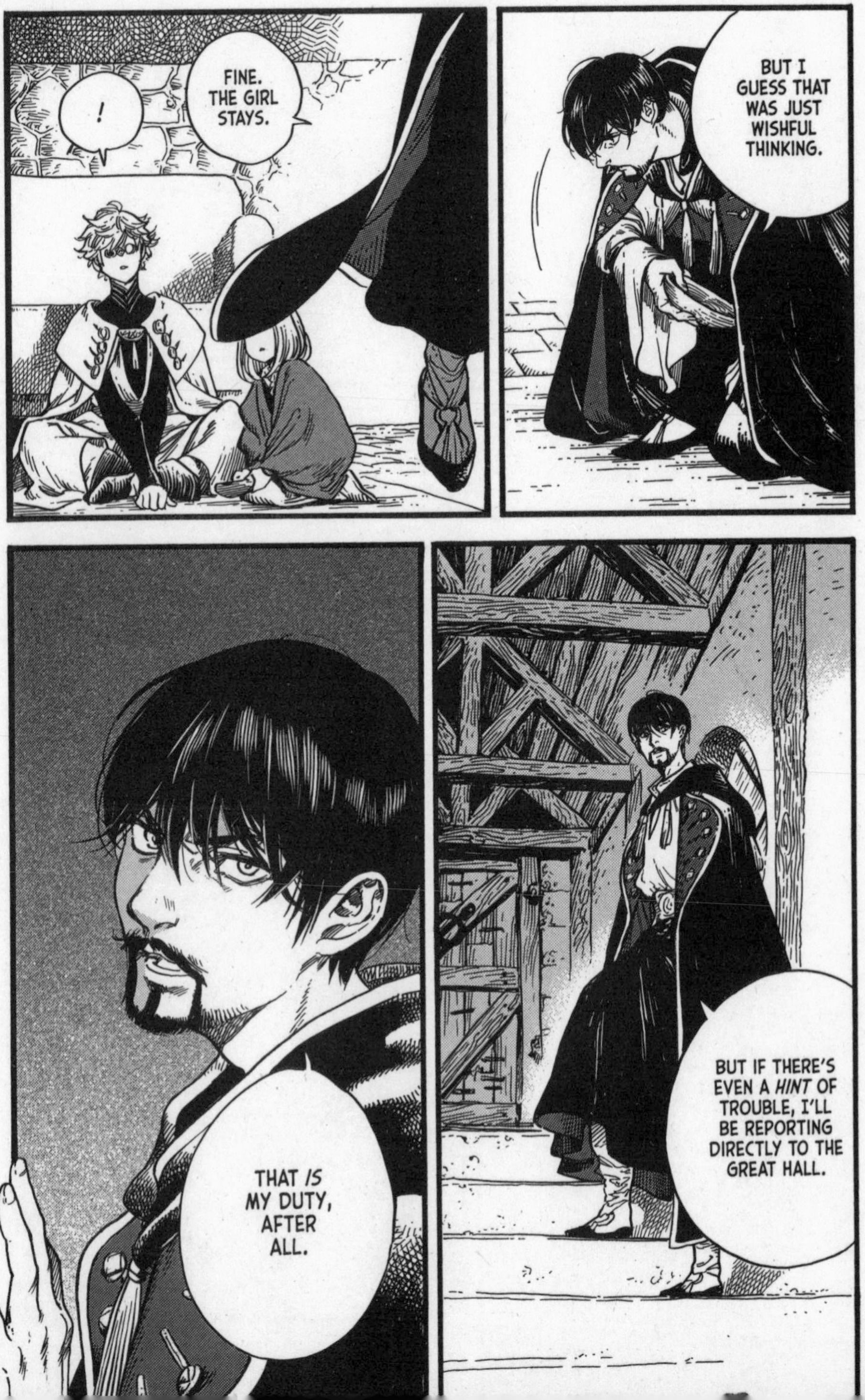
BUT I GUESS THAT WAS JUST WISHFUL THINKING.
FINE. THE GIRL STAYS.
!
BUT IF THERE'S EVEN A *HINT* OF TROUBLE, I'LL BE REPORTING DIRECTLY TO THE GREAT HALL.
THAT *IS* MY DUTY, AFTER ALL.

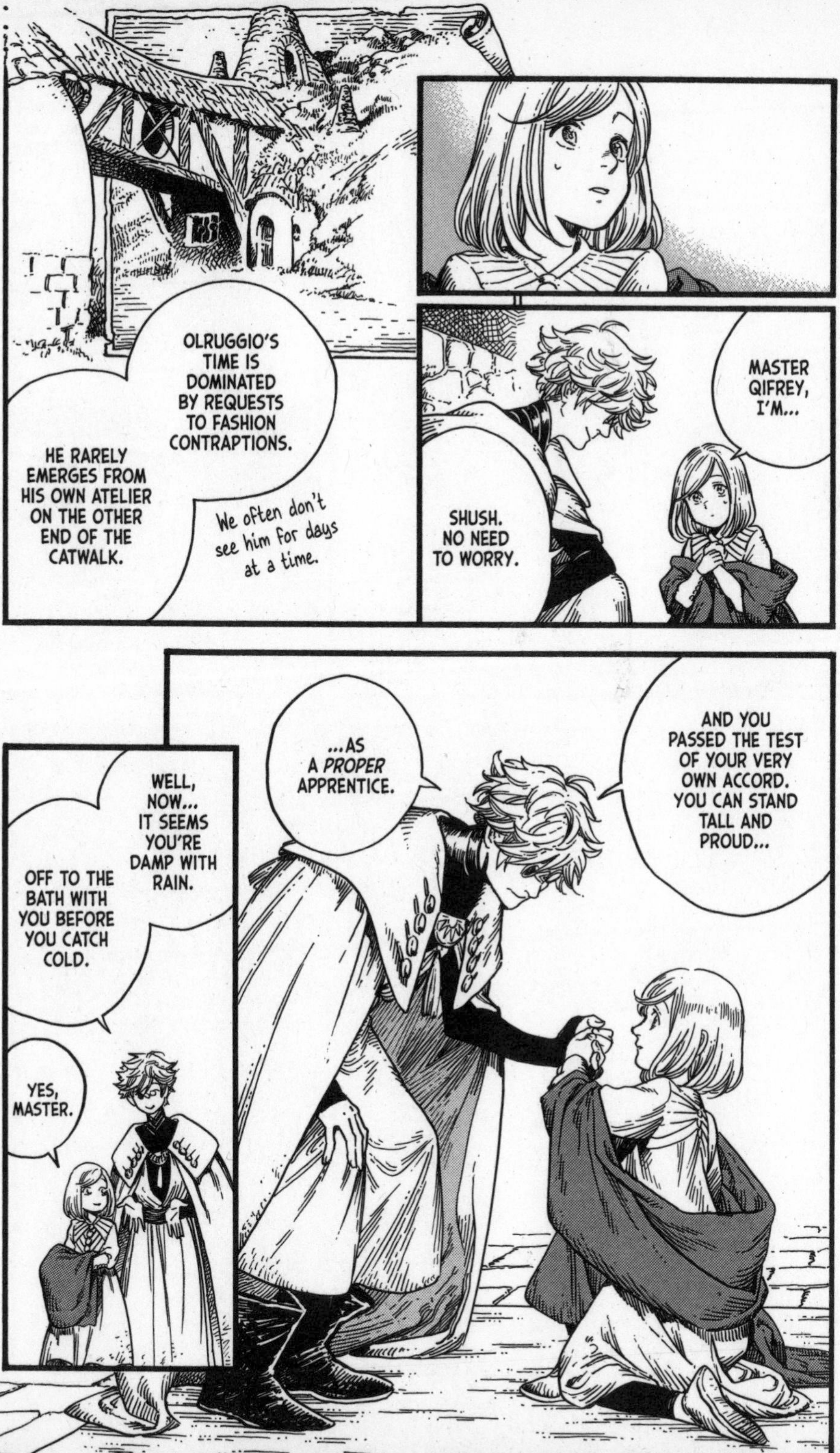

MASTER QIFREY, I'M...
SHUSH. NO NEED TO WORRY.
OLRUGGIO'S TIME IS DOMINATED BY REQUESTS TO FASHION CONTRAPTIONS.
HE RARELY EMERGES FROM HIS OWN ATELIER ON THE OTHER END OF THE CATWALK.
We often don't see him for days at a time.
AND YOU PASSED THE TEST OF YOUR VERY OWN ACCORD. YOU CAN STAND TALL AND PROUD...
...AS A *PROPER* APPRENTICE.
WELL, NOW... IT SEEMS YOU'RE DAMP WITH RAIN.
OFF TO THE BATH WITH YOU BEFORE YOU CATCH COLD.
YES, MASTER.

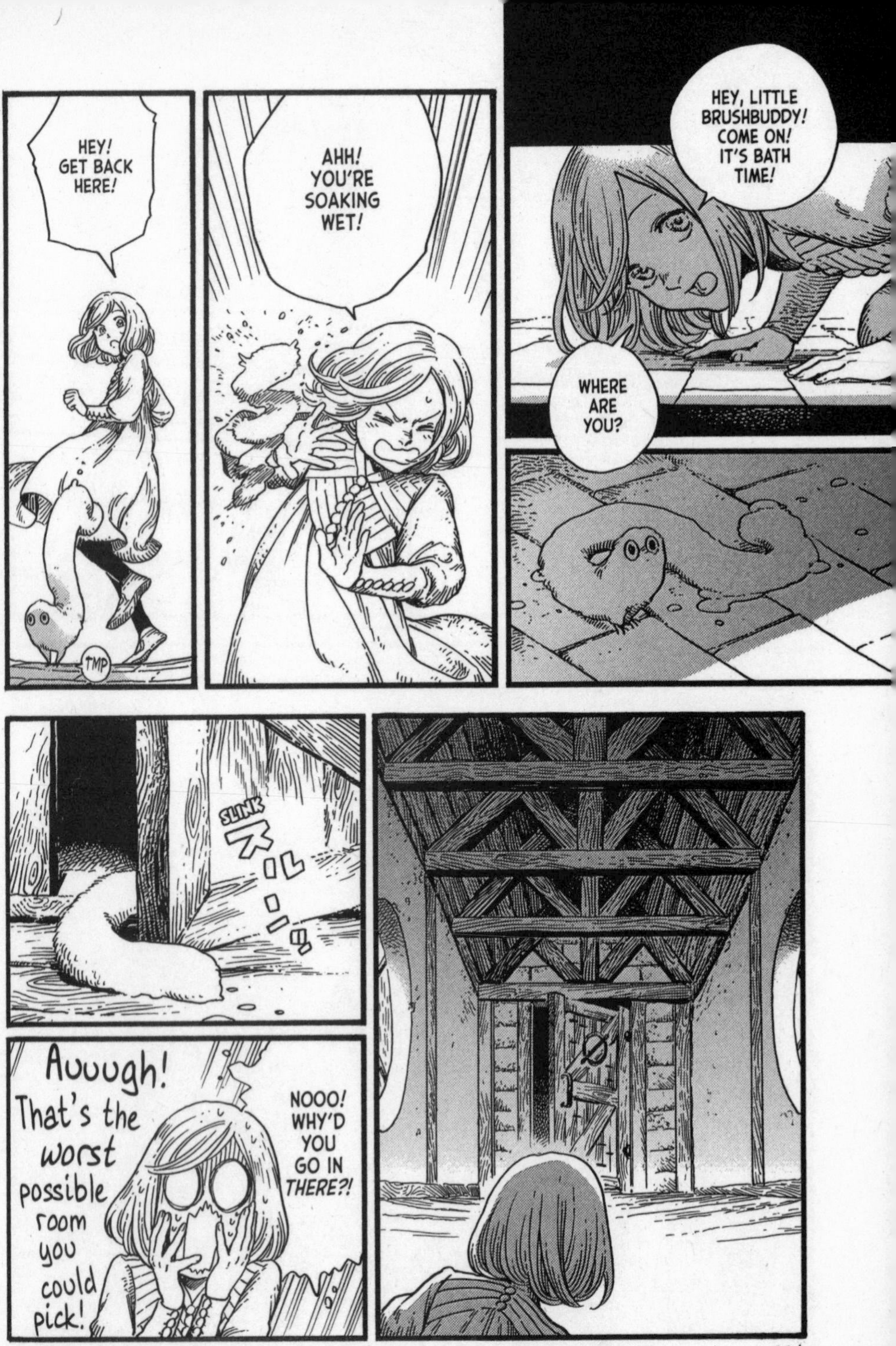
HEY, LITTLE BRUSHBUDDY! COME ON! IT'S BATH TIME!
WHERE ARE YOU?
AHH! YOU'RE SOAKING WET!
HEY! GET BACK HERE!
TMP
SLINK
スル
NOOO! WHY'D YOU GO IN THERE?!
Auuugh! That's the worst possible room you could pick!

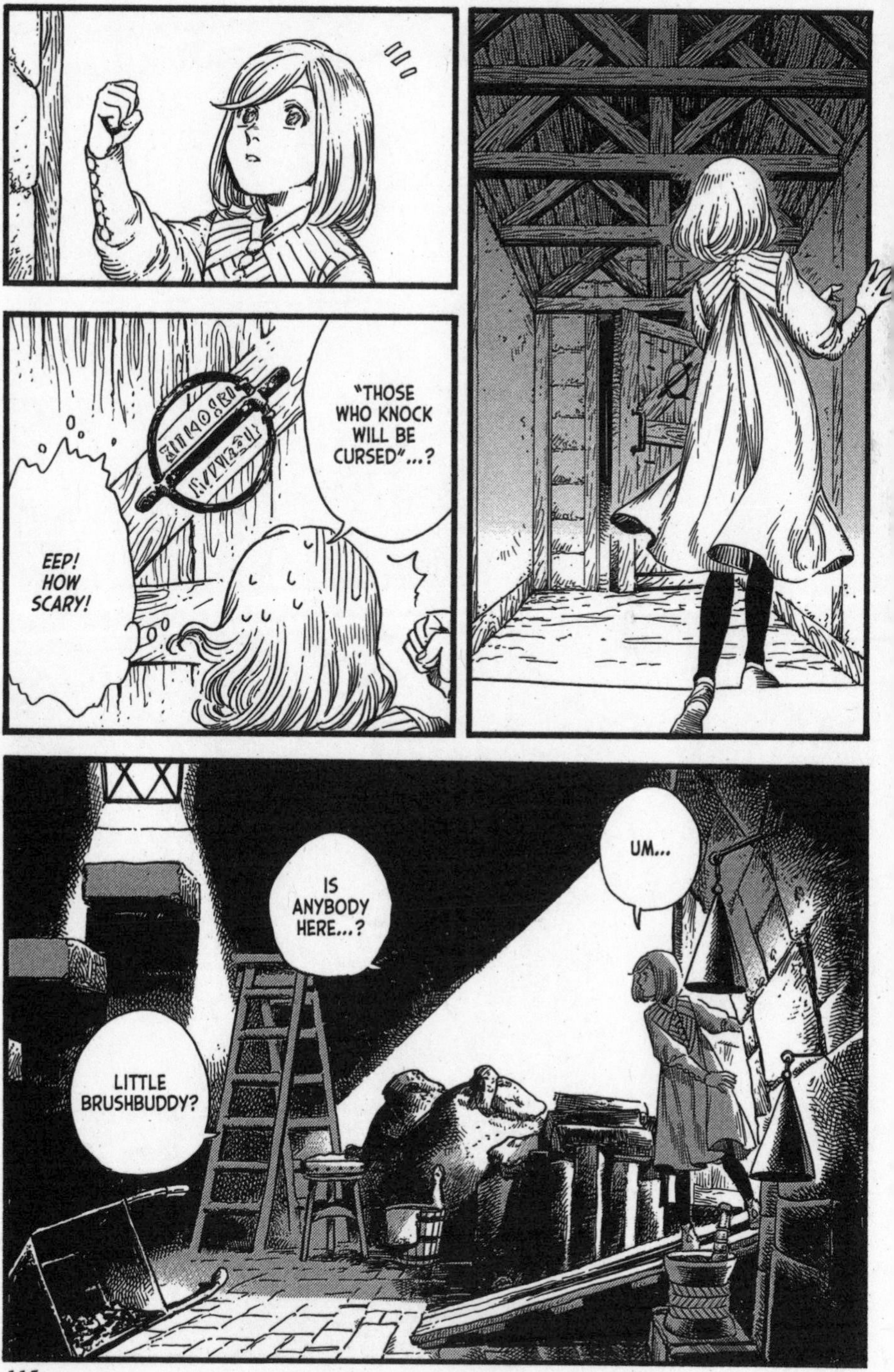
"THOSE WHO KNOCK WILL BE CURSED"...?
EEP! HOW SCARY!
UM...
IS ANYBODY HERE...?
LITTLE BRUSHBUDDY?

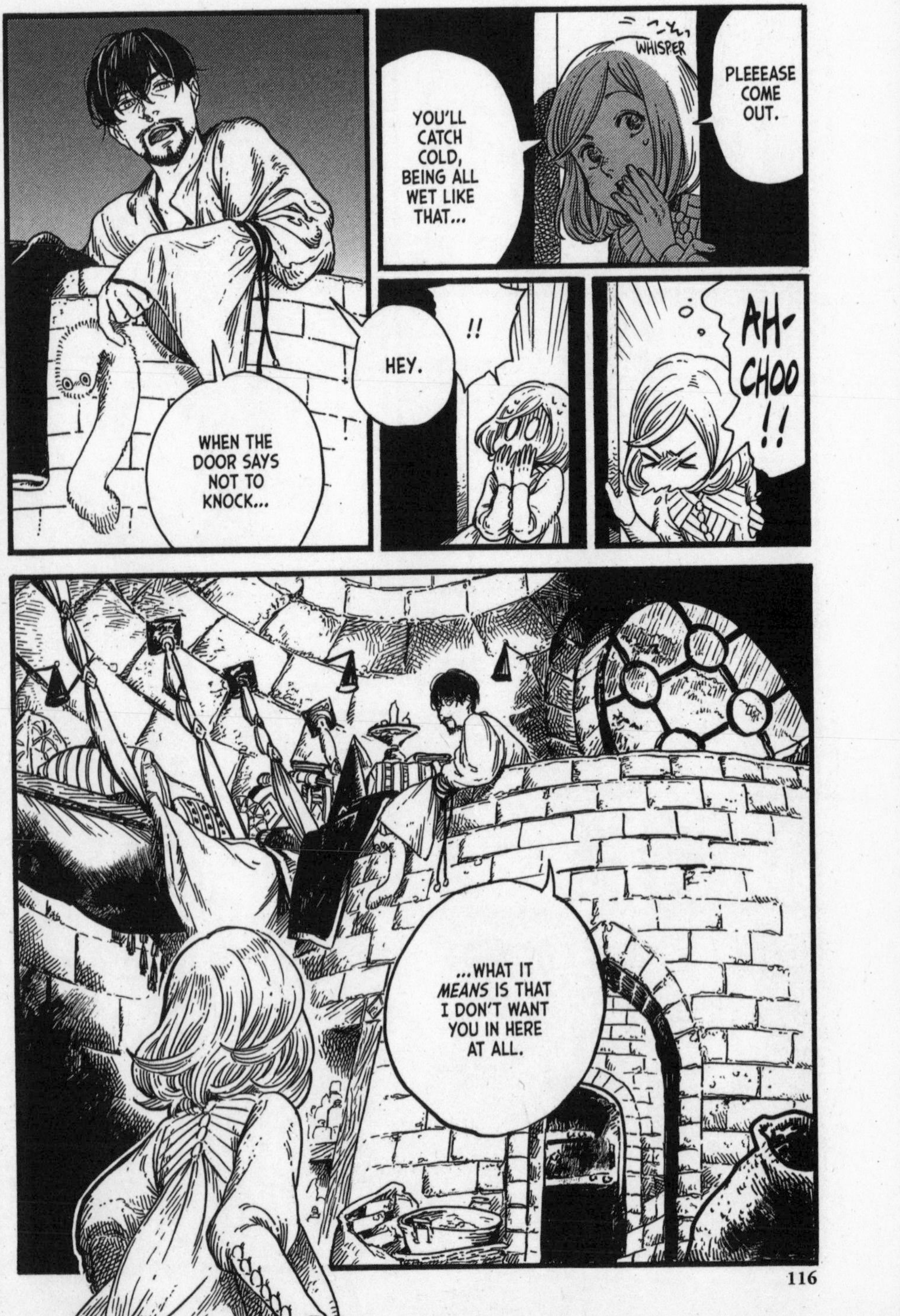
WHISPER
PLEEEASE COME OUT.
YOU'LL CATCH COLD, BEING ALL WET LIKE THAT...
AH-CHOO!!
!!
HEY.
WHEN THE DOOR SAYS NOT TO KNOCK...
...WHAT IT *MEANS* IS THAT I DON'T WANT YOU IN HERE AT ALL.

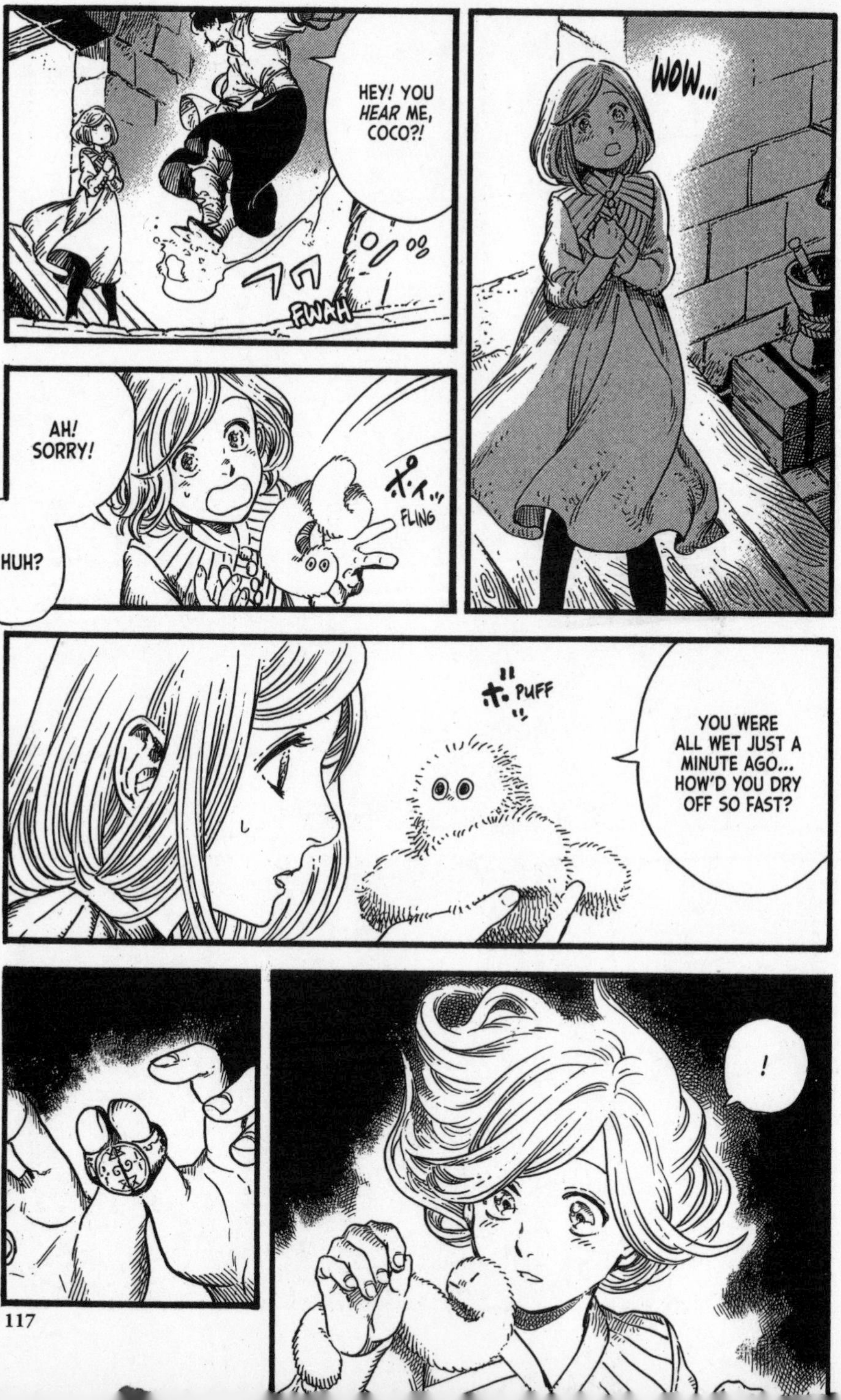
WOW...
HEY! YOU HEAR ME, COCO?!
FWAH
AH! SORRY!
...HUH?
FLING
PUFF
YOU WERE ALL WET JUST A MINUTE AGO... HOW'D YOU DRY OFF SO FAST?
!

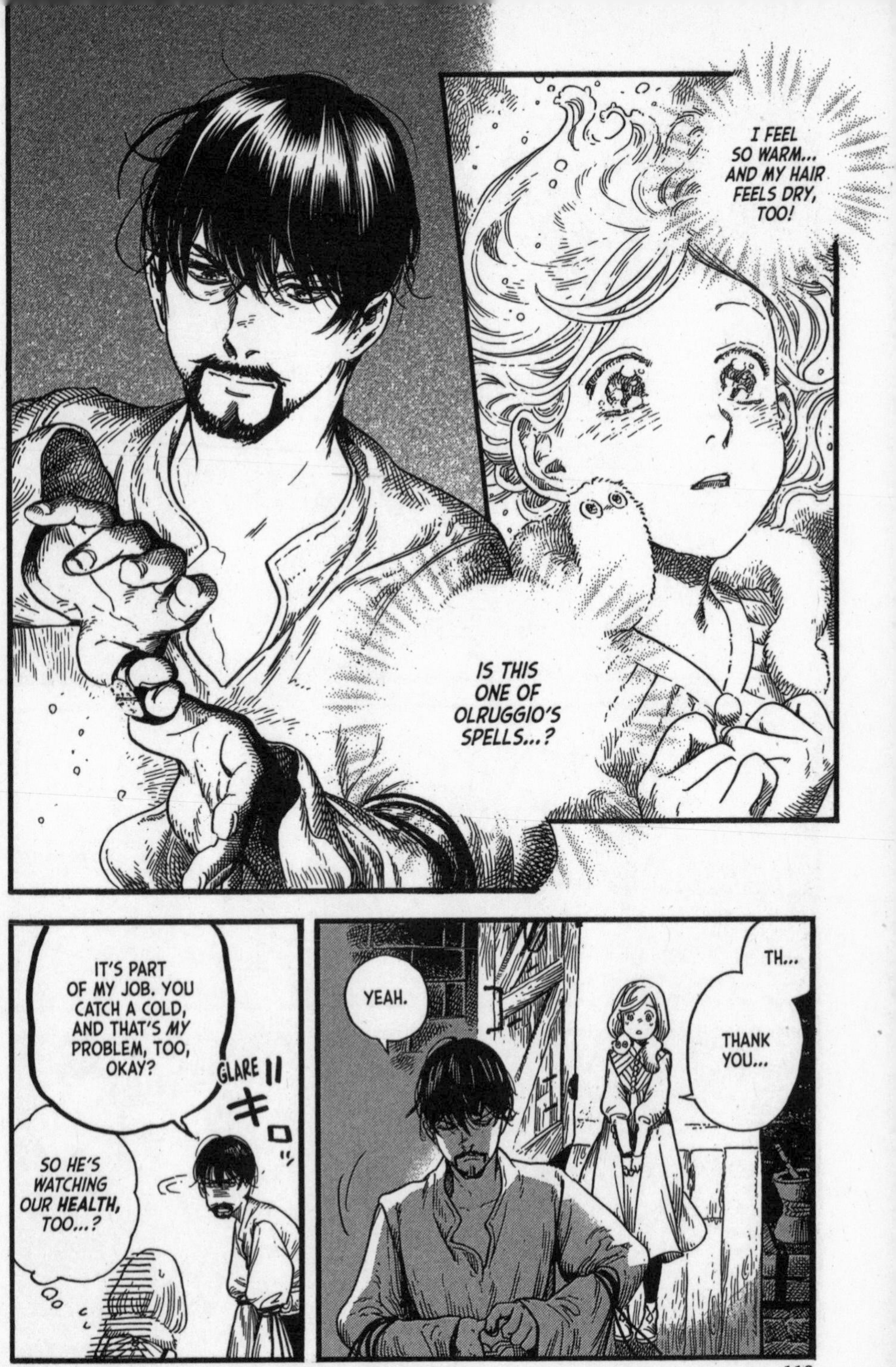

I FEEL SO WARM... AND MY HAIR FEELS DRY, TOO!
IS THIS ONE OF OLRUGGIO'S SPELLS...?
TH...
THANK YOU...
YEAH.
IT'S PART OF MY JOB. YOU CATCH A COLD, AND THAT'S *MY* PROBLEM, TOO, OKAY?
GLARE
SO HE'S WATCHING OUR **HEALTH**, TOO...?

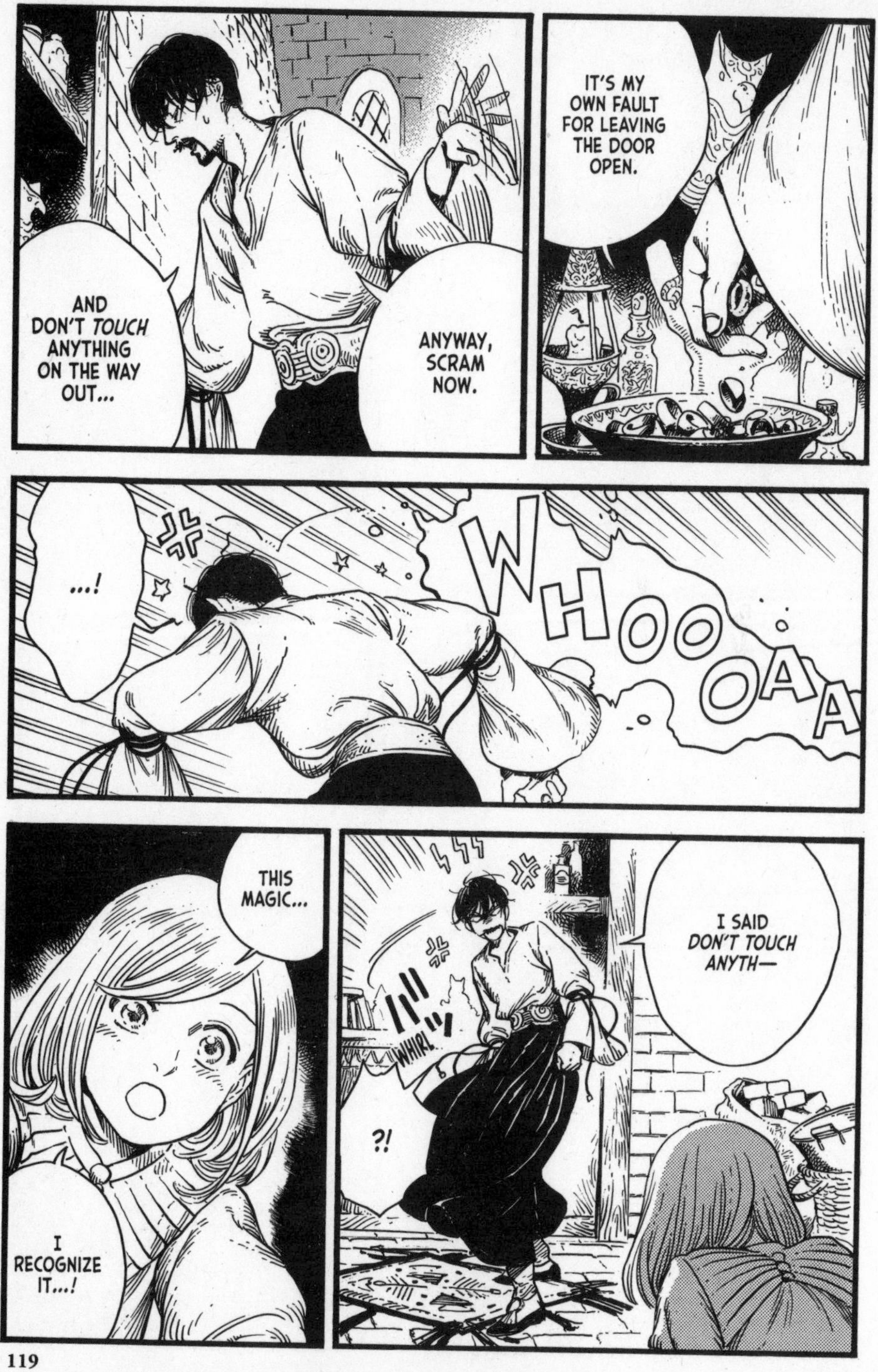
IT'S MY OWN FAULT FOR LEAVING THE DOOR OPEN.
ANYWAY, SCRAM NOW.
AND DON'T *TOUCH* ANYTHING ON THE WAY OUT...
WHOOOAAA
...!
I SAID *DON'T TOUCH ANYTH—*
WHIRL
?!
THIS MAGIC...
I RECOGNIZE IT...!

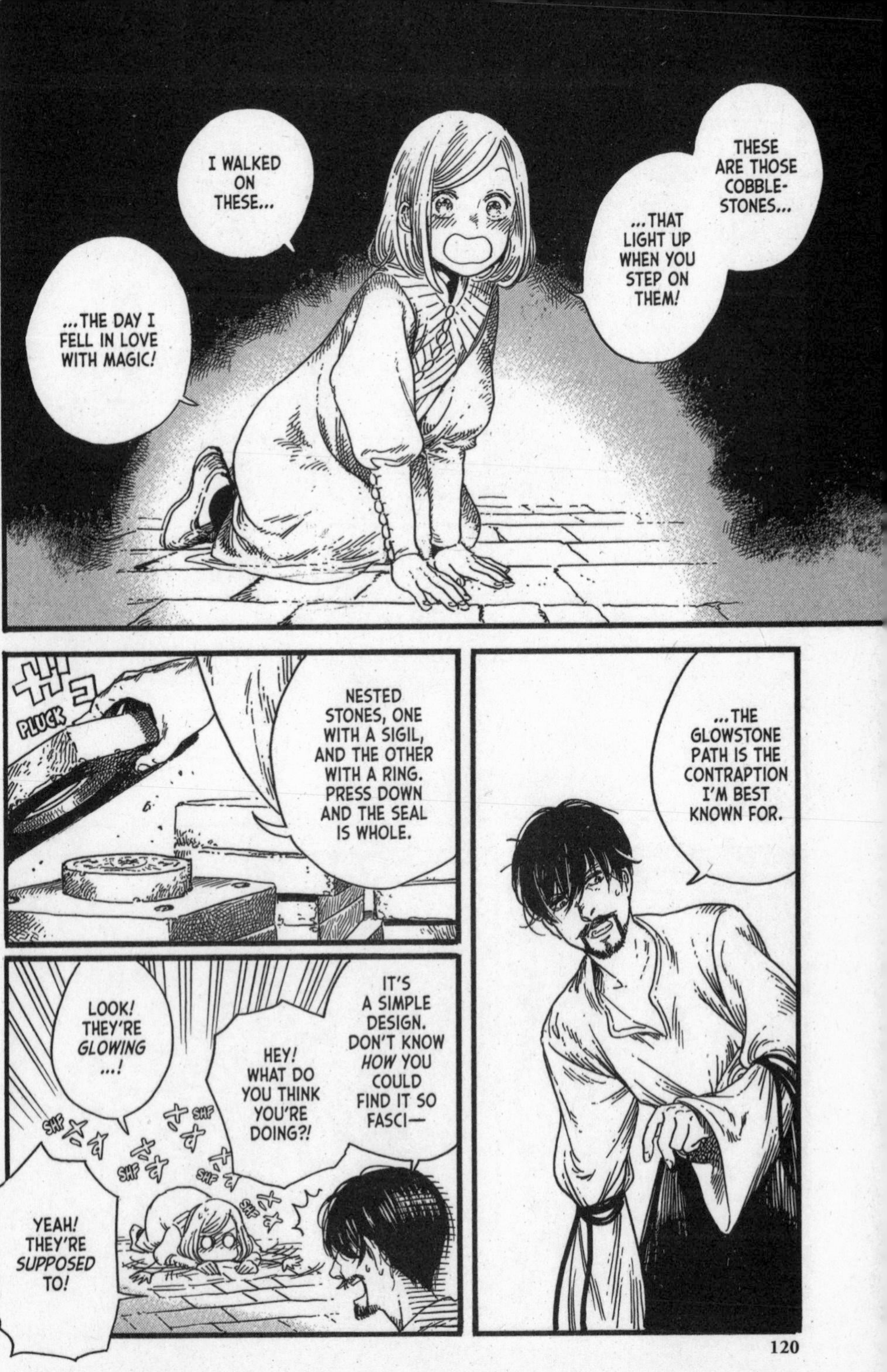
THESE ARE THOSE COBBLE-STONES...
...THAT LIGHT UP WHEN YOU STEP ON THEM!
I WALKED ON THESE...
...THE DAY I FELL IN LOVE WITH MAGIC!
...THE GLOWSTONE PATH IS THE CONTRAPTION I'M BEST KNOWN FOR.
NESTED STONES, ONE WITH A SIGIL, AND THE OTHER WITH A RING. PRESS DOWN AND THE SEAL IS WHOLE.
PLUCK
IT'S A SIMPLE DESIGN. DON'T KNOW *HOW* YOU COULD FIND IT SO FASCI—
HEY! WHAT DO YOU THINK YOU'RE DOING?!
LOOK! THEY'RE *GLOWING* ...!
SHF SHF SHF SHF SHF
YEAH! THEY'RE *SUPPOSED* TO!

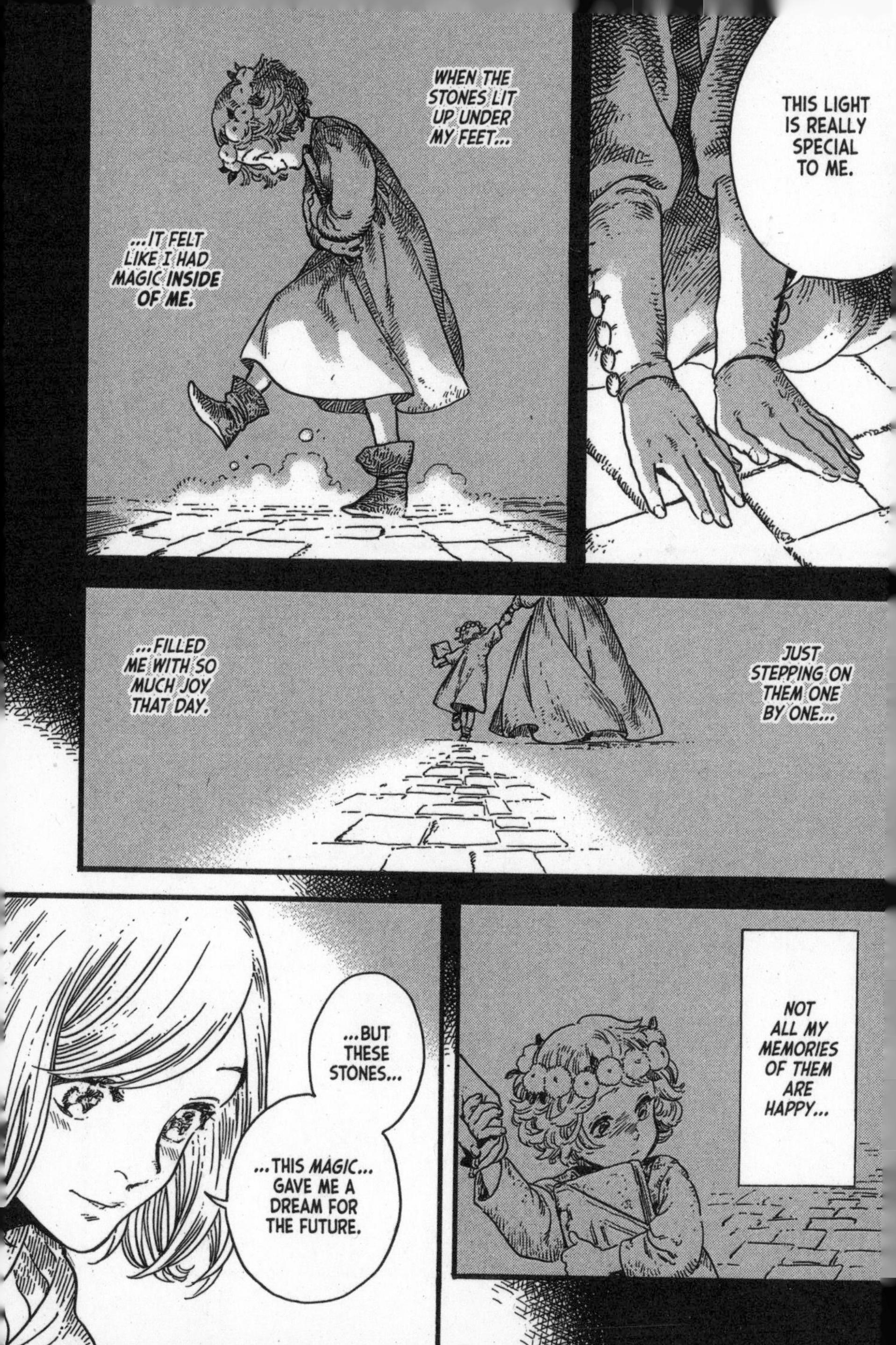
THIS LIGHT IS REALLY SPECIAL TO ME.
WHEN THE STONES LIT UP UNDER MY FEET...
...IT FELT LIKE I HAD MAGIC INSIDE OF ME.
JUST STEPPING ON THEM ONE BY ONE...
...FILLED ME WITH SO MUCH JOY THAT DAY.
NOT ALL MY MEMORIES OF THEM ARE HAPPY...
...BUT THESE STONES...
...THIS MAGIC... GAVE ME A DREAM FOR THE FUTURE.

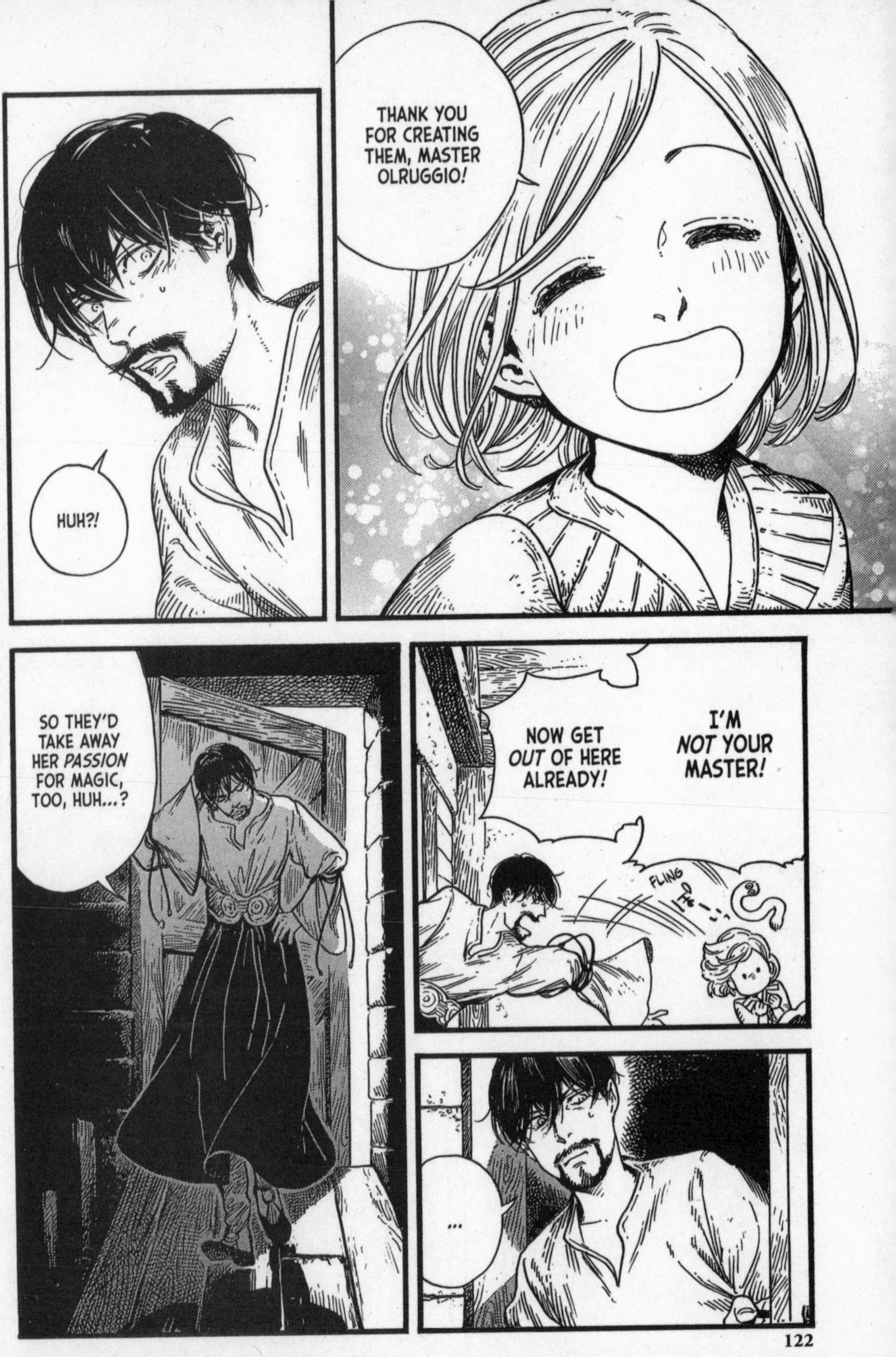
THANK YOU FOR CREATING THEM, MASTER OLRUGGIO!
HUH?!
I'M *NOT* YOUR MASTER!
NOW GET *OUT* OF HERE ALREADY!
FLING
...
SO THEY'D TAKE AWAY HER *PASSION* FOR MAGIC, TOO, HUH...?

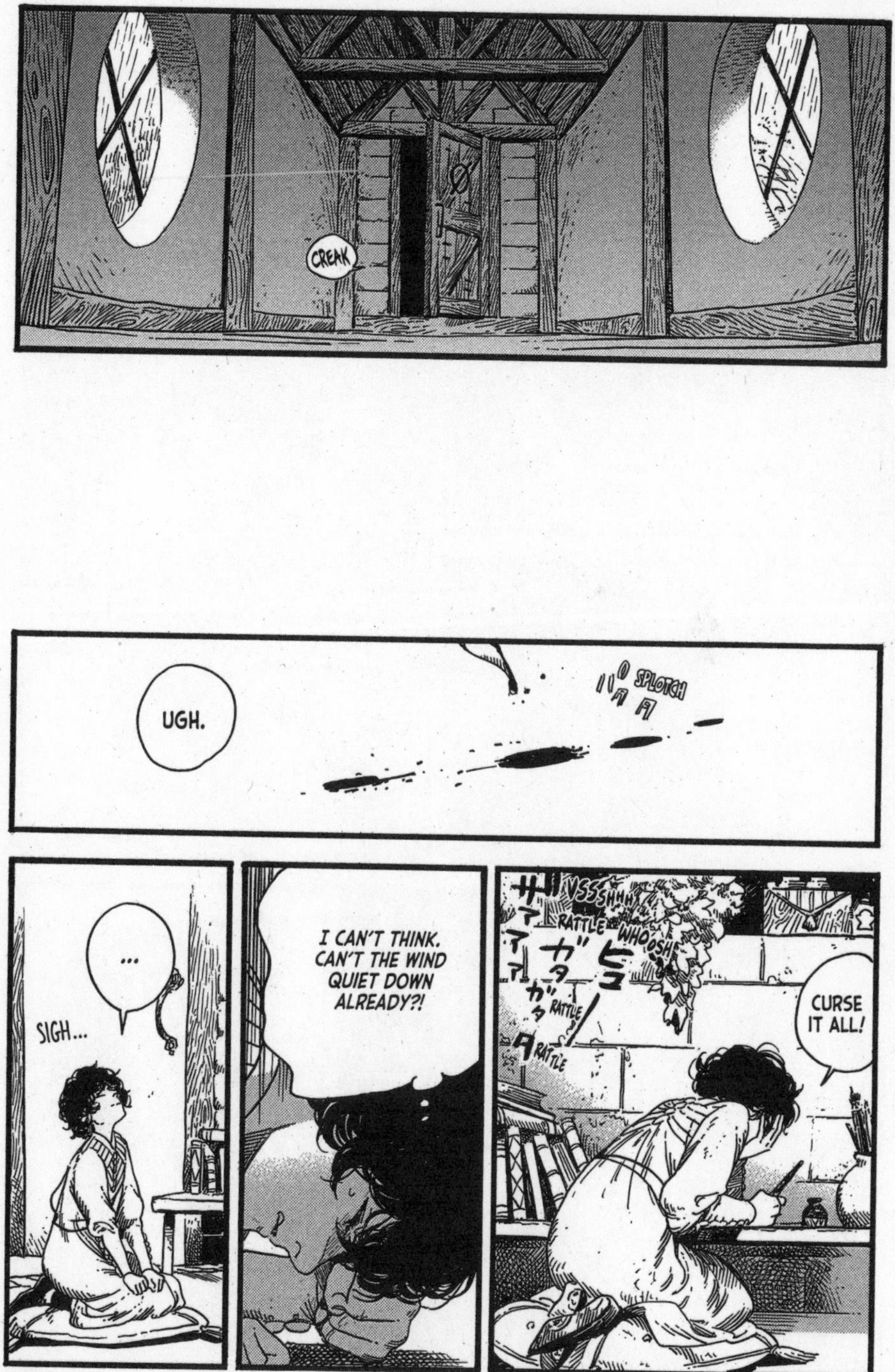
CREAK
SPLOTCH
UGH.
VSSSHHH
WHOOSH
RATTLE
RATTLE
RATTLE
CURSE IT ALL!
I CAN'T THINK. CAN'T THE WIND QUIET DOWN ALREADY?!
...
SIGH...

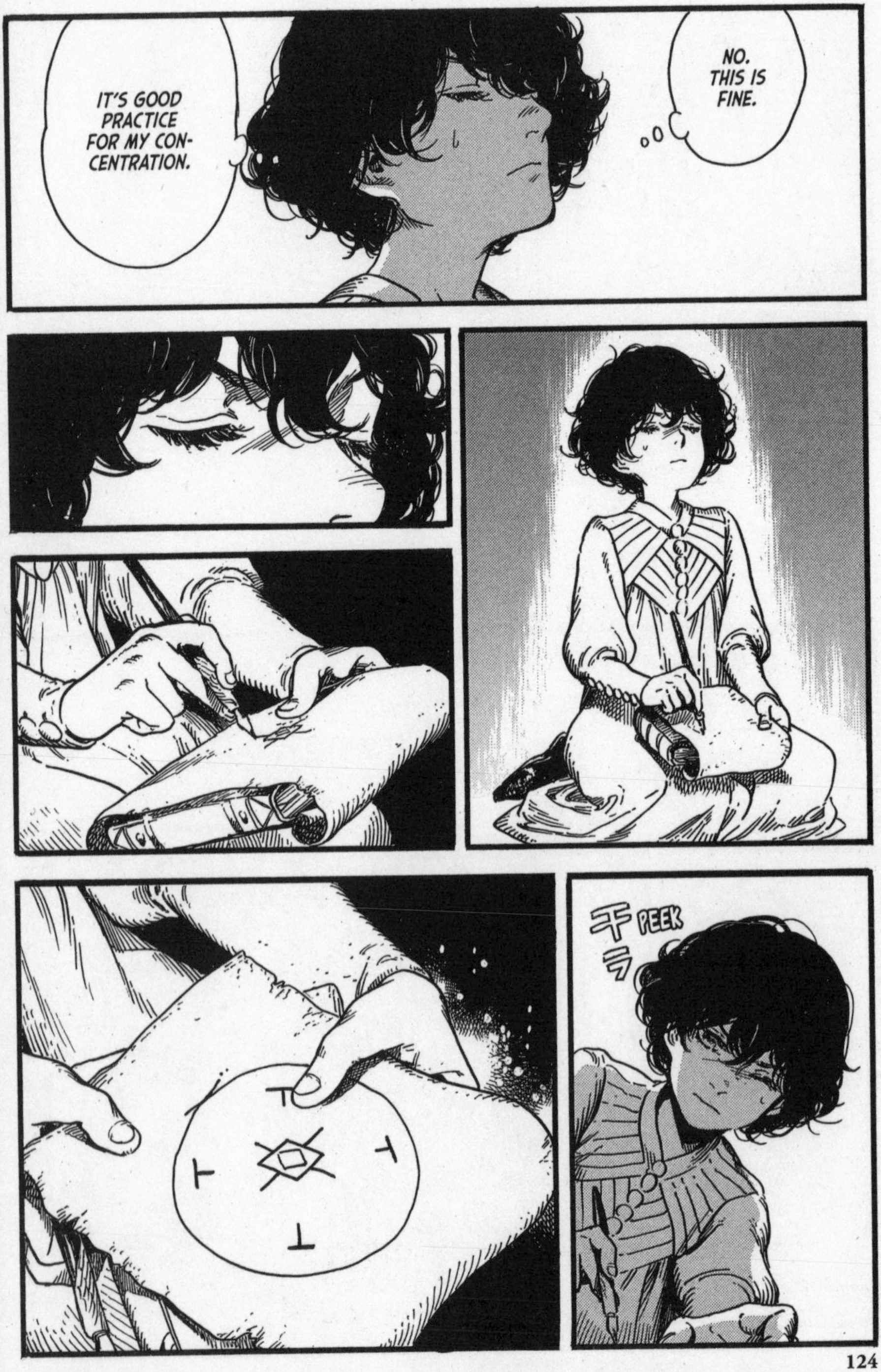
NO. THIS IS FINE.
IT'S GOOD PRACTICE FOR MY CONCENTRATION.
チラ PEEK

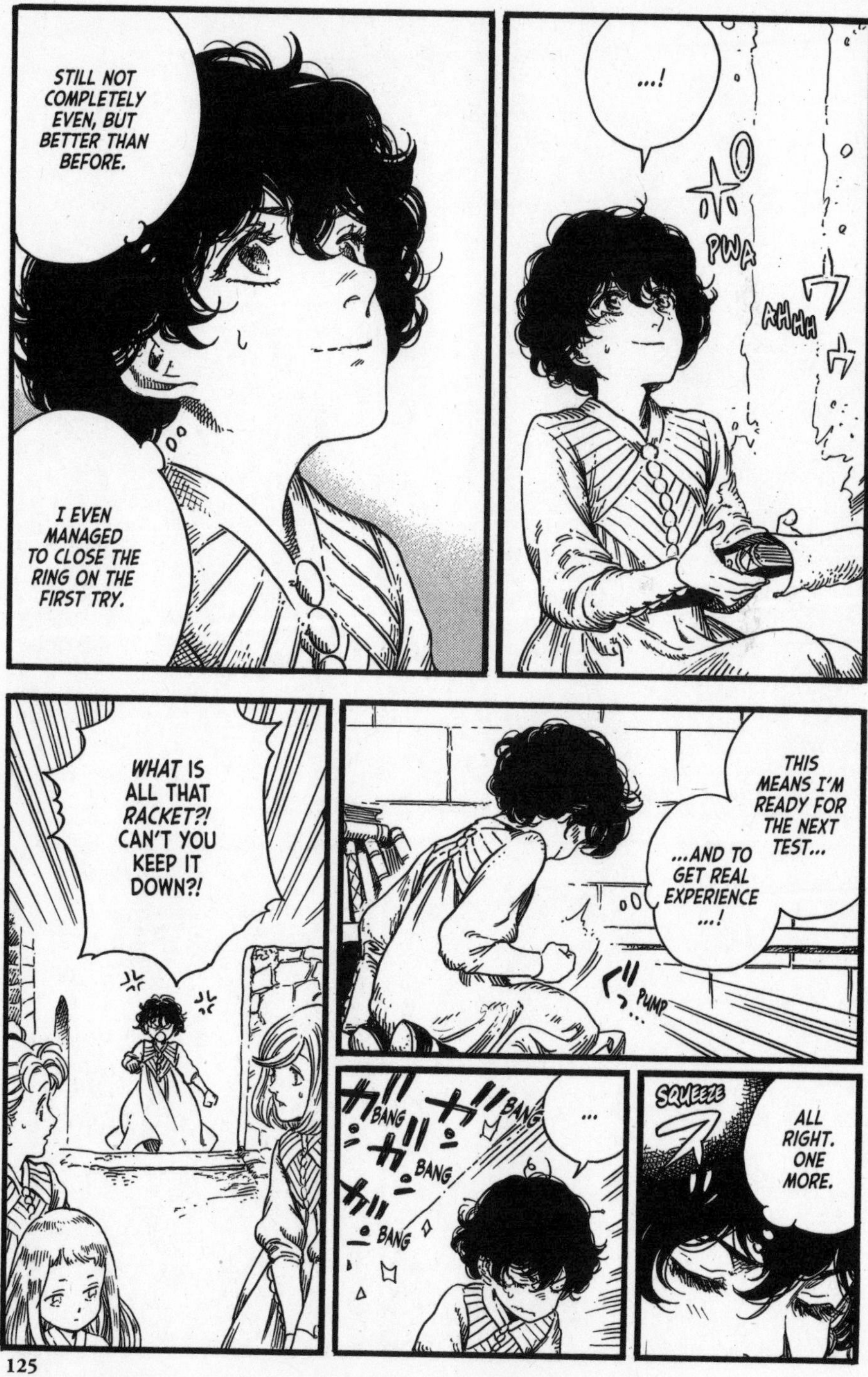

...!
PWA
AHHH
STILL NOT COMPLETELY EVEN, BUT BETTER THAN BEFORE.
I EVEN MANAGED TO CLOSE THE RING ON THE FIRST TRY.
THIS MEANS I'M READY FOR THE NEXT TEST...
...AND TO GET REAL EXPERIENCE ...!
PUMP
SQUEEZE
ALL RIGHT. ONE MORE.
BANG
BANG
BANG
BANG
...
WHAT IS ALL THAT RACKET?! CAN'T YOU KEEP IT DOWN?!

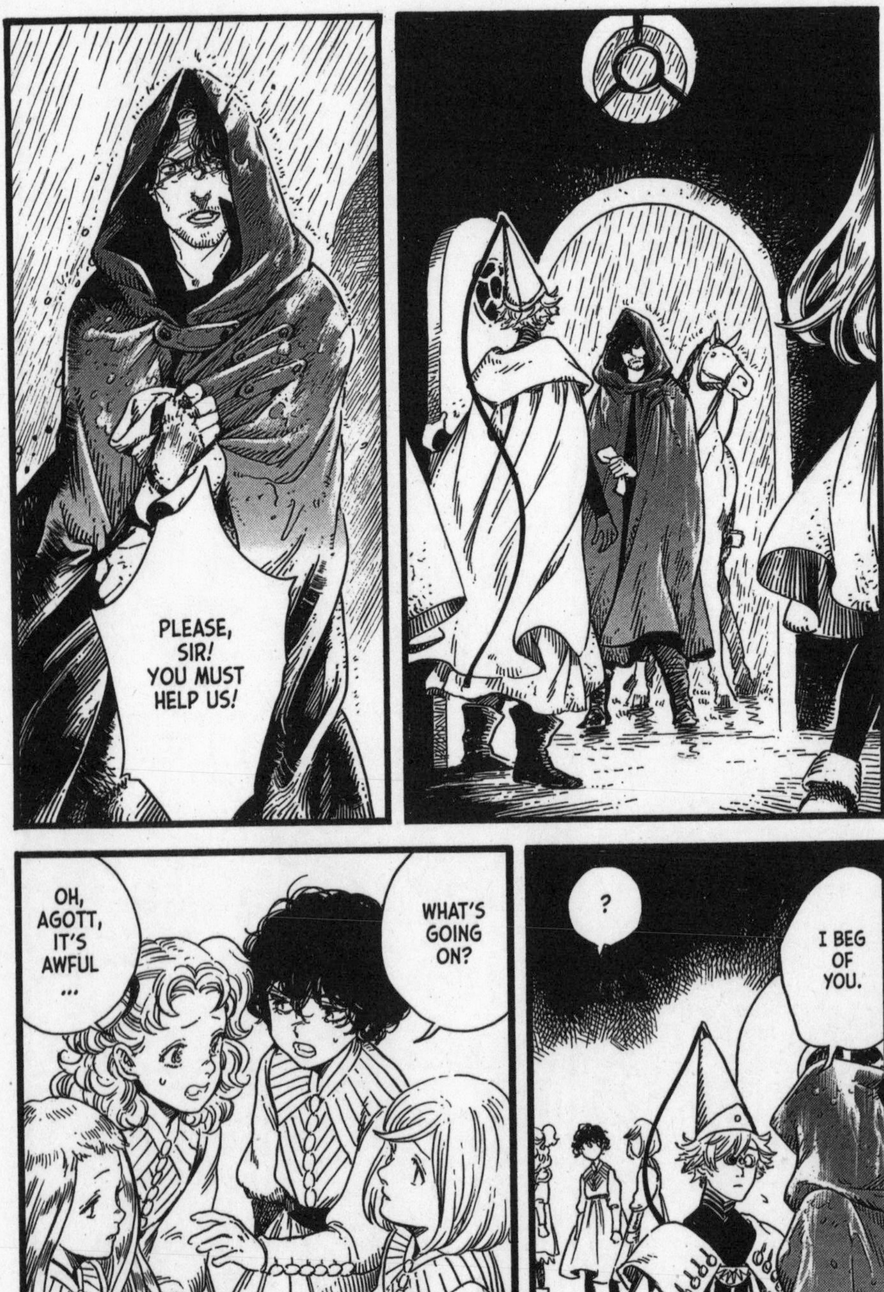
PLEASE, SIR! YOU MUST HELP US!
I BEG OF YOU.
?
WHAT'S GOING ON?
OH, AGOTT, IT'S AWFUL ...

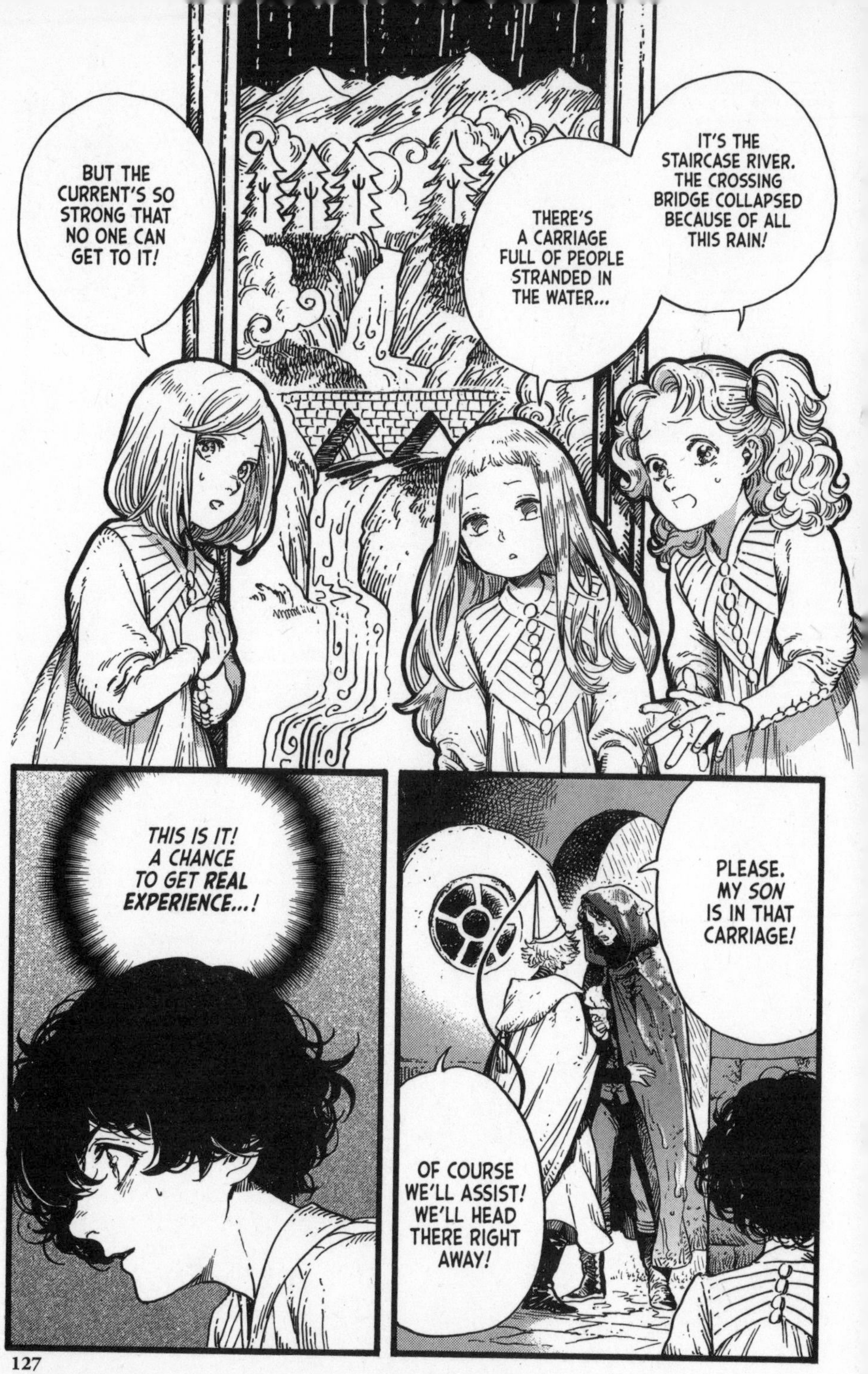
IT'S THE STAIRCASE RIVER. THE CROSSING BRIDGE COLLAPSED BECAUSE OF ALL THIS RAIN!
THERE'S A CARRIAGE FULL OF PEOPLE STRANDED IN THE WATER...
BUT THE CURRENT'S SO STRONG THAT NO ONE CAN GET TO IT!
PLEASE. MY *SON* IS IN THAT CARRIAGE!
OF COURSE WE'LL ASSIST! WE'LL HEAD THERE RIGHT AWAY!
THIS IS IT! A CHANCE TO GET ***REAL EXPERIENCE...!***

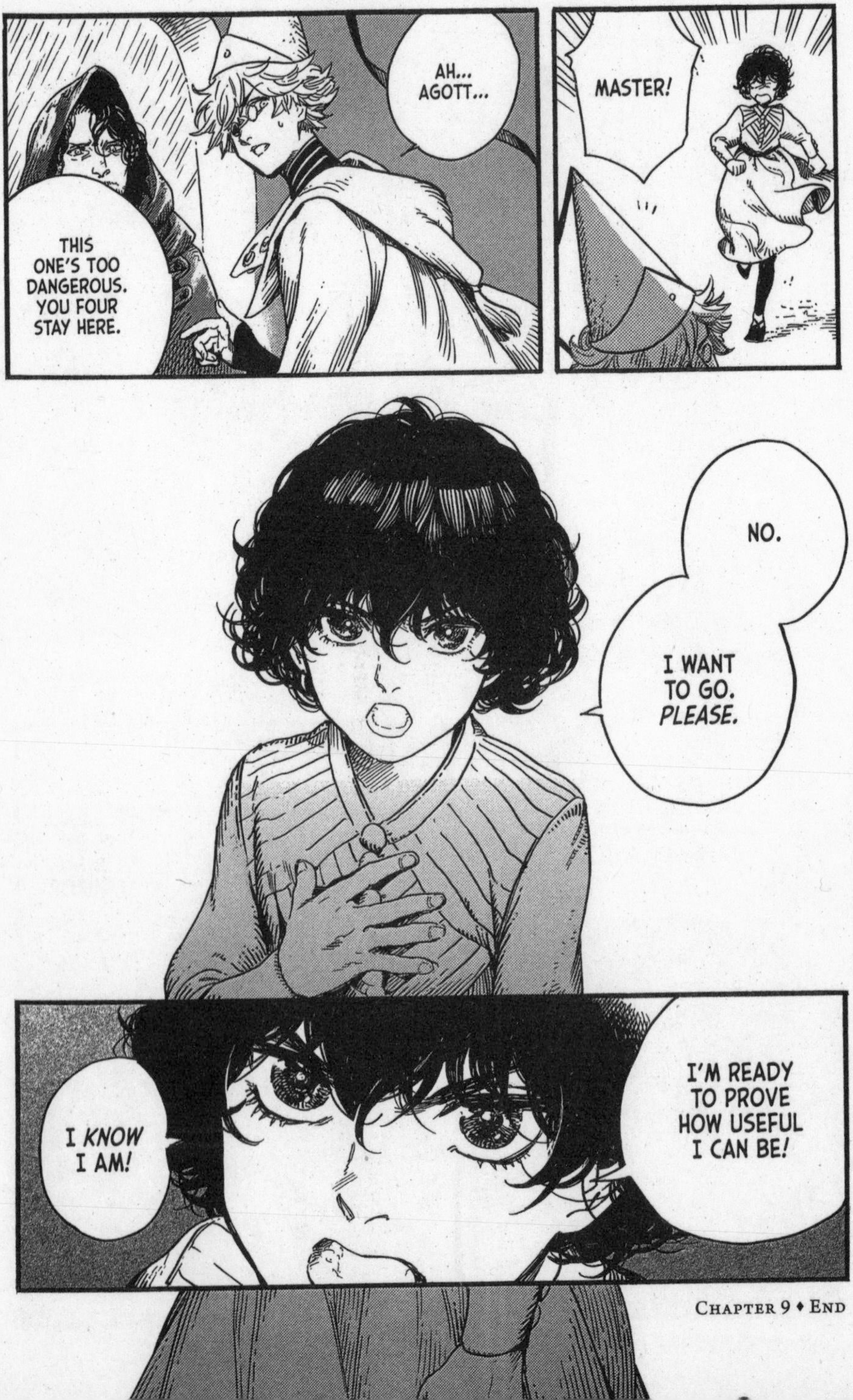
MASTER!
AH... AGOTT...
THIS ONE'S TOO DANGEROUS. YOU FOUR STAY HERE.
NO.
I WANT TO GO. *PLEASE.*
I'M READY TO PROVE HOW USEFUL I CAN BE!
I *KNOW* I AM!

CHAPTER 9 ♦ END

Witch Hat Atelier

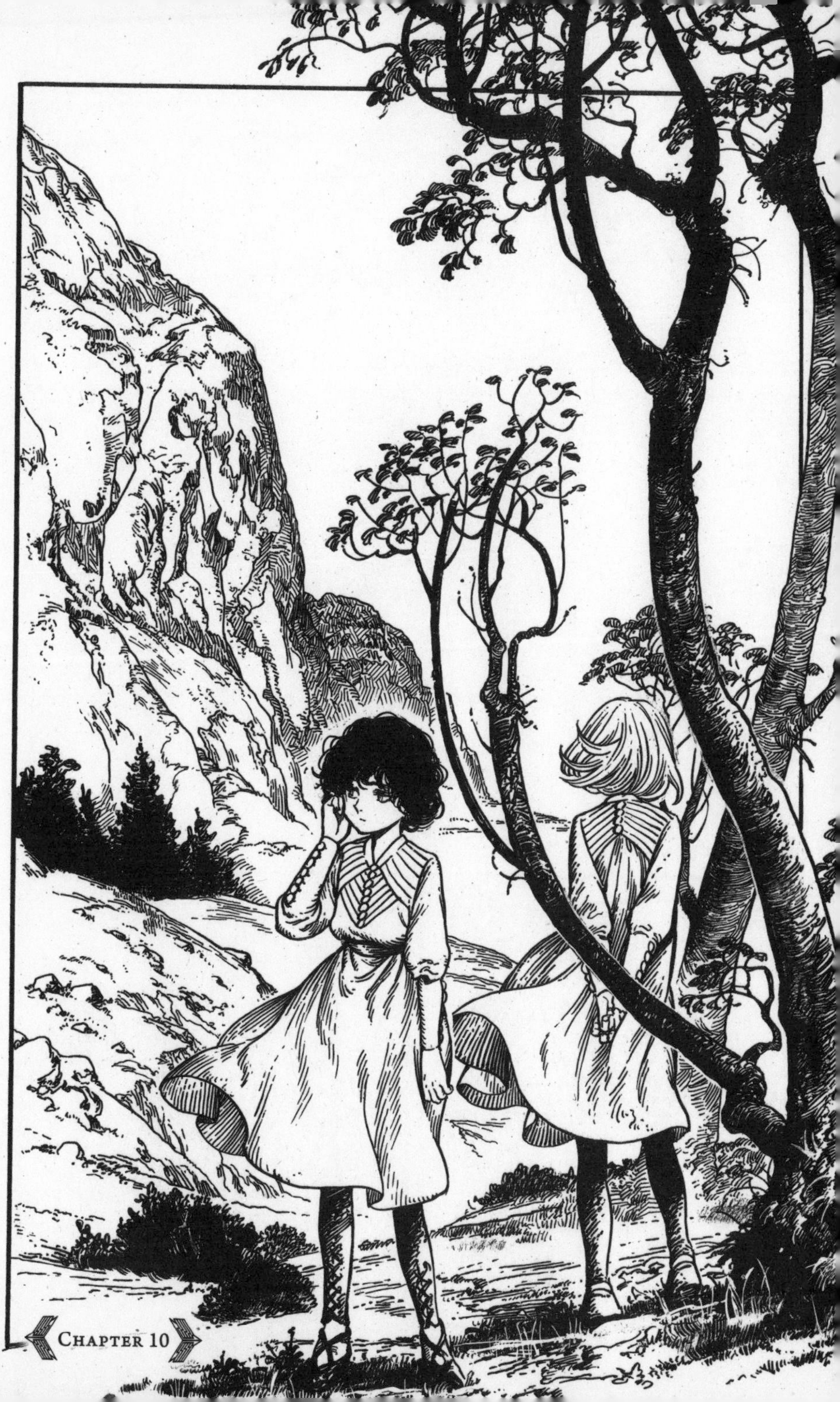
Chapter 10

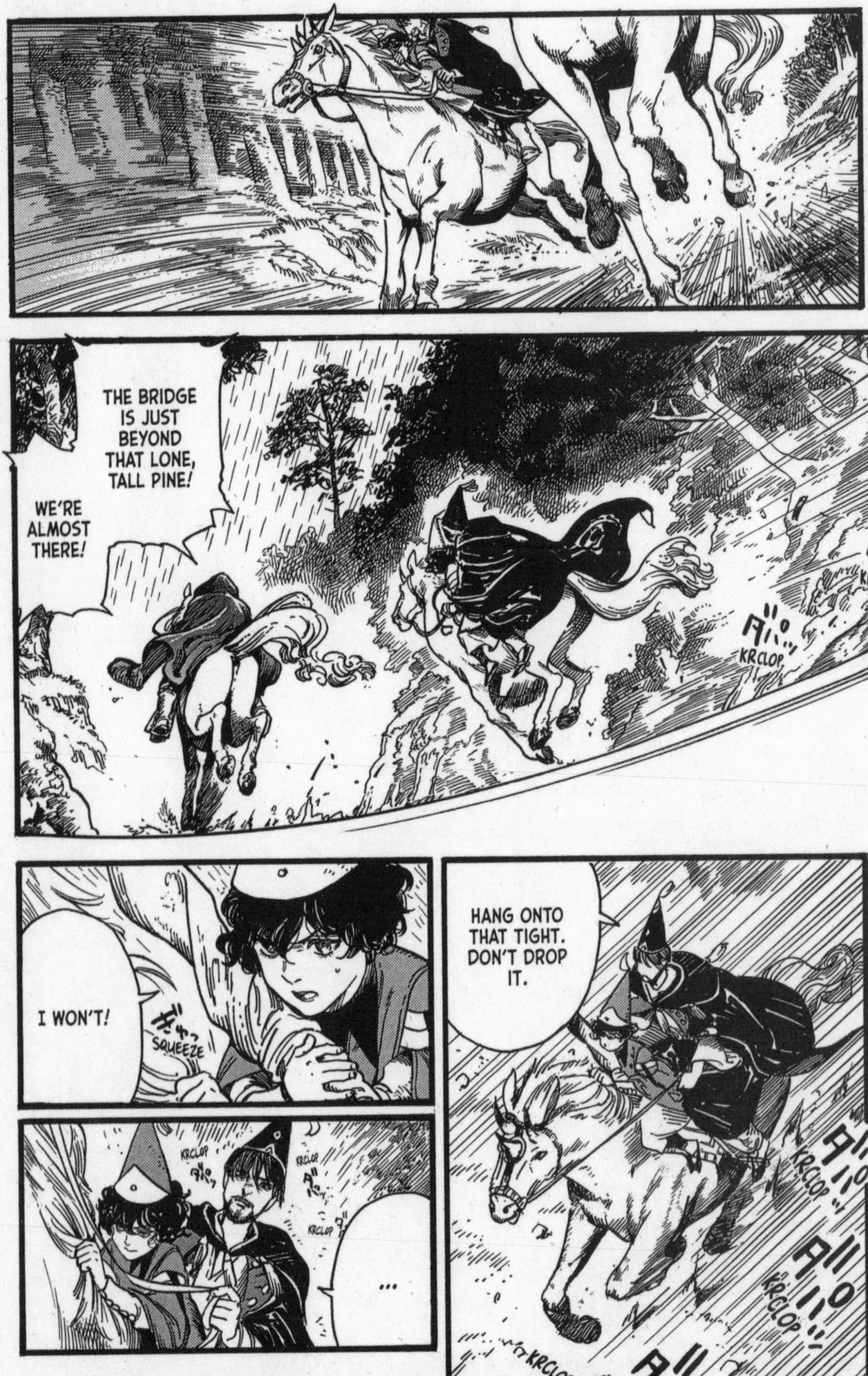
THE BRIDGE IS JUST BEYOND THAT LONE, TALL PINE!
WE'RE ALMOST THERE!
KRCLOP
KRCLOP
HANG ONTO THAT TIGHT. DON'T DROP IT.
KRCLOP
KRCLOP
KRCLOP
KRCLOP
I WON'T!
SQUEEZE
KRCLOP
KRCLOP
KRCLOP
...

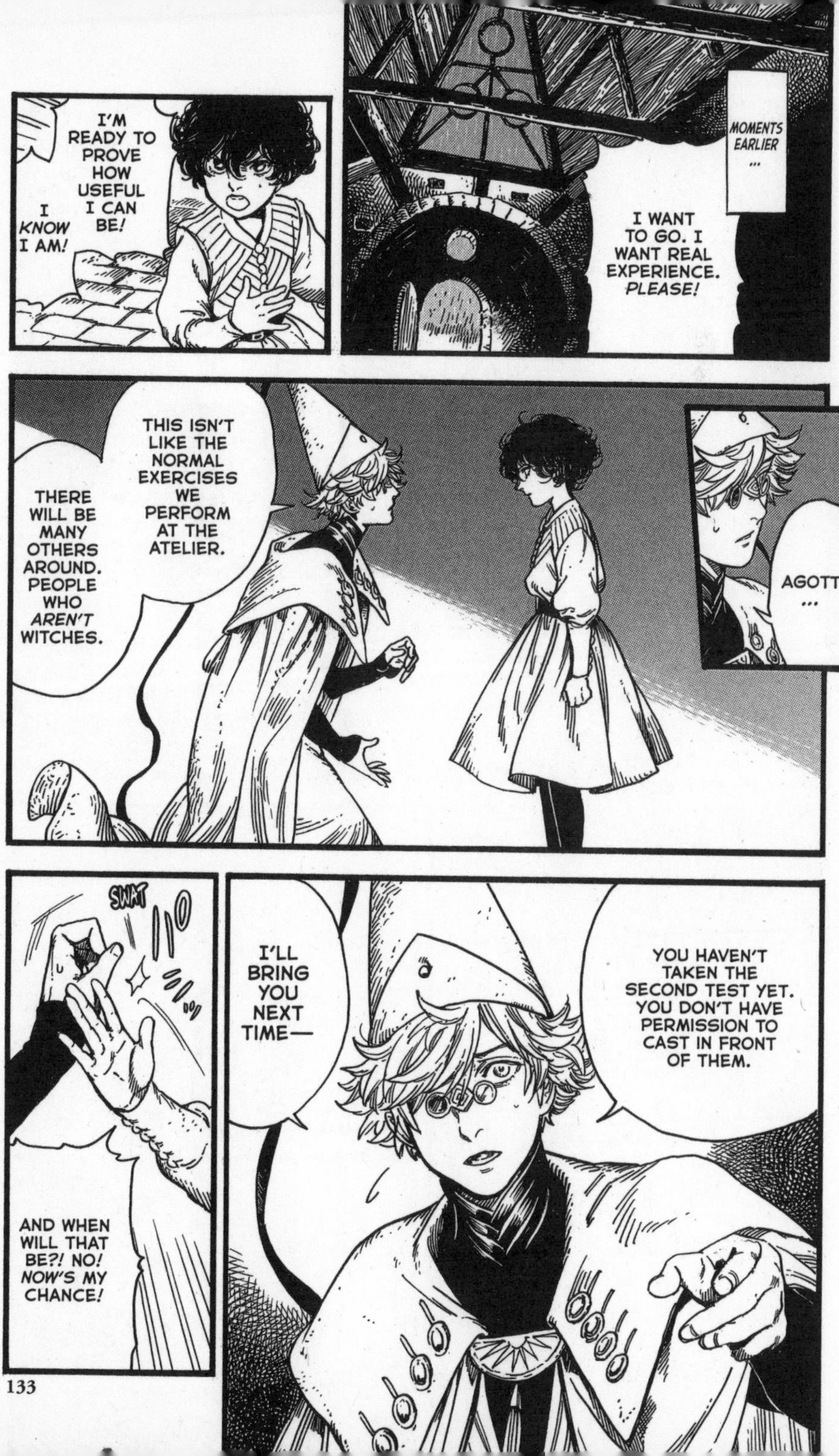
MOMENTS EARLIER ...
I WANT TO GO. I WANT REAL EXPERIENCE. *PLEASE!*
I'M READY TO PROVE HOW USEFUL I CAN BE!
I *KNOW* I AM!
AGOTT ...
THIS ISN'T LIKE THE NORMAL EXERCISES WE PERFORM AT THE ATELIER.
THERE WILL BE MANY OTHERS AROUND. PEOPLE WHO *AREN'T* WITCHES.
YOU HAVEN'T TAKEN THE SECOND TEST YET. YOU DON'T HAVE PERMISSION TO CAST IN FRONT OF THEM.
I'LL BRING YOU NEXT TIME—
SWAT
AND WHEN WILL THAT BE?! NO! *NOW'S* MY CHANCE!

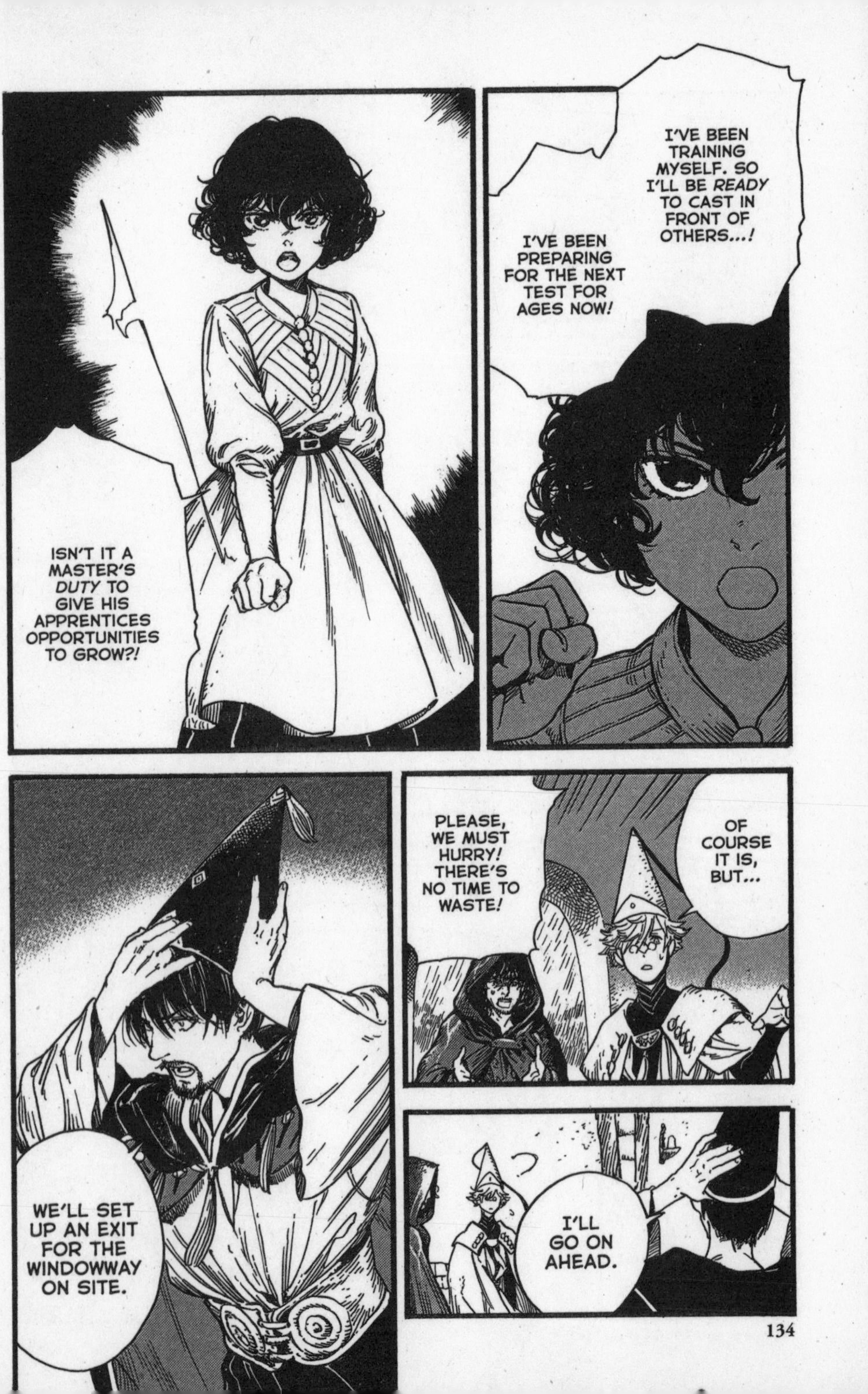
I'VE BEEN TRAINING MYSELF. SO I'LL BE *READY* TO CAST IN FRONT OF OTHERS...!
I'VE BEEN PREPARING FOR THE NEXT TEST FOR AGES NOW!
ISN'T IT A MASTER'S *DUTY* TO GIVE HIS APPRENTICES OPPORTUNITIES TO GROW?!
OF COURSE IT IS, BUT...
PLEASE, WE MUST HURRY! THERE'S NO TIME TO WASTE!
I'LL GO ON AHEAD.
WE'LL SET UP AN EXIT FOR THE WINDOWWAY ON SITE.

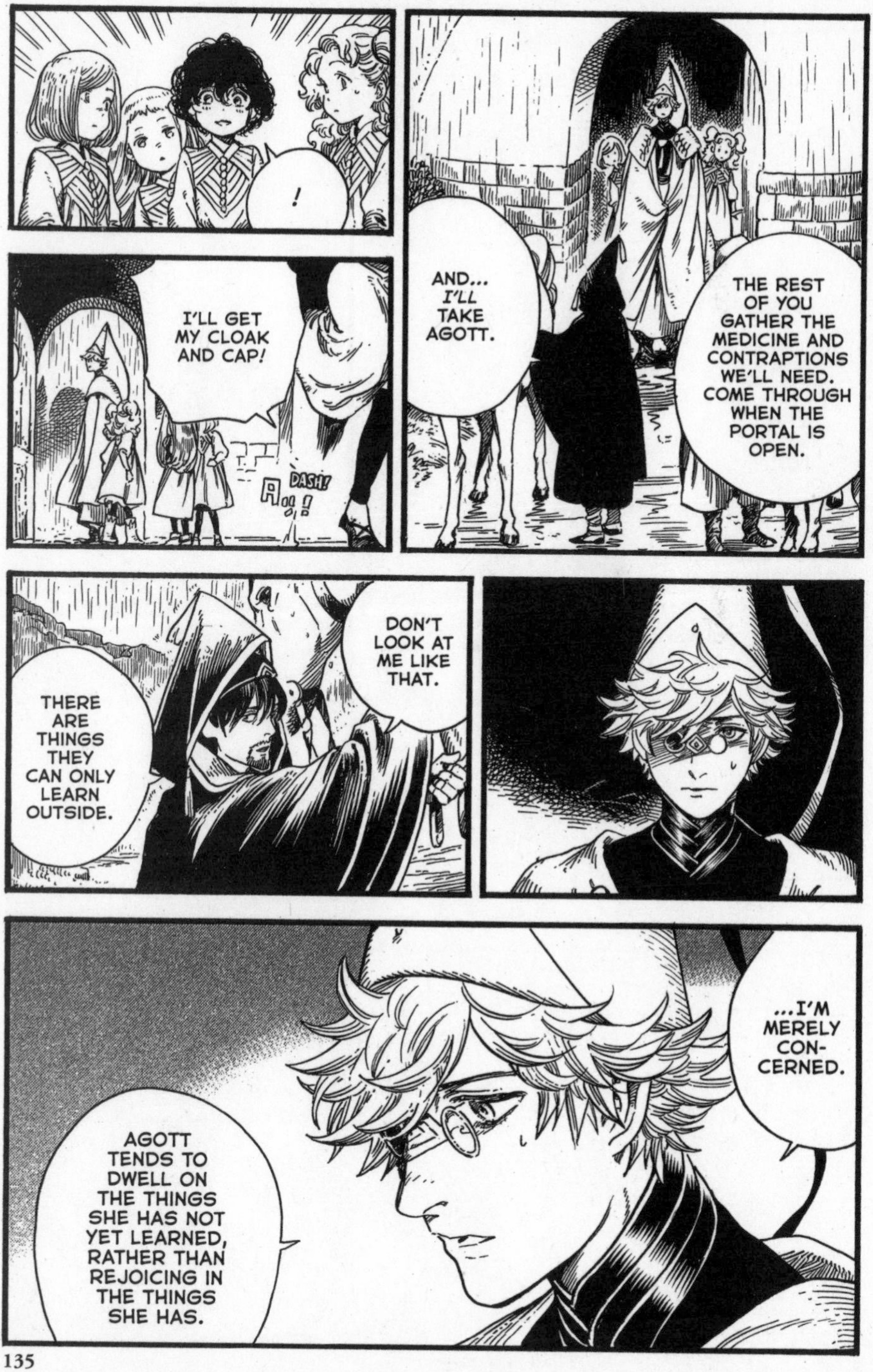
THE REST OF YOU GATHER THE MEDICINE AND CONTRAPTIONS WE'LL NEED. COME THROUGH WHEN THE PORTAL IS OPEN.
AND... *I'LL* TAKE AGOTT.
!
I'LL GET MY CLOAK AND CAP!
DASH!
A..!
DON'T LOOK AT ME LIKE THAT.
THERE ARE THINGS THEY CAN ONLY LEARN OUTSIDE.
...I'M MERELY CON-CERNED.
AGOTT TENDS TO DWELL ON THE THINGS SHE HAS NOT YET LEARNED, RATHER THAN REJOICING IN THE THINGS SHE HAS.

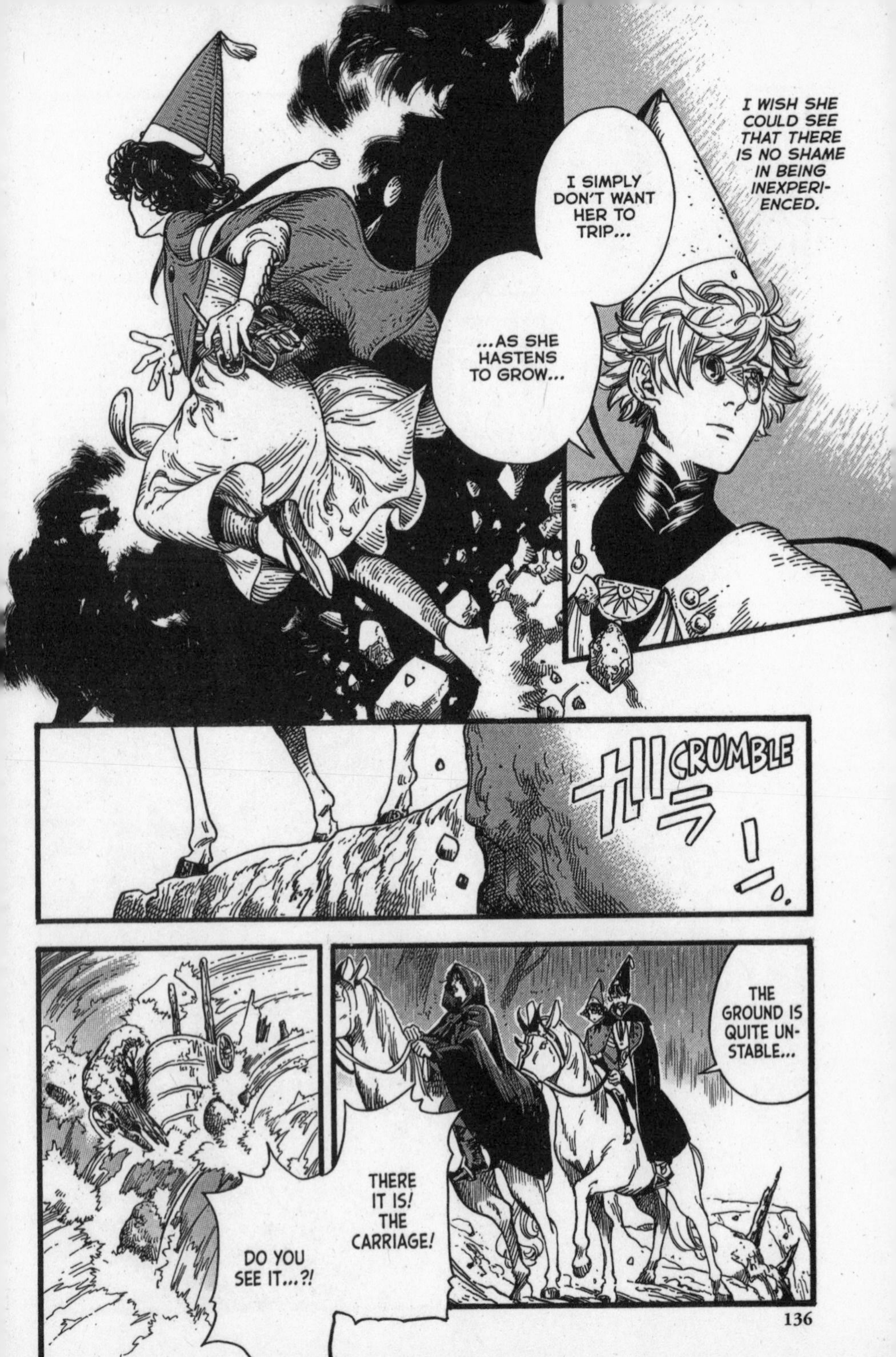
I WISH SHE COULD SEE THAT THERE IS NO SHAME IN BEING INEXPERI-ENCED.
I SIMPLY DON'T WANT HER TO TRIP...
...AS SHE HASTENS TO GROW...
CRUMBLE
ガラ
THE GROUND IS QUITE UN-STABLE...
THERE IT IS! THE CARRIAGE!
DO YOU SEE IT...?!

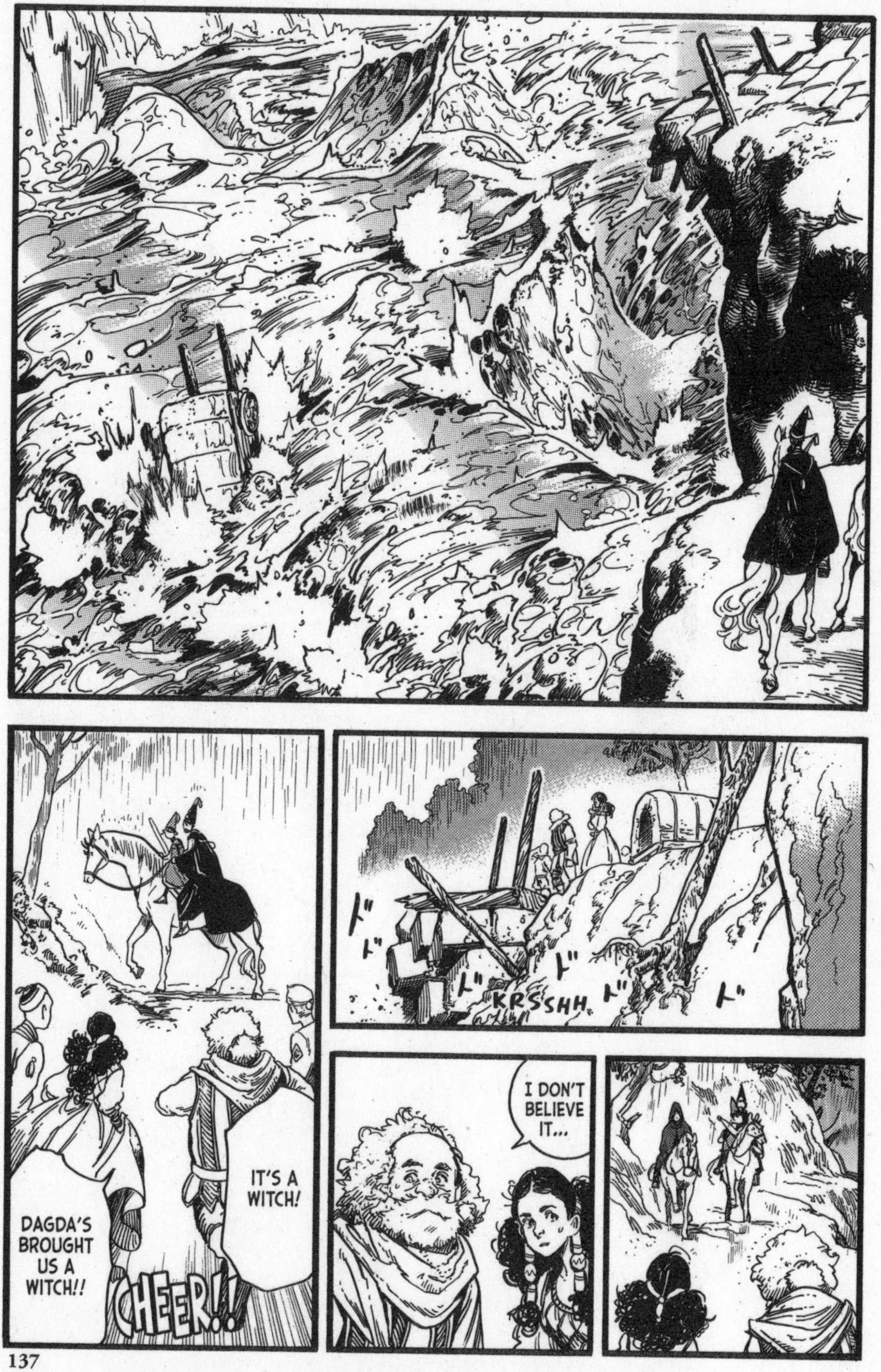
ドドドドドド
KRSSHH
I DON'T BELIEVE IT...
IT'S A WITCH!
DAGDA'S BROUGHT US A WITCH!!
CHEER!!

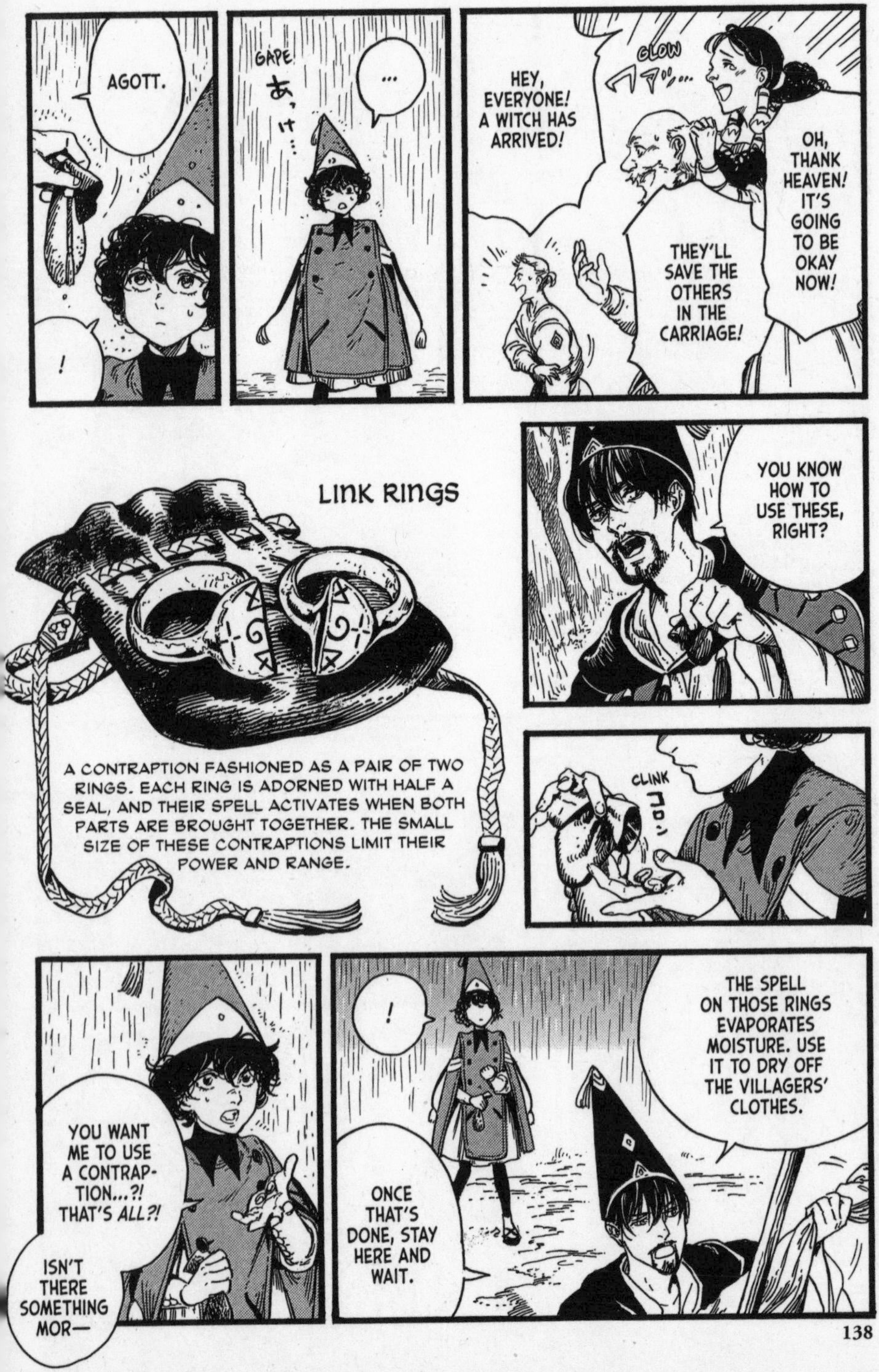
GLOW
ワァッ…
HEY, EVERYONE! A WITCH HAS ARRIVED!
OH, THANK HEAVEN! IT'S GOING TO BE OKAY NOW!
THEY'LL SAVE THE OTHERS IN THE CARRIAGE!
GAPE
あっけ…
...
AGOTT.
!
YOU KNOW HOW TO USE THESE, RIGHT?
CLINK
コロン
LINK RINGS
A CONTRAPTION FASHIONED AS A PAIR OF TWO RINGS. EACH RING IS ADORNED WITH HALF A SEAL, AND THEIR SPELL ACTIVATES WHEN BOTH PARTS ARE BROUGHT TOGETHER. THE SMALL SIZE OF THESE CONTRAPTIONS LIMIT THEIR POWER AND RANGE.
THE SPELL ON THOSE RINGS EVAPORATES MOISTURE. USE IT TO DRY OFF THE VILLAGERS' CLOTHES.
!
ONCE THAT'S DONE, STAY HERE AND WAIT.
YOU WANT ME TO USE A CONTRAP-TION...?! THAT'S ALL?!
ISN'T THERE SOMETHING MOR—

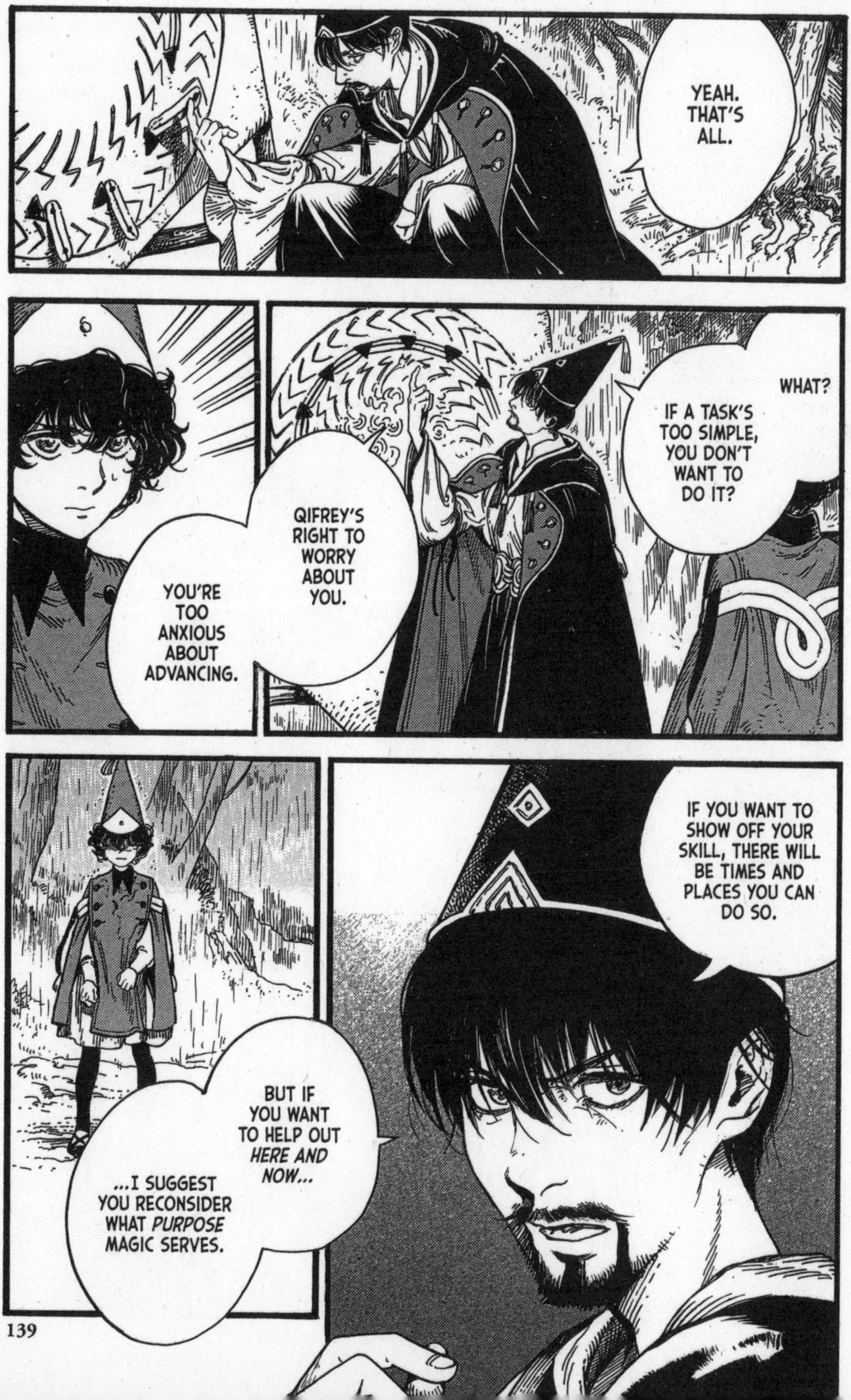
YEAH. THAT'S ALL.
WHAT?
IF A TASK'S TOO SIMPLE, YOU DON'T WANT TO DO IT?
QIFREY'S RIGHT TO WORRY ABOUT YOU.
YOU'RE TOO ANXIOUS ABOUT ADVANCING.
IF YOU WANT TO SHOW OFF YOUR SKILL, THERE WILL BE TIMES AND PLACES YOU CAN DO SO.
BUT IF YOU WANT TO HELP OUT *HERE AND NOW*...
...I SUGGEST YOU RECONSIDER WHAT *PURPOSE* MAGIC SERVES.

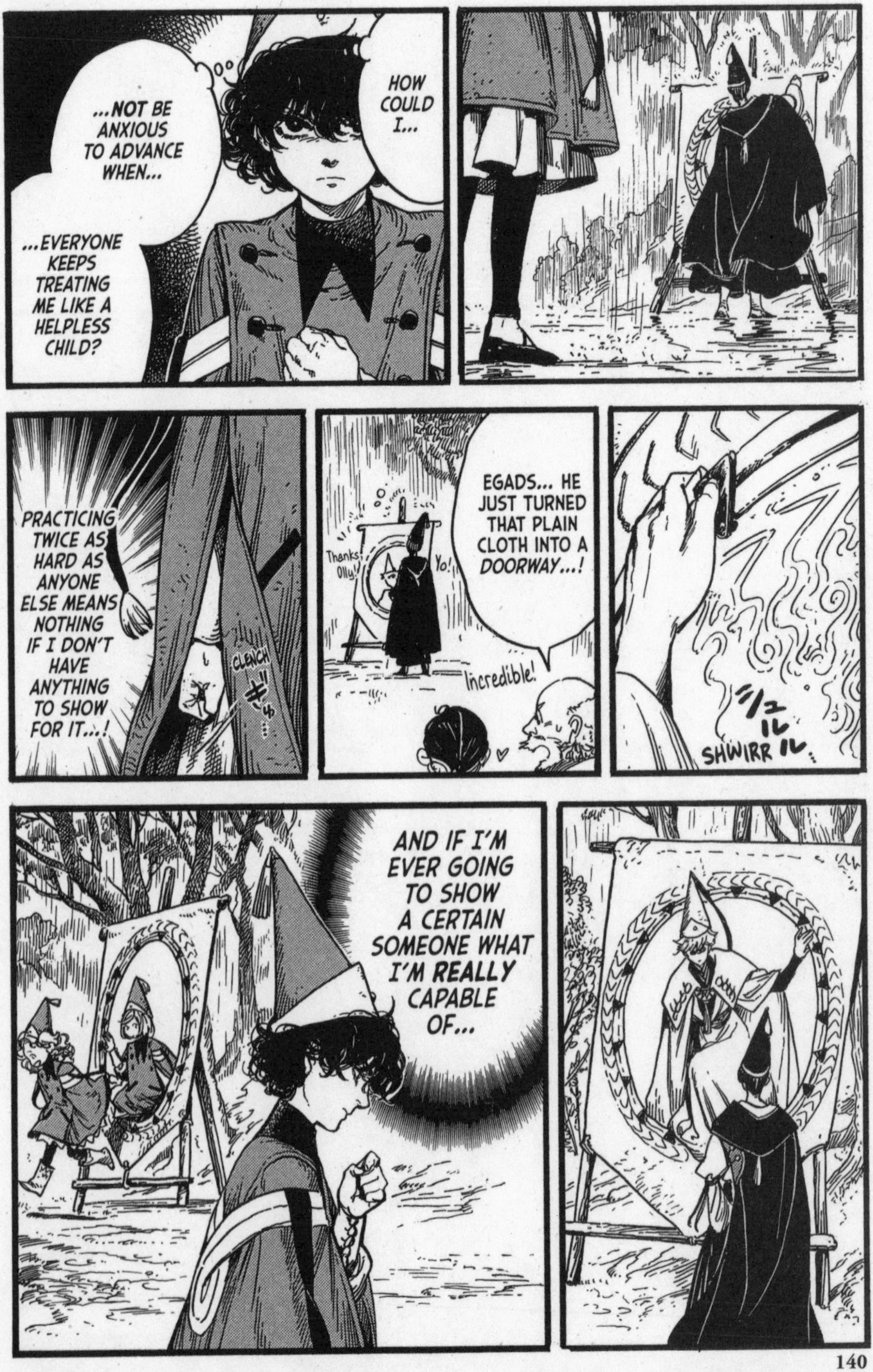
HOW COULD I...
...NOT BE ANXIOUS TO ADVANCE WHEN...
...EVERYONE KEEPS TREATING ME LIKE A HELPLESS CHILD?
シュルル
SHWIRR
EGADS... HE JUST TURNED THAT PLAIN CLOTH INTO A DOORWAY...!
Yo!
Thanks, Olly!
Incredible!
PRACTICING TWICE AS HARD AS ANYONE ELSE MEANS NOTHING IF I DON'T HAVE ANYTHING TO SHOW FOR IT...!
CLENCH
ぎゅ...
AND IF I'M EVER GOING TO SHOW A CERTAIN SOMEONE WHAT I'M REALLY CAPABLE OF...

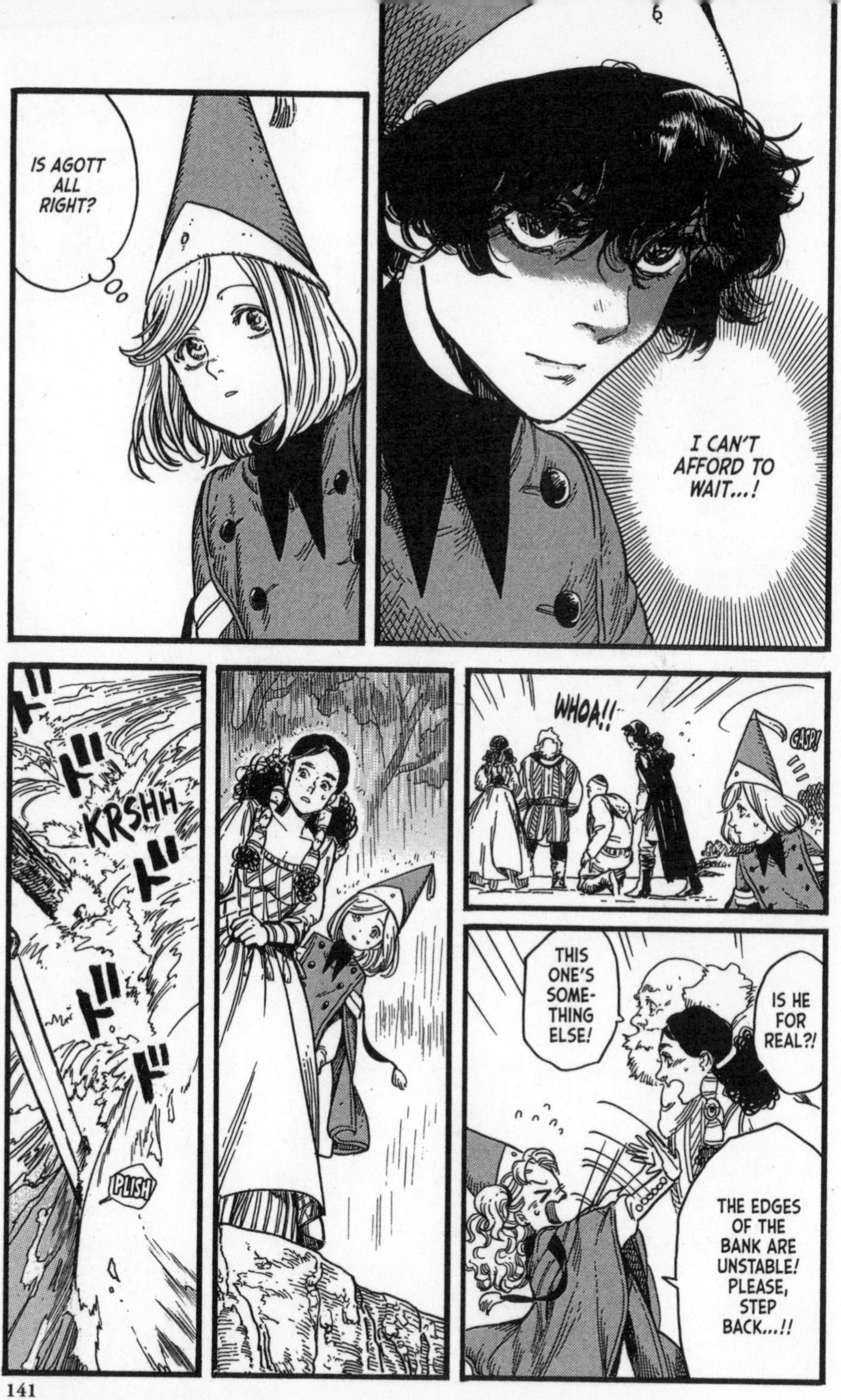
I CAN'T AFFORD TO WAIT...!
IS AGOTT ALL RIGHT?
WHOA!!
GASP!
IS HE FOR REAL?!
THIS ONE'S SOME-THING ELSE!
THE EDGES OF THE BANK ARE UNSTABLE! PLEASE, STEP BACK...!!
KRSHH
PLISH

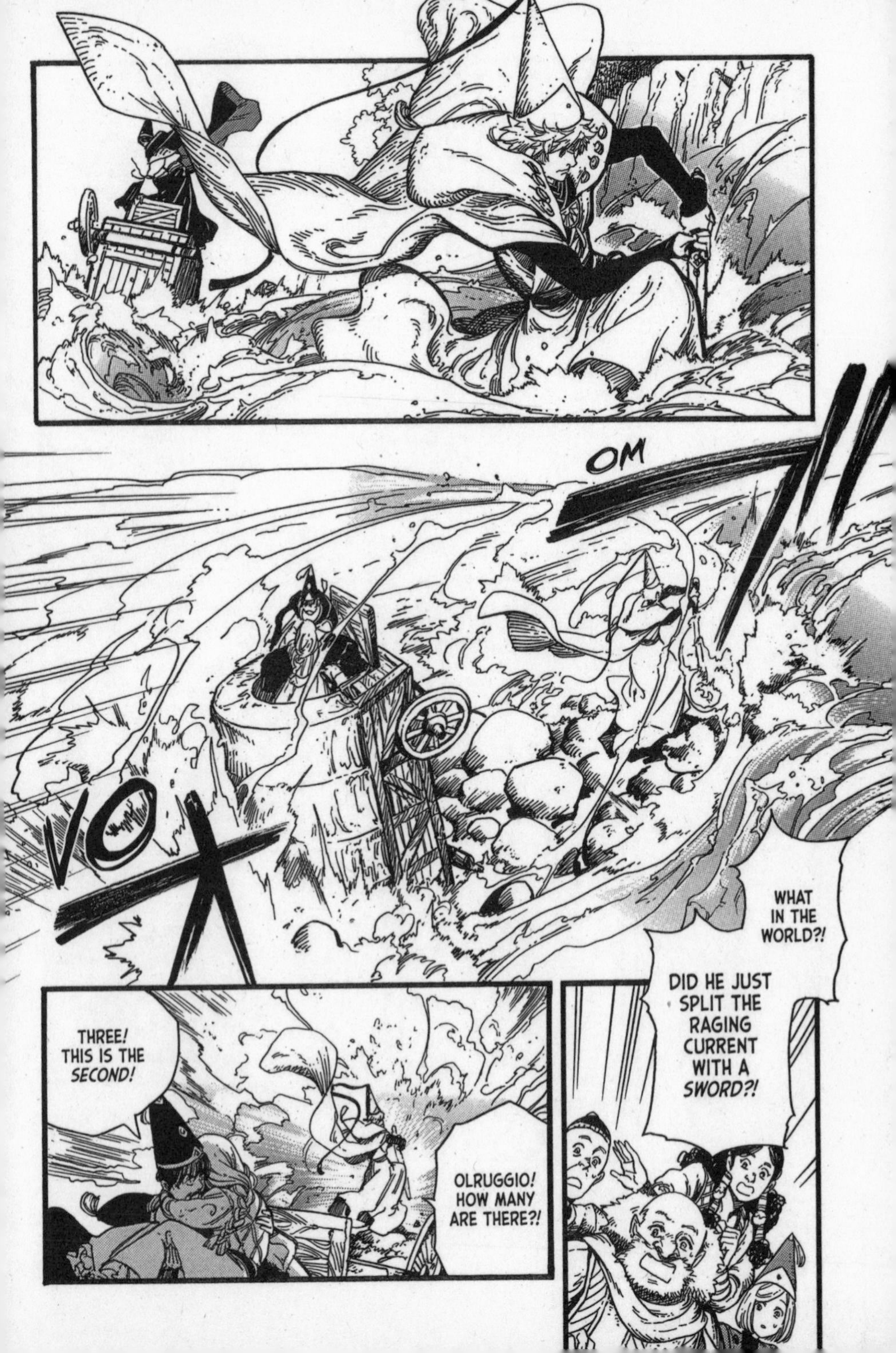
OM
VO
WHAT IN THE WORLD?!
DID HE JUST SPLIT THE RAGING CURRENT WITH A *SWORD?!*
OLRUGGIO! HOW MANY ARE THERE?!
THREE! THIS IS THE *SECOND!*

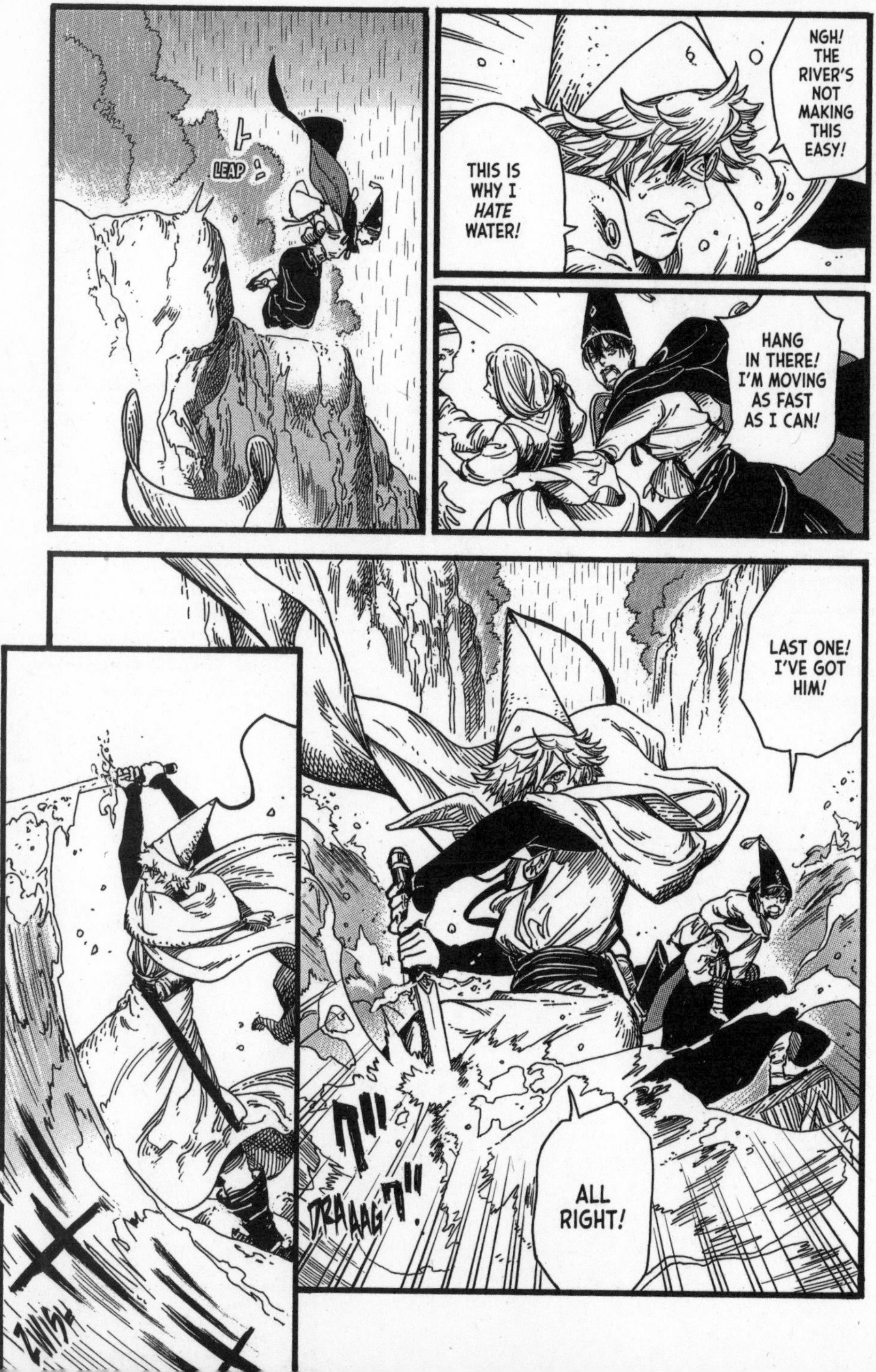
NGH! THE RIVER'S NOT MAKING THIS EASY!
THIS IS WHY I *HATE* WATER!
HANG IN THERE! I'M MOVING AS FAST AS I CAN!
LEAP
LAST ONE! I'VE GOT HIM!
DRAAAG
ALL RIGHT!
ZWISH

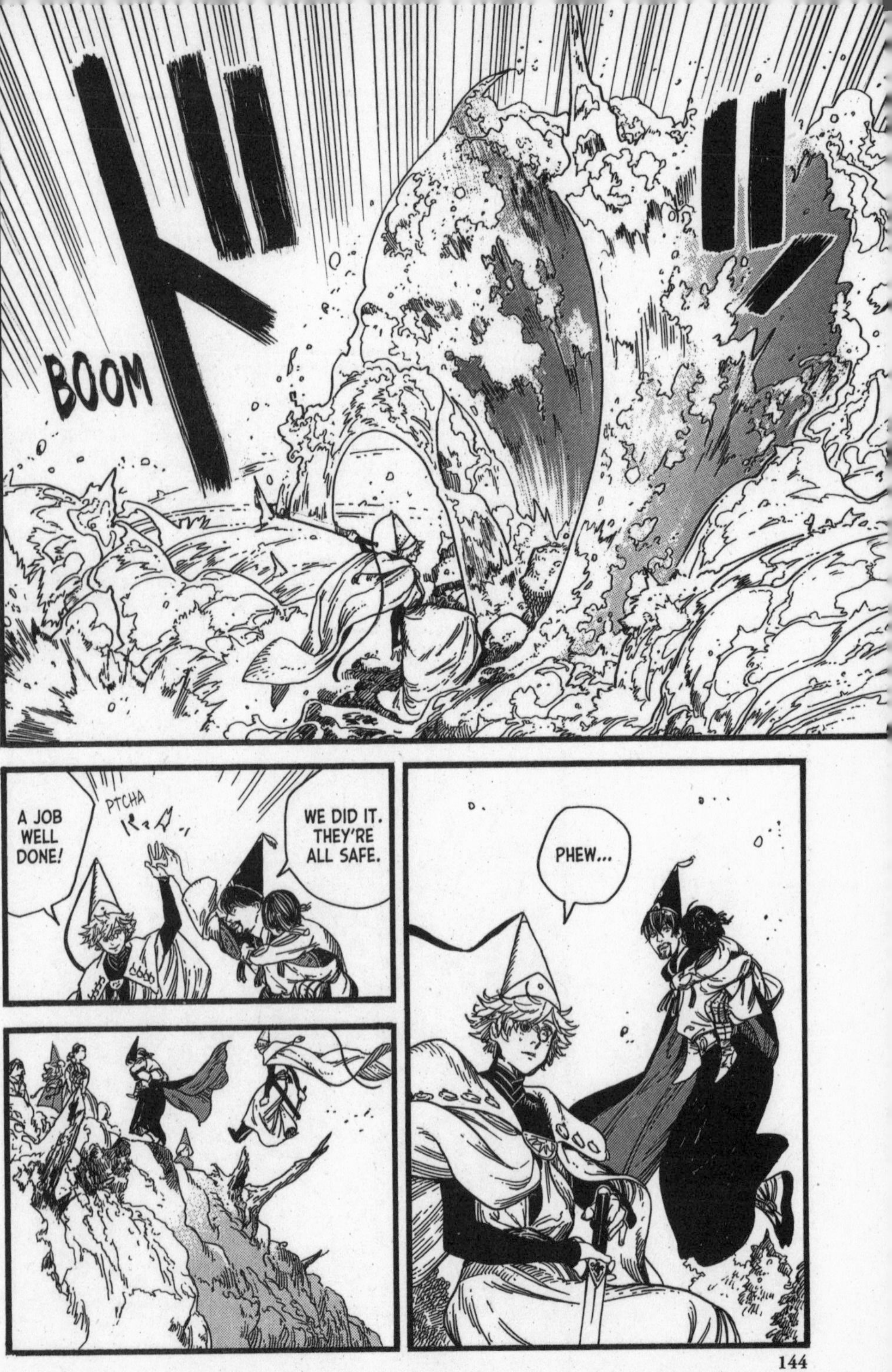
BOOM
PHEW...
WE DID IT. THEY'RE ALL SAFE.
PTCHA
A JOB WELL DONE!

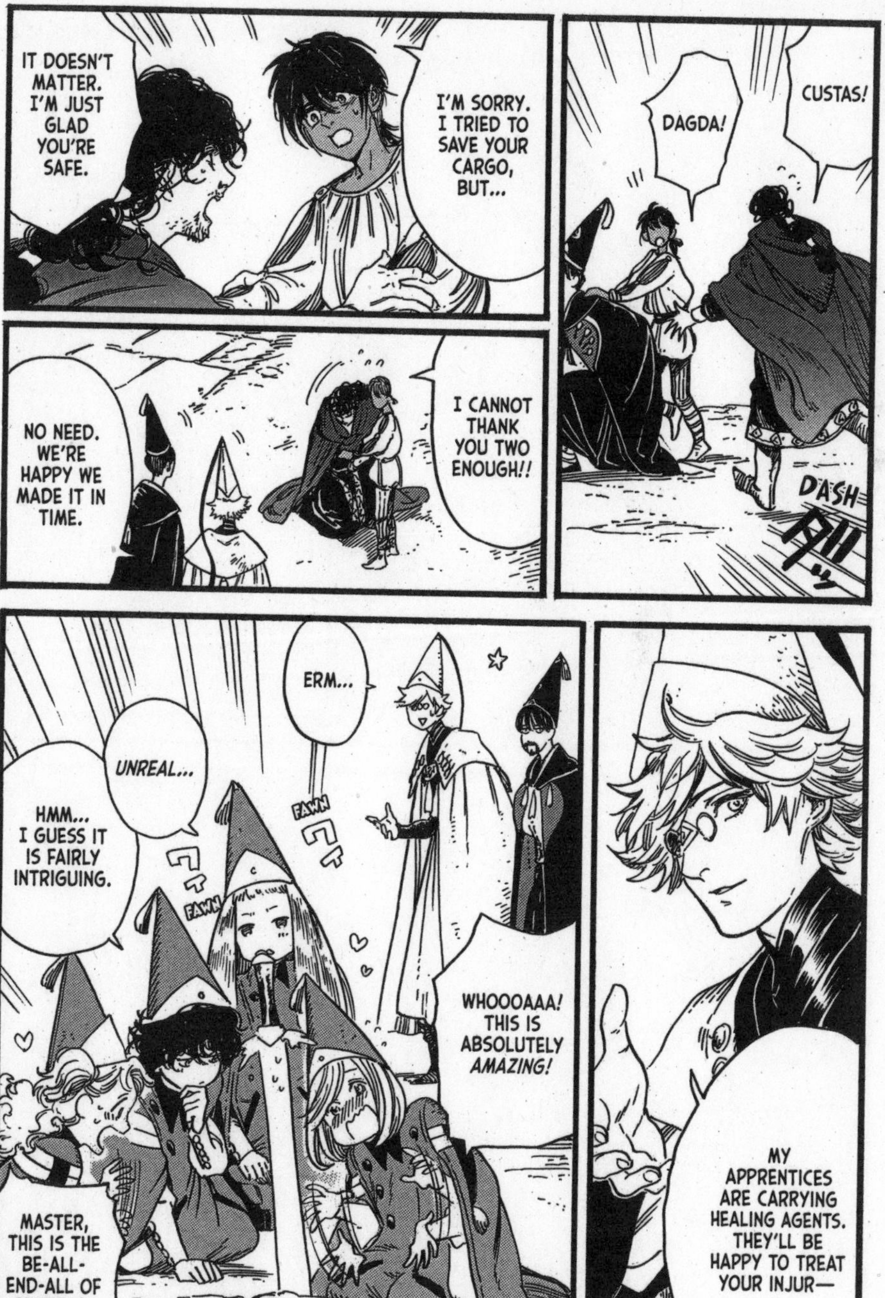
CUSTAS!
DAGDA!
DASH
I'M SORRY. I TRIED TO SAVE YOUR CARGO, BUT...
IT DOESN'T MATTER. I'M JUST GLAD YOU'RE SAFE.
I CANNOT THANK YOU TWO ENOUGH!!
NO NEED. WE'RE HAPPY WE MADE IT IN TIME.
MY APPRENTICES ARE CARRYING HEALING AGENTS. THEY'LL BE HAPPY TO TREAT YOUR INJUR—
ERM...
FAWN
UNREAL...
HMM... I GUESS IT IS FAIRLY INTRIGUING.
FAWN
WHOOOAAA! THIS IS ABSOLUTELY AMAZING!
MASTER, THIS IS THE BE-ALL-END-ALL OF CONTRAP-TIONS!!

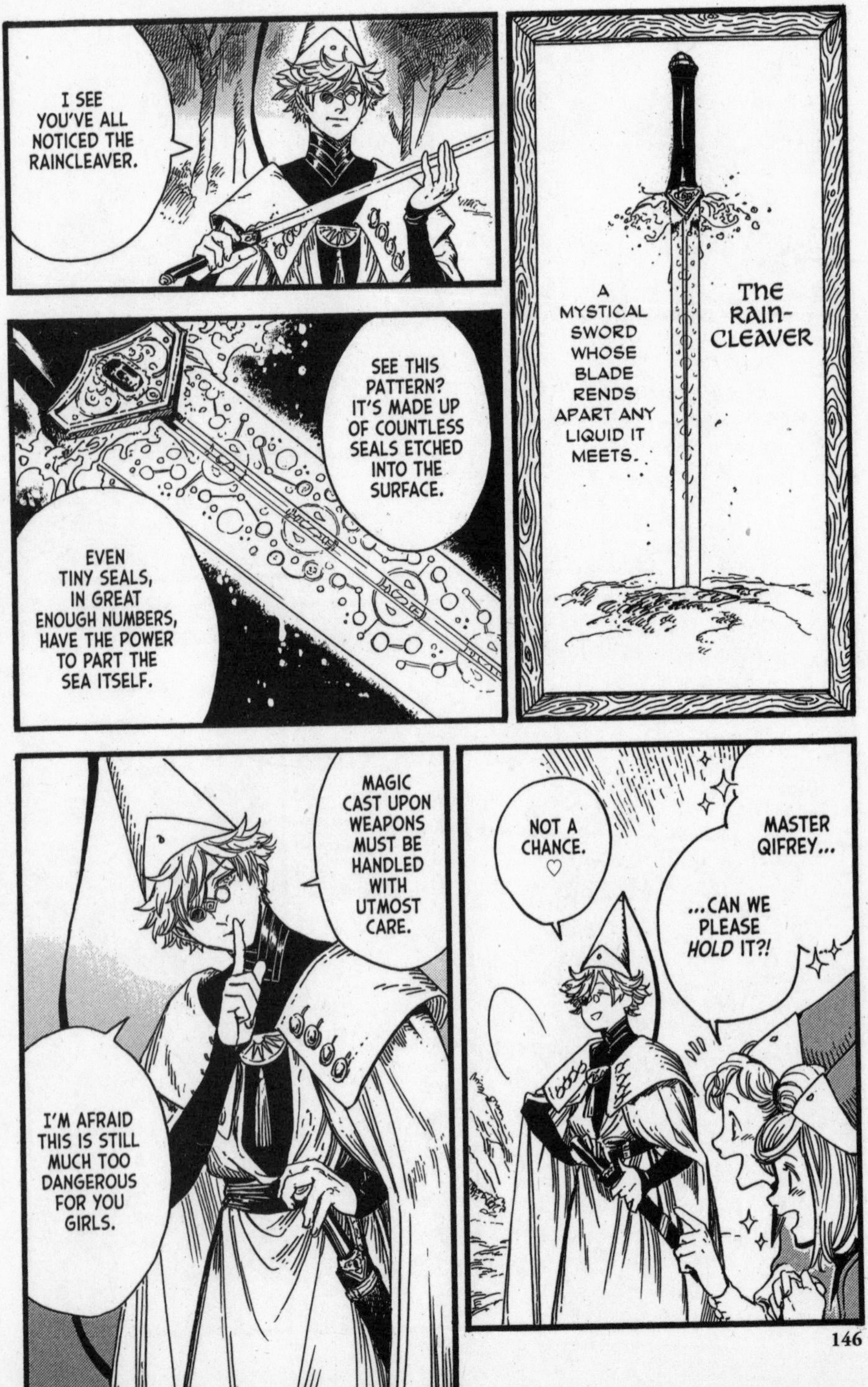
THE RAIN-CLEAVER
A MYSTICAL SWORD WHOSE BLADE RENDS APART ANY LIQUID IT MEETS.
I SEE YOU'VE ALL NOTICED THE RAINCLEAVER.
SEE THIS PATTERN? IT'S MADE UP OF COUNTLESS SEALS ETCHED INTO THE SURFACE.
EVEN TINY SEALS, IN GREAT ENOUGH NUMBERS, HAVE THE POWER TO PART THE SEA ITSELF.
MASTER QIFREY...
...CAN WE PLEASE *HOLD* IT?!
NOT A CHANCE. ♡
MAGIC CAST UPON WEAPONS MUST BE HANDLED WITH UTMOST CARE.
I'M AFRAID THIS IS STILL MUCH TOO DANGEROUS FOR YOU GIRLS.

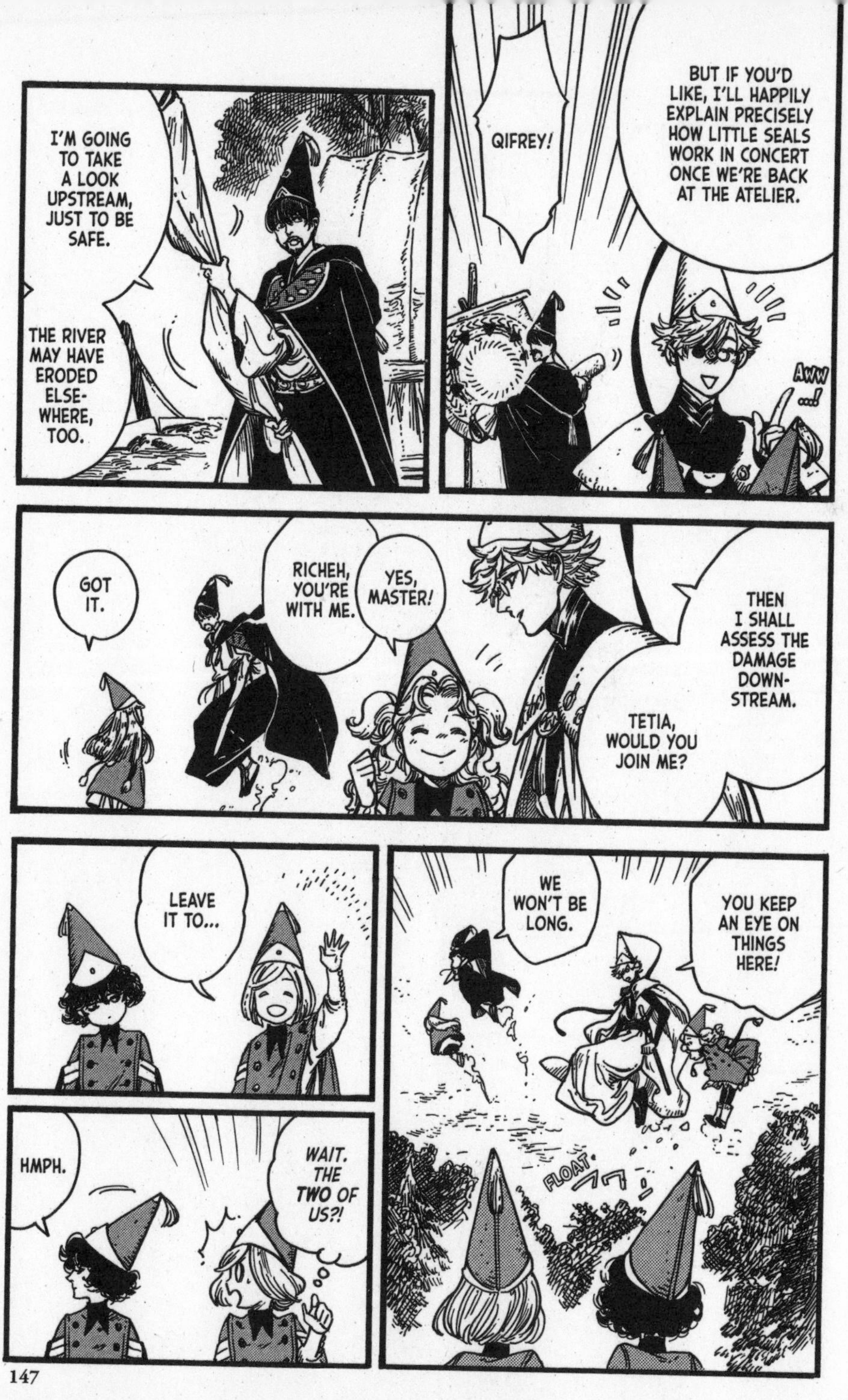
BUT IF YOU'D LIKE, I'LL HAPPILY EXPLAIN PRECISELY HOW LITTLE SEALS WORK IN CONCERT ONCE WE'RE BACK AT THE ATELIER.
QIFREY!
AWW ...!
I'M GOING TO TAKE A LOOK UPSTREAM, JUST TO BE SAFE.
THE RIVER MAY HAVE ERODED ELSE-WHERE, TOO.
THEN I SHALL ASSESS THE DAMAGE DOWN-STREAM.
TETIA, WOULD YOU JOIN ME?
YES, MASTER!
RICHEH, YOU'RE WITH ME.
GOT IT.
YOU KEEP AN EYE ON THINGS HERE!
WE WON'T BE LONG.
FLOAT
LEAVE IT TO...
WAIT. THE TWO OF US?!
HMPH.

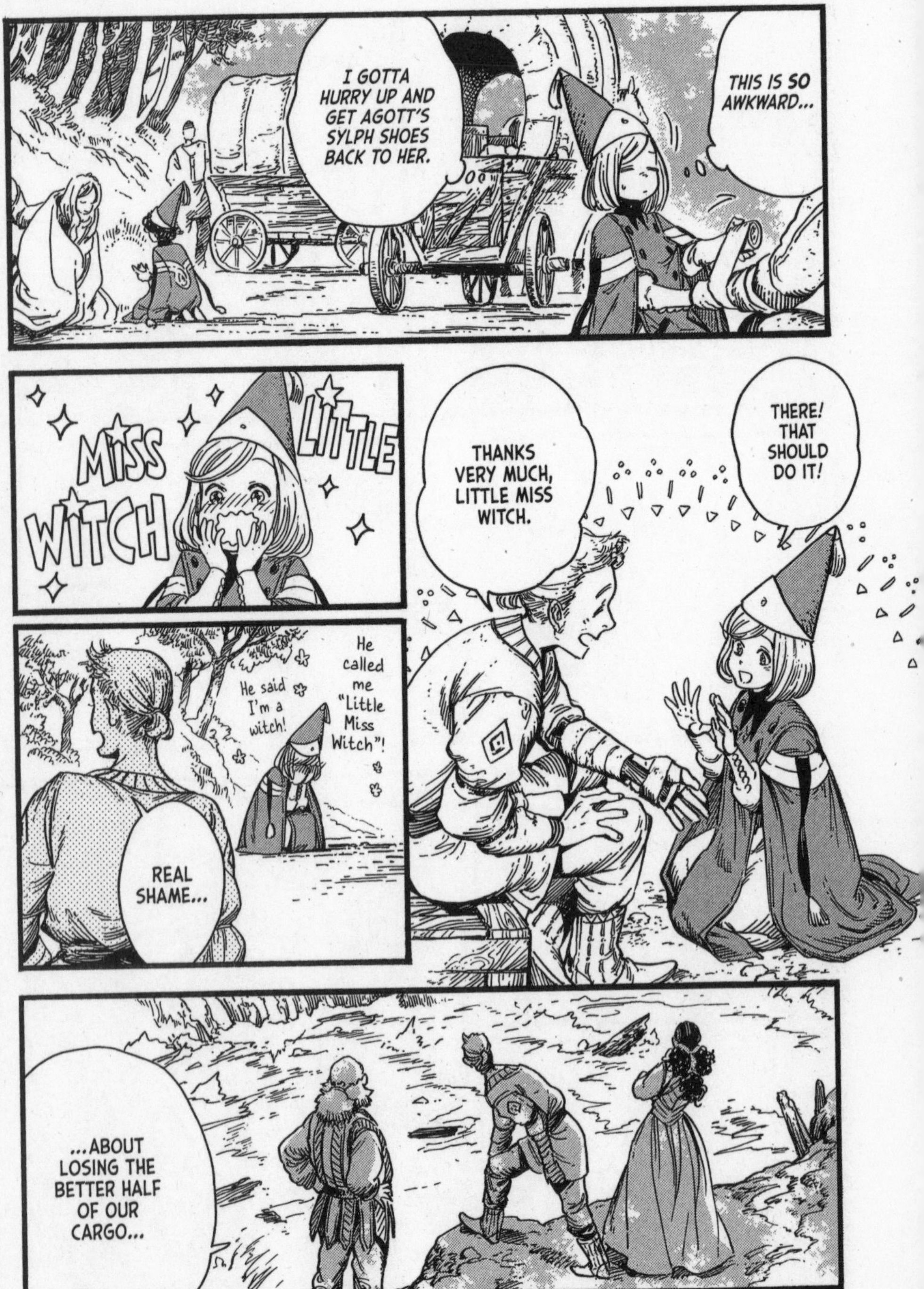
THIS IS SO AWKWARD...
I GOTTA HURRY UP AND GET AGOTT'S SYLPH SHOES BACK TO HER.
THERE! THAT SHOULD DO IT!
THANKS VERY MUCH, LITTLE MISS WITCH.
LITTLE MISS WITCH
He called me "Little Miss Witch"!
He said I'm a witch!
REAL SHAME...
...ABOUT LOSING THE BETTER HALF OF OUR CARGO...

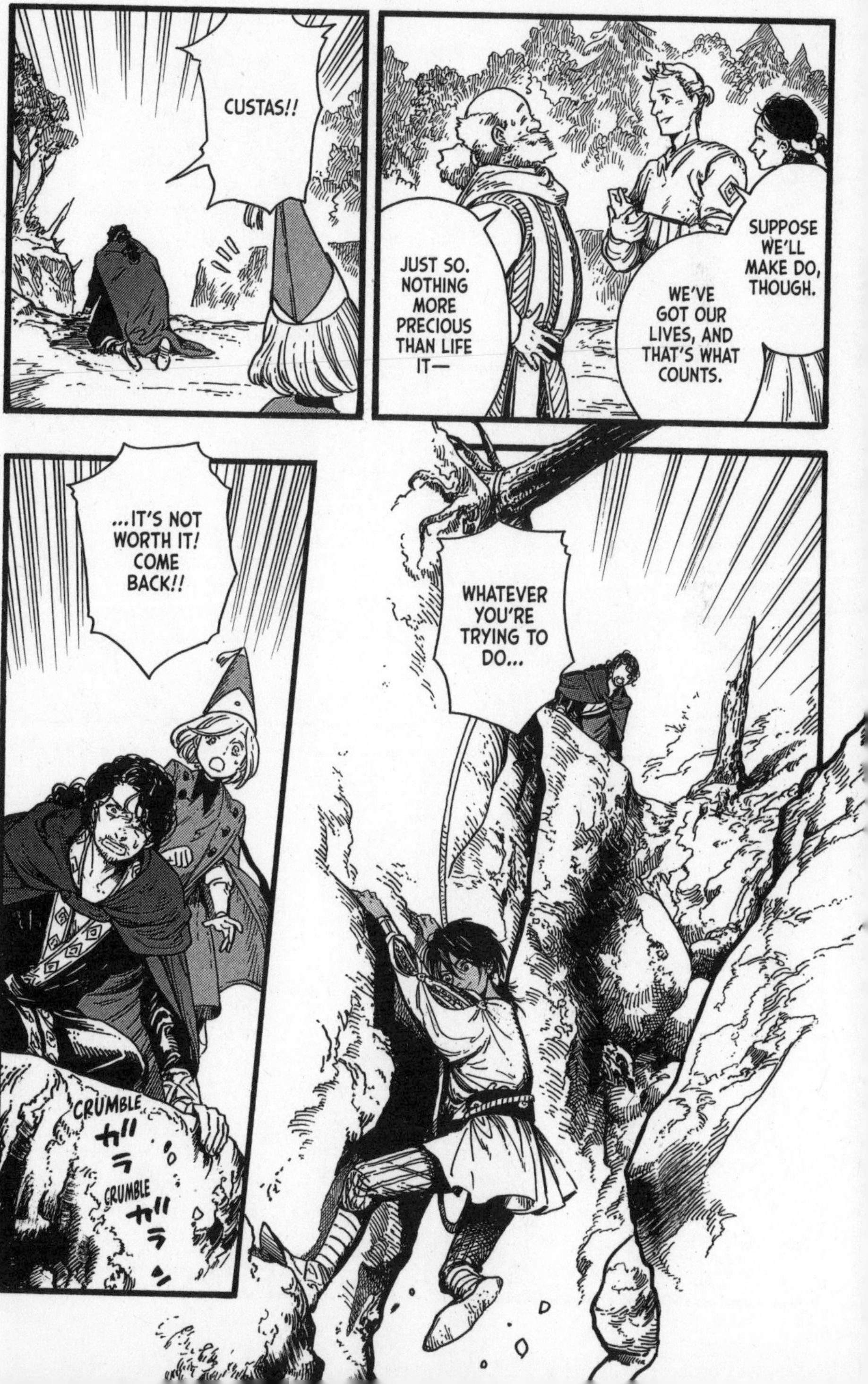
SUPPOSE WE'LL MAKE DO, THOUGH.
WE'VE GOT OUR LIVES, AND THAT'S WHAT COUNTS.
JUST SO. NOTHING MORE PRECIOUS THAN LIFE IT—
CUSTAS!!
WHATEVER YOU'RE TRYING TO DO...
...IT'S NOT WORTH IT! COME BACK!!
CRUMBLE
ガラ
CRUMBLE
ガラッ

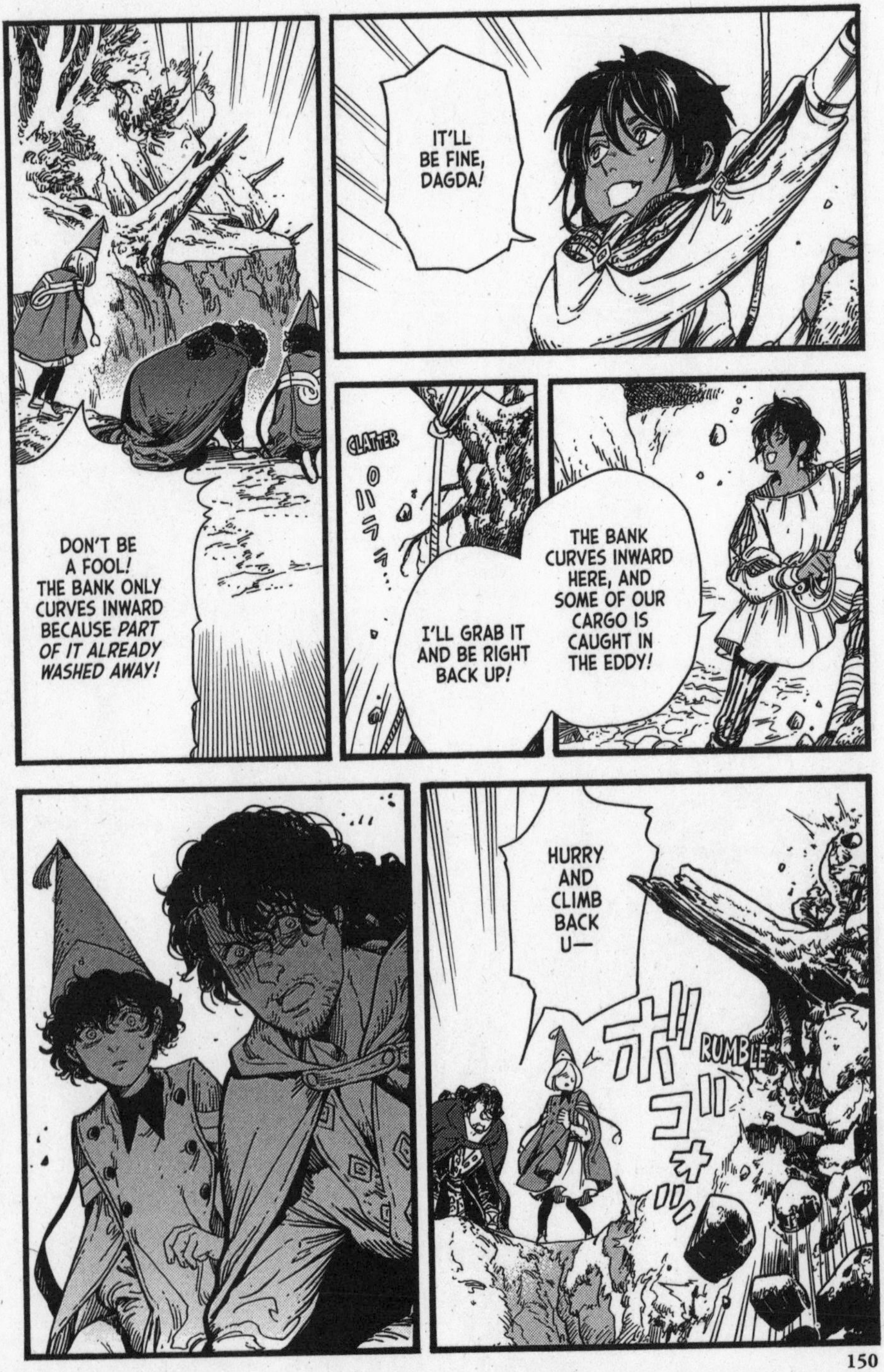
IT'LL BE FINE, DAGDA!
THE BANK CURVES INWARD HERE, AND SOME OF OUR CARGO IS CAUGHT IN THE EDDY!
CLATTER
I'LL GRAB IT AND BE RIGHT BACK UP!
DON'T BE A FOOL! THE BANK ONLY CURVES INWARD BECAUSE *PART OF IT ALREADY WASHED AWAY!*
HURRY AND CLIMB BACK U—
RUMBLE

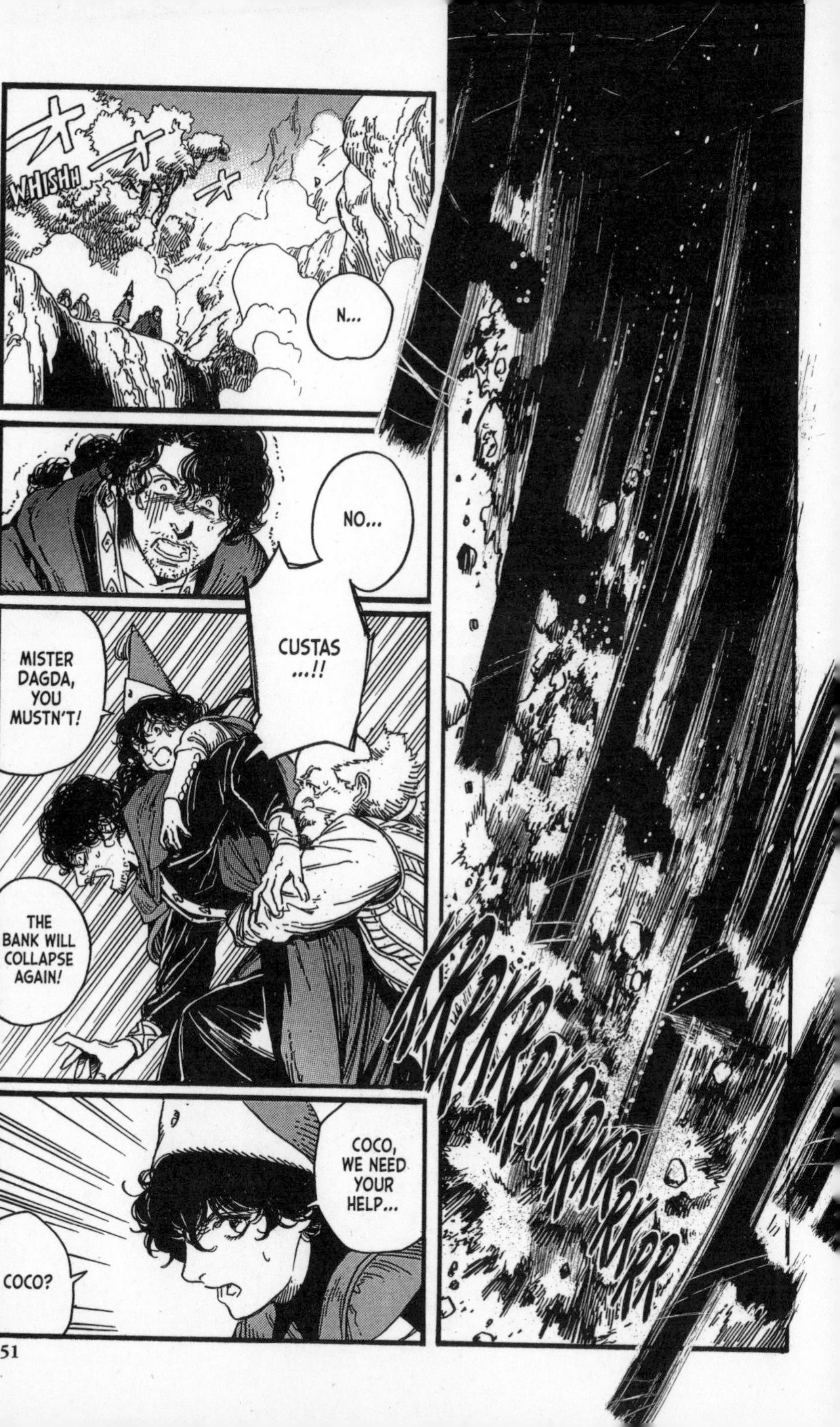
WHISHH
N...
NO...
CUSTAS ...!!
MISTER DAGDA, YOU MUSTN'T!
THE BANK WILL COLLAPSE AGAIN!
COCO, WE NEED YOUR HELP...
COCO?

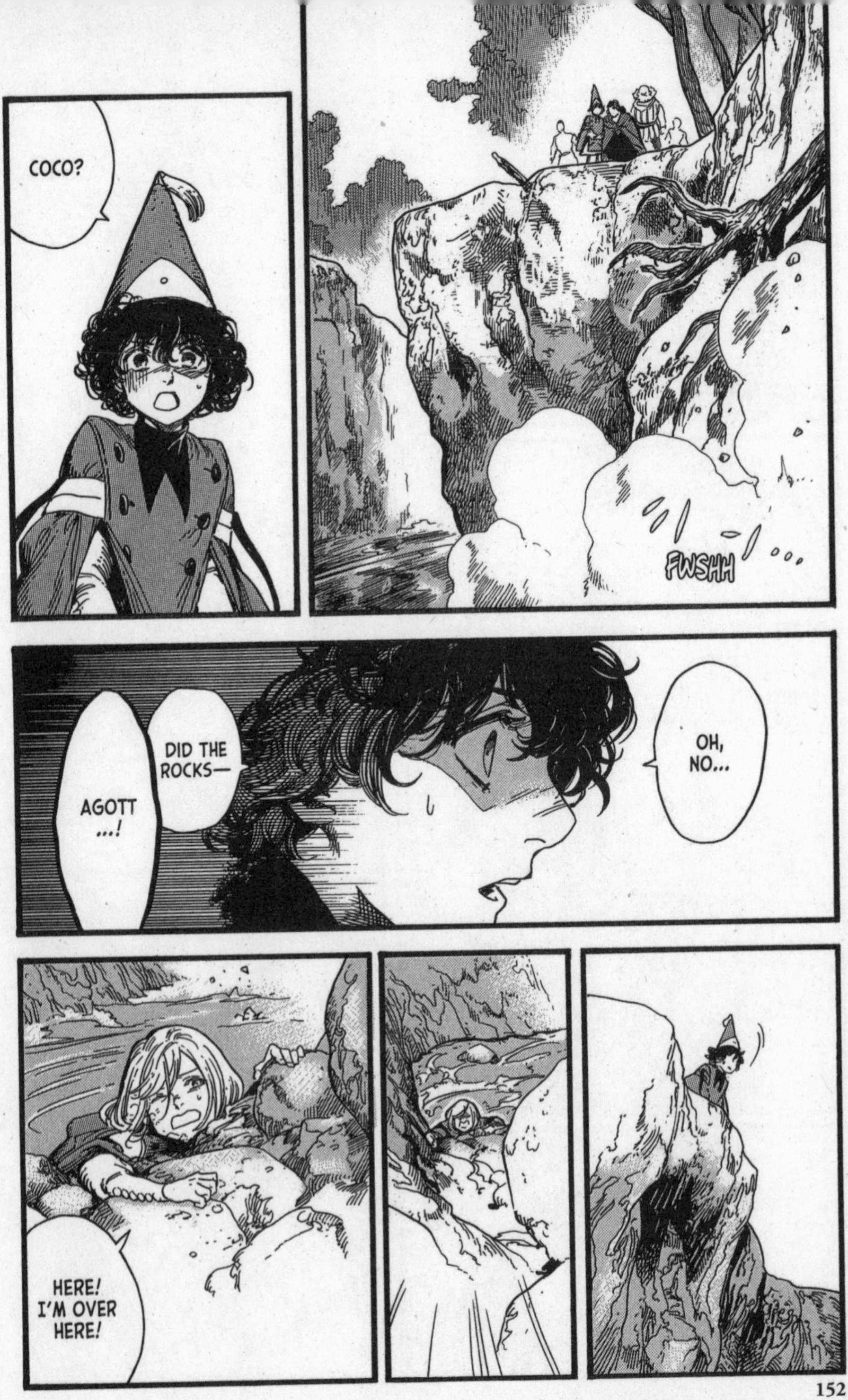
FWSHH
COCO?
OH, NO...
DID THE ROCKS—
AGOTT ...!
HERE! I'M OVER HERE!

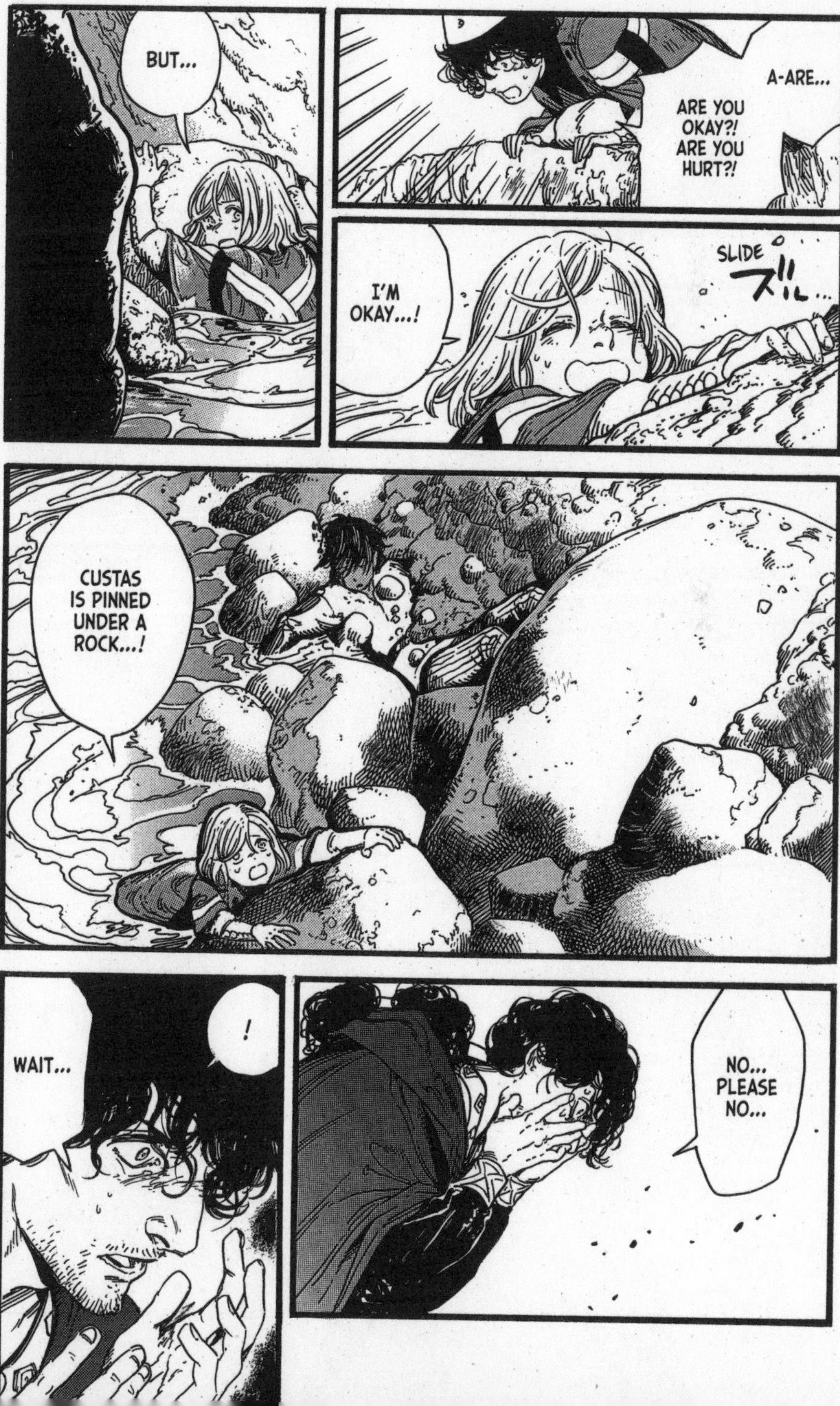
A-ARE...
ARE YOU OKAY?! ARE YOU HURT?!
SLIDE
ズル...
I'M OKAY...!
BUT...
CUSTAS IS PINNED UNDER A ROCK...!
NO... PLEASE NO...
!
WAIT...

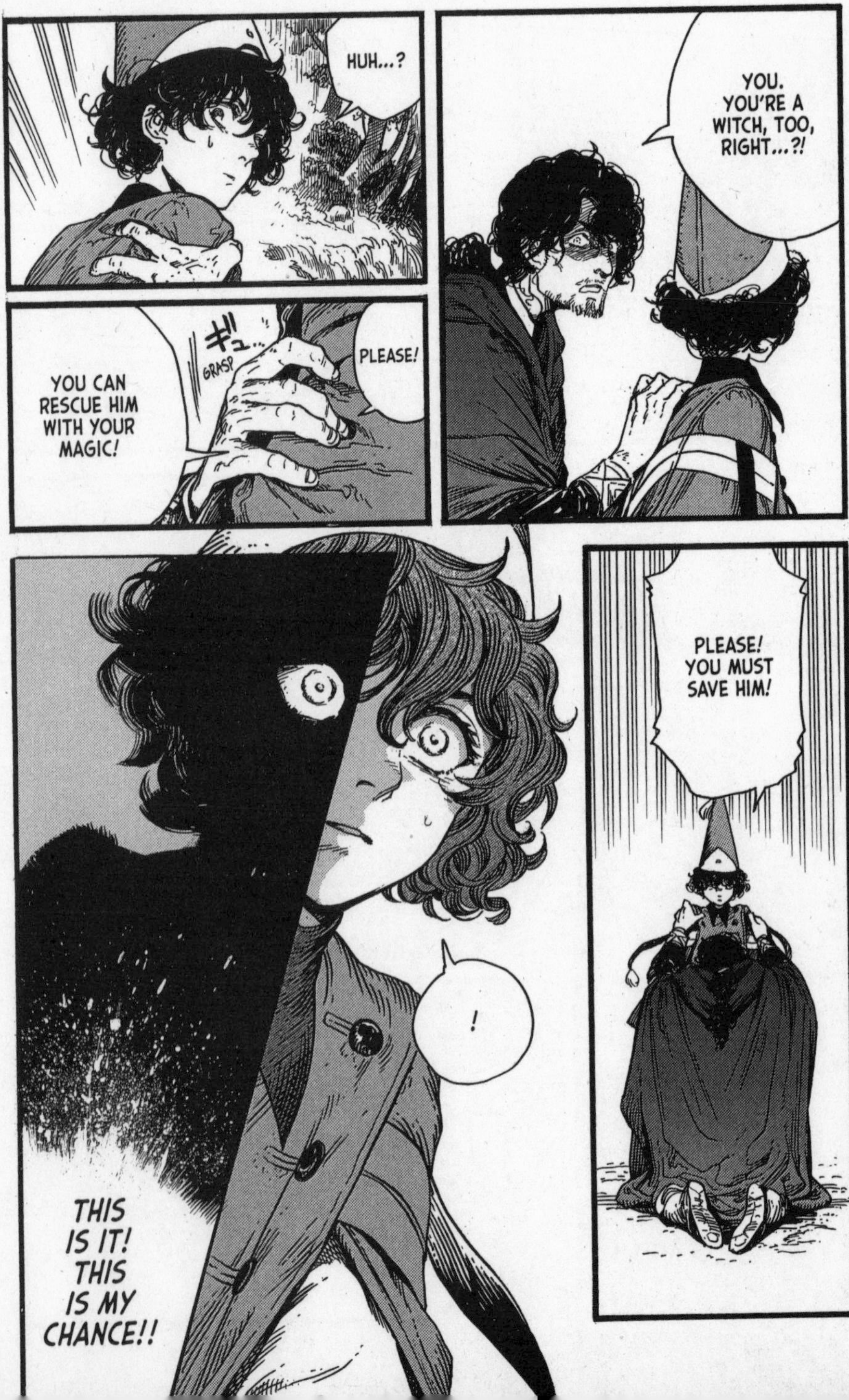
YOU. YOU'RE A WITCH, TOO, RIGHT...?!
HUH...?
PLEASE!
ギュ... GRASP
YOU CAN RESCUE HIM WITH YOUR MAGIC!
PLEASE! YOU MUST SAVE HIM!
!
THIS IS IT! THIS IS MY CHANCE!!

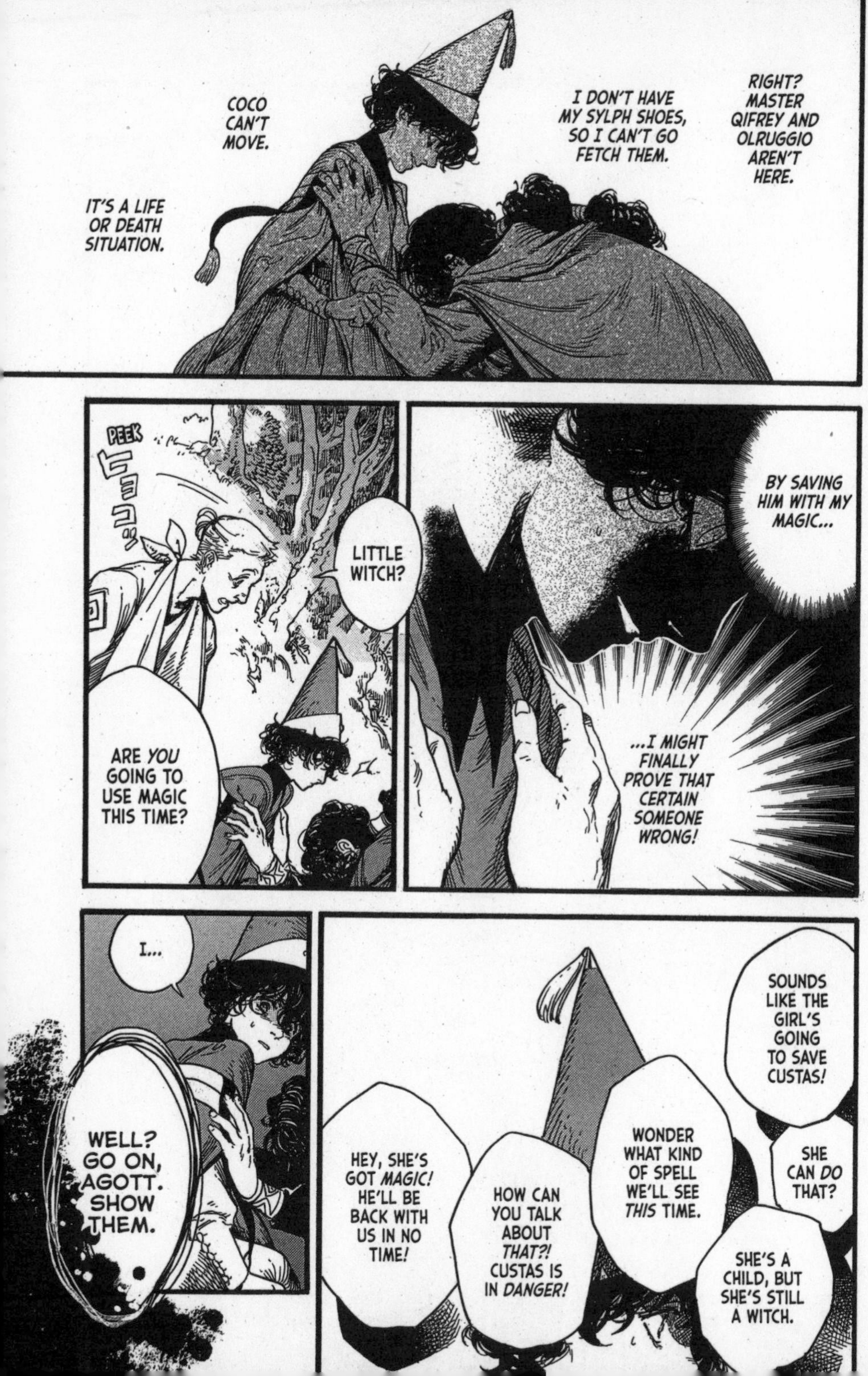
RIGHT? MASTER QIFREY AND OLRUGGIO AREN'T HERE.
I DON'T HAVE MY SYLPH SHOES, SO I CAN'T GO FETCH THEM.
COCO CAN'T MOVE.
IT'S A LIFE OR DEATH SITUATION.
BY SAVING HIM WITH MY MAGIC...
...I MIGHT FINALLY PROVE THAT CERTAIN SOMEONE WRONG!
LITTLE WITCH?
PEEK
ARE *YOU* GOING TO USE MAGIC THIS TIME?
SOUNDS LIKE THE GIRL'S GOING TO SAVE CUSTAS!
SHE CAN *DO* THAT?
WONDER WHAT KIND OF SPELL WE'LL SEE *THIS* TIME.
SHE'S A CHILD, BUT SHE'S STILL A WITCH.
HOW CAN YOU TALK ABOUT *THAT?!* CUSTAS IS IN *DANGER!*
HEY, SHE'S GOT *MAGIC!* HE'LL BE BACK WITH US IN NO TIME!
I...
WELL? GO ON, AGOTT. SHOW THEM.

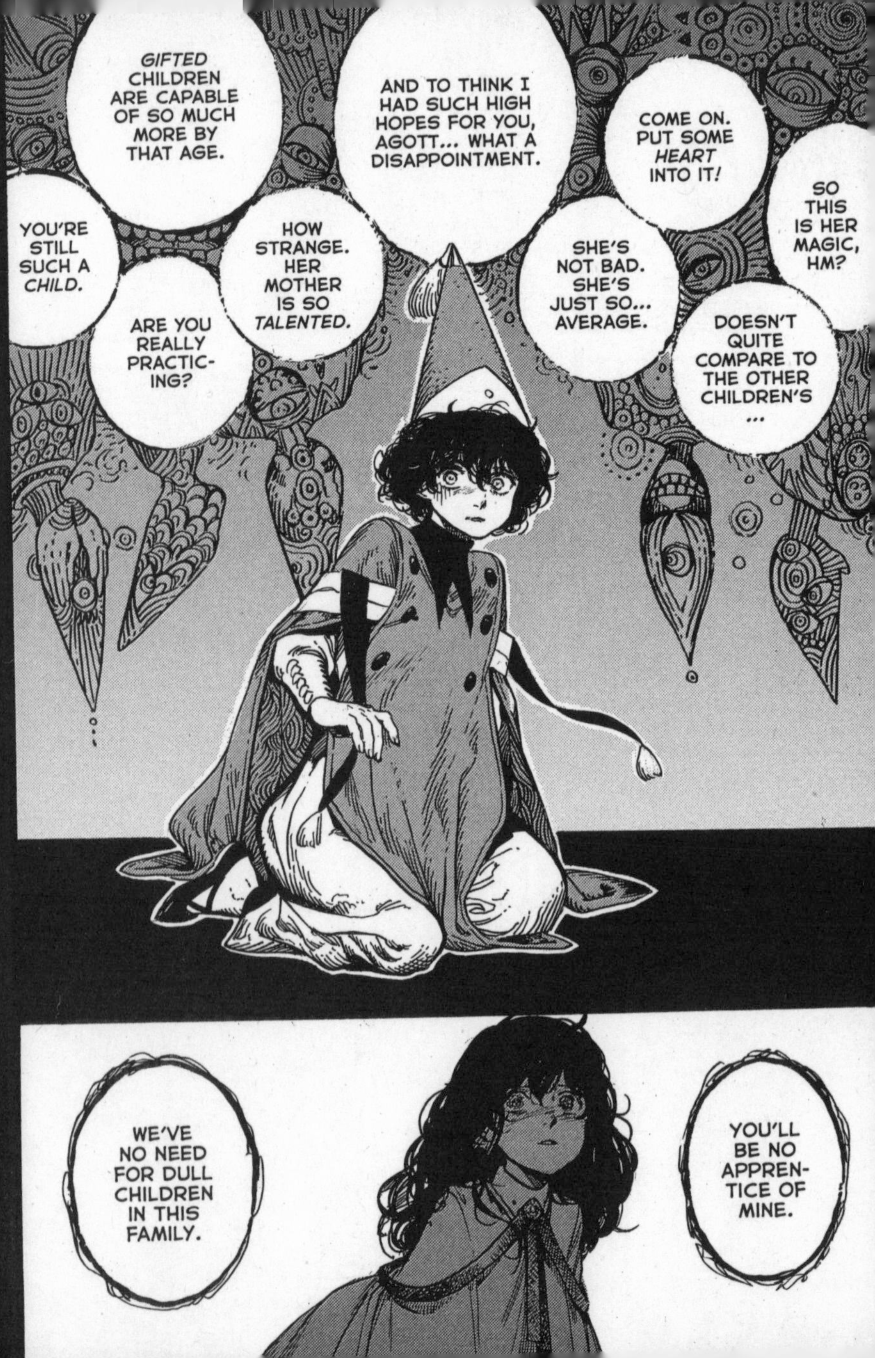
COME ON. PUT SOME *HEART* INTO IT!
SO THIS IS HER MAGIC, HM?
AND TO THINK I HAD SUCH HIGH HOPES FOR YOU, AGOTT... WHAT A DISAPPOINTMENT.
GIFTED CHILDREN ARE CAPABLE OF SO MUCH MORE BY THAT AGE.
DOESN'T QUITE COMPARE TO THE OTHER CHILDREN'S ...
SHE'S NOT BAD. SHE'S JUST SO... AVERAGE.
HOW STRANGE. HER MOTHER IS SO *TALENTED*.
YOU'RE STILL SUCH A *CHILD*.
ARE YOU REALLY PRACTIC-ING?
YOU'LL BE NO APPREN-TICE OF MINE.
WE'VE NO NEED FOR DULL CHILDREN IN THIS FAMILY.

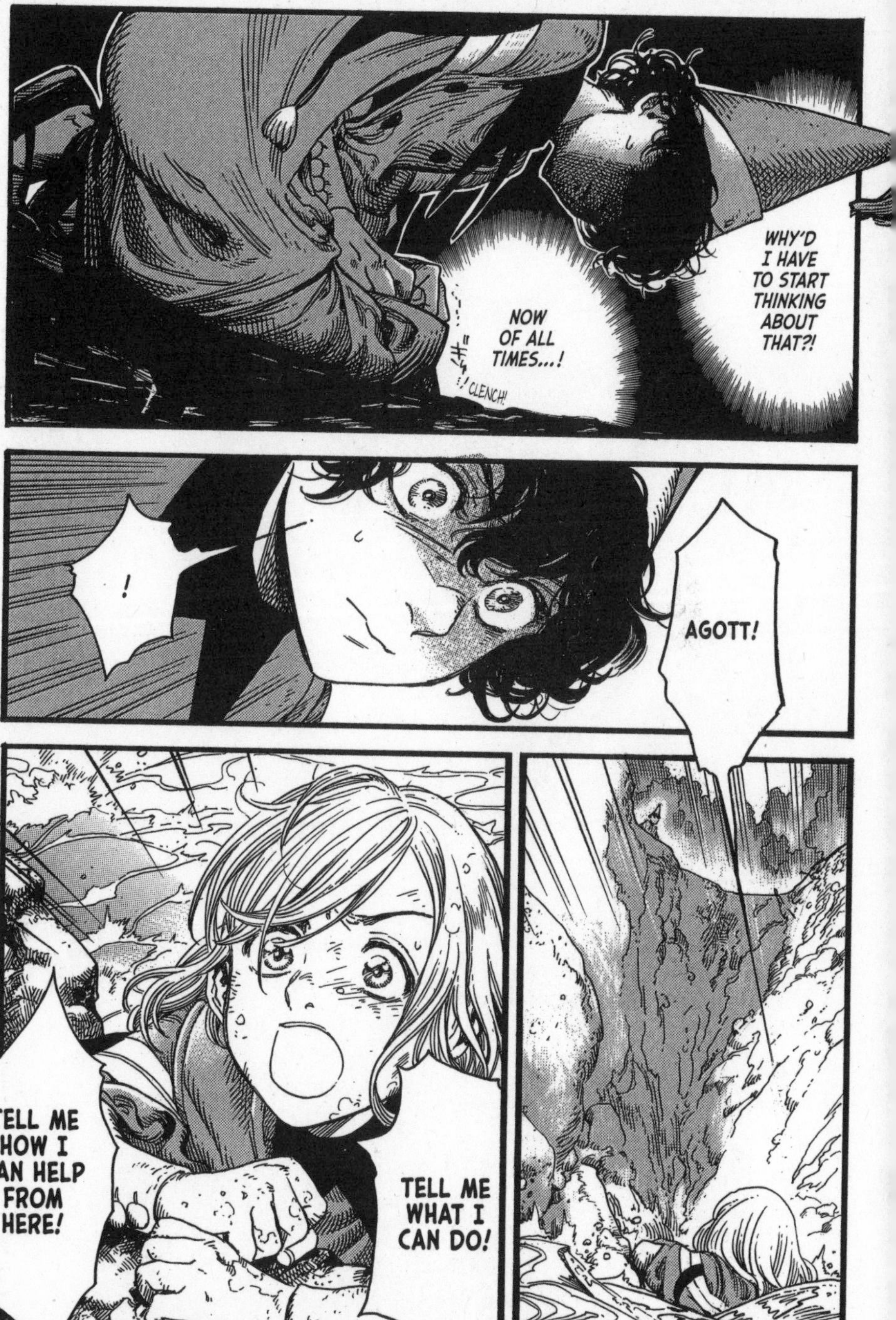
WHY'D I HAVE TO START THINKING ABOUT THAT?!
NOW OF ALL TIMES...!
CLENCH!
AGOTT!
!
TELL ME WHAT I CAN DO!
TELL ME HOW I CAN HELP FROM HERE!

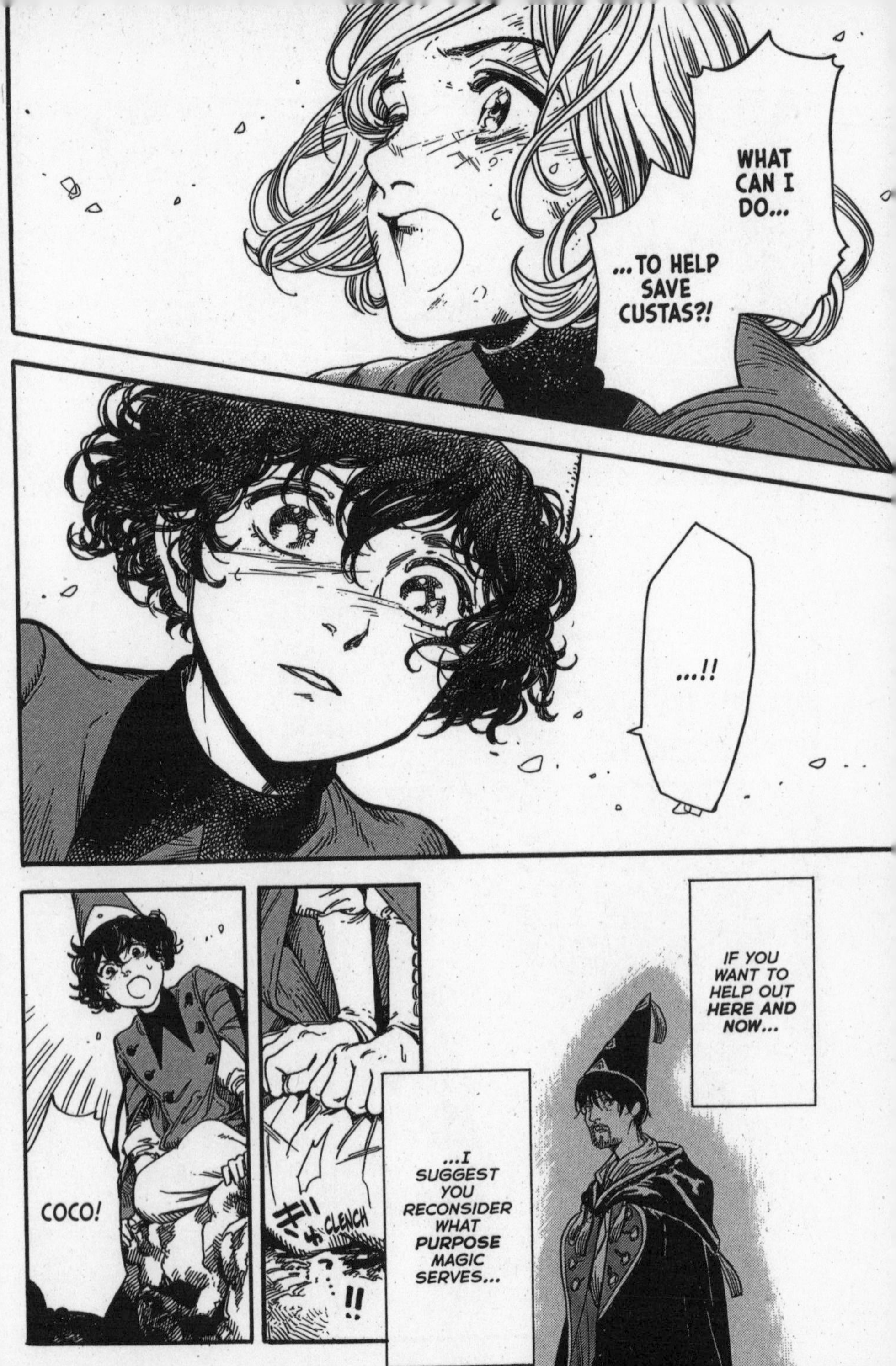
WHAT CAN I DO...
...TO HELP SAVE CUSTAS?!
...!!
IF YOU WANT TO HELP OUT HERE AND NOW...
...I SUGGEST YOU RECONSIDER WHAT PURPOSE MAGIC SERVES...
ぎゅ CLENCH
!!
COCO!

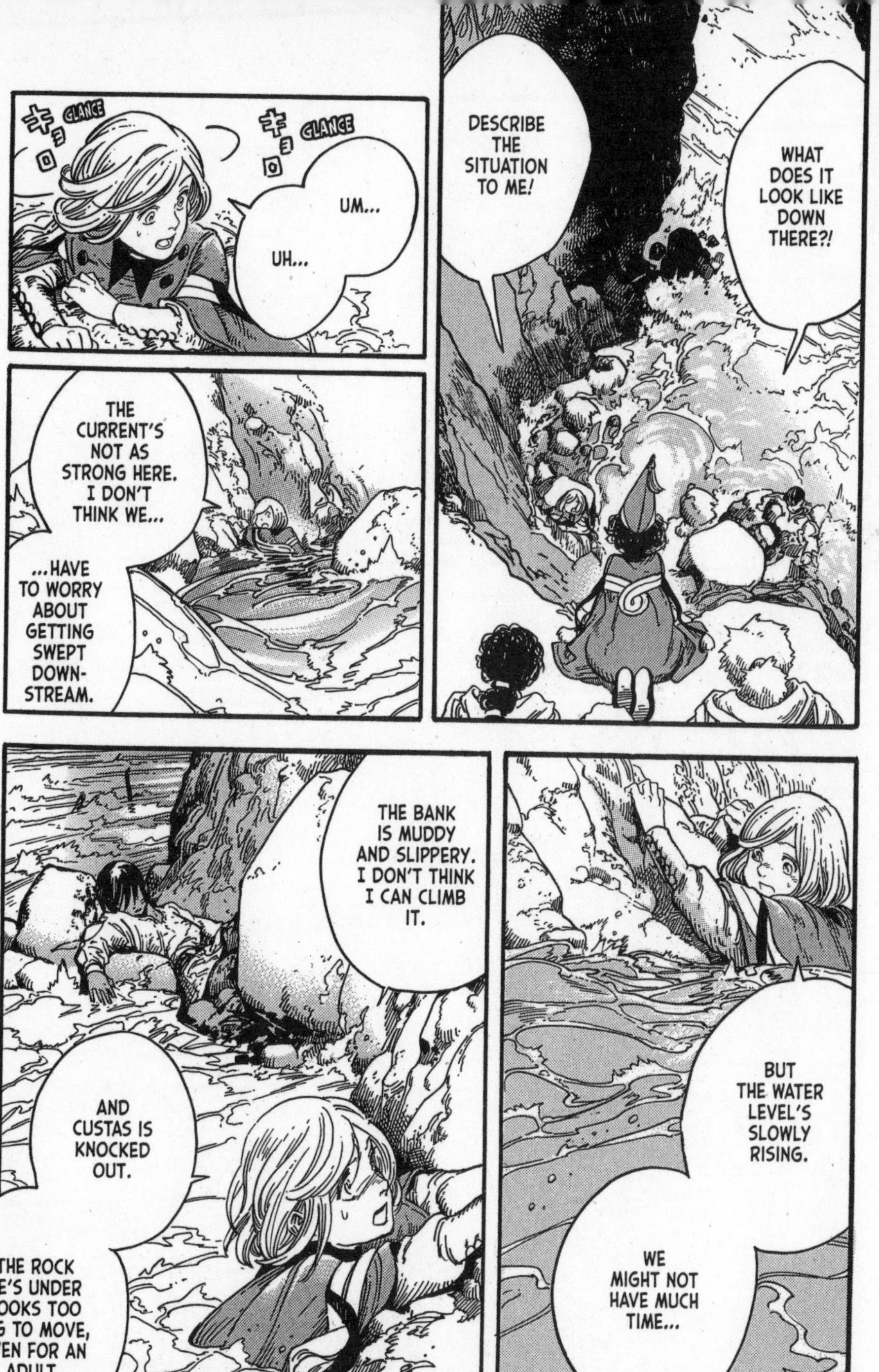
WHAT DOES IT LOOK LIKE DOWN THERE?!
DESCRIBE THE SITUATION TO ME!
キョロ GLANCE
キョロ GLANCE
UM...
UH...
THE CURRENT'S NOT AS STRONG HERE. I DON'T THINK WE...
...HAVE TO WORRY ABOUT GETTING SWEPT DOWN-STREAM.
BUT THE WATER LEVEL'S SLOWLY RISING.
WE MIGHT NOT HAVE MUCH TIME...
THE BANK IS MUDDY AND SLIPPERY. I DON'T THINK I CAN CLIMB IT.
AND CUSTAS IS KNOCKED OUT.
THE ROCK HE'S UNDER LOOKS TOO BIG TO MOVE, EVEN FOR AN ADULT.

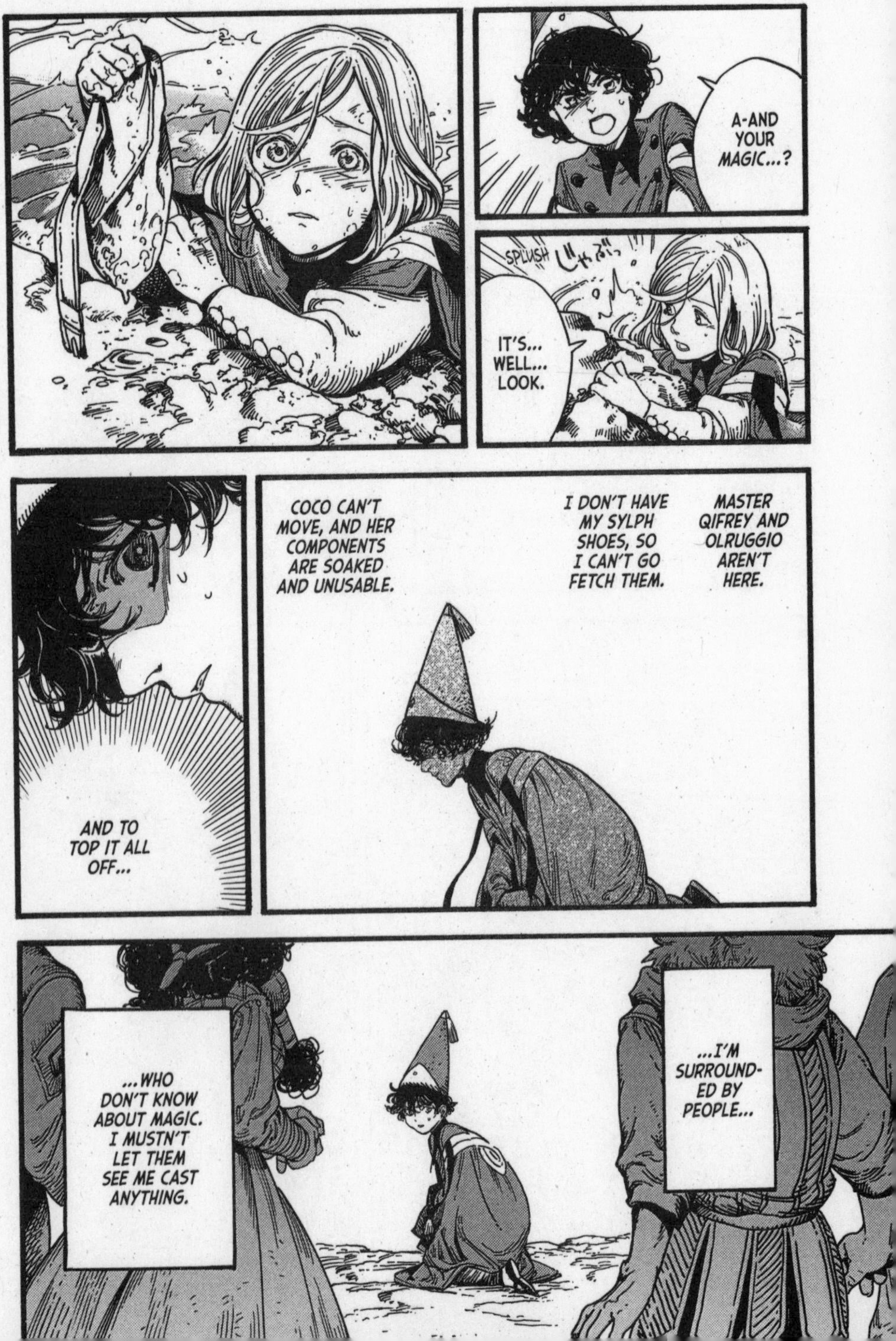
A-AND YOUR MAGIC...?
SPLUSH じゃぶっ
IT'S... WELL... LOOK.
MASTER QIFREY AND OLRUGGIO AREN'T HERE.
I DON'T HAVE MY SYLPH SHOES, SO I CAN'T GO FETCH THEM.
COCO CAN'T MOVE, AND HER COMPONENTS ARE SOAKED AND UNUSABLE.
AND TO TOP IT ALL OFF...
...I'M SURROUND-ED BY PEOPLE...
...WHO DON'T KNOW ABOUT MAGIC. I MUSTN'T LET THEM SEE ME CAST ANYTHING.

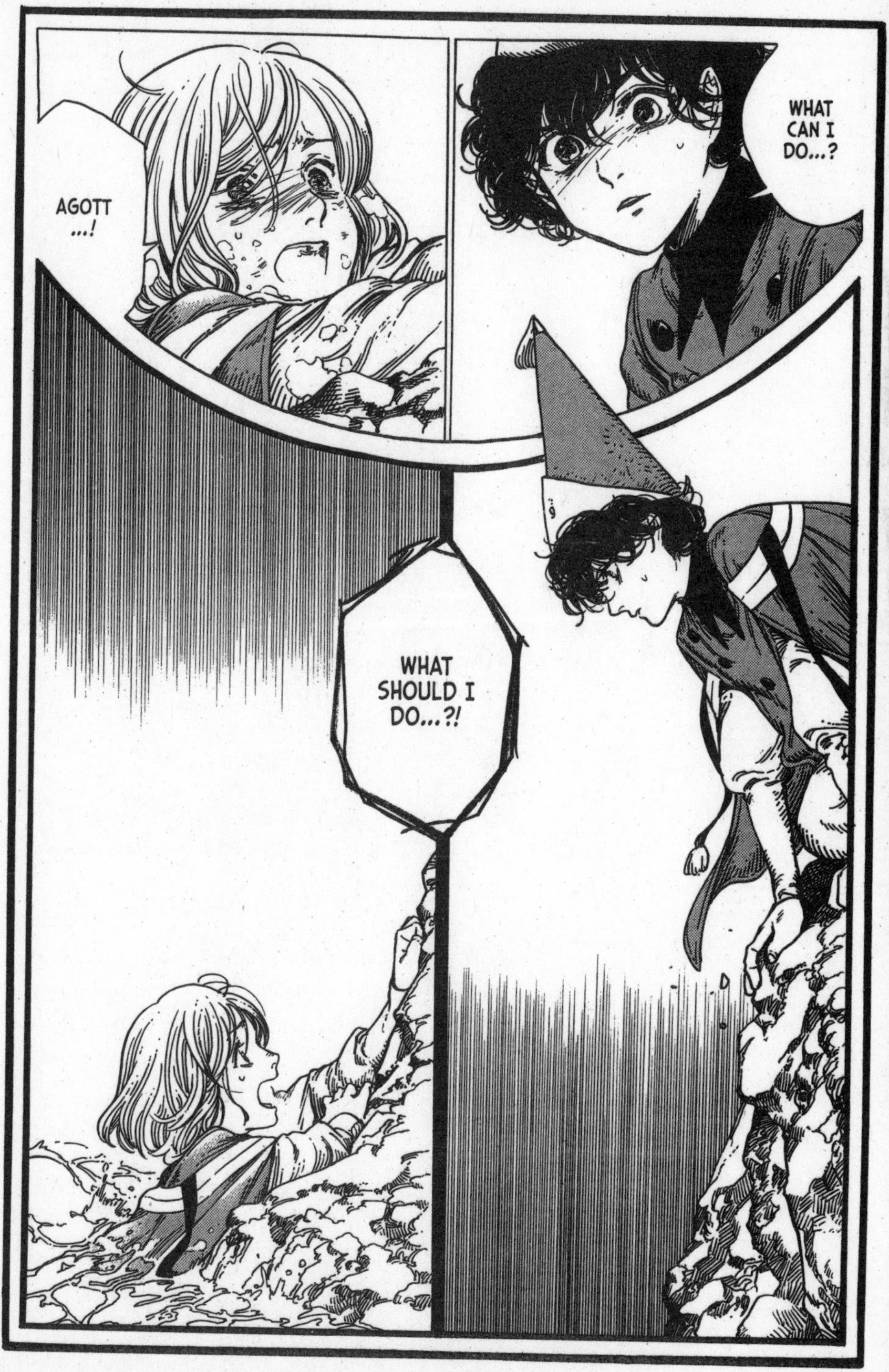
WHAT CAN I DO...?
AGOTT ...!
WHAT SHOULD I DO...?!

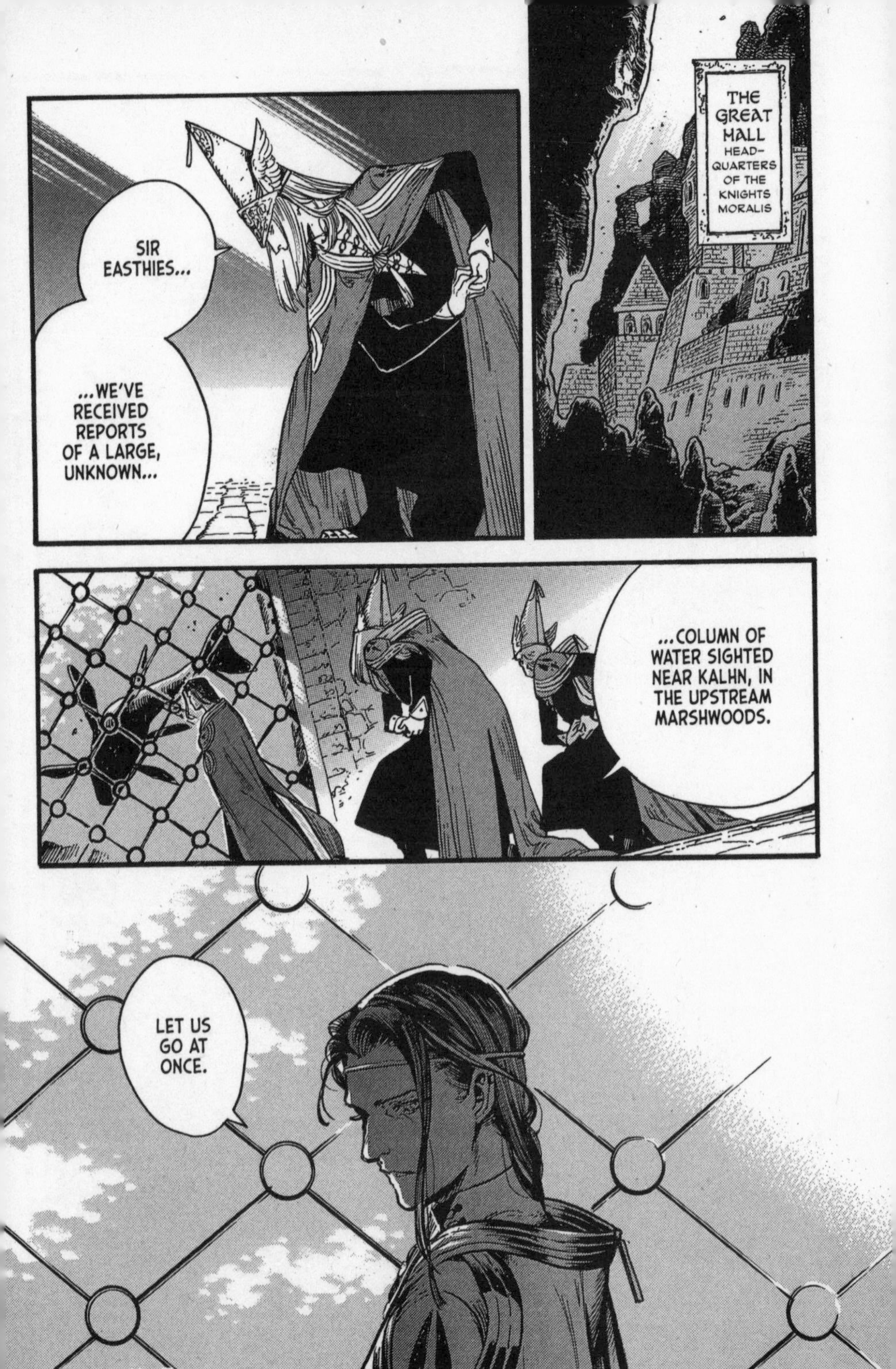
THE GREAT HALL
HEAD-QUARTERS OF THE KNIGHTS MORALIS
SIR EASTHIES...
...WE'VE RECEIVED REPORTS OF A LARGE, UNKNOWN...
...COLUMN OF WATER SIGHTED NEAR KALHN, IN THE UPSTREAM MARSHWOODS.
LET US GO AT ONCE.

CHAPTER 10 ♦ END

Witch Hat Atelier

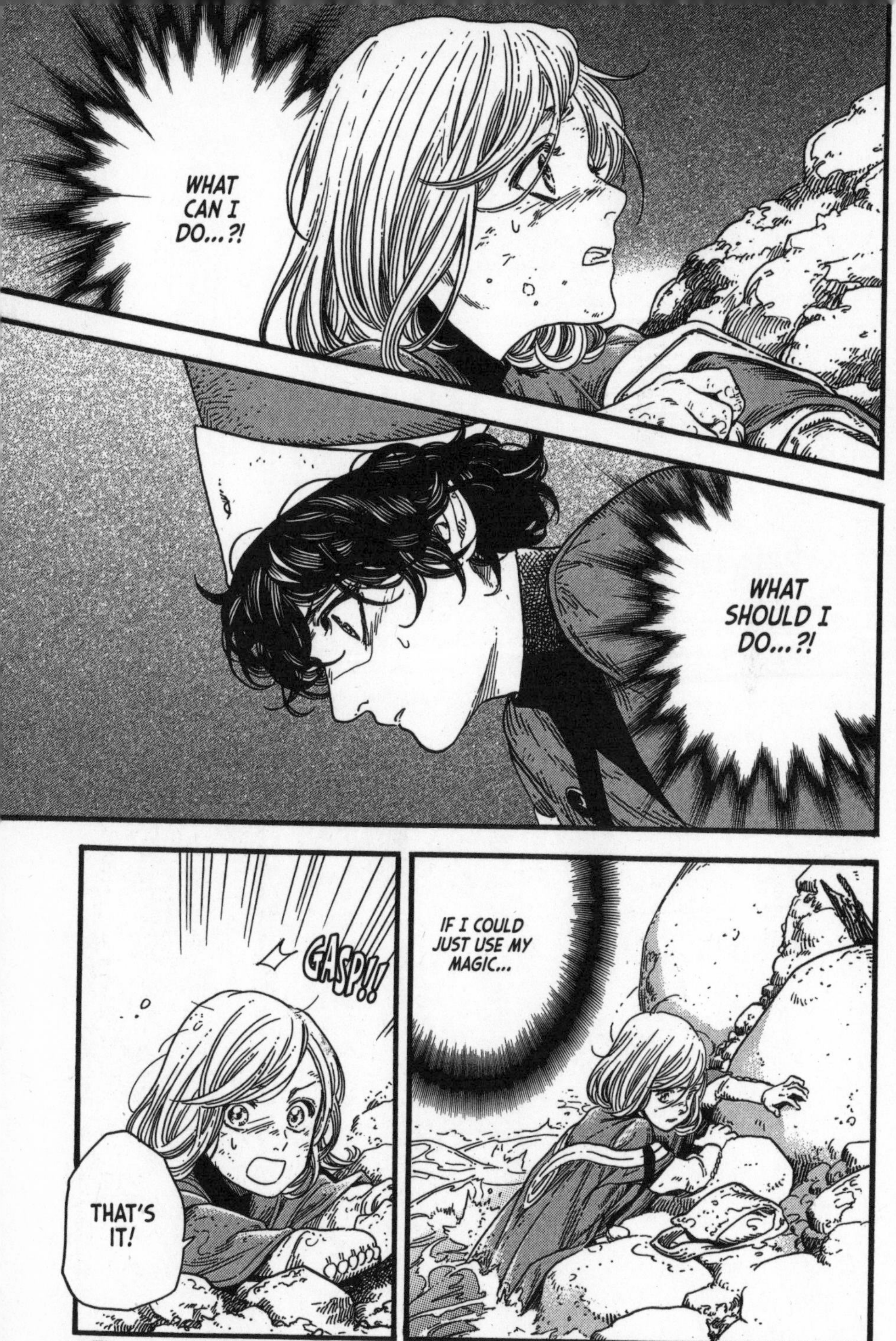
WHAT CAN I DO...?!
WHAT SHOULD I DO...?!
IF I COULD JUST USE MY MAGIC...
GASP!!
THAT'S IT!

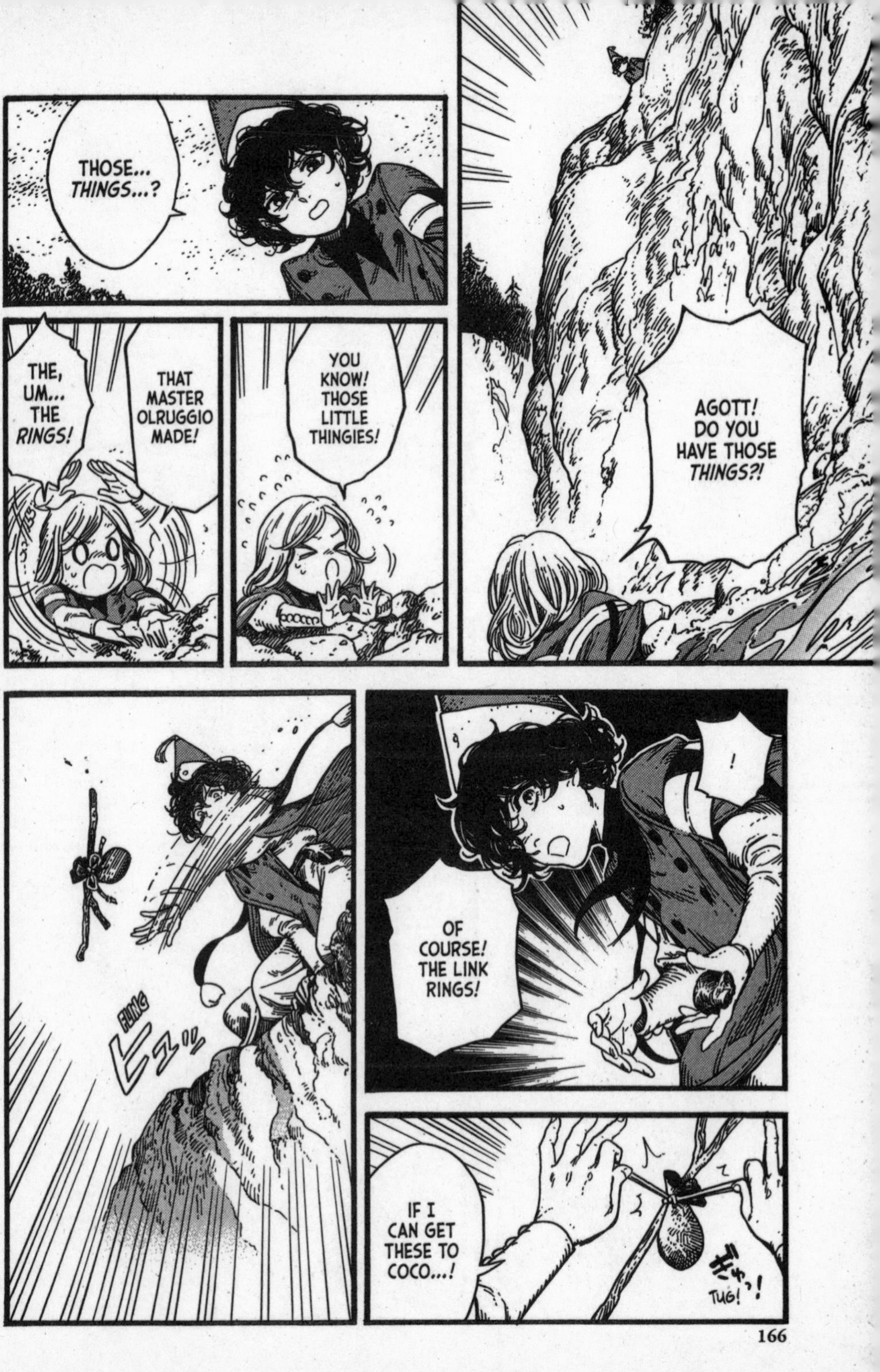
AGOTT! DO YOU HAVE THOSE *THINGS?!*
THOSE... *THINGS...?*
YOU KNOW! THOSE LITTLE THINGIES!
THAT MASTER OLRUGGIO MADE!
THE, UM... THE *RINGS!*
!
OF COURSE! THE LINK RINGS!
IF I CAN GET THESE TO COCO...!
TUG!
FLING

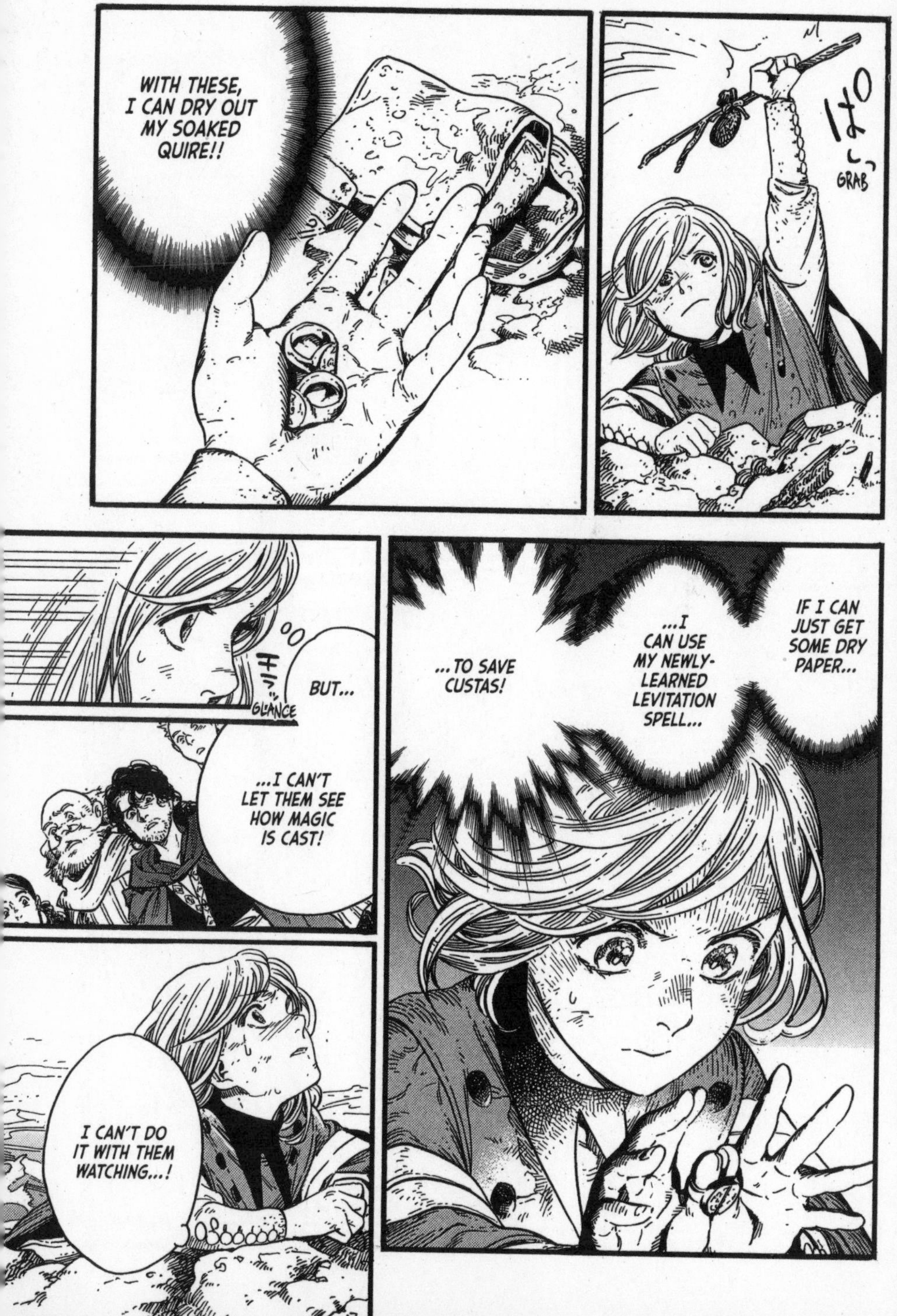
ぱしっ
GRAB
WITH THESE, I CAN DRY OUT MY SOAKED QUIRE!!
IF I CAN JUST GET SOME DRY PAPER...
...I CAN USE MY NEWLY-LEARNED LEVITATION SPELL...
...TO SAVE CUSTAS!
GLANCE
BUT...
...I CAN'T LET THEM SEE HOW MAGIC IS CAST!
I CAN'T DO IT WITH THEM WATCHING...!

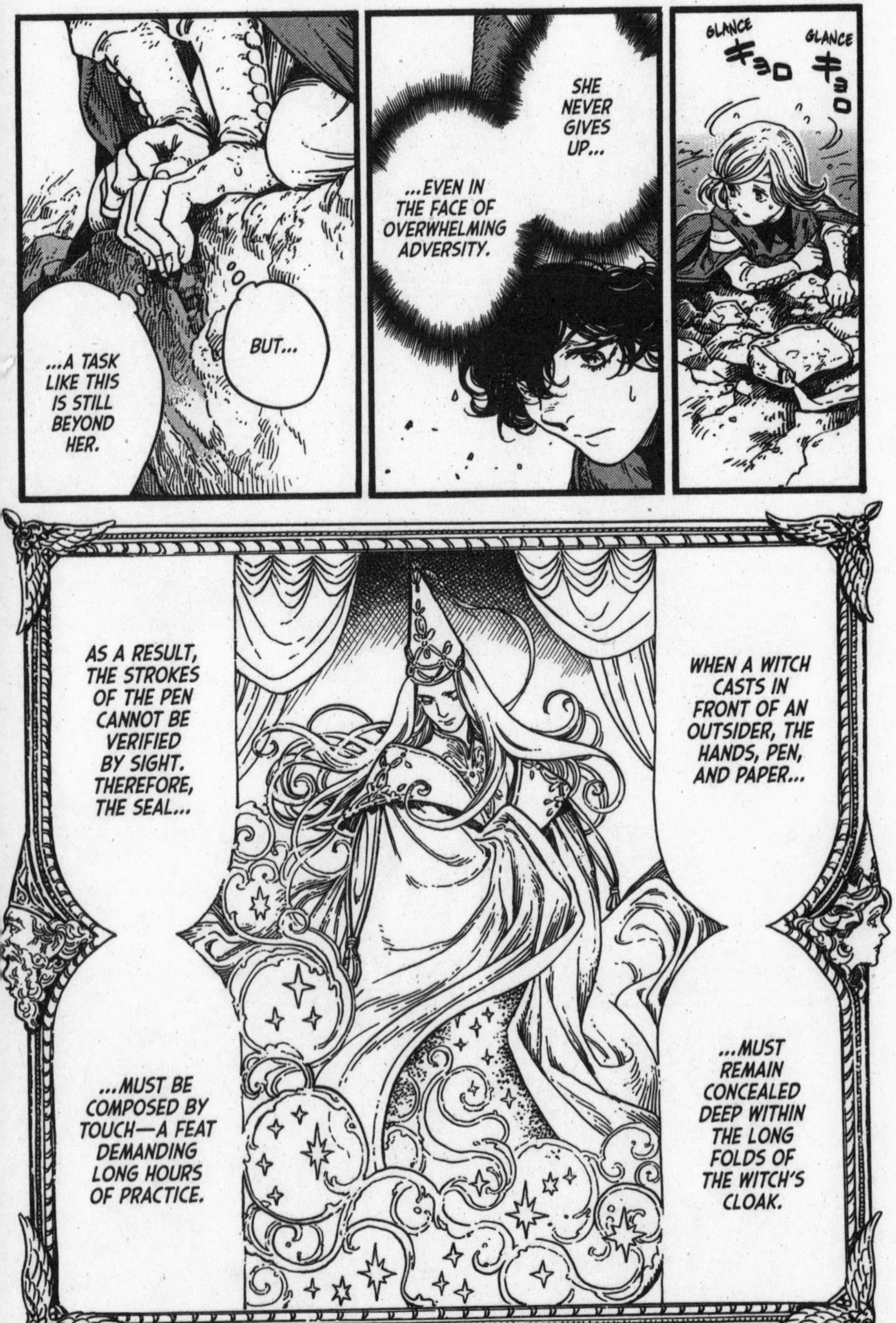
GLANCE
キョロ
GLANCE
キョロ
SHE NEVER GIVES UP...
...EVEN IN THE FACE OF OVERWHELMING ADVERSITY.
BUT...
...A TASK LIKE THIS IS STILL BEYOND HER.
WHEN A WITCH CASTS IN FRONT OF AN OUTSIDER, THE HANDS, PEN, AND PAPER...
...MUST REMAIN CONCEALED DEEP WITHIN THE LONG FOLDS OF THE WITCH'S CLOAK.
AS A RESULT, THE STROKES OF THE PEN CANNOT BE VERIFIED BY SIGHT. THEREFORE, THE SEAL...
...MUST BE COMPOSED BY TOUCH—A FEAT DEMANDING LONG HOURS OF PRACTICE.

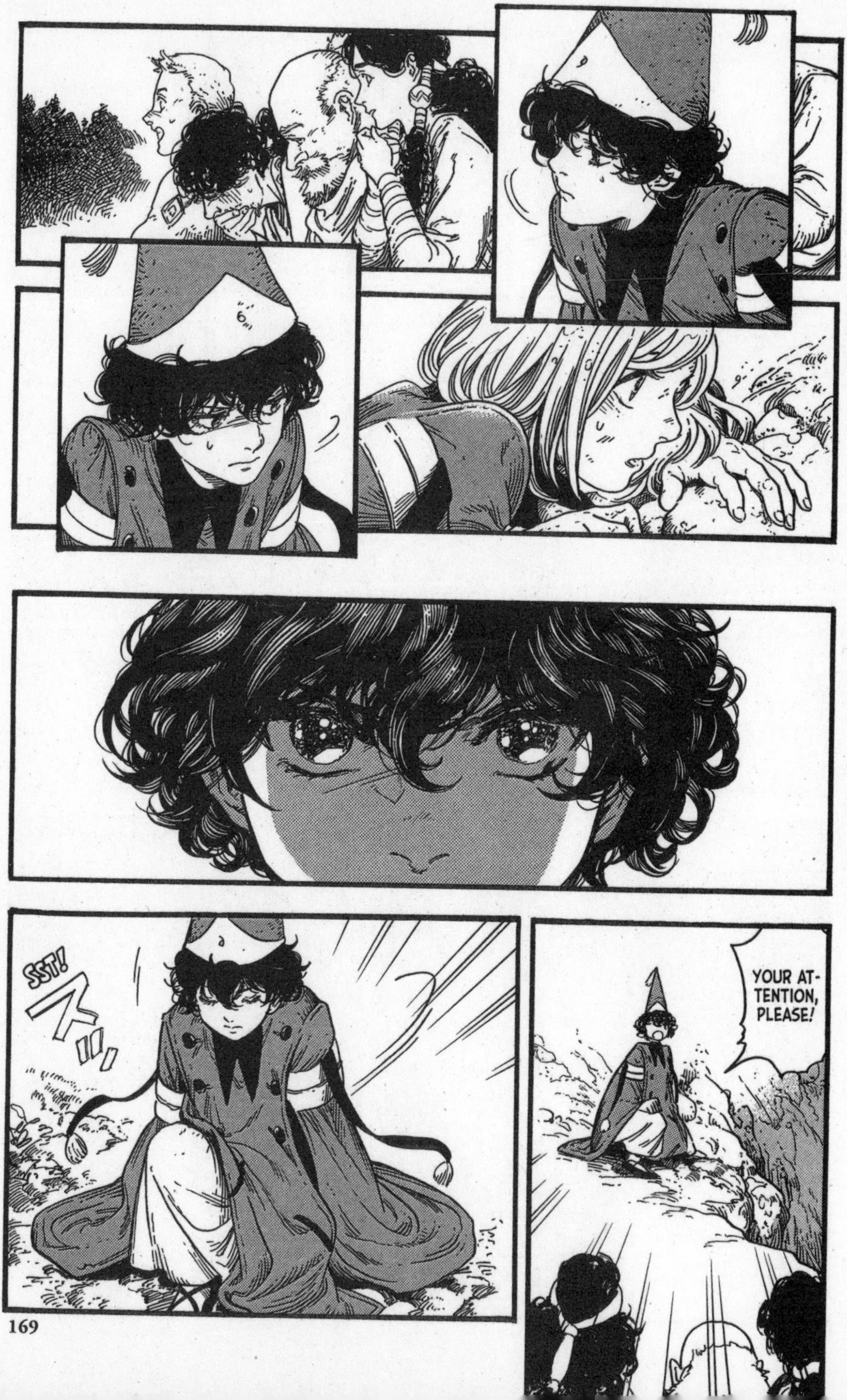
YOUR AT-
TENTION,
PLEASE!
SST!

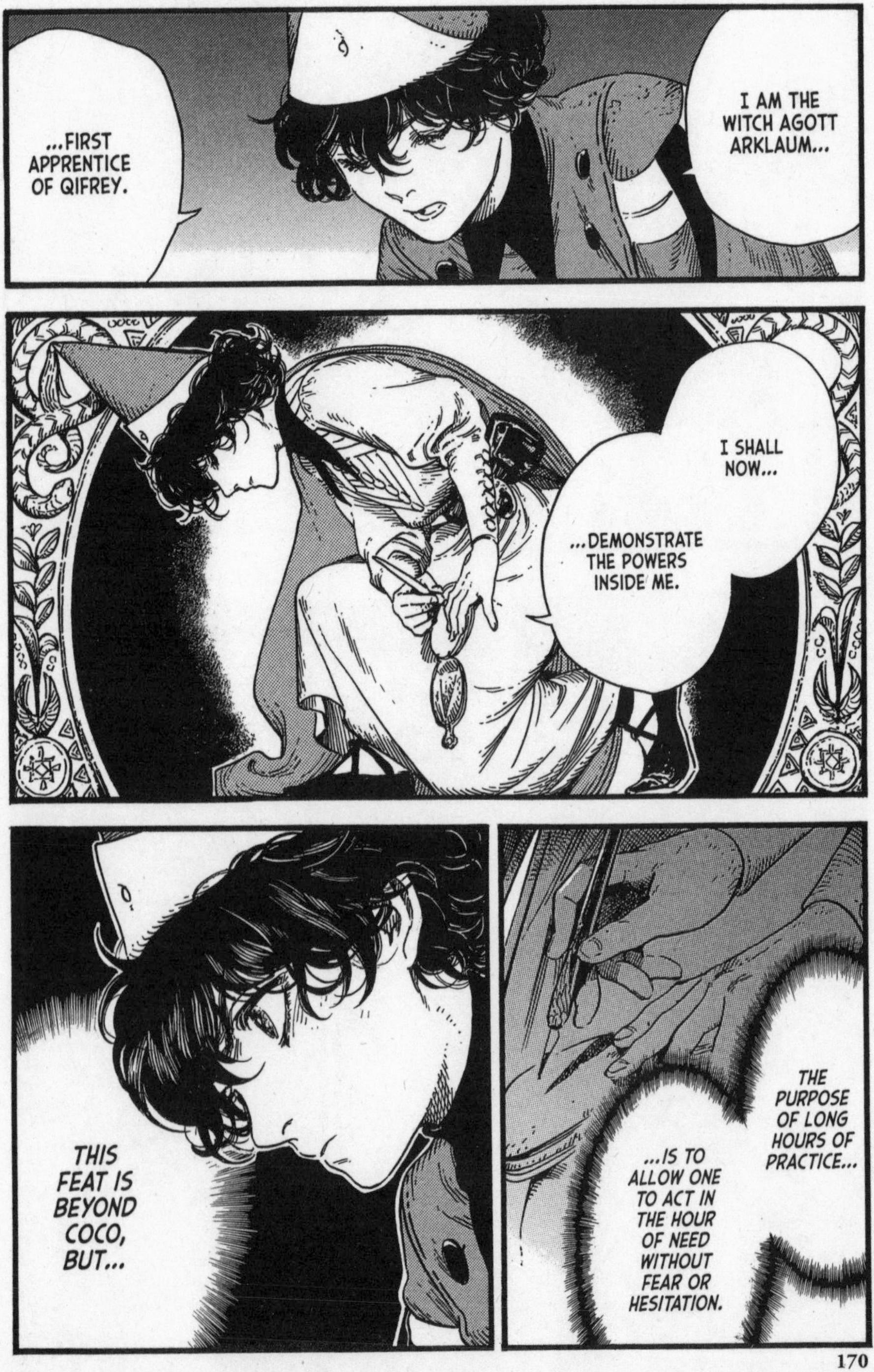
I AM THE WITCH AGOTT ARKLAUM...
...FIRST APPRENTICE OF QIFREY.
I SHALL NOW...
...DEMONSTRATE THE POWERS INSIDE ME.
THE PURPOSE OF LONG HOURS OF PRACTICE...
...IS TO ALLOW ONE TO ACT IN THE HOUR OF NEED WITHOUT FEAR OR HESITATION.
THIS FEAT IS BEYOND COCO, BUT...

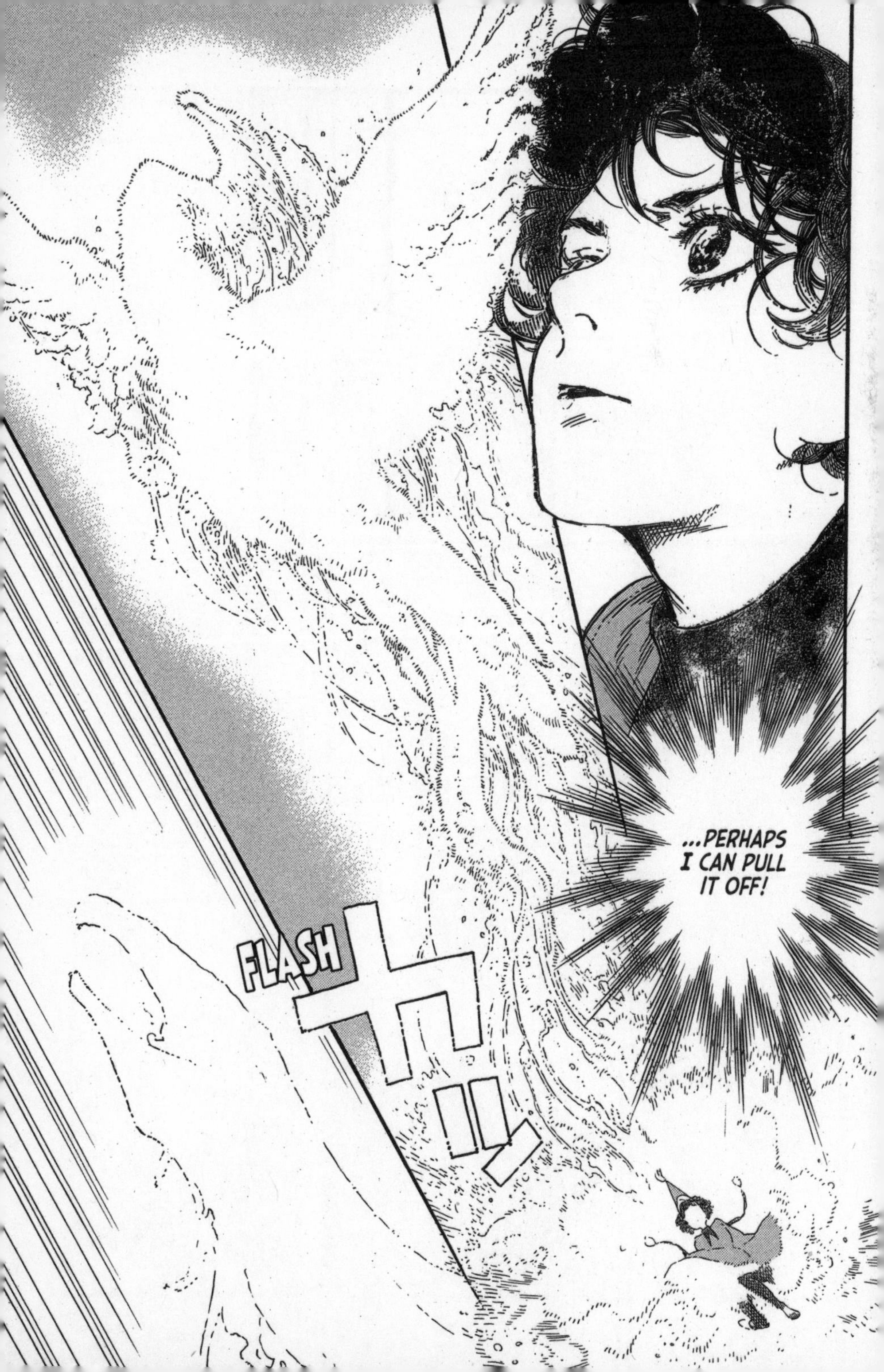
...PERHAPS I CAN PULL IT OFF!
FLASH

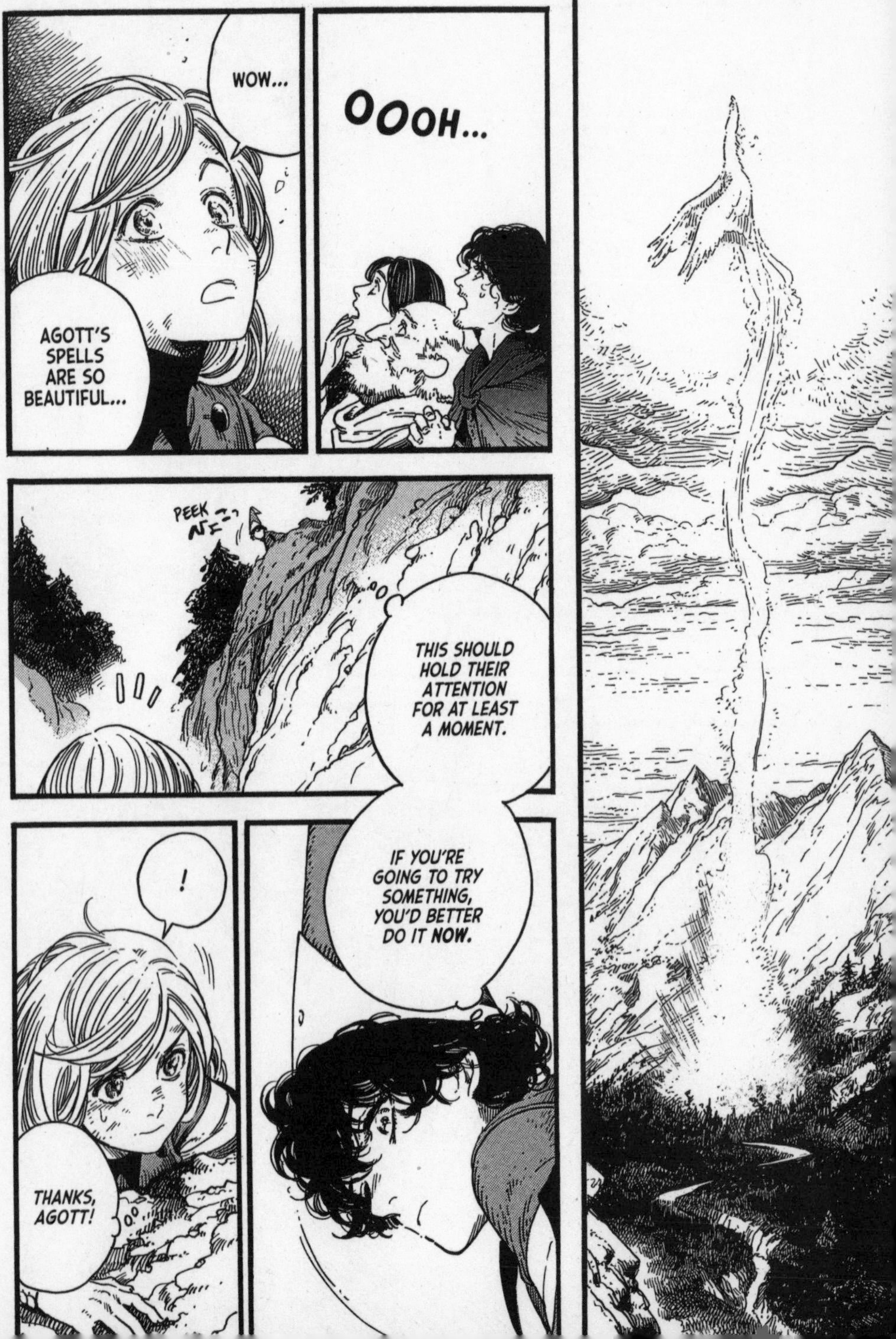
OOOH...
WOW...
AGOTT'S SPELLS ARE SO BEAUTIFUL...
PEEK
THIS SHOULD HOLD THEIR ATTENTION FOR AT LEAST A MOMENT.
IF YOU'RE GOING TO TRY SOMETHING, YOU'D BETTER DO IT NOW.
!
THANKS, AGOTT!

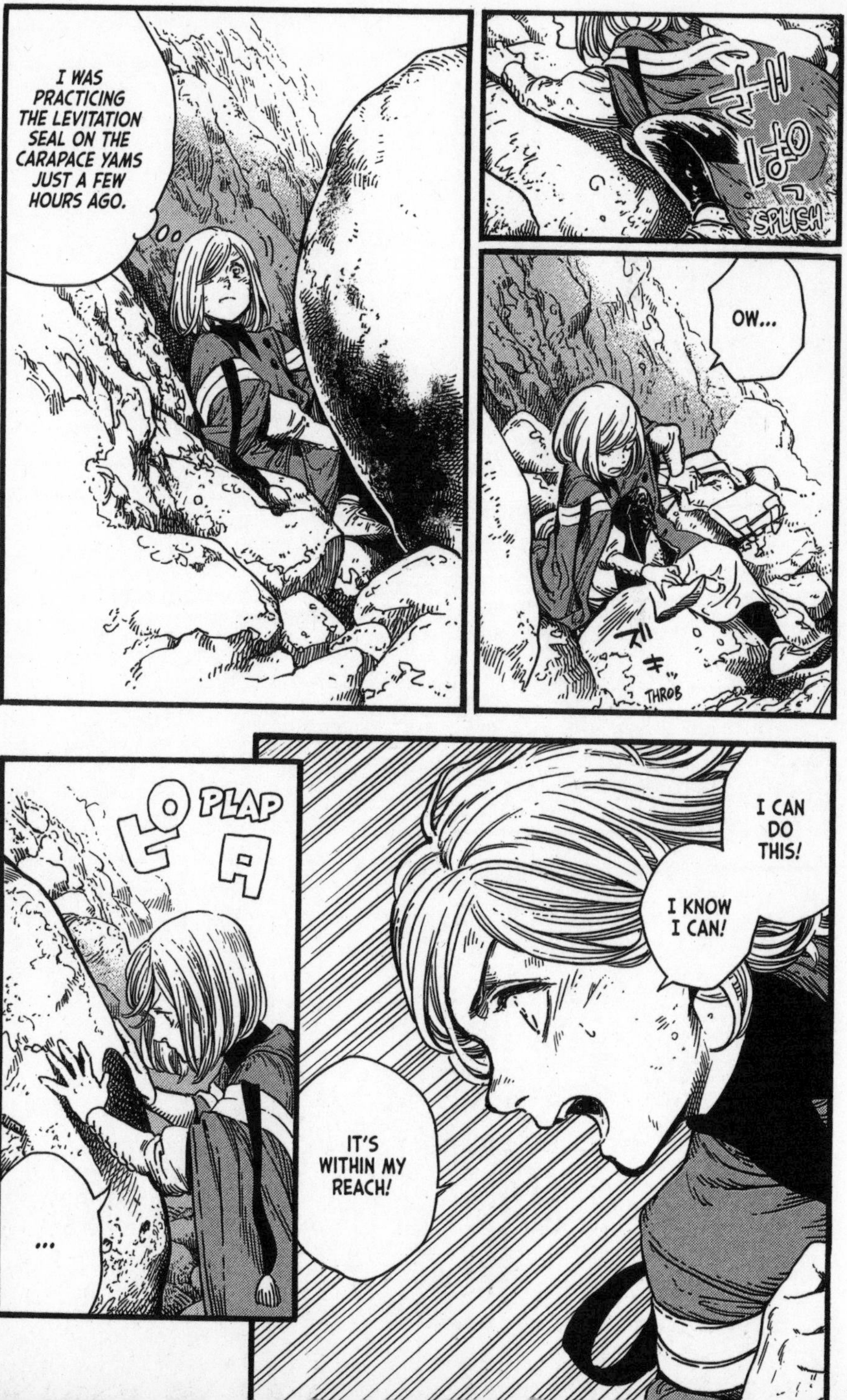
SPLISH
OW...
THROB
I WAS PRACTICING THE LEVITATION SEAL ON THE CARAPACE YAMS JUST A FEW HOURS AGO.
I CAN DO THIS!
I KNOW I CAN!
IT'S WITHIN MY REACH!
PLAP
...

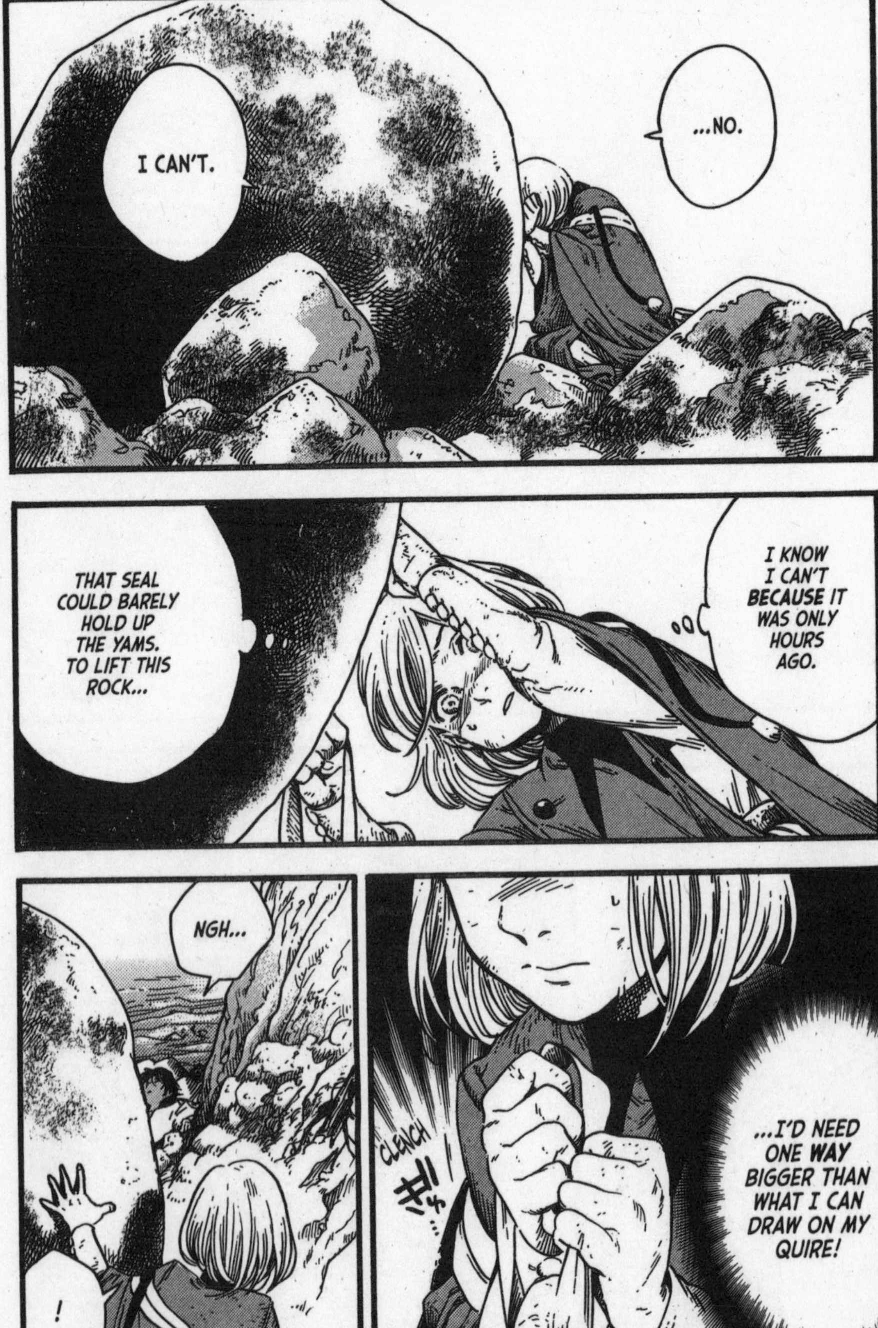
...NO.
I CAN'T.
I KNOW I CAN'T BECAUSE IT WAS ONLY HOURS AGO.
THAT SEAL COULD BARELY HOLD UP THE YAMS. TO LIFT THIS ROCK...
...I'D NEED ONE WAY BIGGER THAN WHAT I CAN DRAW ON MY QUIRE!
CLENCH
NGH...
!

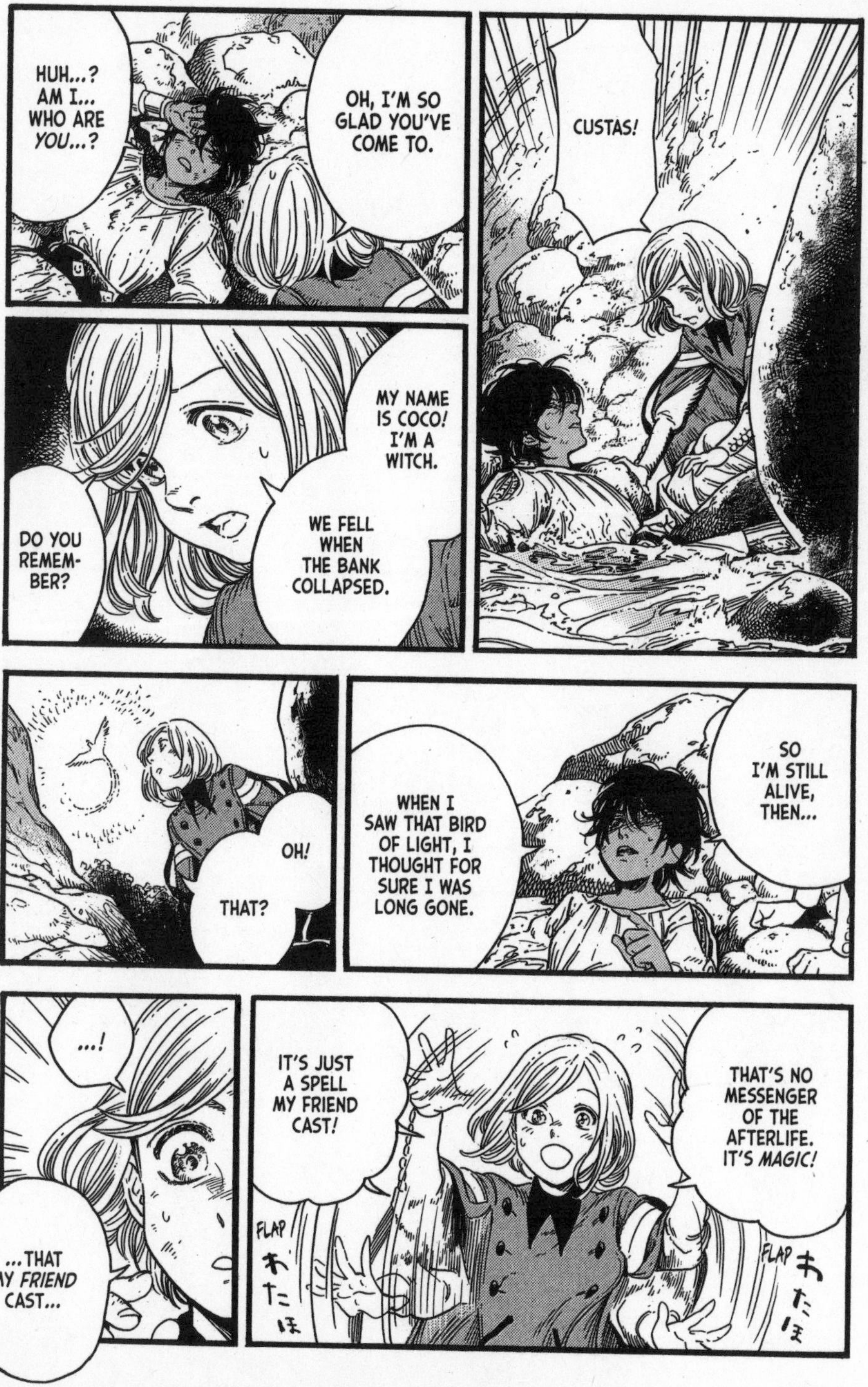
CUSTAS!
OH, I'M SO GLAD YOU'VE COME TO.
HUH...? AM I... WHO ARE *YOU*...?
MY NAME IS COCO! I'M A WITCH.
WE FELL WHEN THE BANK COLLAPSED.
DO YOU REMEMBER?
SO I'M STILL ALIVE, THEN...
WHEN I SAW THAT BIRD OF LIGHT, I THOUGHT FOR SURE I WAS LONG GONE.
OH!
THAT?
THAT'S NO MESSENGER OF THE AFTERLIFE. IT'S *MAGIC!*
FLAP
IT'S JUST A SPELL MY FRIEND CAST!
FLAP
...!
...THAT MY *FRIEND* CAST...

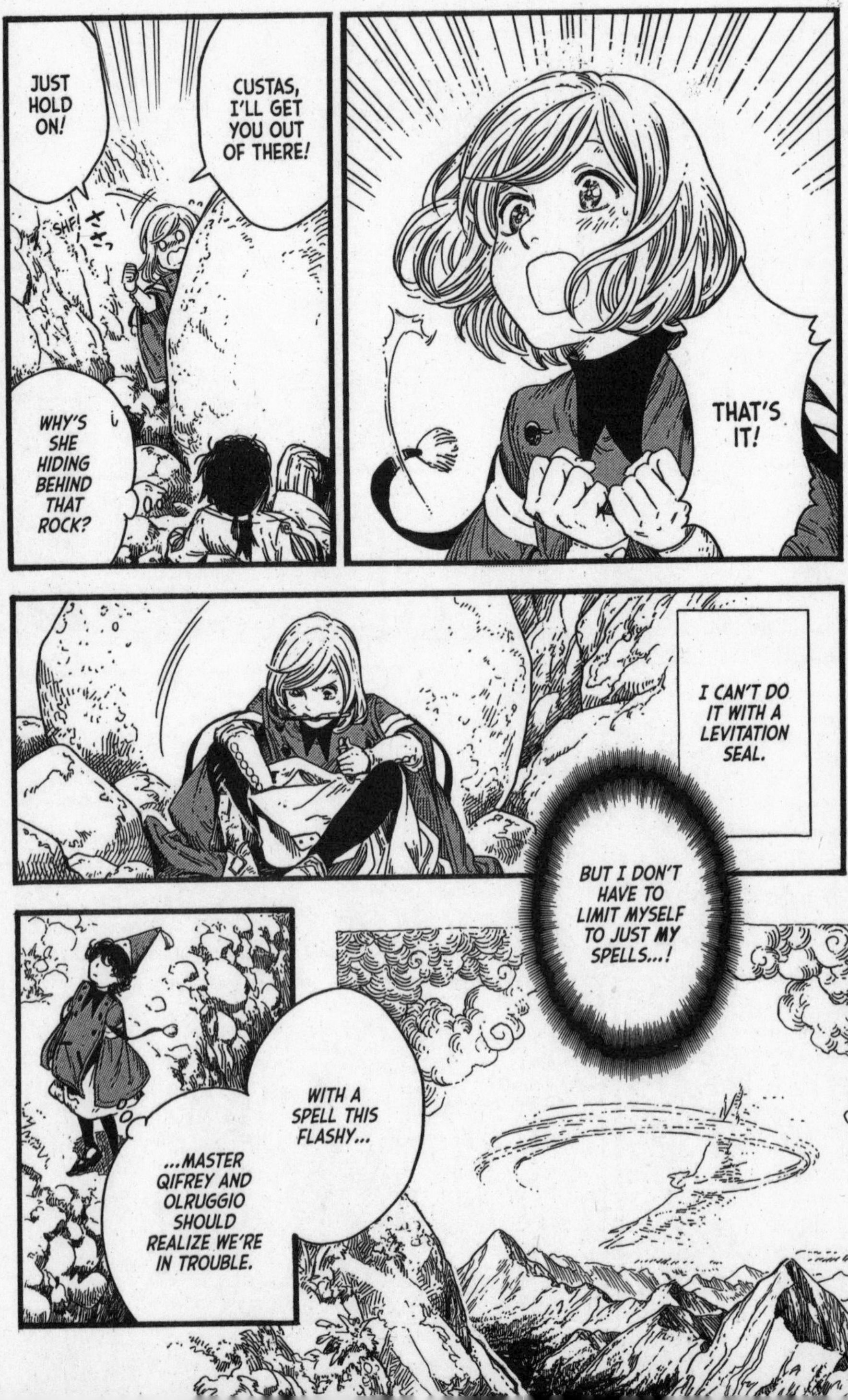
THAT'S IT!
CUSTAS, I'LL GET YOU OUT OF THERE!
JUST HOLD ON!
SHF! さっ
WHY'S SHE HIDING BEHIND THAT ROCK?
I CAN'T DO IT WITH A LEVITATION SEAL.
BUT I DON'T HAVE TO LIMIT MYSELF TO JUST MY SPELLS...!
WITH A SPELL THIS FLASHY...
...MASTER QIFREY AND OLRUGGIO SHOULD REALIZE WE'RE IN TROUBLE.

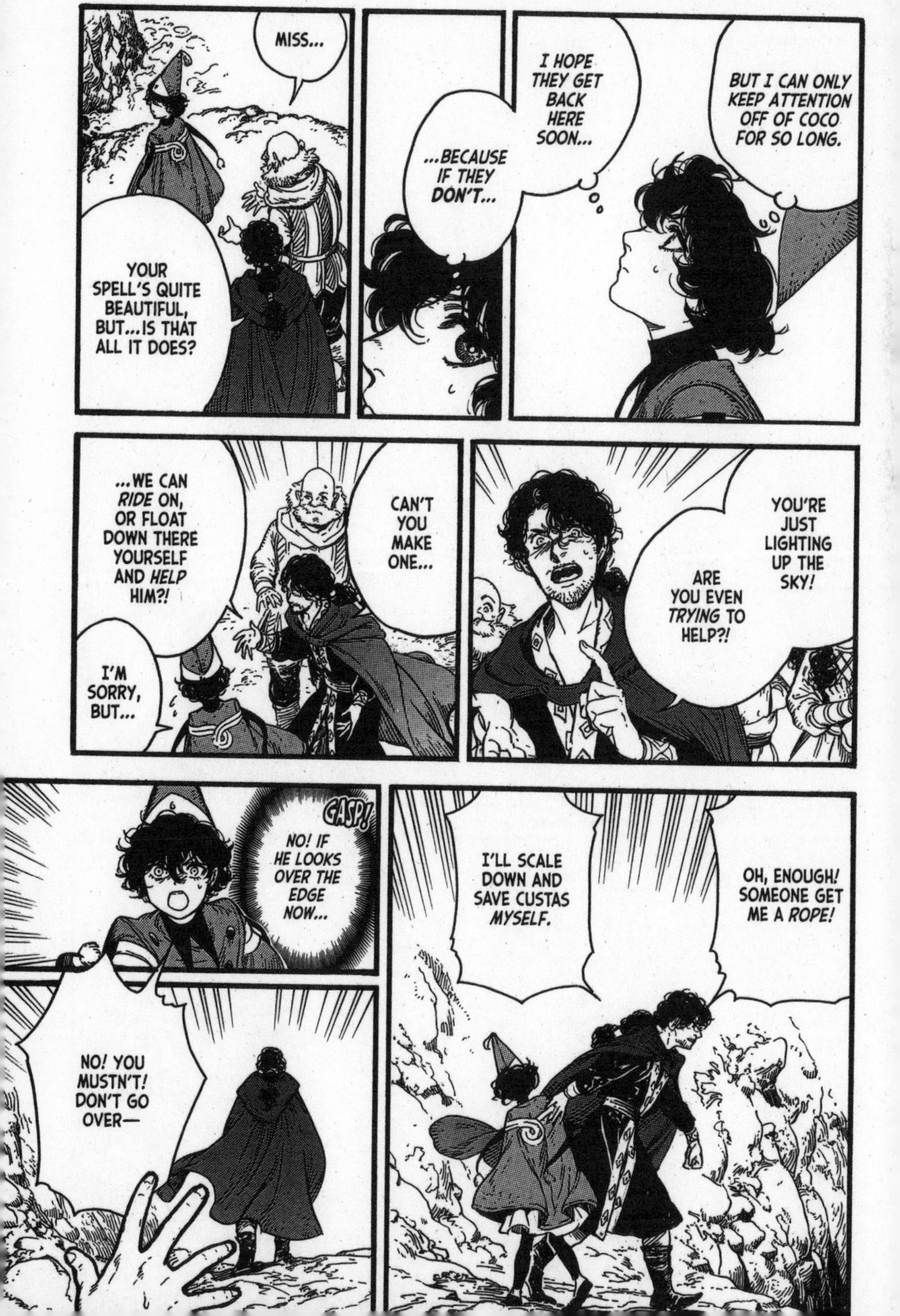
BUT I CAN ONLY KEEP ATTENTION OFF OF COCO FOR SO LONG.
I HOPE THEY GET BACK HERE SOON...
...BECAUSE IF THEY *DON'T*...
MISS...
YOUR SPELL'S QUITE BEAUTIFUL, BUT...IS THAT ALL IT DOES?
YOU'RE JUST LIGHTING UP THE SKY!
ARE YOU EVEN *TRYING* TO HELP?!
CAN'T YOU MAKE ONE...
...WE CAN *RIDE* ON, OR FLOAT DOWN THERE YOURSELF AND *HELP* HIM?!
I'M SORRY, BUT...
OH, ENOUGH! SOMEONE GET ME A *ROPE!*
I'LL SCALE DOWN AND SAVE CUSTAS *MYSELF.*
GASP!
NO! IF HE LOOKS OVER THE EDGE NOW...
NO! YOU MUSTN'T! DON'T GO OVER—

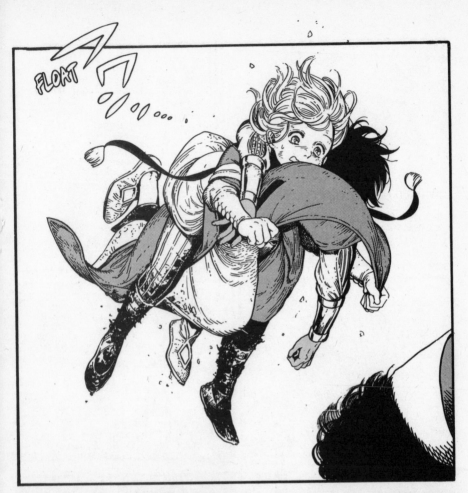

FLOAT

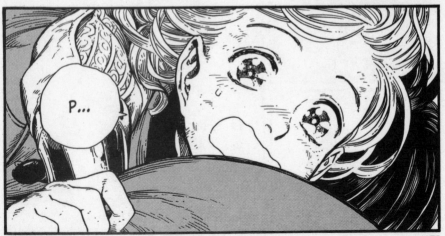

P...

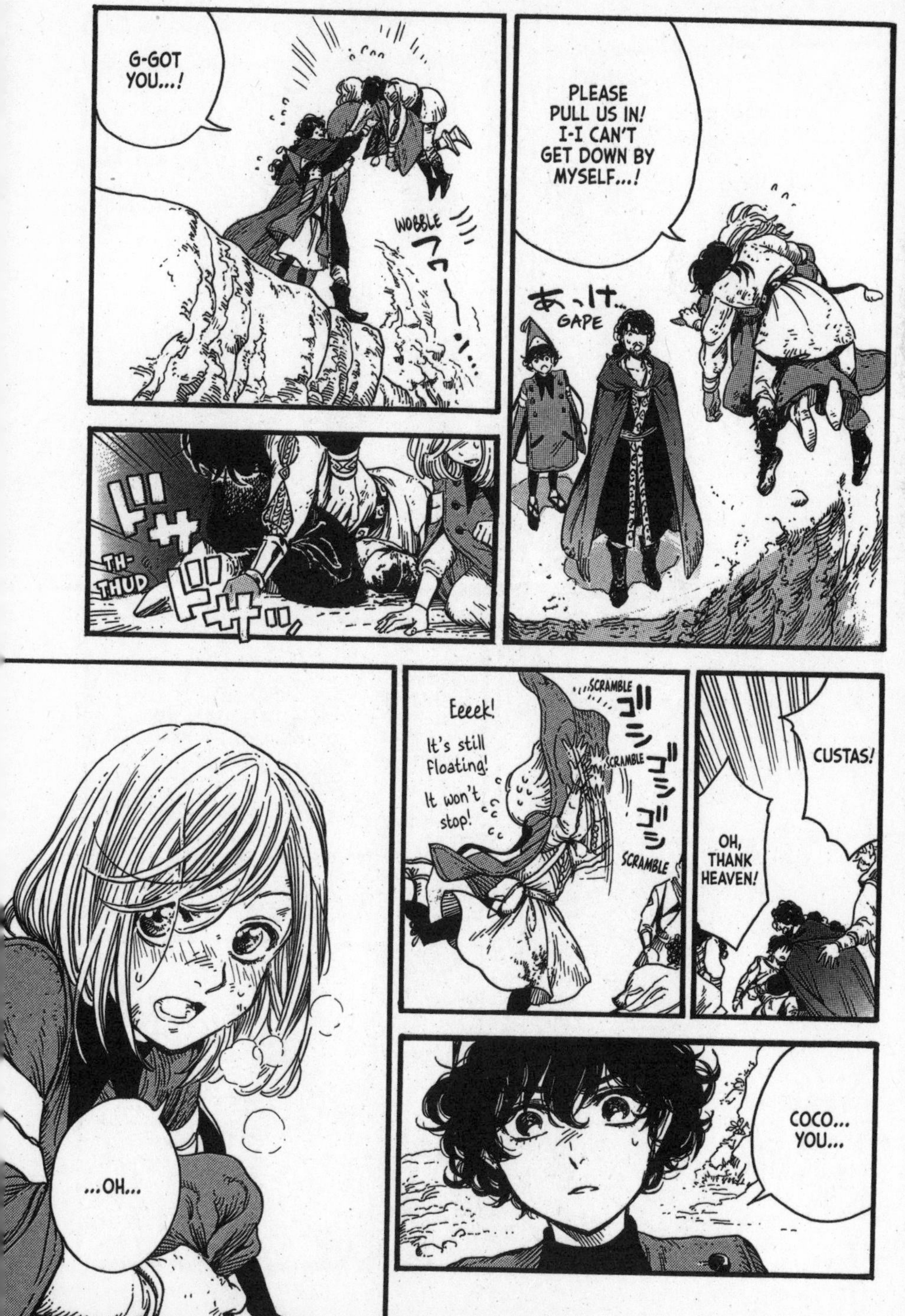
PLEASE PULL US IN! I-I CAN'T GET DOWN BY MYSELF...!
あっけ..
GAPE
G-GOT YOU...!
WOBBLE
フワー
ドサ
TH-THUD
ドサッ
CUSTAS!
OH, THANK HEAVEN!
ゴシ
SCRAMBLE
ゴシ
SCRAMBLE
ゴシ
SCRAMBLE
Eeeek!
It's still floating!
It won't stop!
COCO... YOU...
...OH...

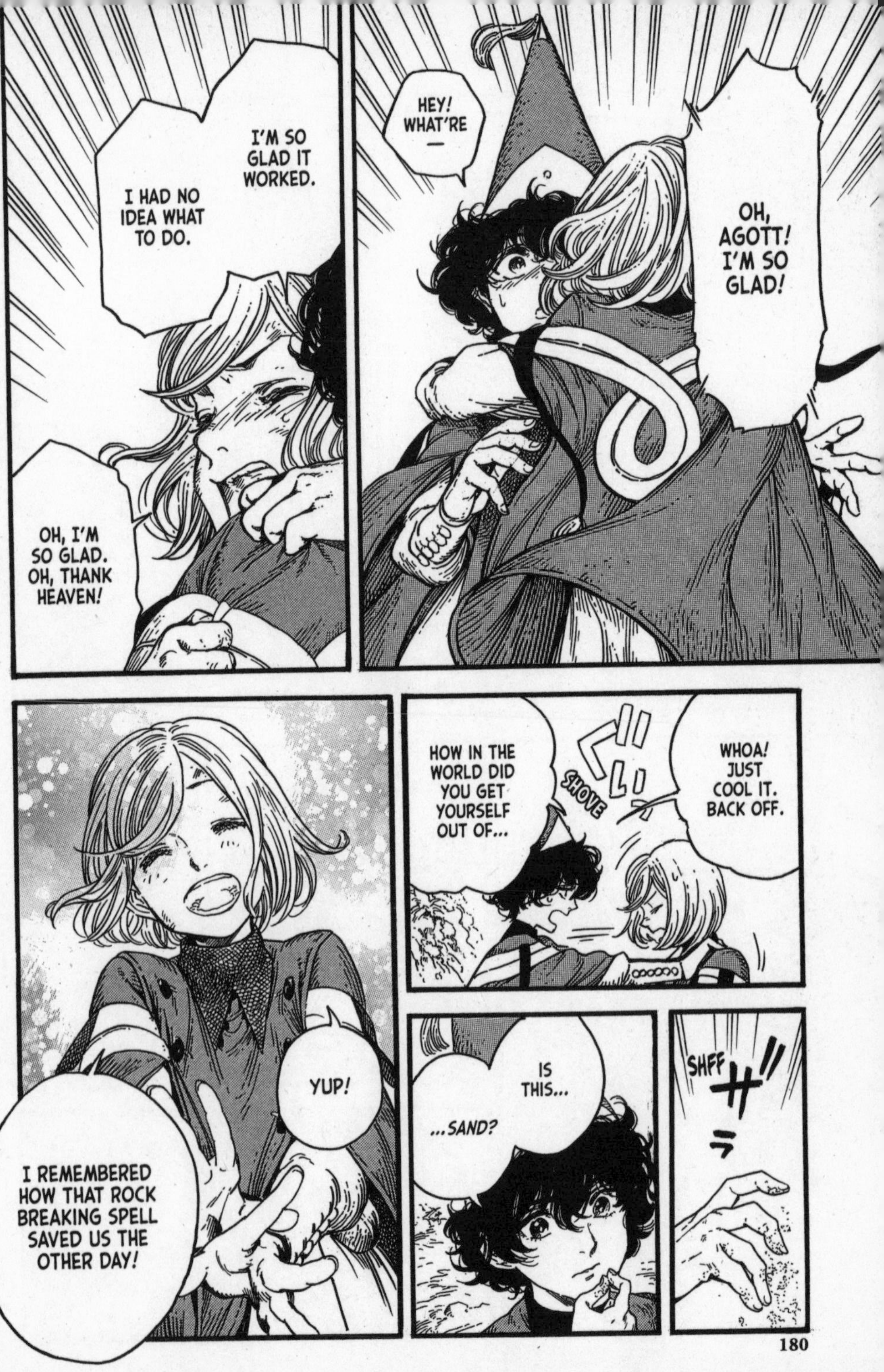
OH, AGOTT! I'M SO GLAD!
HEY! WHAT'RE —
I'M SO GLAD IT WORKED.
I HAD NO IDEA WHAT TO DO.
OH, I'M SO GLAD. OH, THANK HEAVEN!
WHOA! JUST COOL IT. BACK OFF.
SHOVE
HOW IN THE WORLD DID YOU GET YOURSELF OUT OF...
SHFF
IS THIS...
...SAND?
YUP!
I REMEMBERED HOW THAT ROCK BREAKING SPELL SAVED US THE OTHER DAY!

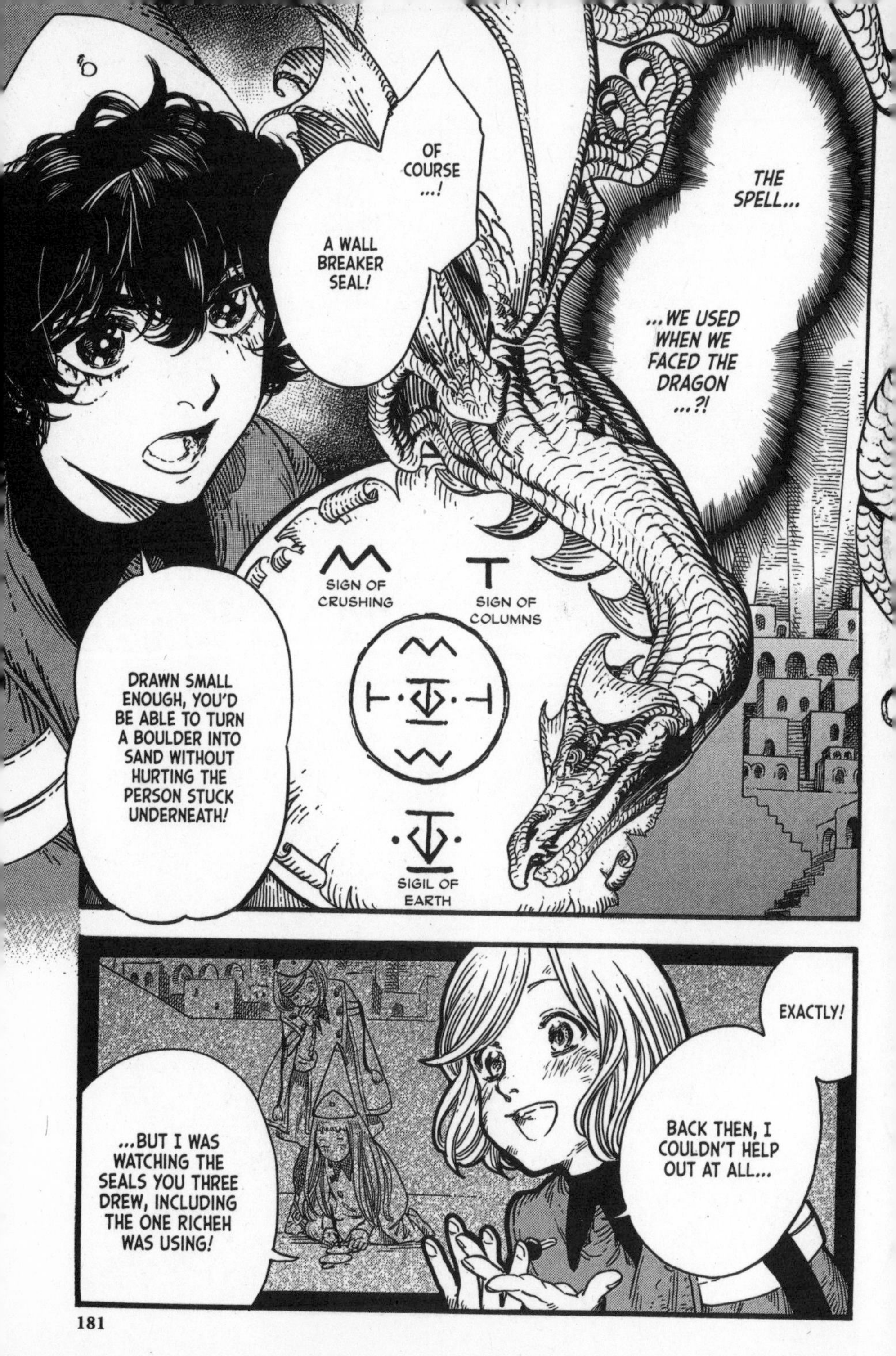
THE SPELL...
...WE USED WHEN WE FACED THE DRAGON...?!
OF COURSE...!
A WALL BREAKER SEAL!
SIGN OF COLUMNS
SIGN OF CRUSHING
SIGIL OF EARTH
DRAWN SMALL ENOUGH, YOU'D BE ABLE TO TURN A BOULDER INTO SAND WITHOUT HURTING THE PERSON STUCK UNDERNEATH!
EXACTLY!
BACK THEN, I COULDN'T HELP OUT AT ALL...
...BUT I WAS WATCHING THE SEALS YOU THREE DREW, INCLUDING THE ONE RICHEH WAS USING!

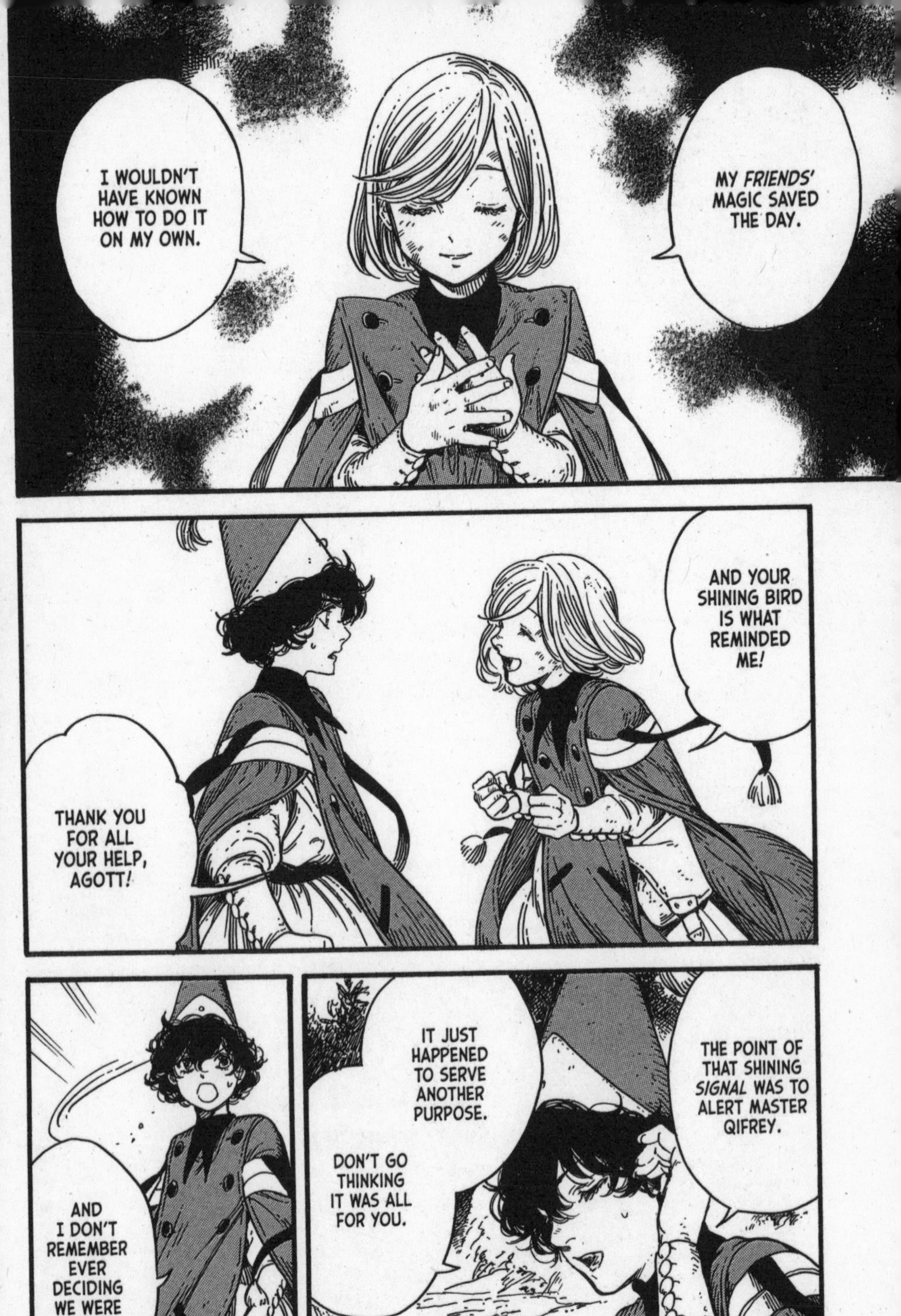
MY *FRIENDS'* MAGIC SAVED THE DAY.
I WOULDN'T HAVE KNOWN HOW TO DO IT ON MY OWN.
AND YOUR SHINING BIRD IS WHAT REMINDED ME!
THANK YOU FOR ALL YOUR HELP, AGOTT!
THE POINT OF THAT SHINING *SIGNAL* WAS TO ALERT MASTER QIFREY.
IT JUST HAPPENED TO SERVE ANOTHER PURPOSE.
DON'T GO THINKING IT WAS ALL FOR YOU.
AND I DON'T REMEMBER EVER DECIDING WE WERE FRIEN—

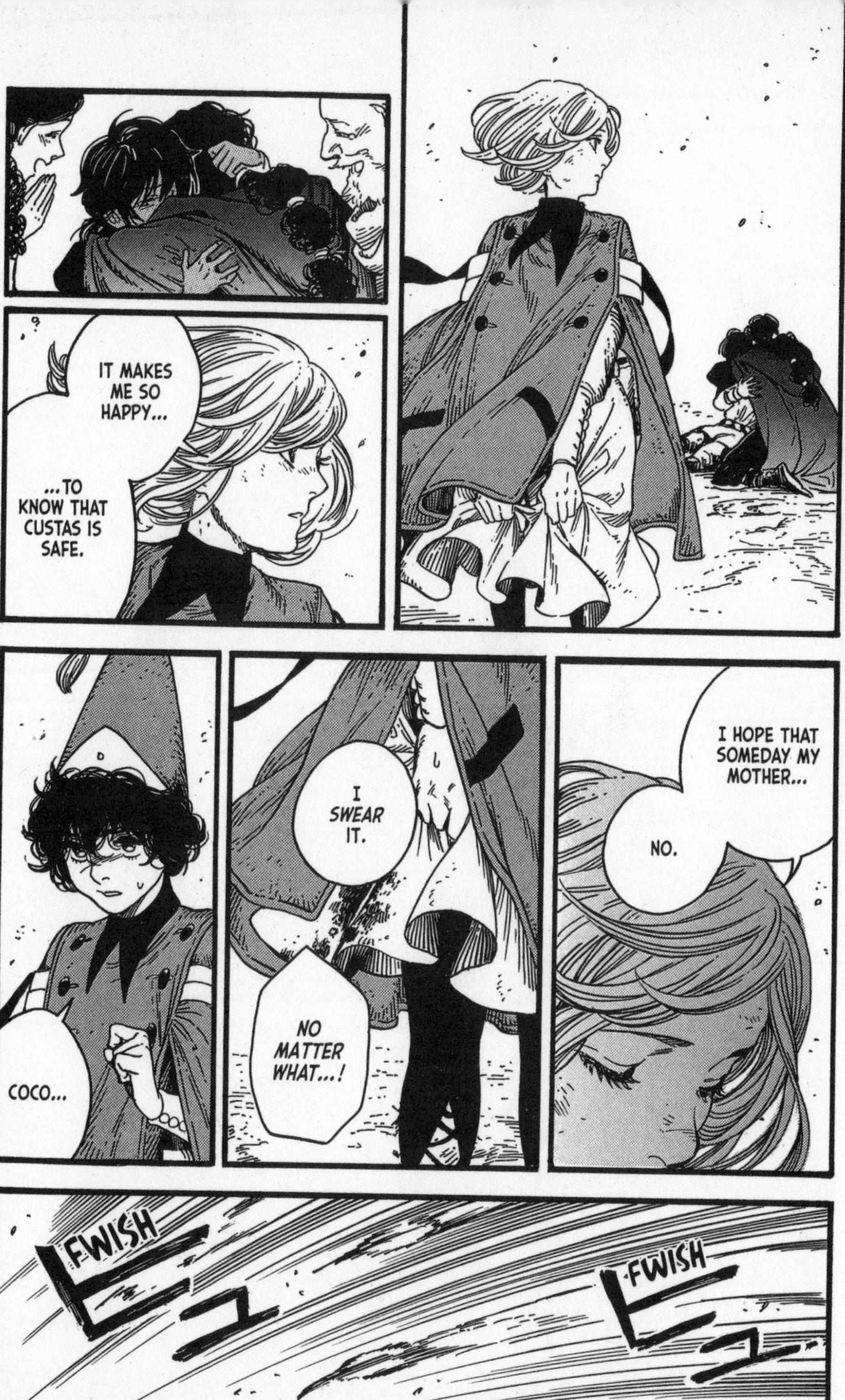
IT MAKES ME SO HAPPY...
...TO KNOW THAT CUSTAS IS SAFE.
I HOPE THAT SOMEDAY MY MOTHER...
NO.
I SWEAR IT.
NO MATTER WHAT...!
COCO...
FWISH
FWISH

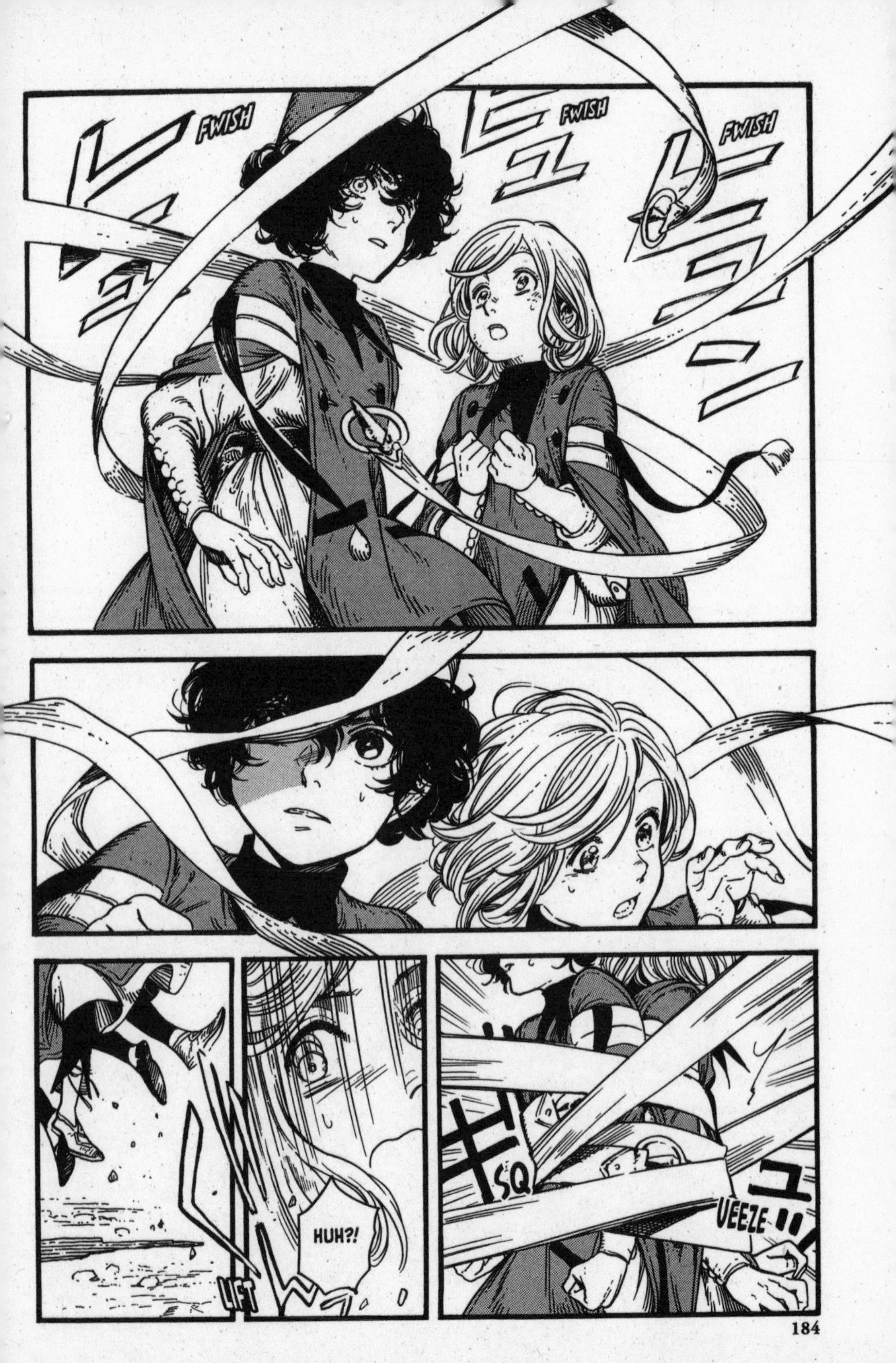
FWISH
FWISH
FWISH
SQ
UEEZE
HUH?!
LIFT

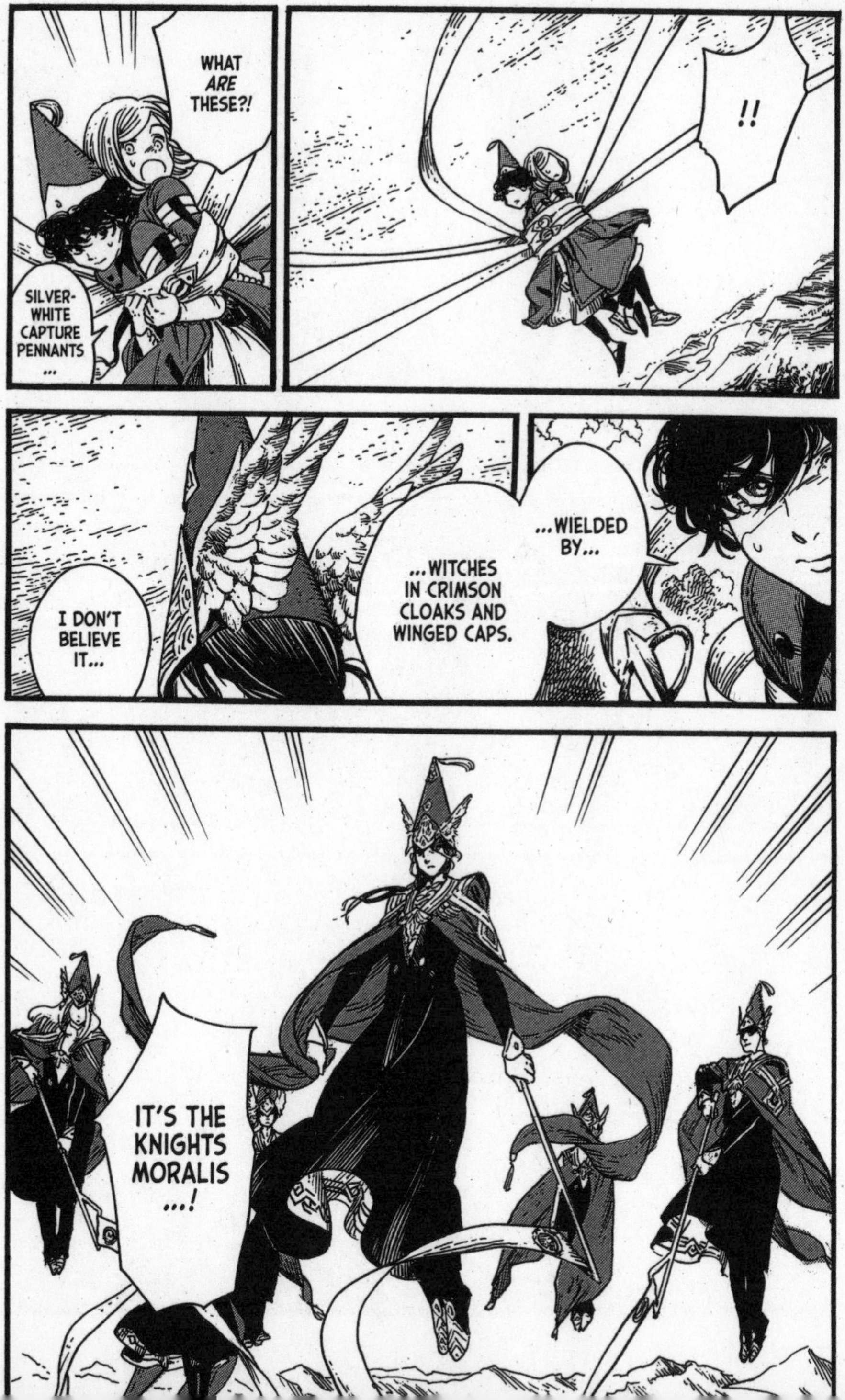
!!
WHAT *ARE* THESE?!
SILVER-WHITE CAPTURE PENNANTS ...
...WIELDED BY...
...WITCHES IN CRIMSON CLOAKS AND WINGED CAPS.
I DON'T BELIEVE IT...
IT'S THE KNIGHTS MORALIS ...!

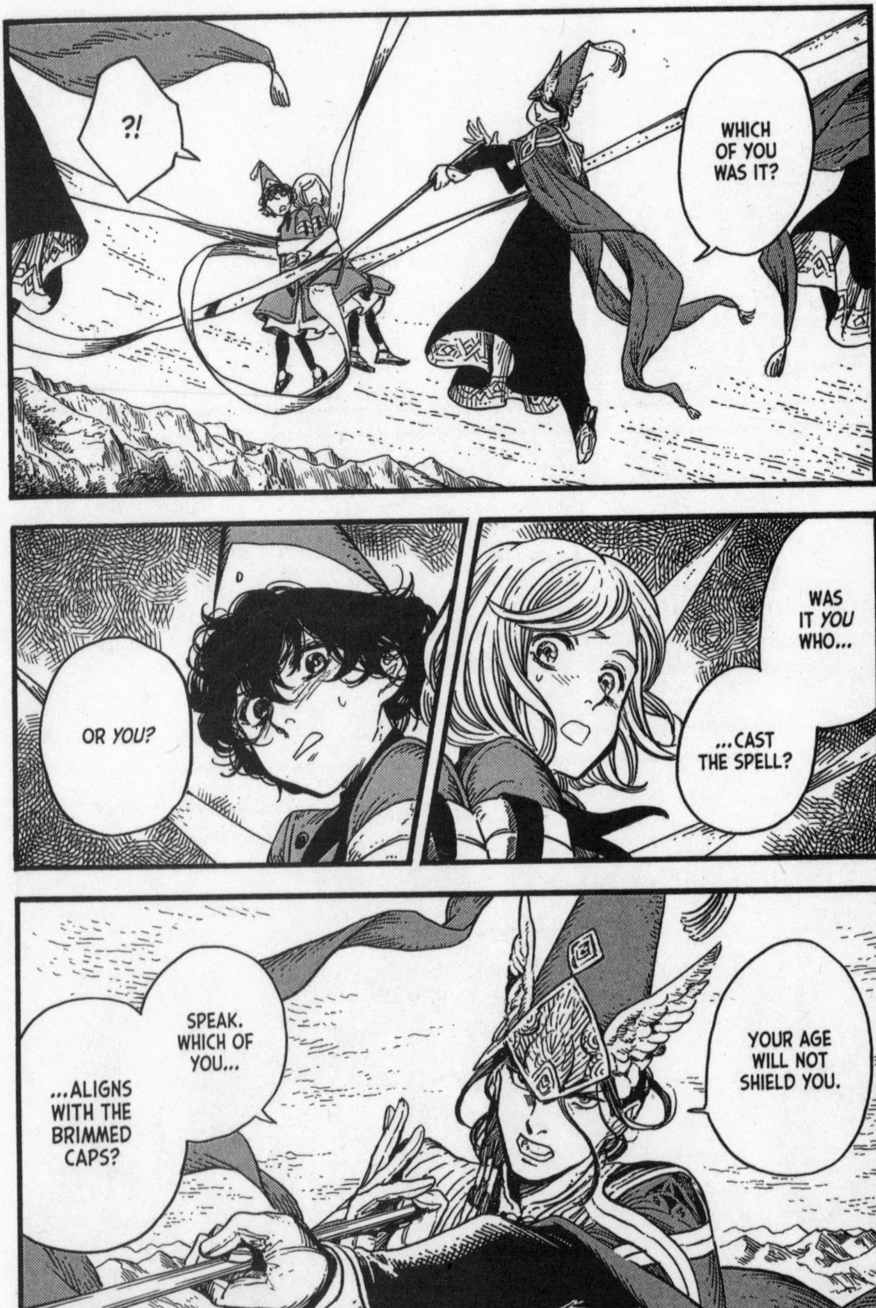
WHICH OF YOU WAS IT?
?!
WAS IT *YOU* WHO...
...CAST THE SPELL?
OR *YOU?*
YOUR AGE WILL NOT SHIELD YOU.
SPEAK. WHICH OF YOU...
...ALIGNS WITH THE BRIMMED CAPS?

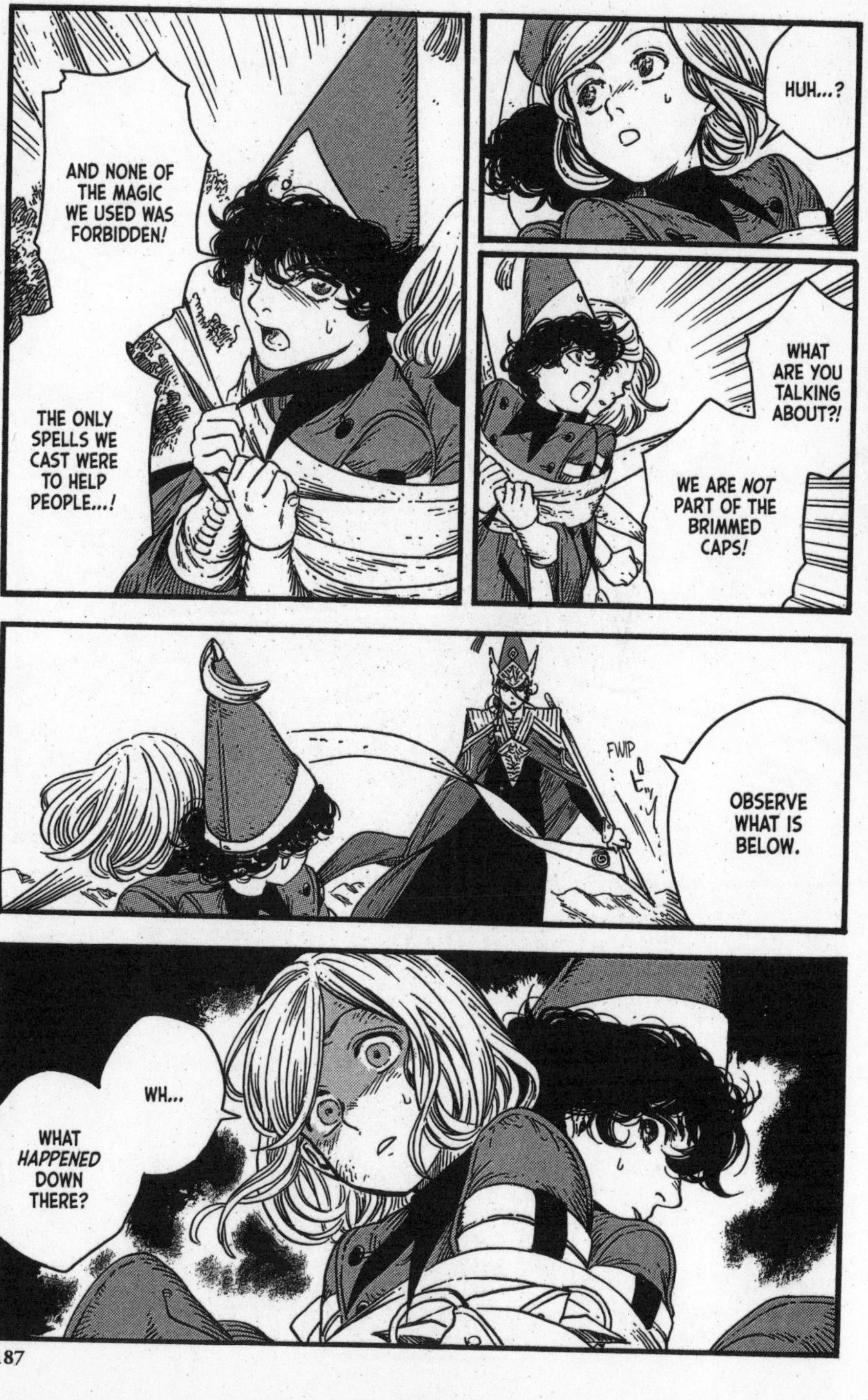
HUH...?
WHAT ARE YOU TALKING ABOUT?!
WE ARE *NOT* PART OF THE BRIMMED CAPS!
AND NONE OF THE MAGIC WE USED WAS FORBIDDEN!
THE ONLY SPELLS WE CAST WERE TO HELP PEOPLE...!
OBSERVE WHAT IS BELOW.
FWIP
WH...
WHAT *HAPPENED* DOWN THERE?

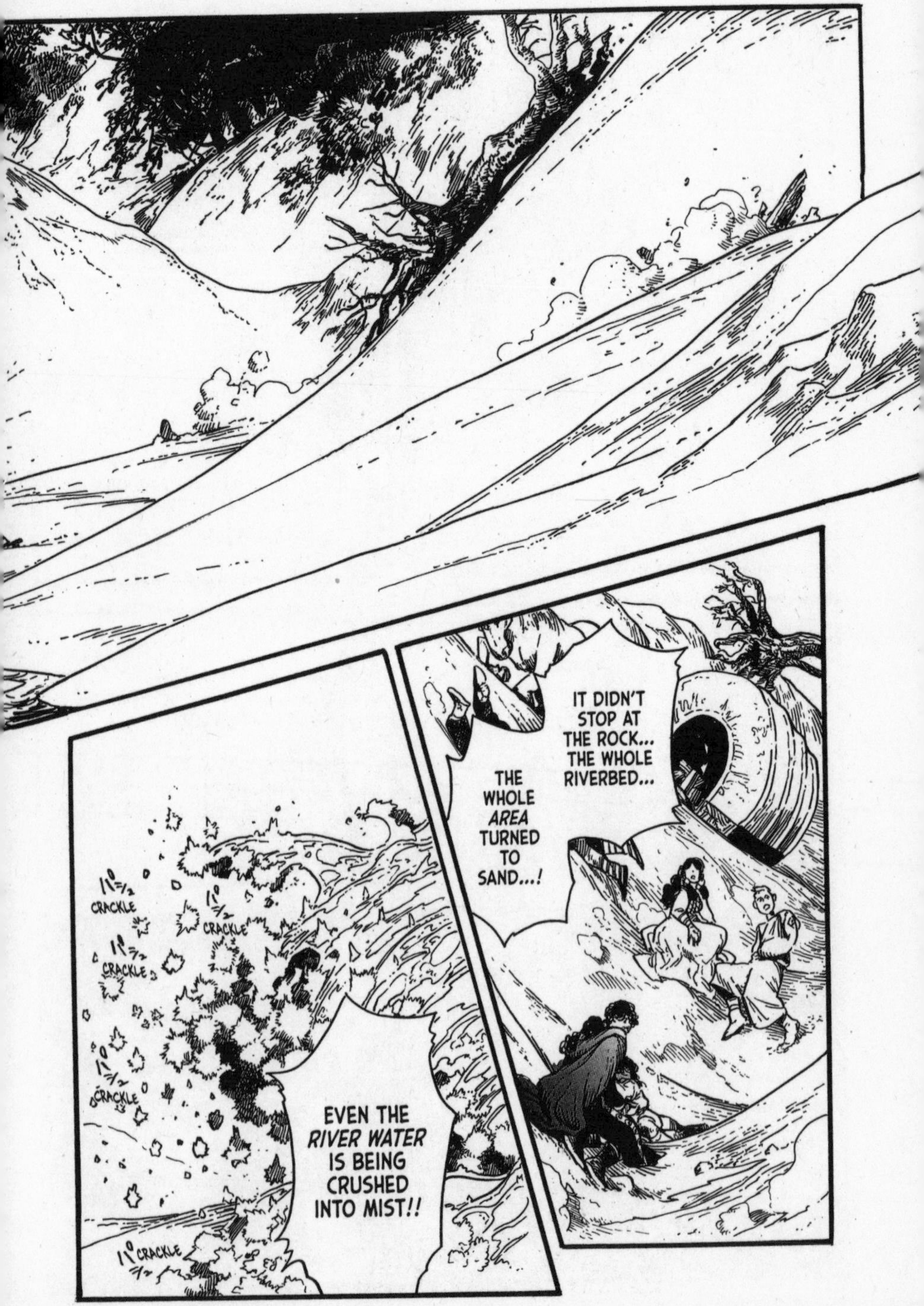
IT DIDN'T STOP AT THE ROCK... THE WHOLE RIVERBED...
THE WHOLE *AREA* TURNED TO SAND...!
EVEN THE *RIVER WATER* IS BEING CRUSHED INTO MIST!!
CRACKLE
CRACKLE
CRACKLE
CRACKLE
CRACKLE

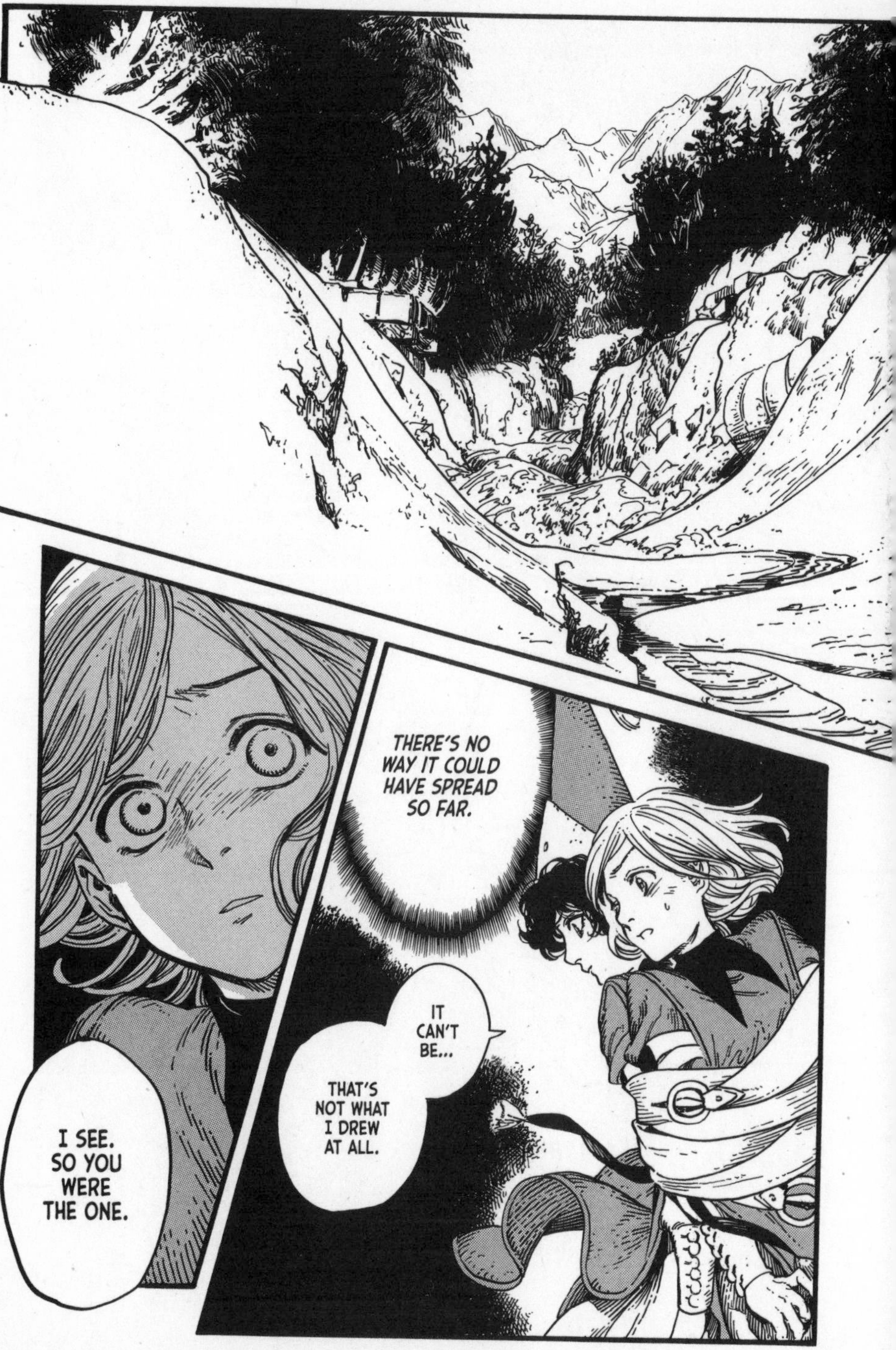
THERE'S NO WAY IT COULD HAVE SPREAD SO FAR.
IT CAN'T BE...
THAT'S NOT WHAT I DREW AT ALL.
I SEE. SO YOU WERE THE ONE.

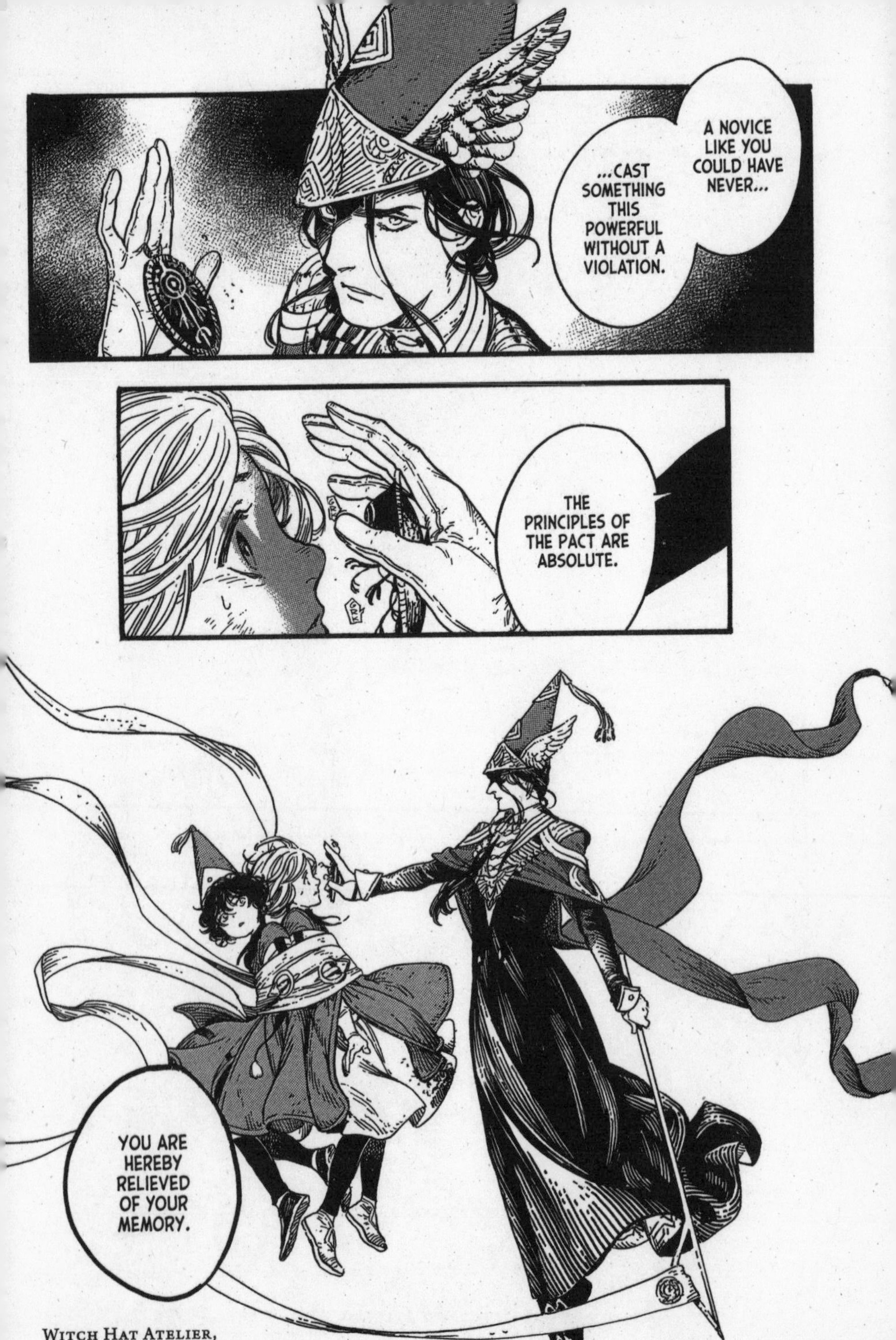
A NOVICE LIKE YOU COULD HAVE NEVER...
...CAST SOMETHING THIS POWERFUL WITHOUT A VIOLATION.
THE PRINCIPLES OF THE PACT ARE ABSOLUTE.
YOU ARE HEREBY RELIEVED OF YOUR MEMORY.

Witch Hat Atelier, Volume 2 ♦ End

HOW TO DESIGN YOUR OWN POINTED CAP

THE DESIGN OF A POINTED CAP DIFFERS DEPENDING
ON THE ATELIER ITS WITCH BELONGS TO!
TRY DRAWING YOUR VERY OWN POINTED CAP IN THE SPACE BELOW!

MY OWN, ORIGINAL POINTED CAP!

RULES FOR POINTED CAP DESIGN:
1. THE CAP MUST NOT HAVE A BRIM ABLE TO CONCEAL THE FACE.
2. THE IDEAL POINTED CAP USES A CONICAL DESIGN THAT FULLY COVERS THE TOP OF THE HEAD.

POINTED CAP

There are many different designs of caps, each representing a certain atelier. The present, brimless shape came into use after it became forbidden to conceal one's face.

CLOAK

Useful for keeping hands and magical tools out of sight.

SYLPH SHOES

Important to size correctly, so they don't fall off in midair!

VOLUME 3: SCHEDULED TO GO ON SALE IN AUGUST 2019!

Witch Hat Atelier volume 2 is a work of fiction. Names, characters, places, and incidents are the products of the author's imagination or are used fictitiously. Any resemblance to actual events, locales, or persons, living or dead, is entirely coincidental.

A Kodansha Comics Trade Paperback Original.

Published in the United States by Kodansha Comics,
an imprint of Kodansha USA Publishing, LLC, New York.

Publication rights for this English edition arranged through Kodansha Ltd., Tokyo.

First published in Japan in 2017 by Kodansha Ltd., Tokyo, as *Tongari Bōshi no Atorie* volume 2.

ISBN 978-1-63236-804-1

Printed in the United States of America.

www.kodanshacomics.com

9 8 7 6 5 4 3 2 1

Translation: Stephen Kohler
Lettering: Lys Blakeslee
Editing: Ajani Oloye
Kodansha Comics edition cover design: Phil Balsman